HOMEFIRES

EMILY SUE HARVEY

THE
STORY PLANT

The Story Plant
The Aronica-Miller Publishing Project, LLC
P.O. Box 4331
Stamford, CT 06907

Copyright © 2011 by Emily Sue Harvey

Cover design by Barbara Aronica-Buck

ISBN-13: 978-1-61188-006-9

Visit our website at www.thestoryplant.com

First Story Plant Printing: June 2011

Printed in The United States of America

DEDICATION

I dedicate this book to the preachers' families of the world. You will recognize in many of my *Homefires* characters your own selves, your children (the PKs), kin, and indeed, those of your flocks. I especially want to honor the parsonage wives, who keep the homefires burning. Who must shift her perception when change comes. And come it does. Moving time comes around swiftly and surely. And once again, amongst a new set of strangers, you find yourself scrutinized, criticized, ignored, or designated to a pedestal from which you will ultimately topple. But then more often than not, you find yourself welcomed with open arms and that makes it all worthwhile. Your focus remains firm as you protect, sometimes with your very life and sanity, your children and your "high-called" husband. Because you know with God-given woman's intuition that without you behind him, the man of the cloth's proverbial row to hoe would be rocky. At the same time, you learn to love each new flock as family and include them in your realm of protectiveness. You will also relate to the successes and the failures of those with feet of clay. The humanity. The despair and the exultation. The loneliness and the sometimes overwhelming needs laid at your feet. You meet each challenge with mercy and grace because you, too, are called.

To beautiful Janeece Wallace, not a preacher's wife but this preacher's wife's armor bearer in years past, who inspired me so deeply that I named my main character after her. Janeece is one of the most loving, generous-hearted of our flocks' women, who nurtured me in my young years, who taught, through example, what real forgiveness and mercy is. What unconditional love is.

To Betty Wallace, the faithful one. To Joyce Griffin, who literally carried me during some of my darkest times.

To Dr. Wayne Miller and his wife, Leslie, for your faithful friendship and encouragement throughout the years. For sticking with us through "thick and thin" when all sometimes seemed lost.

To my own pastor husband, Leland, and our parsonage passel of PKs, I give my heartfelt love and thanks for a life filled with surprises and adventure. It was never dull and always interesting.

In memory of Rev. Danny Wallace, gone much too soon but who left a legacy of beauty and grace for future generations to follow. My parents, James and Dot Miller and my grandparents, Mamie and Will Stafford, who, even when I was unlovable, loved me unconditionally.

To Father God, who made us who we are and forgave our glaring mistakes and blessed our triumphs with the reminder that we "are beautifully and wonderfully made" by Him.

ACKNOWLEDGMENTS

Homefires is fiction. My characters spawn from composites of folks I know and have known throughout the years of my own glass house journey. The actions and words are pure fiction. These of the church "family" remain tightly bonded to my heart in a unique, enduring way that transcends time and distance. Muses for my *Homefires* characters include Eleanor Payne Mitchem, Joyce Griffin, Rev. Bob and Patsy Roach, Roger, Mike, and Jimmy Miller, Karen Bradley, David and Susan Harvey and children, Kaleigh, Lindi, Ashley and Trey, Pam and David McCall, Angie Harvey and Angela Callahan, James and Dot Miller, Will and Mamie Stafford, Alice and Mary Latimer, the late Wayne Matthews, Barbara Ann Newell and daughters Desiree, Lou, and Cindy, Fay, and Cynthia Wiggins, Nathan and Kay Stafford, a passel of kin and a host of others, too many to name. These are the ones who made an indelible impact on my life in my best and worst of times. Each of you loved your parsonage family unconditionally and validated us.

I took the liberty of using fictitious names for settings such as Solomon, South Carolina, as well as other upstate towns. Same with church and school names. I loved every minute of dipping into a smorgasbord of fantasy places and people.

I also love that, in writing, I can reach out and offer hope to those who have "blown it." I can, through my characters' examples, let them know that there is no "hopeless" situation and that anyone who has the remorse, repentance, faith, forgiveness, and determination to hang in there through the devastation, will soon rise above those black clouds into a glorious world of sunshine. Help is always there, dear ones. One must only reach out for it.

Be blessed, reader. Sit back and enjoy the warmth of *Homefires*.

The gravedigger has been at it for at least an hour now. I watch from my car, across the road from the church cemetery where generations of my family rest, separated by six feet of sod from May's warm sunshine. My father's foot marker flanks the newest mound. The digger toils as I observe, experiencing a grief no less than when the earth first opened for the faraway casket that will, tomorrow, change its resting place to here. Twenty years have not dulled my loss. The little village church, where I learned about God and Jesus and the Holy Spirit, overlooks the activity maternally, as she did me when I was a small child.

Melancholy thick and black as old used motor oil floods me and the little girl inside yearns to resurrect. She flounders toward a time when truth was what the preacher said and Mama and Daddy made everything all right. To when the Holy Trinity simply *was* and Heaven was as real as MawMaw's Sunday kitchen feasts. To when loving felt so good, it was like getting feather-tickled all inside and bore no risks.

Risks. That comes with the homefires I keep burning. *Homefires.* Such an innocent word.

The shovel's *ping* against rock jolts me. A small gust of warm air flavored with honeysuckle and tiger lilies ruffles my hair and I inhale deeply, my dull gaze following a jagged stone spooned from earth's gaping hole.

Fact hits me broadside – there is no crawling back into childhood's shelter. Tears gather to blur and mix earth tones.

Thwump. I blink away moisture. The shovel now lies beside the earthen orifice.

The gravedigger's shoulders square off with the red-clay horizon. He pauses to loosen a black scarf tied around his head and uses it to wipe his wet brow. Gloved hands grab hold of firm sod and sinewy arms hoist him up, up until his dirty broganed foot swings over the earth's solid edge and he laboriously climbs out. He turns stiffly to wave at me – a small gesture like the tip of a hat that says, 'it's finished.' For him, it is. Not for me. For me, it just begins.

I hear his pickup's roar as it fades into the distance. I settle my arms over the warm steering wheel, loosely hugging it.

Another beginning. The thought does not lift me. Rather, grim resignation seeps into me.

I take a deep breath and sit up straighter. Thing is, this time, I know I can do it. The old paralyzing fear now has little power over me. I learned long ago not to say, "I could *never* live through that." Seems either Fate or the Devil himself eavesdrops because most of those *never*s came to pass. Little by little, over the years and through circumstances, that curious, finely tuned mechanism inside me grew more and more resistant to threats and dangers. I'm not saying I'll never be afraid again – like I said before, I avoid the word *never.*

At the same time, I know one thing as well as I know oxygen's necessity: nobody else can give me peace. I alone am responsible for it. Another truth: a higher power has and will keep me sane and alive through anything that befalls me.

I shove sunglasses over my small, tilted nose, my best facial feature. The genetic thing that sculpted mine small and straight and – to quote my daughters – spared them from the large Romanesque nose dominating their father's squared off face, softened only by a Kirk Douglas chin cleft.

Kirk Crenshaw: my hero. Kirk calls me a romantic. I suppose I am. Sometimes, he says it like it's good. Other times, when his words seem edged in cedar, they are more an accusation.

"I'm tired of apologizing for living," I've said to Kirk more than once, because that's what it is – living. *Being.* My otherworldliness is both blessing and curse. Lord knows I've tried and tried to harness the thing that lopes away with my imagination. Just when I think I've got it licked, I find myself, mid-task, drifting off to some faraway time or exotic place and writing scintillating dialogue...until Kirk snaps his beautiful male fingers in my face and mutters, "Earth to Janeece...earth to Janeece. Where *are* you?"

I usually end up apologizing. Then, I resent it.

Because Kirk doesn't apologize for living. Ever.

Yet, I refuse to be a scorekeeper.

I'd rather work on me. It's easier. *Safer.*

The spiritual me knows I must forgive to be forgiven. Another part of me is on guard against a vulnerability that hovers, has hovered over me, for as long as I've breathed.

And today, for some reason, that *placelessness* lusts for me. I push the button that raises the car windows and then flip the air conditioner on high, suddenly irked with my stupid, excessive introspection. Air's too heavy as it is.

"You take things too seriously, Janeece," Kirk loves to say, adding, always, a sharp little tweak to my nose or chin. "Let's talk about something lighter." I turn my head quickly to the side, muting some irritated response.

Perhaps I *am* too serious. Perhaps it's just Kirk's way to preserve levity and drive back any need to analyze himself. Kirk loves to soar above troubled waters.

I don't know.

All I know is that I love my husband. That, too, is unalterable. I should know. I park my car at the cemetery and walk slowly to the open sepulcher

Inhaling earth's fecund smell, I blink back tears that blur the chasm. The open grave, the dirt…it's too real…too, too real. I didn't think it could ever hurt this much again.

I was wrong.

PART ONE

"To everything there is a season and a time to every purpose under the Heaven."
Ecclesiastes 3: 8

1960-73

CHAPTER ONE

"A time to love and a time to hate."

Kirk Crenshaw and I graduated from Chapowee High on Monday and wed on Saturday. That we were broke as convicts had no bearing on our full-blown, genuine church wedding. Shoot *no*. Mill village friends and family swarmed like a colony of ants in the little Chapowee Methodist fellowship hall, arranging food offerings, while my two attendants decked me out in the ladies rest room.

"You're *so* beautiful, Sis," sighed Trish, my thirteen-year-old sister, whose bottomless, soulful eyes reflected the robin's egg blue of her bridesmaid dress. Her fingers fluttered gently over my bridal veil as Callie's not so gentle hands grasped the zipper of the candlelight white satin and lace wedding gown and tugged hard.

"Suck in," she hissed and commenced to Saran-wrap me in my pastor's wife's size six gown. Mrs. Hart had weighed one hundred ten pounds when donning it for her own wedding. Eleven years and four children later, it would, she declared, take two angry, strong armed wrestlers to squash and stuff her into it. A couple of inches shorter than hers, my one hundred seventeen pound, five-foot-three frame packed into it solidly. "Just barely," groaned Callie, my co-maid of honor, who shared this role with Trish. She stepped back and, hands on saucy hips, surveyed the hemline.

"My spike heels you're wearing take up almost all the extra length."

"Almost. Lord have mercy, I've *starved* five pounds off in order to wear this thing," I grumbled as the seams seized my flesh. My reflection in the church restroom's long door mirror did not reveal my discomfort and I found when I relaxed, it wasn't so bad. After all, the festivities would be over in a couple of hours.

My buddy Cal's five-foot-eight, Ava Gardner-incarnate presence usually dwarfed and paled me, but today, it didn't. "Spittin' image o' Doris Day," Cal muttered, fluffing her wild, shoulder-length dark-mahogany mane while her sultry brown eyes surveyed me like a chemist's through a microscope.

"Yeah, *right!* With these D-cup hooters and dishwater *bland* hair." I trailed my hands over the snug bustline to the cinched waist. Yet…I angled another look at the mirror. My short sun-streaked hair fluffed becomingly from overnight pincurls. Strawberry pink lipstick glazed my lips and a light brush of Cal's Max Factor Plum Heat rouge focused my features rather nicely. I had to admit, today, I *felt* pretty.

A thrill shot through me at the thought of Kirk in black tux and blue ruffled shirt.

While Cal and Trish fussed with their hair and makeup, I meandered into a Sunday school room of my home church, needing solitude to rhapsodize. I raised the window then perched gingerly on a bench next to it, letting memories waft in on the fragrant, cooling, June honeysuckle breeze.

Kirk, my knight in shining armor, rode onto my horizon atop a cut down peach flat, a clattering Beverly Hillbilly's version, startling and scattering all my romantic dreams of *him* – Mr. Right, a John Saxonish stranger who kidnapped me to his penthouse where he ravished me, then forced me to elope with him. 'Course, I knew that should I succumb to fornication, I'd not only inhabit Hell in the hereafter but would immediately become earthly discarded slop, which surpasses leftovers and is only good for hogs.

Such was the aftermath of underground sex in the fifties. Partly mine was spiritual restraint, but in large part, it was because of my dad, hovering next to God-almighty in my conscience cranny, *watching.* And Joe Whitman, with his regal bearing and no nonsense confrontations was a force I cared not to reckon with. His sunny William Holden good looks – which endured into his sixties – evolved, with provocation, to stony Walter Matthau, freezing me mid-stride. No, I did not want to displease him by being loose like Callie.

Anyway, I smiled today, thinking about the night not far into our courtship, when Kirk – not John Saxonish at all – and I nearly crossed the line. We'd parked in a remote corner of thickly wooded Crenshaw forestland, the only collateral standing between them and destitution – hiding from Daddy and the world. "Tell me about your family," I'd coaxed and settled my head against his solid shoulder.

He did. Seemed once it started, it tumbled out like a slot-machine gone crazy, all of it – his dad's alcoholism, his mom's subjugation, his sibling's insecurity and anger and the poverty, the near squalor. He finished in a voice as low and rough as velvet embroidered with thorny vines. I recognized behind the timbre of those words a pulsating, palpable anger. Eclipsing his mortar-set face, green eyes blazed into darkness. A chill rippled up my spine.

The car radio's dim light cast his features into starkly hewed lines and angles while its speakers oozed rhythm and blues from Ernie's Music for Lovers out of Cincinnati and I wondered *who is this person?* for the first time divining that our differences made us virtual strangers. Then he turned his head, caught my gaze and smiled, in a blink dispelling the harshness from his features as he turned me into his arms and began to kiss me.

The night seemed different, more urgent. Soon, I found myself lying beneath him in the seat and for the first time, felt Kirk's hardness against my belly and it was like getting slammed there with a warm, slushing current and everything went white-hot. God knows, I'd always berated girls for being "that way" and pooh-poohed the idea that one gets "carried away" with passion, and here I was, my hormones gone crazy, my limbs gone liquid and my breath coming in spurts. And poor Kirk, in a frenzy, all hands and lips and pelvis, nearly incoherent. And my brain kept saying *"stop, stop, stop"* while my body kept screaming "Yes! Yes! *Now!"*

They were new, the volcanic rapids carrying me away from rationale, away from *me,* whose velocity pinned me to that seat like a gnat against a cyclone. I don't know where it came from, the strength to say *"stop, Kirk."* Probably from the deep down me who knew I could hide from Daddy and the world but not from *Him.* It was a mere wisp of sound Kirk seemed not to hear.

The next *"No, Kirk. Stop!"* carried more momentum and he halted as if startled from a feverish trance to sudden wakefulness. Kirk quickly disentangled himself, apologized profusely, then spread-eagled his arms and plastered his red face to the steering wheel for a long time. His abashment matched my own.

Later, we talked. Both virgins, we agreed that neither wanted to consummate our union outside of marriage. From that time, despite incredible chemistry between us – his look or touch always melted my bones – we honored our commitment to chastity.

Today, on our wedding day, my eyes misted at the wisdom of that decision because what had developed between us was love in its purest form.

Golden afternoon sunlight spilled over the heart pine vestibule floor, where Daddy fiddled with his blue shirt ruffle. "Does it look too *sissy?*" he muttered out the corner of his mouth, his features stricken with apprehension.

"You look just like a movie star," I whispered, "Only *better-looking.*"

He relaxed, became Daddy again. Strong. The rock beneath my wobbly, stilettoed feet.

I clutched his arm and felt his hand squeeze my icy fingers. Lordy, was I nervous. Then I saw the groom's party enter the front of the church, filing to stand before the pulpit. Horace "Moose" McElrath, a barrel of a fellow with corkscrew dark curls and eyes so smiley half-mooned I had yet to detect their color, took his honored place at Kirk's side. As usual, his turkey-necking chuckle – always present when Moose was nervous – pressed a very latent giggle button deep inside me.

Daddy felt me shaking and gazed worriedly at my lowered head. "You okay?" he asked, patting my hand. I drew in a deep breath and brought the uncharacteristic mirth-seizure under control, nodding.

Then I really focused on Kirk. Another fierce thrill flared through me. Lordy – how did I ever *not* think him handsome? His loosely waved, wheat blond head glistened, awash with afternoon sunrays pouring through stained windows. From that distance, past one hundred heads, with me nearly hidden behind attendants, his gaze sought me out, found me. The connection – hokey as it sounds – *szzzzzz*ed.

In a single heartbeat, *I was back on my porch, nearly two years earlier*, that evening Kirk's contraption had idled to a halt before my mill village house, where I rocked and sang gustily along with Fats Domino's *Blueberry Hill* drifting through my bedroom window. Moose, my friend from English class, hopped off the passenger seat and chatted with me when I moseyed to the curb – actually a front yard easily spanned in four giant steps – to join them. I quickly labeled the wiry, sun-bleached guy the Quiet One, who sat behind the wheel of his peach flat, his gaze studiously transfixed to something beyond that bug-splattered windshield.

"What you guys doin'?" I'd asked.

"We been fishin'," Moose replied, grinning.

"Catch anything?" I slid a glance at the Quiet One.

"You kiddin'?" Moose yuk-yukked. "We eat all our Vienna Sausages and crackers and drunk all our Cocolas, then left. Lookin' fer girls, hey, Kirk?"

The Quiet One merely grunted. Or did he? Feeling bad for Moose, I quickly said, "Moose, did you ever learn how to conjugate them danged verbs?" We laughed and guffawed over that because Moose usually copied my homework paper.

The driver of the vehicle remained statue still, arms akimbo, eyes straight ahead like a horse wearing blinders. Frozen, yet relaxed in an odd sort of way. Curiosity ambushed me.

"Who's he?" I asked Moose, not caring what the other guy thought since he wasn't even *trying* to be polite. Least he could do was speak to me, concede that I existed. So my question was in the same pretend-he's-not-here category as his silent disregard.

"Kirk Crenshaw," Moose offered glancing curiously at his buddy.

"He's in my homeroom." I'd just recognized him. "*Hey! You're in my homeroom.*" Let him ignore *that*. A thing that truly nettled me was disdain. It pounced against this thing inside me that simply *must* placate everyone. Fact was, I felt compelled to befriend every danged person I met and would, in fact, have taken them home with me had Daddy been more social-oriented.

For the first time, the wheat blond head turned to acknowledge me and his hard mouth curved slightly, as if in amusement, or annoyance, I couldn't tell which. "Yeah?" he muttered, as in "so what?" Little did I realize that he waved a red flag before me, with his Elk majesty and male mystique. I knew so little of myself in those young days that it was much later before I recognized what that flag represented. *Challenge.*

Monday morning in homeroom, I watched Kirk Crenshaw's brisk entrance just before the bell. His carriage bordered on cocky. But wasn't. His energetic presence affected me, as did his crisp, freshly pressed shirt and slacks – slacks that showcased firm buttocks and long slender legs. It wasn't that he was all that good-looking, though with wavy sun-bleached hair, his rugged features weren't bad. Kinda nice, I decided, in a tousled, inexplicable way. It was something in the way he moved, like harnessed steam, smooth yet forceful. Even the way he shoved his hands in his pockets, infinitely male, held me rapt.

Later, a prickly 'being watched' sensation moved me to suddenly swivel in my desk to face the back of the room, catching Kirk's study of me. Spring-green eyes, set amid olive-complected features, startled me with their intensity, making my stomach turn over as a warm feeling trickled through me like summer branch water.

I smiled. He smiled back, his gaze never wavering. Then a strange phenomenon occurred. The tough guy blushed. Yeah. He really did, though his eyes never left mine. And that blush changed my whole perspective of Kirk Crenshaw.

Today, across the church, I smiled at him. He smiled back. *De ja vu.* Only this time, his blush was because a whole danged church full of villagers eyeballed him flirting with me.

I moved down the aisle to a slightly out-of-tune piano's rendering of the *Wedding March*, thankful for Daddy's strong arm to hang on to. Else, I'd surely have tripped over the long gown or turned my ankle in Cal's danged heels. All those eyes on me terrified me senseless. *Scrutiny* – my worst scenario. The veil helped me feel a tad hidden, but each step was like those in a nightmare where one is partially paralyzed or mired up in quicksand. Even the lush greenery and white mum arrangements, vivid against the crimson velvet-dressed seats and floors of our little village church, blurred before me.

Then, Callie's wink caught my attention – her "*va va vooom,* babyyy" one. And Trish gazed at me so dewy eyed you'd have thought I *really was* Cinderella in my borrowed Victorian cut finery. Moose – whose tux tugged in all the wrong places – looked ready to burst with joy, furiously swallowing back another *yuk-yukk.*

Kirk – well, Kirk's hot look instantly converted my cold fear into anticipation.

Soon, I stood at the altar and Daddy placed my hand in Kirk's, rushing tears to my eyes as I realized the significance of the gesture. Despite my father's "under the thumb" controlling disposition, he'd always been a good, *caring* daddy. At least I *knew* Daddy, could predict him almost to the T. He was actually *giving me away. What* – I wondered in a heartbeat of panic – was I trading him *for?*

Kirk's strong fingers squeezed mine, almost painfully, revealing his own state of nerves. And a certain *danger.* Adrenaline shot through me. *Now where did that come from? Danger.* I sucked in a deep breath, feeling kinda off the wall. Thank *God* only I knew *how* off-the-wall *I* could be. Preacher Hart's voice moved in and out of my overcast reverie, *"….gathered together…join this man and this woman…."*

Man and woman…man…Did I really know this man? At times, I was certain I did. At others, I was equally certain I did not.

Mrs. Tilley, the pianist and soloist, burst into *Whither Thou Goest,* her humongous bosom heaving with emotion, predictably bending my eardrum by going sharp on the high notes. The giggle-button war commenced warbling inside me and I clamped my teeth together and gazed into Kirk's solemn face for focus. He gazed back, as somber as I'd ever seen him, and I no longer heard the cracked operatic vibrato.

The pastor resumed…*"Whom God hath joined together…"*

Joined together. My breath hitched and Kirk's fingers nearly crushed mine.

"I now pronounce you man and wife…"

In the next breath, Kirk was kissing me. *No turning back.*

The thought flitted through my mind like startled ravens. And was gone.

"I miss Chuck," I murmured between greeting wedding guests. Kirk gave me a sympathetic hug, knowing how I adored my older brother, whom he'd never met and from whom I'd not heard a word in months—during which I alternately wanted to hug him and slap his blasted face.

MawMaw, Papa, my Uncle Gabe and his wife Jean, a Chapowee girl, embraced Kirk and me in the church fellowship hall and chatted with my stepmother Anne. Papa, Teddy-bearish in his one and only church-going brown suit and tie, hugged me tightly, then whipped out his brown handkerchief to wipe suspiciously misty blue eyes. MawMaw was gussied up in a new cotton floral dress. Her eyes, so like Mama's, puddled unashamedly with tears. A moment before leaving, she whispered in my ear, "Now you'uns can come'n see me and Papa, Neecy."

I nodded, dodging a deeper analysis of my screwed-up family today. "Gabe told me he'd landed a good job at the Enka Plant near Asheville, North Carolina," I said, brightly changing subjects, "and would be moving there the next week. Sure hate to see him go." Gabe was my late mom's only sibling.

"We'll probably be moving there, too," rasped MawMaw, emotionally. "Gabe needs lookin' after, with diabetes and all. Jean works fulltime and I'll be helpin' them out all I can." My heart sagged. Here, just when I'd not need Daddy's permission to visit them, they were moving two hours away. I felt a bit betrayed. But what with all the wedding festivities, the feeling passed. More than ever, I missed my mom, who'd died when I was eleven, Chuck, fifteen, and Trish, five.

Daddy kept conveniently busy speaking to everybody else except my grandparents – his former in-laws, whom he'd succinctly cut from our lives one week after Mama's death because MawMaw had spoken ill of him within his children's hearing. I viciously pushed the thoughts away. I had to pigeonhole my priorities today. Simply had to. I refused to let loved ones' hateful unforgiveness spoil my wedding day.

"The flowers look so pretty." I smiled desperately at Kirk and he squeezed my hand. Somehow, he understood. His IRS refund check paid for the floral arrangements. Our wedding was lovely yet inexpensive. Relatives and ladies of Chapowee's Methodist Church had prepared food for the reception, which was the way of Mill Hill folk, whose reward for generosity was the change of pace provided by a bona-fide church wedding. Heck, we'd invited nearly the whole danged village.

Daddy and Anne, whom Dad had married in my twelfth year, hugged us. "We waited till the line cleared out," Anne said, eyes reddened from sentimental tears, surprising me with the depth of her feelings.

"Where's Grandma and Grandpa Whitman?" I addressed Daddy, knowing full well he'd excuse his own flesh and blood's flaws, setting my teeth on edge.

"Ma said her rheumatism is acting up. Said to tell you they're sorry they can't be here." Daddy's gaze begged me to understand. I looked away and quickly moved to another subject, knowing Grandma Whitman always went any danged place she truly wanted to. Knowing, too, that she probably hadn't sent me that apologetic message.

"Only Chuck's missing," I said, almost gratified to see hurt spring to Daddy's eyes. Almost. In the next breath, I was hugging him, wanting to erase the hurt. Lord have mercy, today, my emotions felt tossed about like dead leaves in a whirlwind.

Chuck, my handsome brother, who left home a mere three years after Mama died to "see the world," actually to flee Dad's dominion of him, left the family in a *goshawful mess.* 'Course, I couldn't blame all the mess on him but what part he'd sullied, he'd done a bang-up job. I'd watched them pit wills, my zany, adventurous sibling and my logical dad. Daddy's trying to tether his impulsive firstborn was like trying to hold on to a squirming, greased pig.

Sad thing was, I knew theirs was a battle neither could win and neither knew how to back off. One wintry day, following another shouting match with Daddy, Chuck quit his mill job and disappeared. I cried for weeks while Daddy ranted and roared until he ran out of steam, then grew eerily quiet. After that, up until this very day, I'd remained Daddy's primary parental salvation, with him dedicating himself to overseeing every aspect of my life, especially my social diversions, which, during my teens, had peaked.

Today, a part of me rejoiced to escape Daddy's sometimes suffocating restrictions and accountability. Another tiny part grieved being loosed from that same tight rein, one that included infinite, tender care and concern.

But only for an instant. On its heels came a rush of joy so great I thought I would surely explode.

"Neece?" Cole appeared at my side in his little white tux with short pants, tugging at my skirt. "Wuv 'oo," he whispered, his hazel eyes huge with awe and humility. I loved Anne's and Daddy's offspring as though I'd personally birthed him. Had since I'd first laid eyes on him.

I stooped and gathered him in my arms, choking back tears – knowing I'd be leaving him behind. How I'd miss him being there first thing in the morning, seated at the breakfast table, fork in hand, hungrily watching me cook. We hugged fiercely. He puckered and gave me a big juicy kiss on the lips.

"I love you, too, Cole. Thanks for being my ring bearer. You did great!" And he did.

"Hey, buddyroe," Kirk winked solemnly at him as he returned with cups of punch.

Cole flashed us a huge grin, then scampered to join some cousins at the refreshment table. Though Kirk tried hard to hide it, I knew he was jealous of my close bond with my little brother. He wasn't unkind to Cole, he simply wasn't affectionate with him. Thought him "spoiled." Fact of the matter, Kirk was and still is a territorial ol' cuss.

It hurt, his coolness to Cole. But Kirk's good far outweighed his flaws. So I managed to hide my disappointment and take it in stride.

"Come on, you guys!" Callie gestured hugely from the refreshment area, bare toes poking from beneath her blue hem. Well I hope n' I never... I slowly shook my head, grinning that she'd already shucked her shoes. Cal's earthiness was unquenchable. "*Hey ya'll!*" she bellowed, "Time to cut the cake!"

Cal caught the bridal bouquet, nearly knocking Trish over in her pursuit.

"Not fair," Trish shrieked, giggling. "She's already getting married in two weeks."

"All's fair in love and war, doncha know? 'S th' way the mop flops." Cal smugly clasped the arrangement to her bosom then shoved it into Roger Denton's hands. Her fiance flushed magenta and struggled for decorum, as was customary following

Cal's jinks. Even today, after lukewarm congratulations to Kirk and me, Roger's gaze avoided ours. Only our love for Callie kept Rog and me civil toward one another. Only Kirk's love for me made him tolerate either of them. Though, I have to hand it to Kirk – he relented for Cal to be in our wedding party, conceding that mine and Cal's lifelong bonds were unbreakable.

I felt Kirk's arm slide around my waist and tighten possessively. "Whatcha say we do a disappearing act?" he whispered in my ear, raising goosebumps all over me.

Without so much as a fare-thee-well, he grabbed my hand and we took flight.

CHAPTER TWO

Matrimony pulled me from the quicksand of non-belonging, a thing I'd not fully recognized until I stepped into my own house. And I thought how here, I would keep my own home-fires a'burning. My very own.

Here, I *belonged*.

For though Anne and I developed a close friendship during those last two years under Daddy's roof, I'd never regressed to my former assured *dug-in* self. It wasn't her fault nor Daddy's; it was simply something altered in me by God only knows *what all* but, most certainly, what began with Mama's early death.

I'll never know if things would've been different had Kirk not come along because he did and he gave me the greatest of all gifts: strong arms to hold me and this home called *ours*.

"Hey!"

I blinked my eyes, irritated at Kirk's fingers snapping at the end of my nose as I gazed mistily through *our* window into a dusky blue-gray sky whose horizon slowly oozed peach and crimson. I jerked the venetian blind string to, first, close out the world and second, to vent my annoyance at his fingers' abrupt *snap* that always exploded over me, setting off my high-strung nerves.

"Where were you just now?" he asked, taking off his black tux coat, his heavy-lidded eyes glimmering with what I thought was amusement but suddenly realized was more. We'd chosen to forgo other choices to spend our honeymoon here, in our little village dwelling, only a couple of blocks from Daddy and Anne.

"Hmm?" he persisted in his velvety roughness and began to undress me with fumbling gentleness. I promptly assisted him.

"I was thinking about the wedding –" My voice caught when his hands boldly touched my skin in formerly forbidden places. Next thing I knew, we were between new white sheets, naked together for the first time, glorying in freedom, in the *rightness* of it all and we began to laugh, hugging and rocking back and forth, side to side, kissing and laughing and kissing...

until the laughter stopped and primitive urges, long, long denied, emerged.

Kirk stopped and gazed down at me. "I don't want to hurt you."

In answer, I pulled his head down and kissed him. The discomfort I felt soon gave way to the excitement of unfolding wonders and because of Kirk's tender concern, the consummation would not be completed until later that evening.

Instead, he playfully tugged me from the bed. "Get dressed, woman. Cook me some dinner."

We quickly pulled on cut-off shorts and matching white and Crimson Chapowee High pullovers and, excited as three-year-olds, invaded our sparkling, sunny-colored kitchen with its free-standing white cabinet and chrome and yellow dinette set, pulled out shiny new pots and pans and commenced cooking a fantastic dinner.

Kirk peeled potatoes and sliced them for potato salad, his first cooking venture. I showed off my fluffy buttermilk biscuits, lumpless gravy – learned at age nine from MawMaw – and crispy, juicy Southern fried chicken, compliments of Anne's tutelage. We topped off the meal with Kirk's favorite dessert, Banana Pudding with golden toasted meringue icing.

As I put dishes in a sink full of hot soapy water, I felt Kirk move to stand behind me, wrapping me in his arms, his hands doing magical things to my bosom. "Kirk!" My breath caught in my throat as he smoothly turned me into his arms and up against his arousal.

He kissed me deeply, leaving me breathless and clutching at him.

"I never knew," he muttered huskily, "that flour on your nose could be so sexy."

"Mmmm." I rubbed against him. "That move is pretty sexy, too."

He looked into my eyes, his turning dark as the night. "Let's go see," his voice was raspy as a corn cob, "what we can do about it."

❖ ❖ ❖ ❖ ❖ ❖

The kitchen became our home's hub, where we relaxed and chatted, listening to Fats or Johnny Mathis while delectable aromas wafted from the oven and frying pan. It was during those lingering intimate moments that we began to delve past yet another layer of self.

Each day brought surprises. Kirk gazed at my bowl across the dinette, clearly shocked. "You mean you eat *sugar and cream* on your oatmeal?"

"You mean you *don't?*" I shot back, equally astonished at his mound topped only with butter. After a moment of silent impasse, we burst into laughter. Kirk later divulged that the Crenshaw's plain oatmeal was to spare the expense of sugar. Nor did they drink milk in their coffee for the same reason. I began to really see the Crenshaw's poverty level.

Food made *togetherness* ours. The morning hours, before Kirk went to his second-shift mill job, passed swiftly because we slept late and ate brunches concocted with creative zeal, anything from sausage and pancakes to pot roast and potatoes, didn't matter, it was all fun and adventure.

Today was beef stew we'd cooked from a *Good Housekeeping* cookbook, a shower present of mine. "It's delicious," I spooned the last bite from my plate.

"It's great," Kirk agreed, sipping his ever-present coffee contentedly. "Though I'd like to let it simmer for another twenty minutes next time."

"Think so?"

"Yeah. Needs to tenderize just a mite more."

"Mmm." I smiled at him.

He leaned forward on his elbows, gazing at me as though seeing something for the first time. "What's behind that smile?" he asked, genuinely curious.

"Oh…just that everything is so perfect." I drew on my iced tea glass and sighed. "You'll never know how much it means to me to have a place that's truly mine. It's hard to explain."

Kirk reached across the table and took my hands in his. "I love you so much, honey," he murmured, frowning with the effort to verbalize his feelings. "The fact that you didn't have a mother to care for you made me love you even more."

"Thanks," I muttered, growing a tad uncomfortable with the pity I heard in his voice. "I guess I did okay, considering." I thought of sad-eyed Trish – then pushed away the thought.

Kirk's laser turquoise eyes pinned me with a look I'd seen sporadically – an unreadable, dissecting gaze that did not let up simply because I grew fidgety. "Anne…" he hesitated, uncertain, then forged ahead, "Anne's okay – least she's been nice to me. But she doesn't treat you and Trish like she does her own kid."

"I don't think that's true," I said, desperate to dispel his claim. "Cole's a baby and –"

"Look," Kirk held up a hand. "Let's just drop the subject. You don't want to see…"

"I think we *should* drop the subject." I gave Kirk an appealing look and reached for his hand.

His large, beautiful square fingers curled with mine. "I'm sorry, honey," he said. "I don't mean to hurt you. Ever."

"It's just that – Kirk, family is so important to me. And it seems that those most important to me – I lose them." I shrugged awkwardly, fighting back tears

"What if you had a family like *mine?*" Kirk's eyes glimmered suddenly with dark humor. "A sot for a daddy and a mama who doesn't see anything but her misery? And brothers and sisters who wouldn't spit on each other if they were all on fire. Living in a house where Christmas went by unnoticed." He chortled. "I'd have *died* for just a box of chocolate-covered cherries, y'know? *God a'mighty*, I love those things. And there were never any hugs or 'I love yous.' We just survived. Yanked up by the hair o'the head. You want to talk about *mess*, we'll talk about mess."

We both cracked up. That always did it when I got soppy and sentimental about things I couldn't change. Kirk could always dredge up down-dirty *real* scenarios from his life, which were infinitely more desperate than anything I'd ever experienced.

"Anyway," he spoke as he moved around the table, took my hand and pulled me up and into his arms, "this – *us* – we're family now. And I won't leave you. I'll always be here for you, Neecy,"

"And I'll always be here for you, Kirk. You'll never have another Christmas without chocolate-covered cherries. That's a promise."

On most Sundays now, Kirk and I attended worship services at Chapowee Methodist Church, along with Daddy, Anne, Trish and little Cole. My feelings for my stepmother Anne remained ambivalent, at once affectionate yet vigilant. Vigilant because of Trish's ongoing quandary. Nothing blatantly obvious. Just a feeling I got. And things Trish, on rare occasions, hinted at.

Before Dad and Anne's marriage ceremony, everything was bliss, quite backward from fabled versions. Afterward, all hell broke loose. Daddy's homefront sovereignty hit big potholes when he and Anne toed off. The same *take control* Mama had found romantic and masculine, his new bride found archaic and intolerable and many's a skirmish Trish and I stumbled into. I fended okay, but Trish, little Trish who crooned to any creature *hurt*, found herself wandering about a bloody minefield, dazed and indefensible to what the next step might set off.

In a nutshell, it was Daddy's excessive protectiveness that set his baby up for rejection, for that's the way he viewed Trish: *my baby*. Just as he related to me and, earlier, to Chuck as *mine*. Possessive. Subjugated. For in those days, one side of my father knew only absolutes. The more he insisted Anne heap affection on Trish, the more he sequestered the two. I've thought many a time how, had he left it alone, it might have healed itself sooner.

"Do you want the kids to call you 'Mama'?" he asked one day during a rare truce.

Anne looked at him for long moments pondering, measuring. I held my breath, finding that, surprisingly, I missed calling someone "Mama." I did not like being half-orphan. I'd never, ever forget my precious mother, but at the same time, I didn't like the pity being motherless brings. In fact, I detested pity.

Anne's fair brow, set below flaming titian hair, furrowed. "No, that wouldn't be right."

My heart plunged and a new, sharp ache formed inside me.

Something flickered in Daddy's face, a shade of grief. "Okay." He gave a limp shrug, that in itself uncharacteristic. But I knew, it was not okay. And Daddy could – *would* hold a grudge as long as he breathed.

"Blood's thicker'n water," sprang Grandma Whitman's litany to mind, one she'd always muttered during family loyalty tests. Now, the implication smacked me broadside as I dealt, again, with the changes inaugurated by Mama's sudden death. I had, until now, attained a measure of continuity in my life, a sense of *me*. I'd desperately convinced myself that I remained intact, despite that the pain of losing her still sat heavily upon me. Youthful resilience had mimed healing, using other things to help divert me from the immediacy of loss.

Until that moment, when Anne said, "No."

That's all I heard. *No*. Rejection. It proved one thing I'd suspected for some time now.

I was unlovable.

Everything flooded in on me in that moment, transporting me back to a day or two after Mama's burial. We'd remained at the home of my mother's parents, Daddy and the three of us, nurturing and grieving through the difficult raw days following death. That May day was incredibly bright and sunny, deriding our sorrow and sending Daddy out alone for a drive.

It was while Daddy was gone that Chuck, Trish and I overheard MawMaw's weepy version of my mother's crisis when birthing me years earlier. Seems the inexperienced intern who delivered me had overlooked the afterbirth, then sent Mama home.

"Joe let her lay there and nearly die," MawMaw's quiet sobs wafted through her open bedroom window to where we huddled together on her small front porch. "If you'n me hadn't a' gone to see her when we did, she'd a'died. You could *smell* the infection when we walked in. Poor lil' thing was a'burnin' up with fever, all alone. Joe was nowhere around." I heard Papa trying to hush her.

Her jaded view shocked and disappointed me but knowing MawMaw's propensity to being swept away with emotion made me tolerant. Besides, I knew with eleven-year-old logic that her venting was for Papa's ears alone, was not about Daddy at all but about her dead child, about *loss*. MawMaw was not known for tact when passion seized her, but that same passion, flavored differently, propelled her to love a grandchild as *offspring.*

And when my brother Chuck, for reasons known only to him, later that afternoon took Daddy aside to repeat MawMaw's comments, my father's face had emptied before he whisked us away from loving grandparents whose worst sin was loosed-tongue ignorance.

The *betrayal* devastated Daddy because he'd loved Mama more than life itself and had endured MawMaw's *pprrkk*ing through early honeymoon days and on through the years, respecting her still for Mama's sake.

Now, Mama was gone. Daddy's resolution was simple. "I don't have to put up with it anymore. I didn't neglect your Mama. I'd gone to the store the day her folks came a'visiting. I was only eighteen years old, for heaven's sake. Didn't know nothing about afterbirths and such." He grew quiet as the car hummed us away from MawMaw's house. "That old battle-axe's had her last go at me" was his final comment as he drove us to Grandma Whitman's, who hated MawMaw, a mutual thing generated when their offspring married, both certain all the newlywed's trouble spawned from the other in-law.

Daddy proceeded to excise my grandparents from our lives as succinctly as a surgeon's knife and reinforced with every stubborn gene at his dispatch. Within a week, the genetic validating forces of my life – namely those who loved me unconditionally – all but vanished.

Years later, Anne's "no" drove home the significance of those genetic ties and echoed the losses of a short life. Why get close to anybody if it only ended in separation and pain? So I distanced myself from Anne, as I did from anyone who seemed not to value me. I decided then and there I would have to work extra hard to be loveable – to be accepted. No longer would it be a natural, flowing result of being loved.

Thanks, Chucky boy, I thought as I spun on my heel and fled the room, *for stripping away all I had left. You didn't even hang around to help me pick up the pieces.*

I passed the long afternoon hours, while Kirk worked, scrubbing and hunting things to clean, glorying in ironing sheets and pillow cases and at first, even Kirk's briefs and tee-shirts.

Occasionally, Trish got away to come over to visit. Not often. Because Anne kept her busy baby-sitting Cole and helping in the house. I didn't, at the time, consider the latter abusive, since the same duties fell to me up till I married. Callie, my pal, however, thought it *most* abusive and often vehemently told me so. I brushed it off because Prima Donna Cal led a princess' existence with her mother waiting on her hand and foot. What *did* bother me was the fact that mine and Trish's time together was so restricted. And it wasn't Daddy this time. It was Anne.

Trish, so soft-spoken and kind-hearted, rarely complained.

Today was different. "I can't seem to get things right, y' know? She doesn't like me, Sis," she said with infinite sadness, blaming herself, for cryin' out loud. "She just *doesn't*. She never has."

I didn't want to believe it. Fought against it. "Are you sure, honey? Couldn't you be –"

"No," her head moved firmly from side to side. "Anne-does-not-like-me. I don't know why. Maybe she's jealous because Daddy steps in sometimes and reminds her that she's not really my Mama."

"Oh no. I'd hoped he'd stopped that. *Doggone!*" Daddy's way of getting back at her for refusing to let us call her "Mom."

"Uh hmm." Trish sighed. "Well, it's usually when he thinks she oversteps her bounds. You know Daddy. He's –"

"Iron-Hand-Houdini."

Trish chuckled. "That, too. But...." She grew solemn. "I feel guilty all the time because most of their fights revolve around me. I mean – if I wasn't in the picture, they wouldn't fight as much."

"*Hah!* Daddy and Anne will *never* run out of things to fight about. Trust me, Trish. It's not you. It's them." I pondered a moment. "'Course, Daddy is awfully protective over us. Thinks we're *pitiful.*" I snorted. "*Law,* how I *hate* that idea. We're *not* pathetic *things.*"

"Yeah." Trish smiled sadly. "I appreciate his caring – but that only makes things worse for me." We sat quietly, contemplating Daddy's role in our lives.

"Remember how Daddy made me and Kirk stop going on our Sunday mountain drives?" I shook my head. "So unfair. 'Too much time alone,' he said." I recalled Daddy's dissecting gaze stalking Kirk those early courtship days. I laughed suddenly. "Daddy thought if he ignored it – *it* would go away." I sighed. "But Kirk remained as polite and accommodatin' as you please." I chuckled. "Smart. Knew that to get to me, he had to go through Daddy." I shrugged. "It worked. Daddy thinks Kirk can hang the moon and stars now."

"To be fair – Daddy really did worry that I needed lots of rest." I crossed my eyes. "Thinks I'm so *fragiiiile.*"

"Yeah," Trish slanted me a mock-sassy look, "unlike ol' fatso *me,* you're a bit frail."

"You're not *fatso,*" I said, ignoring her rolled back eyes, "Heck, I only look frail to Daddy 'cause most of the Whitman women are hefty as oxes."

"But you *do get* hay fever and bronchitis, Sis," Trish insisted.

"Yeah," I conceded. "Many's a night he woke me spooning that awful whiskey-lemon-sugar crap down my throat." I shuddered and screwed up my face, then admitted, "But it did stop the cough."

"And though money's short," added Trish, "he always took us to the doctor at the first sign of sickness." She looked directly at me. "He's a good Daddy."

"The best," I agreed whole-heartedly. "*Despite* his heavy-handedness." I grinned wickedly. "One battle Anne won – she got pregnant, in spite of Daddy's objections that he didn't want more kids to raise. He roared and kicked up a fuss about feeling used like a 'stud bull.'"

The phone rang, interrupting our belly laughter. It was Anne.

"Neece, is Trish over there?"

"Yeah. She is." I handed the receiver to Trish, who listened and quietly hung up.

"What did she say?" I dreaded the answer.

Trish looked bleakly at me. "Said to come home. I had no right to sneak off like that." Tears sprang to her stricken eyes. "*Why,* Sis? Why can't I spend time with you? It's not *fair.*"

"No," I said quickly and hugged her at the door. "No, it's not. But I'll tell you like MawMaw told me. When you get old enough, you can come see me when you dadgum well please."

I sent her off with a smile. When I closed the door, I cried.

"Hey, sweetheart, I'm home!" was Kirk's nightly greeting when he burst through the door near midnight, carrying his empty lunch box and coffee thermos. I always said if Kirk couldn't get to coffee, it would be apocalypse. Having cut his baby teeth on a coffee cup, he is novocained to caffeine's effects. I always met him at the door with a kiss and had food on the table.

"Any pickles?" he asked as he munched into a ham and cheese sandwich. I went to the fridge and pulled out a dill to slice in two for us to share. This nightly snack ended our day on a sweet, mellow note.

In bed, Kirk and I grew more adventuresome, exploring new erogenous anatomy. Recently, my mammary glands in particular, fascinated him. Then *me. Wow!*

"Gosh, honey," he murmured one night while driving me mad, "If only I'd known about this while we dated." He lifted his head and peered dazedly at me. "I could've gotten *anything from you I wanted.*"

"True. We probably would've had a shotgun wedding," I gasped, pulling him back for more.

"Yeah," he rasped, burying his face in my bosom, "Good thing I was so innocent."

That Kirk's weekly Chapowee Mill paycheck was fifty-two dollars and our expenses were fifty, failed to dampen our sense of adventure. I shopped frugally for foods that stretched, like hamburger at thirty-nine cents a pound. Five pounds served three to four meals, ranging from spaghetti to grilled hamburgers cooked over open grills at Spartanburg's Cleveland Park, where we'd use our two extra dollars for gas to take us on our one weekend outing.

Heck, we had it all worked out. Kirk handled the money, the little we had, which pleased me because overseeing finances was infinitely foreign to me, and I managed the food purchasing with my ten-to-fifteen dollars allowance.

Laughter propelled us through the days and titillating discoveries through the nights. How *abandoned* we were to each other and to the sheer joy of *being.* Kirk's blundering quest for cooking skills gave me hilarious tidbits to jot down in my writing tablet and many a laugh to share.

How I embraced that period of sterling trust and openness.

"You look so pretty, Callie." I buttoned her red silk blouse up the back and turned her around for a hug. "But you always *do.*"

Late afternoon sunlight painted Chapowee First Baptist Church's Sunday School room walls golden and shimmered across heartland pine floor, where Mollie Pleasant, Cal's mom, devoutly attended, tugging at and praying for Cal and her Dad

Callie's folks, like mine, worked the mill's second-shift, only difference being I had baby-sat Trish while Cal, an only child, had been virtually unaccountable for her time. That gal could lie with the purest face among saints and Mollie and Ed Pleasant, seemingly intelligent folk, took everything she said as gospel.

I'd always espied Cal's mastery with a blend of awe and horror because *me,* I couldn't even carry off a half-truth because Daddy's all-seeing gray eyes could arrest and x-ray me without him uttering a sound and he always *knew.* Oh, yes, he knew. His wordless condemnation made my insides squirm like a stuck caterpillar, my eyes unable to hold his gaze, and his discipline, usually a rumbling baritone diatribe of disappointment, reduced me to a shredded, smoldering heap of shame.

Here I am, I thought, *still* having to remind myself I'm married. Out from under Daddy's rule. The abrupt transition still, at times, made my head reel.

As though reading my mind, Callie murmured, "C'mon, now, aren't you glad to get away from your bossy Dad? Don't know how you ever stood being *watched* all the time. *Ssshsuzzzz.*" She shuddered hugely.

I laughed and ignored the question. She knew I adored Daddy.

Callie and Rog's wedding ceremony had ended more than an hour and a half ago.

Outside, friends and buddies bedecked the getaway car while the bride dressed for a honeymoon trek to the mountains. Callie slid stockinged feet into black pumps. "Was the wedding – you know, really *nice?*" Large amber eyes implored me for reassurance.

"Beautiful." It had been. "Pigeon Forge will be great, Cal. Cool nights but," I wiggled my brows wickedly, "*hot* between the sheets."

"You ol' *hussy*, you." A lusty belly laugh tumbled from her throat. "One week from now and I'll be leavin' this place."

I folded the white veil and placed it carefully between tissue padding in the box. "Sure gonna miss you, Cal."

"Yeah. Me, too."

"We'll have to write often. You *will* keep in touch, won't you?"

"'Course I will." We bear-hugged for long moments. "Gotta take off. Rog sure looked handsome, didn't he?"

"Oh, yeah." I reassured her, strangely moved by her need for it. "You're one lucky couple, like me and Kirk. Bye, Cal."

I stared after her as she bounded from the room to the excitement of leave-taking and grieved that behind Callie's dark whiskey irises stretched an endless Mojave Desert.

❖ ❖ ❖ ❖ ❖ ❖

"I brought you some tomatoes." Tom Crenshaw, Kirk's father, stood on our front porch, holding a paper grocery bag brimming with vivid red tomatoes he'd grown in his bountiful garden. A disheveled, blood-shot eyed, graying version of Kirk, he blushed and shuffled his feet awkwardly, embarrassed at having caught us still in bed on a Saturday morning at ten a.m. "I won't come in, I'm dirty," he handed Kirk the bag.

"Come on in, Dad," Kirk insisted gruffly. "At least have a cup of coffee." The magic word. Docilely, Tom followed him to the kitchen where Kirk's pot still offered up another brimming cup. I've never, before nor since, seen a family who devoured java so ecstatically as the Crenshaws.

I quietly moved to the bathroom to bathe and dress, giving them private moments together. As I soaked in the bath tub, I thought *how difficult it is to believe this man's the same one Kirk described as monstrous*, one who drank liquor steadily from Friday after work until Sunday night of each week. A man who raged and pursued his kids like a fiend, chasing them into the woods with his car, where they migrated to thickly wooded areas where he couldn't follow. Who'd dangled a young Kirk by his ankles above a well over some trivial matter. Today, he seemed okay, though I'd whiffed something foreign before escaping to the bathroom.

Moments later, I heard the front door shut and knew he'd left. Kirk joined me and lounged on the commode. Seemed to just want to be near me. As though I could dispel something. Was being with his father traumatic?

"He can be so – nice," I said. We rarely visited them. Tom always drank on weekends and Kirk refused to go after the one time we'd happened up on him stinking drunk and on a wild rampage. It scared me spitless. I'd never seen a raging drunk and it wasn't a pretty sight.

"Oh, there's not a better man than Dad when he's sober. Has one of the prettiest gardens in these parts," he said proudly, then lapsed into stony silence. I got out of the tub and dried off, leaving Kirk still sitting and mulling when I went into the bedroom and dressed in cutoffs and pullover.

"I'm going to gas up the car," he muttered as he breezed past the bedroom.

"Wait up, I'll go with you," I called as his hand hit the front door knob.

"I'm just ridin' to the gas station."

I approached him and searched his unreadable features. Did he mean *no, I don't want you to go?* But it was so at odds with the *can't stay away from you* Kirk. It just didn't – fit.

If anything, his face registered bland impatience.

Suddenly, I felt childish and awkward, like when Daddy'd refused to let me go off in a car. I shrugged. "I just...wanted to ride with you. It gets kinda lonely being by myself so much. But just go on without me...." I fought a rising indignation.

He shifted, averting his eyes, and opened the door. "I don't care. Come on."

"No. I have things to do." I marched stiffly to the kitchen and began puttering, hearing the front door slam and the car leave the drive. Anger battered me for long moments before I realized Kirk's frustration had nothing to do with me.

Or did it?

My busy hands stilled as I recalled the times I'd heard Kirk's Mom's questions go unanswered, ignored by her husband. Few were the times I'd known Tom Crenshaw to take his wife anywhere with him, even on rare *sober* occasions, no more than I'd known him to show her respect or affection. I felt sorry for the poor soul, who'd one time, in her early days, been pretty and full of life and love and enjoyed movies, a diversion denied since she'd married. Perhaps by naming her children after her favorite stars, she reclaimed some of the magic of those carefree, bygone days and so she'd called her first son Roy Rogers Crenshaw. Then, in two-year intervals, they stair-tripped downward: John Wayne, Kirk Douglas, Mitzi Gaynor, Randoph Scott, Lana-Ava and Rex Allen.

Tom's indulgence for his wife's frivolity sprouted and died there in the birthing bed. Betty's fun and free-spiritedness had early on taken flight. By the time I met her, she was a wispy shadow of a woman whose focus seemed affixed to sheer survival. From the time I first saw her standing behind her screen door to welcome me into the clean but shabby Crenshaw dwelling, my heart lurched in sympathy, something in me recognizing her aloneness.

Kirk's love for his parents was solid while his view of them was confused and at times, paradoxical. He spoke of his father in terms of *when he's sober* this and *when he's drinking* that, his features bounding twixt pride and sadness. With his mom, his estimation blurred more – the fact that Betty had hung in there and kept the family intact during all the desolation brought both pain and sorrow.

No wonder Kirk's love signals got muddled. He had lousy role models.

Today, I heard him return and acted busy at the sink. He came up behind me and put his arms around me. Then he laid his head over on my shoulder, gently burrowing, as a child would – a gesture of need.

I turned and gathered him in my arms, hugged him for long moments, then took his hand and went to the den to sprawl on the sofa and talk. Today, Betty was the underdog.

"Mama cried at the drop of a hat, over nothing – over *everything.* I never believed the tears were real. Y'know? Like something out of her danged movies. Felt they were manipulative – to gain sympathy. Mama loved being a martyr." Kirk's vehement stance shocked me, but I kept silent. It was his life and at last, he was opening up to me. I refused to analyze too deeply.

"She shoulda left him years ago, got us kids out of all that misery," Kirk added during the dark moment and I wondered about the times he'd *praised* her for the same tenacity. I wondered, too, why it was that not only he, but his siblings as well, seemed much more tolerant of their dad's drunken railings than of their mother's passiveness. Seemed that, to the Crenshaws, earning power established one's worth and despite Tom Crenshaw's creation of havoc – Hell, his children valued him – the bread winner – more than they did their stay-at-home mother. That mystified me. So did the influence the man had on Kirk, a thing Kirk would stoutly deny, to this very day.

Like today, Kirk's abrupt pivot from *let's be together* to *I need time alone* reeked of Tom Crenshaw. Of course, I realized the senselessness in attributing Kirk's genetic quirks to his father. I dared not give voice to my fears. For though he aired his frustrations with me, he remained, during our early married days, fiercely loyal to his parents.

In the end, I reasoned that this was but one of the potholes all newlyweds faced. Adjustments.

I also reasoned that even with all my family mess, I still had it a hundred and ten per cent better than Kirk. I rededicated myself to making it all up to him.

The whole deal left me feeling that a part of the girl in me vacated to make room for more woman.

"Why, you ain't grown a bit, Sis. Still lighter'n a Gypsy Dandelion." Chuck had popped in today out of the blue, temporarily evaporating my anger at him.

My feet touched the floor and I clung to my brother, steadying myself, laughing and peering through tears into the good-looking face whose blue eyes crinkled with laughter lines. He would be twenty-three now. "Chuck, you're just about the best lookin' guy I've ever seen. A blond John Saxon.

"*Just about?*" he mimicked, wide grin framing perfectly even white teeth, knowing I'd paid him my highest compliment.

"Why isn't – is her name Connie? Did she come with –"

"No. Actually, Honey, Connie ain't with me anymore. Gettin' a divorce," he stated calmly, succinctly flipping a fleck from his shirtsleeve with his fingertip, a gesture that spoke more than words.

"But –" I sucked in a shocked breath. "What happened, Chuck?"

"Oh," he shrugged. "Differences. Just couldn't be helped. What about you? Things goin' okay with yours?"

"Oh – great. Great." I did not pursue why his marriage ended. My heart felt a peculiar heaviness as he plopped down on my turquoise sofa, but he soon had me diverted again, laughing and cutting the fool. Fact was, I was the yo-yo and he pulled the string. He tossed me away and pulled me back. Tossed me away when I mentioned Daddy and pulled me back when I appeased him.

When in his favor, I thought of bygone days when we siblings were the "Three Musketeers," one for all and all for one. It hurt, the change, especially when I knew Chuck had been a Mama's boy. I knew the pain of his loss.

I didn't then and still don't today know what murky trick of genetics caused the disintegration of trust between Daddy and Chuck except that they were both bullheaded and both plagued with tunnel-vision once their minds were made up. I knew Daddy loved Chuck, just as I knew Chuck loved him, but they just couldn't get it together. Unforgiveness and pride eroded their chances of reconciliation.

"How's Trish, by the way?" he asked.

I filled him in on how Trish's weight problem seemed to be escalating, leaving out that the tension between her and Anne still existed. Chuck had locked horns with Anne aplenty on his own before he split – in his case, it was his own smart-aleck rebellion at doing chores he felt beneath him. Like cleaning the bathroom commode. And I'd thought *does he think that should fall to us mere females?* And though Trish's pudgy tendency began long before Anne entered the picture, I was convinced the stress of Trish's position magnified things. I told Chuck Anne had spent a few days in the hospital recently.

"Ulcerative colitis." Anne still fought her own emotional battles with Daddy.

Chuck's eyes glimmered when he looked up from the wedding pictures we were going through. "Ol' man still giving her a hard time?"

"They just don't always – see eye to eye on things is all, Chuck." I tried not to sound prim, but Chuck's nostrils reacted to my defensiveness.

"Tell me somethin' new, why doncha?" He tossed a picture aside and, whistling through his teeth, opened another album. I bit my tongue, determined not to say anything to drive him away. *Why?* Why did I so tenaciously carry this virtual one-sided commitment.

All I knew was that this was my brother. That *had* to mean something.

I didn't share my disappointment that our grandparents moved away so soon after I was free to visit them without Daddy's permission. Despite his animosity toward Daddy, Chuck sympathized to the point of shunning MawMaw and Papa, augmenting their grief.

The vicious cycle spun on. Chuck's anger roiled restless and indiscriminate, settling in senseless ways.

My brother left as abruptly as he came, his hostility lingering like a dank gray, choking fog. That he could turn off his love for Daddy and MawMaw and Papa – and now, Connie – baffled and terrorized me. Was it only a matter of time before I displeased him and he stopped loving me?

A chill rippled up my spine. I rushed to get the tablet I wrote in when things built up.

Later that night in bed, I shared my fears with Kirk.

"Chuck's got a lot of junk to get rid of," Chuck said grimly then kissed my forehead. " I'll take you to see MawMaw and Papa, honey, any time you want. Kirk will take care of his girl," he murmured against my temple, ruffling my hair as I spooned back against him. " Didn't I promise?"

"Mm hm." My lids drooped as his strong arms closed around me, securing me to him.

I was safe.

CHAPTER THREE

I felt *like a bird out of prison*, as the old country gospel song goes.

Kirk and I took our liberties. In the following months, we did everything *if* and *when* we darn well wanted to. We ate, slept and made love that way – even attended church sporadically when it pleased us. After my extreme *daddy-ordered* life and Kirk's self-parenting existence, we were ready to do our own thing.

Our own thing was each other. It was building a new, better life, seeing only the good in one another. Tonight, on a cool October evening, it was going to Jimbo's Nook and spending our last two dollars on his incomparable minced barbecue sandwiches, holding hands and listening to *Silhouettes* from someone else's jukebox-deposited change.

"Let's dance." Kirk took my hand and turned me into his arms. The place was nearly empty except for a couple of teen girls who watched us wistfully, dreamily. I held my breath, hoping Kirk's second left foot was off duty tonight. He only stepped on my toes twice during that song.

"Here's to the newlyweds," Jimbo said, pulling change from his apron pocket as he came from behind the counter. "What'll it be, Neecy?"

"*Special Angel*," I said, grinning all over myself. It was our favorite. "Thanks, Jimbo." Slow-dancing, we relived high school sock hops, whispering and laughing, reminiscing over Callie's gypsyish, uninhibited behavior and Moose's doofus, sweet ways and silly drunken escapades.

The teen girls put more change into the jukebox and *A Certain Smile* kept our feet moving and our hearts beating as one. "Let's adopt each other's family," I gushed impulsively, warmed and magnanimous and crazy in love.

He gazed into my eyes for long moments, a slow, cool analytical look that suddenly warmed and made my heart do a flip. "Case you hadn't noticed, darlin'," he drawled lazily, "I *have* adopted your family as my own. I feel closer to Joe than I've ever felt to my own father."

That was true. "That's what I wish I had with your family," I said longingly

Kirk's face turned to stone. "Is something wrong?" I asked quietly, my heart thumping hard. He stared over my head now, avoiding eye contact. I felt his withdrawal

"I wish you could accept—reality." His uneasy gaze lowered and swept over my features. "I don't want them to hurt you."

I let it drop. Our wave lengths weren't in the same atmosphere. But that was okay. I was learning our childhood experiences veered us emotionally in totally opposite directions.

"I'm glad, Kirk, that you're close to Daddy," I said, then stopped dancing suddenly. The room was beginning to spin crazily and the lights to blur. "Kirk?" I grasped the front of his shirt. "I'm dizzy...."

"Neecyyyyyyy......"

My name echoed on and on. Then, everything went black.

"Eight weeks pregnant," was Dr. Woodruff's diagnosis.

Pregnant and so sick I turned green. Honest – as Kirk is my witness. My finely tuned senses augmented smells and sights, that'd once enthralled me, into stench.

Suddenly, Kirk's cigarettes stank worse than any other scent in this vast universe. Just a whiff of their smoke – that invaded every molecule of indoor space – sent me scurrying to the bathroom to throw up or as Grandma Whitman would have said, to puke.

Unrefined though she was, I had to agree. There *is* a difference.

Finally, by the third month, I had only to glimpse a Winston to start the violent heaving, not always making it to the bathroom in time.

Kirk was considerate and loving but terribly addicted to nicotine and had to justify *why* he didn't just lay them aside. So, it goes to reason that he decided a part of the nausea was in my head, especially since, at that unenlightened time, some doctors propagated the theory that the nausea was at least partly psychosomatic

"How come you get sick just *looking* at a cigarette, even before smelling it?" he asked in his most guilty moments, wiping my brow with a damp cloth as I sprawled noodle-limp on the sofa.

I could have argued it wasn't only the sight of his cigarettes that set off fierce puking but thoughts of sweet pickles, onions and even innocent golden iced tea, but I was simply too depleted to react.

"Huh?" he'd persist, trying to shift his features from *guilty* to *imposing* by furrowing his brow.

"I don't know." I took the cloth from him and washed my lips. "It just happens."

"Ahh, honey," his expression swung to undiluted anguish. "I'm so sorry you have to go through this." A furious hand swiped through his hair. "It's not fair."

"Sure it is," I whispered, cupping his rigid, frustrated face in my palm. "For whatever reason, that's the way God planned it." I smiled weakly. "I'll be okay. Just give me a few minutes."

He grew quiet after that – *throbbing* with a guilt I could not assuage. I knew he would quit smoking *if* he could. *When* he could. And I knew that just as he wasn't perfect, neither was I. I knew by now there *was* no Knight in shining armor.

But I knew, beyond a doubt, that above anything on earth, Kirk loved me. And quite suddenly, he was as cow-eyed as me over little gurgling, cooing babies.

The day Heather was born, Kirk threw away his cigarettes. "I don't ever want my children to see me smoke," he said in his mind-made-up way, then kissed me like Rhett Butler did Scarlett .

Anne told me that during my final labor, Kirk wedged his face into the crack of the Delivery Room door to watch Dr. Woodruff and his team scurry about while two patients delivered at once.

Kirk was as proud a Dad as a man can be. "I love you a thousand times more than before," he told me in his velvet-gruff voice. "Thank you, Sweetheart."

In those words, he handed me the world.

The next day, leaving the hospital, Kirk won a good-natured tug-of-war with Anne over who'd carry Heather to the car. My stepmother stayed with me for a week, caring for me and the baby, cooking delicious meals and keeping the house tidy for company who paraded through to see the new little Crenshaw.

Motherhood was the most marvelous thing and I reveled in it, loving my child – mine and Kirk's creation – with a passion that surpassed anything I'd ever felt. Within weeks, Heather's round solidness filled my arms and heart with delicious pleasure. Her apple cheeks glowed with perpetual pinch-pink rosiness and, from the beginning, she moved and held herself erect with amazing strength. "Just look at that," Kirk crowed, rounding his chest like Charles Atlas.

Her Aunt Trish, at twelve, was quite good at tending the baby, who could be a tad demanding at times. Daddy, still youthful, did *Papa* with aplomb and beamed when folks declared, "but you're too *young* to be a grandpa."

Sometime during those days, Daddy took Kirk under his wing and began parenting him, giving him the respect missed in younger years and boasting to anybody who'd listen about his great son-in-law and what a hard worker he was.

My heart nearly burst with happiness seeing the two men most dear to me loving one another.

When Heather was six weeks old, Kirk drove us to Asheville to see MawMaw and Papa and they made over the baby as if she were a one-of-a-kind edition. I rocked her on the front porch of their little white, five-room cottage and looked across the vast mountain range and saw a golden castle afar off, etched amid myriad spring greens coating the majestic highlands, glistening in the sunlight, and I felt as if I were dreaming.

"What's that?" I asked MawMaw, who came out her screen door, looking endearingly fluffy in a fashionless, loose-fitting cotton print dress, bearing frosted glasses of iced tea. Papa, more Panda-like than ever in clean overalls and shirt, trailed her with a tray of sliced homemade chocolate cake. He'd long ago taken to growing one side of his salt and pepper hair long at the part, then sweeping it over his bald spot, which stretched from one ear top to the other.

"That's Biltmore Castle. Where the Vanderbilts live."

Kirk fed me cake while I nursed Heather, modestly covering myself with a light blanket and we talked and reminisced until dusk about days gone by, especially capers attributed to Chuck and me. Nobody could work up a celebratory mood like my grandparents, whose laughter rang and bubbled and roared at the humor found in most everything under the sun, didn't matter what, they always ferreted out a funny twist.

MawMaw's laugh billowed out in husky, rhythmic tumbles that tossed back her head, dilated her nostrils and brought tears to her eyes, while Papa's rolled out like popcorn popping, half-mooning his gray eyes and shaking his entire body. I always thought Papa's face looked like the Man in the Moon. Classic caricature. Marvelously loveable. Their mirth showed me a side to life that valued me. Theirs was laughter unbridled yet kind. I do not recall their teasing ever making me feel awkward or diminished.

My uncle Gabe and Jean, who lived nearby, came over to visit and the laughter increased for a spell before everyone on the porch began to settle into a quieter contentment and soon, began to yawn. That brought on more soft chuckles about it being contagious. Kirk mentioned Daddy was leaving the mill to pursue his lifelong ambition to barber, something he'd done during World War Two in the barracks after discovering his talent for it.

"Is that so?" Gabe's interest in Daddy kept Kirk talking.

My grandmother fell deathly silent, and I saw her deflate at the mention of my father's name. Her resistance to affirm the existence of Joe Whitman attacked my spirit with shame and horror and helplessness. *Why?*

"When you seen Chuck?" MawMaw's whispery, choked aside didn't interrupt the men's conversation.

"Not since before Heather was born. Actually – it's been over a year."

MawMaw rocked the cadence of one in a trance, desperate and vacant. "I saw Joe and Anne right before we moved up here," she said quietly so as not to be heard by the men, whose talk flowed. "They run into us at the Company Store. Had that little boy of their'n with 'em."

Cole. Little Cole. Her cold reference to my baby brother chilled my heart.

I knew Anne had fussed at Daddy for feuding with his ex-in-laws. "They're the kids' grandparent's, Joe," she'd kept reminding him. Anne's late mother and MawMaw had been good friends, a thing that drew the two women together. And I knew Daddy'd let up a bit on his hostility, giving me a growing sense of things being set aright.

I did not want to hear this.

But MawMaw continued, rocking maniacally, staring into the night. "Anne said, 'Cole, say *hey* to MawMaw and Papa.' And Joe kinda nudged him to speak to us." Her rocking grew heavier and the air thickened about me until it began to choke me as MawMaw went on. "I thought to myself how Joe'd took my grandchildren away from me and then wanted to push this one at me."

Shock and sick disillusionment cascaded over me at my grandmother's unkind referrals to the innocent little guy I adored. He obviously wasn't anything to MawMaw. But he was my *brother.*

The muddled genetic pool into which I toppled washed a pall over me, a heavy black ooze that snuffed and vanquished all the joy of this visit. Gabe kept the conversation afloat with Kirk as I battled the knot in my stomach. Kirk droned softly on, supplying Gabe with family divulgences, oblivious to MawMaw's stricken features and Papa's concern for her, all barely discernable, all screaming at me.

When MawMaw abruptly rose and went into the house, Papa closely trailed her.

I didn't follow because I knew that MawMaw's grief, though heavy, did not begin to approximate mine. And while her reactions held, to some degree, choices, mine did not.

"I wish they wouldn't do that." The gray night soaked up Gabe's quiet words. Blinking fireflies punctuated them in a surreal way. He'd not been as preoccupied as I thought.

"What?" Kirk asked, his silhouette in the darkness lean and long and tense. I'd discussed little of the family war with my husband, hoping it would go away, not wanting to give him place to take sides, knowing I'd be hurt further.

"Not letting loose of – things," my soft-spoken uncle replied.

After long moments, Kirk replied. "Yeah." I realized then that Kirk knew. He could not know me and *not* know.

Despite Daddy's compulsion to air his in-law grievances within earshot of anybody who'd listen, I still trusted Kirk to not allow my – *our* – turf to be polluted by it all. He'd sensed my desperation and remained as impartial as possible. A difficult thing, especially on those long afternoon male-bonding drives with Daddy. He must have felt torn many times.

I swallowed an egg-sized lump and lay my head back against the oak headrest, rocking harder and snuggling Heather, now swaddled in her blanket, nuzzled to me like a second skin. Seemed my kin were destined to hate. In that moment, I grieved for the joy and contentment of young years, when love was a fact and flowed freely among family.

Oh, how I *despised* their hatred, one that now tainted my affections with guilt, choking spontaneity and pleasure.

Under all that lay the jagged rawness of my *insignificance* that rendered me invisible and soundless in their war arena, where I wailed and howled forlornly for family solidarity. It was a horrible, suffocating place of fetid emotions. A place where Daddy and MawMaw and Papa never *saw* nor *heard* beyond their vendettas and principles.

So there, on that little porch, with Biltmore Castle glowing like a thousand Christmas trees from the black velvet distance, helplessness snaked its way inside me, and on the wings of fireflies, my hope – that forgiveness would restore my family – took flight.

CHAPTER FOUR
"A Time to be born…"

Looking back, I can't recall exactly when Kirk's peaceful surface began to ripple. Certainly, one parallel change was that Kirk stopped wanting to go to church. Oh, occasionally we went, but when we did, Kirk wasn't really *there*. His resistance deeply affected my own commitment. Nobody can wordlessly resist as *vigorously* as Kirk Crenshaw. Perhaps the restiveness had always been there, just on the perimeter of our happiness, but the wonderful love and laughter we shared, and now, little Heather, all had somehow kept it at bay.

Ironically, it was the laughter that began to unearth it, little by little.

Kirk one day dropped a pan of leftover rice on the floor as we cleaned up, then skidded and fell butt first into the heap of it. I leaned to help him up and burst into giggles.

It wasn't until he shook my hand from his arm as though it were a spider that I realized something was wrong. When I saw his stormy face, I nearly panicked.

"Are you hurt, honey?" I asked, standing awkwardly aside, paralyzed by insecurity.

He didn't reply, just set his icy gaze straight ahead and, gripping the sink ledge, hoisted himself up onto his feet. I began to brush the seat of his pants, but he elbowed me aside and peeled off his jeans, marched to the bedroom closet and tossed them into the laundry hamper.

"Kirk?" I approached him cautiously, as is my nature in the wake of a storm.

He looked at me then, his green eyes aglitter and fierce. "Don't ever laugh at me." This he said in a near whisper.

"But honey – I wasn't laughing *at* you. I was – "

"Just don't do it again." His granite face relented not one whit.

I blinked, thinking I was hallucinating looney toons gone tragic. Moments earlier, we'd been laughing over silly things, now we stood squared off, my husband looking as though prepared for mortal combat.

"Kirk, you *know* I'd never make fun of you. I love –"

He spun on his heel to tread succinctly away from my declaration of devotion, back straight, gait proud, to our closet for starched, freshly pressed slacks and plaid button-up shirt.

Numb, I watched him briskly dress, then slam through the front screen door to his car and drive away. I slouched down on the couch and fumed for long moments. I'd never, in all my days, seen such offense taken over something so – so *piddly*.

Sure I had. My brother, Chuck, had erupted with Daddy over things as trivial.

Kirk stayed gone an hour, a bewildered interval, etched in the shimmery terror of abandonment, and I met him at the door, trying to read from his face some sense into the strange episode.

"Kirk?"

He walked past me, hesitated, then turned, looking hollow-eyed and exhausted. "Janeece," he ran a hand through his tousled hair. "I just – I can't stand to be laughed at." He shrugged limply, looking so miserable my heart went out to him. And I knew.

His pain spawned from a darkness unknown to me, where drunkenness and violence and betrayal pilfered anything humane and kind, where one learned to hide hurts and walk through storms alone.

I silently went to him, slid my arms around him and felt his slowly encircle me, then tighten. "I'm sorry," I whispered, though why I felt I should apologize, I wasn't certain.

He didn't say a word. Just kissed me and soon, made me forget the weird incident.

From there, things spiraled downward. I called Kirk's angry lapses "black moods" where nothing I said seemed right. His scrapping experience was eons ahead of my own, which was practically nil. So, mostly, I backed off. I loved peace *too, too* much, I suppose, because I kept making excuses for my husband's sharp edginess until that Christmas Eve, when Kirk pushed me too far. He and I had each opened one of our gifts from one another. Mine was *Estee Lauder's Youth Dew* cologne, for which I'd shamelessly hinted. I'd spent hours looking for Kirk's gift before finally making a selection. I was not prepared for his reaction. He was livid.

"You mean you went and bought me a *hunting coat* when I'd bought one just months ago?" He glared at me as though I had rocks for brains.

"But Kirk, I didn't know you'd bought —"

"I *told* you, Janeece."

He *had?* I honestly didn't remember it. "I do *not* remember you saying a word."

He paced to the window and back and braced hands on hips, staring me down. "You don't *listen* to me."

I opened my mouth to say something, but the words fizzled. Suddenly, I was so weary I could hardly stand up, much less respond to something so.... So *what?*

"What, exactly, are you angry about?" My voice seemed to come from far away.

His nose nearly touched mine. "Because my wife can't even go out and buy me a Christmas present right." His words were quiet. "I work hard. I deserve more."

That quiet timber told me how despicable he considered me. *Unloveable...unloveable.*

I turned, went to the gifts piled underneath the tree and pulled out one.

"Here," I said numbly, holding it out to him. He seemed ready to refuse but then glumly snatched it from my hand.

I turned and went into the bedroom, pulled out a little overnight bag I'd used for my hospital stay and into which I quickly stuffed underwear and a change of clothes. Then I grabbed seven-month-old Heather's diaper bag and packed in extra diapers.

She was asleep, but I bundled her and was at the front door when Kirk spoke.

"Where you going?" His voice didn't sound so certain any more. I didn't give a tinker's damn.

"To Dad's."

"Why?"

"Because, being so obviously *beneath* you, I don't deserve to be under the same roof as you." To my horror, my eyes puddled. I angrily swished them away. I could just hear him lambasting his mother…. *"Mama cried over everything…I never believed the tears were real."*

I turned and dashed out the door. *Unloveable…unloveable… unloveable.*

"Janeece!" he called. "Don't do something you'll be sorry for."

I didn't look back.

I had to hand it to Daddy and Anne. They treated my barging in, red-eyed from crying, at ten-twenty on Christmas Eve night, as a common occurrence. They asked no questions, thank the good Lord. Trish took Heather to her bed and soon the baby slept again.

I bedded down on the couch. Through tears, I watched the tree lights twinkle and run.

Why, I wondered, was Kirk so angry? Was I so difficult to love? *Still?*

Apparently so. I tried to squash down the terrible, terrible gut-crush of rejection. I tossed over and knotted up, staring at the ceiling. Exhaustion won out. I dozed.

At twelve-ten, a rap on the door brought me awake and upright, trembling. I pulled Trish's yellow robe around me and padded barefoot across the pine floor. "Who is it?" I asked.

Silence. Then, "Kirk."

I hesitated, then unlocked the door and flipped on the porch light. He looked as miserable as I felt. "Come on in," I said stiffly and stepped back to let him pass.

I turned from the door and his arms were *there*, open and without warning, pulling me into their embrace. I stiffened for long moments, still *stung* from his hateful words, and then I felt him trembling. "Oh, Neecyyy," he sobbed against my neck. "I can't live without you."

Crying? *Kirk?* I tried to pull back and look, to make sure, but he wouldn't loosen his grip.

I felt my neck grow wet. "Ah, Kirk," I whispered and slid my arms around him. "Don't."

"I'm so sorry," he murmured against my shoulder. "I'm such a – a…."

"Butt," I flatly finished for him.

He lifted his head, gazed at me, tears dripping and all, and said, "The *worst*. When I opened that last gift" he stopped for a moment to pull out his handkerchief and wipe his eyes and nose. Then I saw fresh tears and the way he was trying to swallow them and failing. I reached up to touch his cheek.

"I felt like the worst scum on the face of the earth. Please," he stepped toe to toe with me, "forgive me, honey? It's not you. *Never you.* The demons are all *mine*. God couldn't have given me a better wife than you."

In answer, I pulled him to the couch and down beside me. That's when I heard the crinkle of paper and cardboard from beneath his jacket. He pulled out the still sealed box – my present to him.

Chocolate covered cherries.

BamBamBam.

We'd just finished supper that Saturday evening when the loud banging at our door startled us. Kirk frowned and arose from the table just as the banging recommenced.

"Coming!" boomed Kirk, his brow furrowing as he strode to the door. I washed red spaghetti sauce from Heather's plump little fingers, removed her bib and lowered her to the floor. Her knees *bumpbumpbumped* their cadence as she crawled off to explore nooks and crannies from her knee-high angle.

Curious, I keened to hear what transpired between Kirk and the caller. Suddenly, Kirk's voice projected – and it had that deadly quiet timber. "You're welcome to come to my home anytime when you're sober, Dad. But don't you *ever* come here again when you're drunk."

"Y – you can't talk li'that to me. I'm your *daddy*, you little—"

"*Shut up*, you sorry excuse for a man," Kirk spoke through clenched teeth. "Listen up good. I lived in that mess all my life. Now, I don't have to put up with your drunkenness. I won't have you around my family like this. Do you understand?"

Kirk's dad sounded like some kind of mewling, evil beast as he cranked up with more foul scorn. Heather had crawled right up to her daddy's legs, where she now sat, her saucer-eyed gaze bounding back and forth betwixt Kirk and her Grandfather. At

Tom's angry bellowing, her lips began to pucker and her chest to puff soundlessly in and out with panic.

"Heather, baby," I crooned and rushed to lift her into my arms.

I froze inside at the violence I sensed, *heard* in him. Heather began to bawl. And to think – he *sired* Kirk. My Kirk. Heather's father. Kirk didn't deserve this. He looked around and saw Heather's distress and clenched his fists as he whirled on his father.

"How *dare* you come here and upset my baby. Get out!" Kirk hissed. "And don't come back unless you're sober. Go on." He gestured to the road. "*Git!*"

He slammed the door in his father's snarling face and Kirk – who rarely swore – cursed soundly.

I hugged Heather to me, cooing and calming her, fighting my own disgust and anger at the man. *Dear Lord, please make him leave quietly.* I knew God heard me when Tom turned on his heel, staggered to his car and spun away without another word.

Kirk's shame was palpable as he plopped down onto the sofa. He propped his elbows on his knees and buried his face in his palms for long minutes. I quietly left the room and changed Heather's diaper, put on her nightgown and lay her in her crib. I wound up her musical crib-angels that circled overhead to *Lullaby,* before I tiptoed from her room.

Only thing that'd shifted about Kirk was now he sat sprawled on the sofa, head thrown back like a dead man. Eyes sealed shut, nothing moved about him except when his body vibrated with each heartbeat. I stared fascinated at his hair quivering rhythmically, his shirt, his fingers – everything. Like a dead man, I thought, except for that volcano roiling inside him that threatened to blow him to bits.

"Kirk? You okay, honey?" I asked softly, lowering myself beside him.

Long moments later, he muttered. "Yeah," still like one comatose. But his voice was strong. I took heart at that.

"Want some coffee?" I asked, needing to do something – *anything* to draw him from that dark place he now inhabited.

"Huh uh."

I felt helpless, wanting to console him but not knowing how. I'd learned by now that what comforted ninety-nine point seventy five per cent of the population did *not* placate Kirk Crenshaw. I had yet to find that particular formula.

"Well," I said, shrugging limply. I stood, and turned to leave. "I'll turn in, honey." *Give you time to execute your own healing.*

"It's a terrible thing, Neecy." The words floated out so softly I barely caught them. I turned to look at him. His eyes slowly opened, staring into a void somewhere.

"What's terrible, sweetheart?" I asked.

He looked at me then, his eyes so desolate my breath hitched.

"Wishing my father dead."

The next morning, Kirk was already dressed for church by the time I gave Heather a bath. I quickly stacked breakfast dishes in the sink then dressed myself and the baby. Kirk liked to get to church early. A true Type A clock watcher.

As we took our seats in the sanctuary, I noted Daddy and Anne's absence. Again. Daddy had recently taken up smoking again. For Daddy, not a good spiritual sign. Anne was not, at that time, a particularly spiritual being anyway, so playing hookey wasn't difficult. Trish, however, came in late and sat with us for the opening hymns. Then she whisked Heather away to the nursery.

The service was ordinary. Adult Sunday School Class. After that, three hymns, the offertory and sermon. Only difference was, today Kirk was *there.* Seemed to hang onto every word of the message about how we shouldn't just be just *pew-warmers.*

Preacher Hart, short and squat, yet peculiarly imposing, had really worked himself up by the time he read from the third book of Revelation, in verses fifteen and sixteen where John wrote to the Angel of the Church of the Laodiceans. His face was red as he paced, holding his bible aloft, and his deep voice raised the hair on my neck: "I know thy works, that thou art neither cold nor hot: I would thou *wert* cold or hot. So then, because thou art neither cold nor hot, *I will spew thee out of my mouth!*"

He halted dramatically, pulling his handkerchief out and wiping his entire face while catching his breath. "Do you want God to spew you out of his mouth on that day?"

I felt Kirk shift beside me and resettle stiffly as the altar call was issued. Mrs. Tilley, her round hefty bottom nearly hanging over the ends of the piano bench, played and led the congregation in *Just As I Am* for the invitational. Standing now, I glimpsed Kirk's hands gripping the pew in front of us, his knuckles white as chalk.

Why, he's fighting conviction. The realization shot through me like a bullet. He'd been adamant about attending church, even if sporadically, but he'd never in his life had a conversion experience. Me, I'd absorbed it all along, from the age of five when I'd knelt at this same altar.

The music ended. I heard, *felt*, Kirk's relief that he was off the hook. For now.

As we drove home, Kirk's mood grew blacker. I tried to ignore the thickening air and overcast emotions.

Ignoring Kirk's darkness is like trying to walk through a hailstorm without blinking.

Finally, I could stand the roiling silence no longer. "What's wrong, Kirk?" I blurted.

He was quiet for long moments. Then, angrily, "That's *it.*"

"What's *it?*"

"I'll not sit and listen to a preacher who preaches *at me.* Calling me a *pew-warmer.*" He huffed a grim laugh. "That *entire* message was aimed directly at *me.*"

I stifled a giggle. What an *ego*, I thought, gazing at him in amazement, knowing the futility of trying to convince him otherwise. I faced the front and crossed my arms. *Let him stew in his own juices.*

I knew what was coming next. He did not disappoint me.

"I'll never," he snarled, "*ever* darken the door of that church again."

We visited Dad and Anne that afternoon, to get out of the house. Kirk seemed especially restless. We'd spent our last two dollars Saturday afternoon on banana splits at the Dairy Queen so walking to see my family was all there was left to do. Lordy, those splits were good. Heather had smacked her lips ecstatically on the gooey rich treat and bawled when I said, "enough."

We all sat around in the den talking, while in the background, the television, a new nineteen-inch, played an old forties flick starring Roy Rogers and Dale Evans. The Sons of the Pioneers sang *Tumbling Tumbleweeds* and I spent a nostalgic moment listening, remembering singing that song around MawMaw's piano as her little fingers flew over the keys, with Papa, Gabe, Daddy and Mama playing guitars and harmonizing....

Then, Mama died. I gulped back melancholy and quickly pushed the thought away.

"Where's Trish?" I asked, gazing about, turning Heather loose to toddle around, dimpled fingers latched onto the furniture.

"Cleaning out the storage closet," Anne replied. "She was supposed to've done it last week and didn't."

I remembered that Trish had been nearly down with a cold. "Wasn't she sick?"

"Not enough to stay home from school." Anne replied a bit edgy. "Trish felt like doing everything she *wanted* to do."

I wondered what, exactly, Anne referred to but buttoned my lip. After all, I wasn't around to know everything first hand. I hesitated to challenge Anne on disciplining Trish because, number one, she dealt fairly and lovingly with me. Number two, Trish said that would only make things worse for her. I still wondered at the *where* and *why* of the subtle cold war between those two.

"Well, I guess I'm just an old transplanted Baptist," Daddy's rising voice splintered my mulling. I noted his Walter Matthau candor – with the word "Baptist" tacked on.

Being of the Methodist camp, knowing what I knew of Daddy's recent decline into former vices, the entire thing reeked of spiritual rebellion. I rolled my eyes and crossed my arms against what I knew was coming: Daddy's straddle-the-fence, balance-act, with one leg hanging in the Methodist camp, the other dangling in the Baptist. He wanted the best of both worlds.

His justification was that he grew up a Baptist and only switched to Methodism when he married Mama. So, dredging up his old Calvinism doctrine assured him of his eternal security – regardless of his slide back into the cigarette habit and an occasional cuss word. And his stance on "once saved, always saved" as opposed to being "a lost backslider" directly related to how willing he was to give up his smokes.

"Why," he continued testily, "there's not a thing in the Bible about cigarettes."

"There is about cussin'," I mumbled under my breath as I arose and headed for the bathroom. Me? I believed doctrinal truth lay somewhere *between* the extremes of Calvinism and Arminianism. I relieved myself and on impulse headed for the closet used for storage, off the kitchen.

I found her sitting on the floor inside the dim chamber with one hanging light bulb, her back to me, surrounded by out-of-season boxed clothing, Christmas and seasonal decorations, magazines and books, an old end table, chairs with broken legs and endless paraphernalia usually labeled "junk."

"Hey, Trish," I said softly, warmed to be with her.

She didn't move. Then I noticed her legs were drawn up and she hugged her knees.

"Trish?" I moved around her and gazed down into her face. "What's wrong, honey?"

Nothing moved but her eyes, those huge soulful, bottomless pools of sadness, raining tears. They clutched at my heart. "Honey," I dropped down beside her and slid my arm around her. "What's wrong?"

Her head slowly moved from side to side. "I-I d-don't know," she whispered, holding back sobs, blinking with confusion. "I-I j-just can't seem to get anything d-done."

I looked about us at the clutter and my stomach knotted. My aversion to clutter was and is classic. In fact, Trish usually – the rare times I charmed Anne into allowing it – helped bail me out when things piled up, finishing the job in no time flat. No, today's paralysis was emotional.

"Trish," I gathered her to me, "I had these – spells, too, after Mama died, you know, when Daddy kept us away from MawMaw and Papa? It's just nerves – frustration." I rolled my eyes. "*Just* is not a word to put in front of *nerves*. It's a tough thing to handle, Trish, but I'm here for you. And Daddy is." The silence stretched out. I sighed heavily. "Would you like for me to talk to Anne?"

"*No!*" This almost vehemently. Then she said more softly, "No, Sis. It won't help."

I silently cursed the genes that conduct and spawn these danged cat-on-a-hot-tin-roof nervous systems that pick up on the tiniest nuances of sentiments as a *threat*, that blast one's adrenaline level to kingdom come, that take a look or a phrase and blow it up to wide-screen, 3-D horror, that suck away at self-esteem 'til one's time is consumed with just surviving each moment, that make victims of good, otherwise *strong* people.

"I'm okay," she awkwardly arose and commenced to attack the task. "I'm just tired. This old cold seems to be hanging on longer than usual." She looked pale and beneath her eyes looked as if shaded by a dark crayon.

"Has Anne – ?"

"No." Trish looked me in the eye. "It's not anything she's *done*. Honest. It's just me."

"Promise me you'll come to me if I can help you."

"Okay, Sis." She turned from me and began shuffling things around.

Back in the den, things were still hopping. "I know he was preaching right at me," Kirk divulged to a militantly sympathetic Daddy.

"Yep." Daddy's recliner tipped back and his chin rose another notch. "Know whatcha mean. Last time I was at church, he preached on smoking and I know, *by golly*, he was aiming it right smack *between my eyes*." His nostrils flared regally, a precise measure of Daddy's indignation.

"Now, Joe," Anne scolded, "Pastor Hart didn't ever come out and *say* 'cigarettes.'"

"That's cause 'cigarettes' ain't in the Bible." Daddy's hand slapped the chair arm. "*Dangit all.* Preachers shouldn't oughta *meddle.*" *Law me*, I thought, he's gaining steam.

"Trish doesn't look like she feels well," I said to Anne, not able to hold my tongue.

"It's that old cold." Anne's face had, like, no expression, like shuttered.

"Kirk, can we go now? Heather's getting sleepy and I need to put her down for a nap."

"Bye, darlin' face," Anne hugged Heather and kissed her soundly on her plump cheek. I felt so torn. I knew beyond doubt that Anne's love for me and my family was genuine.

What about Trish?

Our walk home was silent, except for Heather's *Dada and Mamama jabber,* which usually perked Kirk up. Today, I knew my usual teasing him about dada's little girl would be pointless, futile. So I left him be. I'd known, since the Christmas Eve incident, that his deep funks had nothing to do with me. My thoughts kept ricocheting back to Trish, my little sis.

Please…help Trish. And Anne. Somehow, Lord, make things better.

Kirk's walk, I noticed, lacked its usual peppy cadence. It actually sloughed.

And while you're at it, fix Kirk up, too.

Kirk rolled over in bed later that night. "You awake?" he asked softly.

I roused from the doze closing in on me. "Mm hmm." I turned over to face him, anticipation fluttering like scattered butterflies through me because my husband seldom wasted words, especially at bedtime when he usually – after we made love – promptly fell asleep with me spooned back against him, his arm firmly draped around my midriff. And when he wanted to talk, it heralded something significant.

Suddenly, I was fully awake…and I remembered his present angst.

Was tonight different? I knew a moment's apprehension.

"Remember when I said I wanted us to go to church and all – that day at the lunch table at Chapowee High?"

I did and had wondered many times if he remembered. "Yes."

He shifted onto his back and folded one arm under his head. "Well, I want us to."

"To – what? We go to church every – well, *most* Sundays, anyway."

"I know. But not to be just *pew-warmers.*"

Bingo. I suppressed a grin.

"I mean – I want us to be born again." He turned his head to gaze at me through nighttime's sooty veil, silvered by outside streetlight filtering through venetian blinds. There was, in his statement – because that was what it was, a statement – a resoluteness that was Kirk's when his mind was made up.

"Okay." I gazed back, knowing his decision was right. He did nothing lightly and when he was convinced, so was I. Though I'd found Christ at five, kneeled at the church altar, I sensed Kirk's awe of this newly unearthed reverence. Too, I'd drifted in recent years. It was time.

And so we slid from bed onto our knees and prayed together and went to sleep wrapped in each other's arms – and a new peace.

I shall never forget arising the following morning and seeing the sun, already warm and golden in a sky bluer than I'd ever remembered, and thinking how brilliant the world looked with dew-soaked verdant grass. Colors shimmered and danced and twirled as they had when I was a child.

Kirk's transformation was instant. It was as though his soul had passed through a spiritual dialysis machine where most of the junk filtered out. Not all – but certainly most. Heather's unconditional, adoring love had already boosted my self-esteem. Now, as Kirk viewed me through different eyes, my old feeling of unloveableness began to recede.

In the weeks and months to come, that aura of *rightness* grew and burgeoned and when I learned I was pregnant again, Kirk and I considered it a holy seal on our new start.

As it turned out, *both* Anne and I were pregnant. Anne, whose only symptoms were sleepiness and an increase in appetite, didn't know for weeks that she'd conceived. Her delivery date was four months prior to mine. Anne seemed mellower, somehow. Her eyes, the ice-blue of a clear-day sky, cut through Daddy's nonsense with scalpel perception but would – amazingly – turn incredibly warm and teary by something touching. Pregnancy seemed to agree with her on all levels. I convinced myself things between her and Trish were improving. At least, I prayed they were.

This time, I weathered the nausea stage a bit more stoically and the months passed swiftly. Kirk now served as deacon and Sunday School teacher and took seriously his duties. But he always had time to cuddle and romp with Heather, who adored her daddy.

Trish spliced her duties between me and Anne, who gave birth to Dale in February.

"He's not a pretty baby, Neecy," Anne stated matter-of-factly of the little red-faced bawling brother who added to Daddy's straining quiver. "But he's a sweetie-pie."

"He's cute as a button," I insisted, kissing and nuzzling his sweet-smelling neck. I was thrilled that my family kept growing and growing and growing.

It helped offset, to some degree, my loss of Mama's folks. As time passed, Anne and I bonded more closely and though I'd learned to love her family clan, the *belong*-thing evaded me. Unlike me, young Trish synthesized with the Knight kids. Looking back, I believe they loved me. They could not have been nicer. I simply missed the affectionate spontaneity that came so naturally from MawMaw and Papa. The Knights were great people with a strong sense of *family*. But was I, to them, family? Was Grandma Whitman right? *Was blood* thicker than water?

Maybe, I decided. Chuck – well, Chuck didn't even concern himself with blood-ties, much less with step-status. "What is, *is,*" was his cynical commentary before he fled home.

I conceded that perhaps, in this instance, Chuck was right. *What is, is.*

Just minutes before midnight, on Heather's second birthday, Kristabelle – Krissie – came into the world with the serenity of cherubs in religious paintings. Tiny and doll-like, she seldom cried. Rosebud lips yawned and minute limbs stretched and arched like a kitten's. I never thought I could adore another baby as I did Heather, but from the beginning, I felt love equally as intense for this wee one. Kirk's devotion to our girls matched my own, swelling him to giant proportions in my eyes and laced even tighter the love bonds connecting us.

Gentle Krissie flowed with everything, from traveling to nursing. She was a wise little grown-up in an infant's body, whose big soulful blue eyes said she'd simply not feed if it was a bother to me. Months later, I would lay her in her crib during busy times, then get sidetracked with laundry or dishes or whatever and an hour later, remember.

Krissie. Gripped by guilt, I'd bolt to the nursery and peer in, to find her lying contentedly, cooing at the crib's bunny rabbit decal or gumming a rattle. The blond curly head would swivel to seek me out and sunshine would burst over her face. How I loved her. As the months passed, my two girls became inseparable playmates. Heather, a natural leader, was always *Mama* in their play-likes and Krissie, *Baby.*

Mymymy, how revealing to hear Heather's Mama-dialogue. "If you do that again, I'll *spank* you, young lady," delivered in just the right touch of steely authority and then the steady, climbing, shrill, "Stop that! Stop that this *instant.* Just you wait until your Daddy gets home!" always stopped me dead in my tracks, eyes wide with disbelief. Yet on some level, I recognized the wording, voice inflection, and note of frenzy as *me.*

That piece fell into the incomplete *Who Am I?* puzzle. Neecy, the Role Model.

Spooky.

Like it or not, what I said in haste and impatience *would* come back to haunt me.

Kirk was, I discovered, a mathematical genius. Against my lackluster math background, Kirk shone brilliantly. By the time I scurried for a pencil to write down the numbers, figures raced through his head, calculated and spouted out his mouth like a slot machine.

Eventually, I asked him to do equations for me to save time and quite honestly, face. My ineptness embarrassed me. The upside was that my praise and deference to his skills pleased him, as did my being home with the children and having a delicious table set for his homecoming. "I don't want my wife working," he'd say in that "it's settled" voice.

I felt special. Protected and coddled. Later, in the next decade, when Women's Libbers shrieked of being suffocated and buried in the home, I was astonished. Why, at that time, I wouldn't have traded places with another female on the planet because Kirk's sentiments flowed from peace and contentment. What more could a woman ask for?

"Thanks, Sis," Trish gushed and hugged me. She'd come by after school to pick up the package I held for her.

"Now if you need me, let me know. Here's the calorie chart and here's Dr. Crane's instructions."

"I'll get right on it. I'm so sick of being fat I could –"

"Trish," I stopped her. "I would love and respect you even if you were the *circus fat lady*. But you've said so many times you wish you were slim like Callie or Marsha and so – I wrote to the newspaper doctor and got his diet plan. Now, don't go overboard. It's the same one I went on when I was thirteen and getting pudgy. Just be careful to not drop your calories too low."

Trish giggled and hugged me again. "Don't worry about *that*." She sobered. "Gosh, I hope I can do it, Sis."

"Lookee – you can do anything you *want* to do, Trish. Don't ever forget that *you* control your destiny." I blinked a couple of times, mentally backtracking. "At least to a certain degree. God does the rest."

"I know." She kissed me and left with a new spring in her step.

Kirk worked the graveyard mill shift, came home, slept a few hours and spent afternoons in JOE'S BARBER SHOP, training with Daddy. Soon, his clientele grew and with the salary increase, Kirk planned a weekend excursion to a new gigantic theme park, Six Flags over Georgia. By now, he served as Church Deacon and taught a teen Sunday School class.

During the drive to Six Flags over Georgia, I relaxed to radio music, humming *The Girl from Ipanema* and singing along with the girls to the Beatles' *She Loves You*. I rode the waves of Kirk's sizzling enthusiasm as he snapped photos and accompanied the girls on daring rides while I – a self-professed, devout *coward* – sat in the shade, feet up, waving as they screamed to the daredevil fun.

Kirk's drive always astounded me. While my energy is deep and inward, stirring slowly and thickly, his is everywhere, all over him at once, crackling the air about him. In his presence, one is smote by it. I've seen folks drawn to him because of it and discerned their frustration when he evaded closeness. Because, while he is a wonderful husband, father and in-law, Kirk Douglas Crenshaw is an entity unto himself. I've seen few dare to enter his fortress. Those who did failed to tarry long. His is not unkindness, rather he simply moves in his own aura, not needing, not seeking enhancement.

In all my years with him, boredom never had time to light because I moved in the momentum of his exciting discoveries.

I alone know the intricacies, darkness, brilliance and complexities that form Kirk's world. My knowledge is not an easy one. There were times I'd rather not have known it all. I'd rather have remained in my dream world, as he calls it, whose background is marshmallow clouds and willowy lace, where everybody loves everybody and there're no such things as bias and bitterness.

"You need to get out into the real world just *one* day, Neecy," he's often told me, "and have to work under a foul-mouthed supervisor. Then, you wouldn't be so Pollyanna."

I rued the day I'd defined *Pollyanna* for him.

At times, my ultra-forgiving spirit seems to slightly annoy, to threaten him in some way. He cannot come to terms that it's just not my nature to harbor anger. Just as it's Kirk's nature to react. He is passionate in both the good and bad. And when he has a run-in with someone and I seek to calm him by showing him another perspective, it's like pouring gasoline on a smoldering log. That's when he gives me the "real world" diatribe.

Frustration stalks me because I cannot change my nature and it often casts us on opposite sides. I hate fights and dissension. Kirk is his most magnificent in the heat of battle. I get a knot in my stomach, *craving* his approval while he blissfully goose-steps to his own drum roll.

Yet...Kirk is not immune to my opinions. Following confrontations, he disappears to mull. Despite his autonomous spirit, Kirk will fairly assess matters. His resistance, I know, is sheer reaction, a conditioned thing. Without fail, he returns, either to accept my view or to freely compromise.

I think back on it and realize it was our spiritual walk that balanced the scales in our favor. It tempered Kirk's volatile drive and helped me sense how tightly it lay coiled inside him. It made us teachable and gave us a deep *giving* love for one another. It allowed me to thrill to my husband's strengths and complement him by being resilient and easily entreated.

We each basked in the other's differences.

There was a certain mellowing in him about that time that showed in everything he did. His eyes, those marvelous green pools, spoke eloquently to me. Their fire gave way to such devotion that it took my breath. His passion was no less – just different. His voice, his touch, everything emanating from him spoke of a commitment and protectiveness I'd never felt before. Not the fathering kind. It was a total thing, laced with everything male and powerful and tender.

And I knew in my heart of hearts that his promise to me years earlier stood firm: *I'll always love you and take care of you, Neecy.*

CHAPTER FIVE
"A Time to Plant..."

I had no warning. Not a clue as parishioners spilled out the door of our little village church and onto grassy grounds steeped in June sunlight. Those same warm rays reverberated off Pastor Cheshire's shiny bald head as he stood just outside to greet each departing parishioner. His was a wide, toothy smile that justified his name and I thought how we'd come to love this round little man, whose English background had initially posed a threat to the unpretentious southern male of his flock. Women, being women, adored his British accent, but the men, Kirk included, took their own good time in warming to him.

"Hard to get past his uppity ways," Daddy'd muttered after Pastor's first sermon. We ate at our house, Kirk's and mine, that Sunday.

"Now, Joe," Anne cut her blue eyes at Daddy reproachfully, "he's not a bit uppity."

"He just *talks* that way," Kirk quipped, winking at Daddy, who missed it while glaring at Anne. Kirk's eyes glimmered that he enjoyed the *bite* of the conversational turn. By now, I knew Kirk's dysfunctional family were scrappers who thrived on fights and got high on crisis.

"Pastor can't help how he talks," I added gently, hoping Kirk wouldn't take umbrage that I'd disagreed with him again. I *always*, to his way of thinking, took the view opposite his when it came to criticism. I think partly he felt I set out to de-spiritualize him, which was not the case. I simply could not go along with anything belittling. This time, however, he didn't seem to mind.

"Yeah," he agreed, leaning his elbows on the table and sipping coffee. "He's not such a bad fellow. I dropped by his office this week and visited with him for a spell. Smart guy. Knows the Bible like the back o' his hand."

"Hmm," Daddy looked thoughtful for long moments then shifted decisively in his chair. "I really liked what he said about the Lord's Prayer getting a reputation for being almost Pharisaical and repetitious. The way he taught us to use it, you know – elaborating on 'Our Father,' using all the names of God and dwelling on each one is – well, a whole new twist."

I relaxed and released my held breath. "Can't wait to hear the rest of his series on it."

Today, more than a year later, on the church steps, our Pastor's plump black-robed figure inclined itself like a teetering tent to Krissie, our flaxen-haired tot who gazed, enthralled, up at his huge, bared teeth.

"Ahh, Krissie, my girl. You're still my sweetheart, aren't you?"

Sky-blues stared fixedly at the white piano-key squares a moment and missed the exaggerated wink.

"Yessir, Pas'r Che'sir." I watched, horrified, the giggle that rose up in her, threatening to explode. Before I could move, a sharp little elbow poked her in the back, swiveling her small face to address her sibling's frown of disapproval.

"Heather!" Pastor Cheshire straightened to half-mast and extended a thick hand to my darker haired daughter. Nearly five, Heather emitted a pulsing cynicism that gave Pastor pause before he drew in his lips and inclined his shiny pate in a totally sincere way. "And how are you today, my dear?"

"Fine, thank you." Her mouth pursed and her gaze sliced down to Krissie's slack jaws, as if to say, *that's how you do it. Cool and polite as you please.*

"Pastor Cheshire," Kirk's big hand grasped the plump one and I watched his face, now elongated into my fantasy of Viking features with sea-green eyes, whose corners crinkled in the sun or upon scrutinizing. They were incapable of evasion or dishonesty. In his gray-blue suit, my husband's presence whammed my awareness in a way that, after six years of marriage, still took the wind out of me.

His virility stunned and excited me. He never seemed to get enough of me and at bedtime, even when I was tired from diapering, and later, chasing lively toddlers and unable to converse or eat heartily of imaginative meals I set before him, I welcomed his eagerness. Kirk's lovemaking melted me to liquid and tossed me to the galaxies. Unsullied, we'd learned together ageless mysteries in their purest forms.

"How about it, Honey?" The turquoise eyes swam before me, their crinkles deepening, while the strong mouth twitched slightly at one corner. "Janeece to earth...."

I blinked at the sun-washed Viking and tail-spinned to reality.

"Where were you, Neecy?" Kirk grinned knowingly at me.

"I'm sorry." I cast Pastor an embarrassed glance and shrugged. "What did I miss?"

"About the children's registration for Vacation Bible School," came Pastor's soft reply.

"Oh, I've taken care of it."

Kirk's arm slid around my shoulder and the squeeze of his strong fingers on my upper arm pulsed all the way down to my toes as his voice rumbled near my ear, "I figured you had. See you tonight, Pastor."

We drove a detour home, through the countryside with the windows of our little white Volkswagen open. I slipped off my black pumps and wiggled my cramped toes, allowing balmy breezes to play with them. I inhaled deeply of Tigerlilies and honeysuckle sweeping past.

"Such a pretty day," I sighed.

"Mama," Krissie wailed, cherubic face poked between the two bucket seats, her breath ruffling my hair, "Heather *push* me."

"Did not." I turned to investigate, finding Heather seated very lady-like in the farthest corner of the backseat.

"Did, *too*." Krissie craned her little neck to glare from her perch on the edge of center seat, her small patent-leather shoes planted squarely on the risen hump that centered the car floor.

The *hump* battle raged once again.

"Heather, you *know* Krissie fits the space there better, so let her enjoy it, okay? We've discussed it before anyway." I faced the front again, suddenly weary. What was so *darned coveted* about that spot? But I knew – it was to see the passing scenery. Before Krissie came along, it had been Heather's roost. Now, tiny Krissie perched on the raised center with her little face poked between the seats, giving her full view through the front windshield.

I looked over my shoulder and glimpsed Heather's plump jaw set into a pout and her stormy gray eyes fixed on the sky beyond moving landscape. Krissie's turned-up nose rose a notch higher as she settled with tenacious smugness into her turf. I stifled a grin.

"Janeece."

Just that, my name tumbling from Kirk's lips, snared my focus. He'd been silently contemplating during the drive. Now, I *felt* something happening inside him.

"I've got something to tell you. Something terribly important to me – to us."

My ears, my senses lurched.

"I – I hardly know how to say it." His broad shoulders shrugged, heightening the suspense.

"What, honey?" I touched his arm, growing alarmed.

He darted me a look I'd never seen before. "I've received the High Calling on my life," he softly declared and turned his attention back to the road.

I stared at him for long moments while confusion, like an angry waterfall, rolled over me, then blurted, "The *what?*"

"The call. To the ministry."

"Oh." My lips remained in Cheerio position as I stared at his set profile, his "mind made up" stamp already in place. And for a moment, his blurred silhouette was vintage Abraham Lincoln. The unexpectedness, the *blow* of his words made him seem a stranger. I struggled to dispel my befuddlement by facing the front and concentrating on what day it was. *Sunday....*

"Wh-when –" I whispered, cleared my throat and tried again. "When did this happen?"

I gazed at him again and saw one corner of his lip curl up. He looked incredibly serene, as lucid as I was addled. "I've felt it for awhile now. It was just this morning, at church, that I knew for certain. As I prayed." His brow, between green eyes, wrinkled. "I hope you're happy about this, Janeece."

I shifted my numb body until he vanished from my perimeter, until all I saw was the expanse of rolling hillside passing. Yet I could not escape the appeal in his statement – I felt it with every bone, every atom that comprised *me*.

My vocal chords refused to give the words he yearned to hear.

Dear Lord. *He* had received the High Calling. Where did I fit? Why hadn't Kirk prepared me, at least given me a small hint that my – *our* lives were about to do an abrupt left flank? No – an atomic rearranging.

With rising dread, I envisioned the fish-bowl milieu of the Cheshire family...and that of Pastor Hart's family before them. *Scrutiny.* The very idea rained terror on me. All my struggles to keep *me* tucked away from prying, *pitying*, interference and hatred, only to now watch my privacy dangled over a keg of nitroglycerine.

Privacy. I gulped back hysteria. My self-exile was a luxury to be short-lived, like a wickedly sweet milk chocolate bar in the dimpled hands of Krissie.

Dread, thick and heavy as lava fell over me. *This is crazy.* I took a deep breath, trying to get a grip. The High Calling – nothing could be more wonderful. Could it? More honorable. Then why wasn't I feeling wonderful about it? Why this crazy sense of splitting off from my husband, of being set adrift while he sailed ahead like a highborn porpoise?

Into his sunset. Not mine. *His.* And what could be more incredible than Kirk, the howling loner, thrusting himself into humanity? Would he still be Kirk? *My* Kirk?

For, complex as it was at times, I'd found my place at his side

The passing landscape blurred as the enormity of it all hit me again. My peaceful little world was about to somersault. God only knew how it would land. And I couldn't do doodly-squat about it. Who could argue with the *High Calling* and *Whither Thou Goest I Will Go?*

Was it only yesterday things were certain? *Safe?*

Kirk – why didn't you prepare me for this? A vague sense of betrayal swelled within me. While he was the Loner, I was the Dug-in Kid who loved the day-to-day tranquil *flow* of life. Didn't he fathom at all what this trail blazing would cost me?

"Of course," Kirk's sudden lapse into speech, as though I'd gushed an enthusiastic, *I'm elated, darling!* startled me. "I'll have to enroll into Spartanburg Methodist College right away. I'll work at the barber shop part time and go to school in the evenings and –"

I listened as plans tumbled from him like popcorn and realized the seed had taken root long before now. If only he'd enlightened me, it would have made all the difference in the way I now felt.

But that was not Kirk's way.

Strong. Silent. Closemouthed.

Not so now. "It's such an honor, Neecy," he paused for breath and shook his sun-streaked wheat hair that waved more with age, "I'm overwhelmed by it all. Y'know? Why *me?* An old country boy who can barely spell."

I swung my gaze to the road ahead, still unable to speak. I, too, was overwhelmed, but not with awe. *Mrs. Kirk Crenshaw*, after six years, *fit. Preacher's wife* was a whole new frontier. I honestly didn't know if I had it in me.

In that moment of cataclysmic, timeless suspension, my mind leaped backward to high school days when Kirk teased that he'd captured me before any other males got to me, grinning that foolish grin, one I'd grown to love because it revealed a side to Kirk Crenshaw reserved for only *me.* And his character smote me anew, the kind that dictated integrity, honesty and kindness. It was what snared me in the very beginning. It had to do with the direct openness of the sea-green eyes. And the level-headedness. The wisdom of when to laugh and when to be serious.

"...and I need to talk with Pastor Cheshire right away. He can notify the District Superintendent." Kirk efficiently steered the Volkswagen into our drive. We piled out of the car, the girls dashing to their room to change into play clothes before Anne, Daddy, Trish and the boys arrived. It would be a few minutes because they, too, switched to comfortable attire and Anne gathered her fill-in dishes, usually as many as I'd prepared.

Has he noticed? I wondered as I quickly slid into cool jeans and a pullover. But Kirk silently shed his suit, donned jeans, abstractedly slid his wallet into his back pocket and vanished. While I took the roast from the warm oven, I overheard Kirk on the bedroom phone, talking with Pastor. My insides tail-spinned into a bottomless ocean. No time to discuss – I turned from the thought and, with shaking fingers, pulled potato salad from the refrigerator to join steaming garden peas on the table.

Get past it, Neecy. It's out of your hands.

The door slammed and small feet tripped swiftly to my side. "Dale!" I swept my little brother up into my arms to plant a kiss on his puckered-up lips and feel his arms squeeze my neck until my eyes bulged. "I wuv you, Tweetie Pie."

"I wuv you, too, Neecy." His hoarse little belly laugh was like a warm brook washing over me and I felt soppy as usual that my carrot-topped lil' brother adored me. I set him down and he toddled off to play with the girls.

"Oomph!" Cole's arms tackled me affectionately around the waist. "Hey there, pal," I leaned to nuzzle his neck, now at my chest level. Where had the years gone? "You might be eight but you're still –" I paused, smiling at him.

" – your baby," he finished for me, grinning from ear to ear.

"Hey, Neecy!" Trish swooshed in the door, planted a soft kiss on my cheek and hugged me soundly. "Mmm, food smells good." Trish, now in high school, had managed to lose twenty pounds after several start and stop failures with the calorie diet. She needed to lose at least fifteen more. I gave her pep talks all along, telling her to hang in there.

Her beautiful facial bone structure was beginning to protrude through diminishing flesh. Trish is the real beauty of the family.

"Sure does," Anne chimed in, sliding her brown 'n serve rolls into my preheated oven.

"Say," Kirk appeared, "I've got to test this." He nabbed a spoonful of Anne's bubbling hot macaroni-cheese pie, cheddar stringing a trail from bowl to mouth, and with facial contortions to protect his tongue, managed to ingest it. "Lordy," he proclaimed," that's good enough to make you want to slap your granny, Anne."

He snatched a slice of cantaloupe and I cuffed him playfully on the shoulder, a mere tap. "Stay outta that. Else we won't have enough." I tried to keep the edge from my voice, hoping he wouldn't take offense since he was in such a good mood.

"It'll be okay, Neecy," he rejoined playfully and stuffed half of it into his mouth, darting his hungry gaze about in search of something else to pilfer. I was relieved my little reprimand bounced off him this time. Kirk equated generosity – mine – as a test of love and any infraction upset our delicate balance.

Kirk found it intolerable that I concerned myself with everybody else getting his or her fair share of a delicacy. I found it just as intolerable that he *not concern* himself. I suppose being from a large family, in which survival-of-the-fittest rules, makes one that way. Kirk was, I often told him, probably the little pig at the head of the trough, unaware of the other little pigs that got there too late. It was ingrained in him.

And yet, he was, and is, in every other way the most generous person I know.

Within moments, glasses of iced tea frosted beside my best cornflower dishes while we took seats at the table.

"Let us pray," Kirk said and all around the table, we joined hands. "Father, thank you for this food of which we are about to partake. And thanks, too, for making your will known to me. I thank you for the High Call on my life. Amen."

I felt that jerk in my plexus region again as a frozen silence struck the family. *We look like a Norman Rockwell painting,* was my inane thought. Dad spoke first, "When?", then Anne, "You don't mean it, Kirk. Really?", then Trish, flashing her dimples, "I can't believe it – my brother-in-law – a *preacher!*" Then everybody was talking and laughing and rushing to embrace Kirk, who took it all with a little boy grin on his face. Heather and Krissie raced, Heather nudging and winning the 'first hug' spot and even insisting Cole and little Dale hug Kirk before Krissie. I sat glued to my chair, emotions gyrating, but managed a wide smile when his eyes searched out mine.

Instinct took over and the actor in me rose to the occasion. I could find no button to push and stop the building dread whose litany played over and over in my head; *Things are going to change...to change...to change.* I operated on automatic, giving such a convincing performance of support that nobody seemed to notice I had nothing to say.

The visit that day stretched interminably long. I needed to be alone and when Anne hugged me goodbye, she looked me in the eye and said, "You'll make a great preacher's wife, Neecy."

"Thanks," I replied and smiled as though it were the sweetest compliment in the world.

After they left, I escaped to my bedroom. Kirk had gone for a walk, no doubt to enjoy his new status, one already fitting him like a soft elastic suit that breathed and caressed.

I kicked off my shoes and stretched out on our white chenille bedspread, hearing the girls in their room's big climb-in closet, enlarged by their Daddy, doing a *play-like* scenario of church. Heather was the song leader, of course, with Krissie sitting on the bench, actually a twelve-inch-high shoe shelf stretching along each side of the closet floor. When they pushed back the hanging clothing to one side, *presto,* they had a sanctuary...or house...or *whatever.*

I closed my eyes and tried to relax, to let my mind go. *Lord, help me.* Several deep breaths later, I felt the tension begin to loosen and I uncurled my fingers and pictured an enormous vat of Jell-O, sitting beside a still lagoon, where a soft breeze wafted over my skin, cooling and soothing.

Rationale kicked in. I handled the facts. Tradition and religion dictated that a man dislocate the universe, if necessary, to follow the High Call – a wife or children never being mentioned in the variables. Only thing I'd ever heard was that a man forsake all to take the gospel to the world. And woe unto that wife who dared to interfere or come between her husband and the Hand of the Almighty.

My eyes popped open. I, Janeece Crenshaw, walked on shaky, Holy ground. Was I questioning God's will? I closed my eyes again and searched my heart the only way I knew how. Honestly. No. I did not question the purpose of Kirk's decision. It wasn't that.

So what *was* bothering me?

I sat up in bed, having seen the mountain. I needed it moved.

First, however, I had to know what the mountain *was.* The front screen door slammed and I saw Kirk walk by the bedroom to the kitchen. He looked so darned noble, already different. *Why can't I switch channels as easily?* I gazed out the window, through drapes stirred mildly by a breeze. Our friends across the street, the Nelsons, sat on their porch, fanning and rocking. I would soon leave all this – my roots. That fact stared me baldly in the face.

"*Pwaise de Lord,*" pealed Krissie as Heather's sermon warmed up. "*How-de-youu-ah!*"

From the mouths of babes....

And in that moment, I felt a warm, warm presence and slowly, like a jammed door screaking open, something inside me shifted. And certainty flooded me that I could, when the time came, cope with whatever faced us.

Deep down where it counted, I was happy for Kirk and tickled by his sense of fulfillment already so apparent. And I knew that, even if I could, I wouldn't lift a finger to change things back to the way they were yesterday.

"Oh Vic-to-ryyy, in Je-sus," chorused my daughters' voices from the closet's church, "my Sav-iorrr, for-eh-ber...He *punched* me, to Vic-to-ryyyyyy —"

I clapped my hand over my mouth and laughter spilled through my fingers.

Moments later, as humor ebbed, it came to me what this was all about. For the first time, I had to sort out things without Kirk. This time, I must come to grips without involving him. It was a new role: protector.

The bedroom door opened, Kirk stood there and I saw it in his hesitancy, his guarded eyes. *He'd noticed.*

"What you doing?" His voice was soft, husky, tentative.

I got up off the bed and moved to stand toe to toe with him, my fingers playing with his shirt buttons. "I was just lying here thinking Lordy, imagine *us* – a preacher's family." I laughed then, a genuine belly one and we slid into each other's joyful embrace.

Over his broad, strong shoulder, I glimpsed beyond the window a world clothed green by springtime and made vibrant by the sun. A new chord, with clear, precise harmony, struck inside me. Heck, I could handle this new role. Kirk would be happier than he'd ever been. And if Kirk was content, so was I.

CHAPTER SIX
"A time to Reap...."

Toby was born during Kirk's second year at Bible College, trailing Anne's infant daughter, Lynette, by eleven months. An adorable replica of Kirk, our son's shock of blonde hair Mohawked for the first six months. He was, like Krissie, affable and resilient. Kirk's resistance to having a *'Kirk Junior'* in the family stemmed from his movie star name. Its frivolity embarrassed him. He'd always liked the sound of "Toby" and so the name took.

We were so caught up in family and school and church that we seldom saw our old friends. Kirk heard Moose had joined the Air Force and was stationed in Japan. Occasionally, Callie wrote me a brief letter, telling me too little of what transpired in her life. It was sad, the wide gulf now separating all of us.

Grandma Whitman once said I was as readable "as a red bird in a snow storm." So were Toby and Krissie, to the point that I knew what they were about in any given situation.

Heather's genetic pool consisted heavily of her father's legacy. Like Kirk's, her face registered little of her true feelings as she grew older.

Early on, Toby and Krissie formed an alliance to breach Heather's stealthy manipulative maneuvers. It was, I kept telling myself, an innate leadership thing built into my oldest child. Overheard now in play-likes was a subtle shift in roles, Heather still being "Mama," while Toby – but a toddler, unable to follow Heather's directions – became "Baby," content to be hoisted from point to point by a huffing puffing petite Krissie, whose role shifted from *Daddy* to *maid* to whatever fit Heather's whim of the moment.

I heard the front door open and shut. I dried off my hands at the sink just as footsteps approached the kitchen.

"Trish! What are you doing here this time of day? Didn't you go to school?"

Then I noticed her swollen, red eyes. She'd lost the last fifteen pounds rather quickly and looked marvelously thin. Today, she looked haggard. "Honey," I gathered her in my arms as she dissolved into tears. "What's wrong? Come on, let's sit down."

I led her to the den couch and settled her, then lowered myself beside her. It was long moments before she could speak. "I-I couldn't get to the bus stop this morning a-and— The sobs renewed, stronger this time.

"Hey, take your time, honey. I'll get you some tea, okay?" The ritual gave her time to collect herself and by the time I set her iced beverage before her, she was able to talk.

"For some reason, I couldn't get it together this morning – one of those anxiety spells, I suppose. Anyway, I wanted to catch the bus so badly, I took that shortcut across the field and my feet sunk into mud. All the way to my ankles. But I kept running anyway. I saw the bus sitting at the stop and was only about a fourth of a block away and so out of breath I thought I'd faint. Well," she paused to take a drink of tea, "that smart aleck Tommy Jones pulled off and left me. I *know* he saw me."

Poor Trish. "That was snotty," I snapped, like a true sister.

"Yeah. Anyway, when I got back home, I slipped off my shoes on the back porch and was trying to clean the mud off my ankles when Anne came into the bathroom." She swallowed back sudden tears and my heart filled with dread.

"What happened?" I asked gently.

"Anne's eyes got really – big? And she asked, 'what are you doing here?' And I said, 'I missed my bus. I just can't seem to do anything right this morning' and," she rolled her watery eyes, "I started crying. Next thing I knew it, she lit into me – slapped me twice across the face."

I turned icy with shock. Anne? "Why?"

Trish gave me this sad little smile, kind of a pitying one. "I wish I knew, Sis."

"Okay," I said, standing. "You're not going back. Not until something drastic changes things."

Trish arose, too. "I'm glad you said that," she declared in a voice I'd never heard her use before, "because I'd already decided not to go back. Can I stay with you, Sis?"

I embraced her and rocked her back and forth standing there in my den.

"My home is your home, Trish. It's time you got away from whatever ails Anne."

To say Daddy was angry would be grossly misleading. He was *furious.*

When Trish refused to go home with him, he left in a huff. An hour later, my phone rang.

It was Daddy. "Trish knows it's wrong for her to tear up our home like this, Neecy. And it's wrong for you to condone it."

I usually didn't argue with Daddy but this was too much. "Do you want to hear what 'wrong' is, Daddy? I'll tell you." I proceded to share the things Trish had tearfully divulged over time. The last thing was an incident I'd repressed until after Trish moved in and reminded me of it.

"Remember that big gold-framed wall mirror Anne bought when you two married? It hung over the mantle. Well, Trish climbed up there to get a little hair ribbon she'd put there, hoping that by placing it there, it wouldn't be moved and get lost. She used the same chair, a platform rocker, that she'd used before to reach the mantle, only this time, when she reached for the ribbon, the chair moved suddenly, throwing her forward, into the base of the mirror. I happened to be standing nearby and saw the mirror break loose and begin to fall. I dashed to get to Trish before the thing crashed over her head, killing or cutting her to ribbons. I whammed the frame and knocked it to the side as Trish hovered there, arms over her head, terrified as that darn thing hit the floor and crashed into a million pieces."

"She began to cry and Anne rushed from the kitchen to see what had happened. I told Anne the mirror had nearly fell on Trish, but Anne just looked at that blasted pile of glass and turned on Trish. Know what she said, Dad? She said, 'Just look what you've done to my mirror!' and stalked away, disgusted."

Daddy had grown deathly quiet. "I'm sorry, Daddy. You know I love you and Anne. She's been great to me since Cole was born. He sort of bonded us, you could say. I don't know what it is with her about Trish. But I can't let you blame Trish for what's happened. Trish has never hurt a fly and she doesn't deserve all this. Do you —"

"What are you doing —" Daddy's angry voice rang out, cutting me off. "Wait a minute, Neecy," he said disgustedly, "Anne's on the war path. She's been on the other phone, listening in on our conversation. I'll get back with you." The line went dead.

I looked at the receiver in my hand for long moments, then quietly laid it down.

Oh, well, whatever happened, I'd followed my heart.

And despite an almost certain estrangement from Anne, I felt peace.

My sister lived with us the last half of her senior year at Chapowee High. How we enjoyed each other! I'd gone over to Dad's house right after Trish moved out, to get her clothes and Anne didn't come to the door, though I knew she was there.

"Why did Anne act like she wasn't home?" I asked Dad later when I called him at the barber shop. "I have no quarrel with her. I'd hoped we could go on as always."

"She's ashamed," he said bluntly. "Anne knows she's not treated Trish right. But I don't think it really hit her *how* bad it was till she heard you telling me all of it on the phone."

"I hate that I was the bearer of such but seems it couldn't be helped. Tell Anne to please not avoid me. She just needs to square things with Trish, is all."

"Yeah." Daddy sounded sad. I knew how hard it had been for him to let Trish out of the tense situation but for once, he'd put her feelings ahead of his own.

"Are you going to drive with us when we take Trish to Spartanburg Methodist? She wants to check it out for the fall semester. She's graduating in a month, you know."

"Can't believe my baby's graduating high school," he muttered, as forlorn as I'd ever heard him.

"Well, she is. You with us?"

"Yep. Count me in."

We'd just finished supper that evening when Daddy walked in. "Have a seat, Daddy," I said. "There's still some steak and potatoes left."

"Naw," he said, "I came to get Trish."

Trish's face fell and she gaped at Daddy as though he'd lost his senses. "I don't *want* to go back there, Daddy." *Spunky,* I thought, feeling warmed by it. *It's about time.*

"Trish," Daddy said imploringly, "meet us half way. Anne promised she'd treat you better. She really is ashamed, Trish. It's hard for her to say it, but I know her. She is. And when she promises something, she comes across. She's changed. Won't miss a Sunday church service, even if I don't go." I had to believe Dad because usually, he relayed the worst about Anne.

Trish looked at me, uncertain, wary. "It's your call, Trish," I said, though I'd miss her like crazy. I knew she missed being with baby Lynette, Dale and Cole. We'd gone over on weekends to visit. At first, Anne had disappeared to the bedroom. Gradually, however, she'd begun to linger with us, quiet as a morgue, but *there.* I'd persisted in treating her as usual and most of the awkwardness between us had diminished.

"Come on, Trish," Daddy gently coaxed. "Let's go home."

Trish seemed to sorta wilt. Just for a heartbeat. Then she squared her shoulders and went to get her things. Within thirty minutes, she was gone. The girls watched her and Daddy leave, their noses pressed to the front screen door. Toby climbed on the sofa and peeked through the blinds. When all three seemed ready to burst into tears, I cried, "Hey! She only lives a couple of blocks away."

That thought bolstered me as well. As did the fact that Anne seemed to be changing and the certainty that Trish had emerged from this entire situation a much stronger, more self-confident person.

Realistically, I knew my sister and stepmother had much to work out between them. But this was a start.

It finally happened. Kirk donned the frock.

In his third year of Bible College, Kirk accepted an interim pastorate at a tiny church in upstate South Carolina, whose former pastor had resigned. And while the country setting offered us a down-home, folksy welcome, the old timers weren't so ready for change.

"He's a good man, Pastor Hanson. We shore hated to see 'im go." Mr. Branson pumped Kirk's hand on the sun-washed steps following our second week of services at Possum Creek Methodist Church. "Course he didn't have no choice, with his bad health and all. Good man."

Kirk's wheat hair inclined and a broad smile broke over his features. "I'm certain he is." College had polished Kirk's vocabulary and manner. Though fiercely loyal to his roots, Kirk was smart enough to use his new ammunition well. Diplomacy fit him nicely.

I stood at his side, face stiff from smiling. We'd risen at five a.m. to allow me time to feed, bathe and dress the children, then drive the hour and twenty minutes to the remote Oconee County spot on the map.

For once, I was glad Kirk liked my fresh-scrubbed look because primping time had melted to brief moments before we'd rushed out the door this morning, only to dash back in to retrieve Toby's forgotten socks. Krissie, excited about gussying up in a new dress, had overlooked them when tying his shoes. She was always scurrying to help me during cramped times. Heather helped with bigger things, cleaning the table and fetching dishes to the sink. Even Toby dusted furniture, picked up clothes and deposited them in the laundry hamper.

Kirk silently meditated as he drove to church while I swiveled to remind Krissie it was Toby's time and right to roost in the hump-center. We'd traded our red Volkswagen for a newer, more efficient navy blue model. She quietly complied but soon had Toby tattling, "Kwiss-ee touch me." Few were the times Krissie resorted to such tactics of revenge and they remained mild and inoffensive. Still – my stomach knotted tighter.

"Krissie, please do not touch Toby."

"Yes, ma'am," she replied softly, her enormous blue kitten's eyes wounded and frustrated. Relinquishing one's territory to another is never easy.

Someday, I thought, I wanted something without a humped floor. I touched my stomach and pressed the tender spot beneath my ribs. I'd played down the stomach thing to Kirk, who spent most of his time settled back in the old beige naugahyde La-Z-Boy, socked feet raised half-mast, partially blocking sight of the moment's required book spread across his lap. I deposited heaped plates of food on the table next to him and later, steaming cups of coffee to ward off drooping lids.

The kids and I improvised, so as not to disturb Kirk's studies. We moved the television into the kitchen or bedroom and piled up on the bed to watch children's specials or an old forties' movie I loved so much. Many's the night I scooped each slumbering child in turn and gently carried them to their own beds.

The rest of the nightly ritual remained fixed. I'd nudge Kirk awake and he'd daze a weaving trail to our bed, shedding clothes along the way, then collapse between clean sheets until dawn's early light when the entire process began anew.

Sex? We simply shifted that into the wee hours, when Kirk usually awakened first and with those marvelous hands and lips, transcended me slowly from a languorous tingling to agonizing climatic pleasure.

"Kirk should help you on Sunday mornings," Babs, my neighbor insisted.

"No, I can't ask Kirk to help with the children. He's bone-tired from rising so early, meeting classes and the hours he puts in at the barber shop. Not counting the long evenings of study. No, I can't ask that of him."

"But, Janeece, he's your husband. I mean – at least on Sunday mornings when you get so hassled, he should help you. You said yourself it takes you till mid-week to unwind after the Sabbath morning war of –"

"I know." I gazed at her, seeing the logic and simplicity of her rendering. "I know, Babs. It sounds good in theory." I chuckled and shook my head. "But what about his time to meditate? He needs that time Sunday mornings to draw strength from God and study his sermon notes. Anyway, we have to leave early to get to Possum Creek for the ten o'clock service – he's already deprived of that early solitude."

Babs, wiry as a crane, peered at me from beneath her frizzed, oak-rust hair. She'd been my Mama's best friend from schooldays and that sentiment extended to me. Then she laughed a smoky, cigarette-coarse laugh. "You're somethin' else, Neecy. The Maker knew what He was doin' when he called Kirk. Not many wives could handle it."

I'd felt strangely embarrassed by her intended compliment.

"Aww, come on Neecy, you're a *basket case* while Kirk sails along undaunted in his pursuit of his calling."

"That's not fair." I didn't fare well when others criticized Kirk.

"So when is life fair? Love goes two ways. There's got to be a compromise somewhere in your great heroic epic."

I marveled at Babs' erudite use of the king's language, a product of her compulsive reading, not only novels and biographies but anything she could get her nicotine-stained fingers on. We were, on that level, kindred-spirits. She wasn't much on church going but I was convinced my daily prayers for her would soon accomplish a big turnaround.

I gazed into Babs' unwavering resolve and forced my tired lips to smile. "There is no solution for the time being. Kirk has to finish school. At the same time, he has the pressure of the interim pastorship at Possum Creek. He's got all he can handle."

Today, I stood beside Kirk as he greeted the last of the departing parishioners.

"Good morning, Mrs. McKonna. You're looking well."

"Hmmph." The pigeon-round chest swelled as the elderly woman's cynical, bespeckled eyes raked Kirk. "Why shouldn't I look well? I'm perfectly well and at peace with life. Except that I *do* miss Pastor Hanson. One of the most *mature* men I've ever known. Sure added a lot here at Possum Creek." She sniffed soundly and with a curt nod of white, nape-bunned head, indicated the exchange over, then hobbled away without so much as a "howdy-do" to me.

I realized my teeth were clamped like a vise and turned in time to catch the amused expression on Kirk's face, the *I know* one, before he turned to enter the church to exchange black robe for suit coat. He knew how rudeness chafed me, especially the rejection kind, and was always curious to see how I would handle it, wondering if my mercy-forgiveness index would persevere.

I think, subconsciously, he sort of hoped I'd lose my temper, just a little bit. That would justify his lapses. It was this very human aspect of Kirk that flavored him even more appealing to me, because had he been perfect in every way, he'd not have been attainable in 1959.

Actually, since Kirk's calling, his biting criticism of folk or situations had ebbed with a daily, steady honing away of his former edge – even when I got on his nerves with mundane bothers. *Mundane* comprised anything outside his scope of work and studies. He already neatly catalogued his priorities: God, Ministry, family. I saw nothing wrong with that, after all God had called him and I needed to be resilient and willing to free him for whatever his role required.

"*Mama!*" Toby bounded around the corner of the old white sanctuary, shirttail flapping loose from his creased pants. At two, his little face was as excitedly transparent as Krissie's. "Come look!" Black scuffed shoes pivoted and kicked huffs of dirt as he dashed back in the direction from whence he came.

I'd grown accustomed to Toby's discoveries that ranged from caterpillars that squirted green stuff when accidentally stepped on to buffalo shapes in puffy white clouds. This time, he took me to a copse of trees, some twenty-five feet behind the old church. Heather and Krissie had their heads poked in the crude door of the makeshift structure.

"It stinks." Krissie pinched her nostrils shut.

"Course it does, silly." Heather looked down her freckled nose. "It's a toilet."

Toby gazed up at me, bustling with curiosity. "Wh-what i-id it, Mama?" His stammer surfaced in direct proportion to his emotions.

"An outhouse, Toby," I carefully explained, "where you – use the bathroom."

Krissie, head still inside the door, pealed, "Can I use the bathroom, Mama?"

"*May* I? Yes, you may." I laughed. Good grief. An outdoor privy in this day and age? I'd noticed the absence of a bathroom in the ancient country parish last Sunday and we'd stopped en route home at a service station to use the restroom.

Heather's smirk drew me to the door, where, inside, Krissie looked bewildered. "How do I use it, Mama?"

"Step back." I ordered the other two outside, then joined Krissie inside the small chamber. A how-to was in order.

Krissie's wonder faded by the moment as dark, fetid reality surrounded her.

"Pull your pants down and – hop up on this step, then up on the platform," I instructed and helped my daughter accomplish the undignified squat. She giggled as her bladder emptied with nary a drop hitting the toilet seat's round wooden border.

"This is *fun*." Krissie's blue eyes danced with merriment.

"*Hummmph.*" Heather's disgust palpitated through the rough wooden door.

"I wanna do it!" screeched Toby, "I wanna do it, too!"

While assisting Toby as creatively as possible, I heard Heather outside muttering, "It's just a dumb ol' *toilet*, Krissie."

"If it's so dumb," Krissie giggled, "How come you gon' use it?"

"You're so *dumb*, Krissie. I'm gon' use it cause I really *need* to go to the bathroom. Not like you and Toby – just cause you're silly and never saw one."

I shook my head while tucking Toby's shirttail in his pants again as Krissie waged vainly for the last word. "Well – you never saw one, either."

"I've seen *hunerds* of 'em."

A short silence, then a curious, "Where?"

I rolled my eyes and made my way from the shaded thicket. Kirk was locking the double front doors when I rounded the corner while Toby dashed off to gaze up into a tree at some mystical rustle of limbs and leaves. Soon, we were driving home. It was a tiring trek, the morning round-trip, then back for the evening service, which gave Kirk little time to rest up in the afternoon before yet another sermon.

Anne had taken it upon herself to have us over every Sabbath now, knowing our early departure didn't allow me cooking time. So I did what I could on Saturdays, things I could refrigerate, and took them over for the Sunday meal. But I wasn't thinking about the cheesecake, fresh sliced peaches marinating in syrup, nor the potato salad as we rode in silence, the children tired from early rising.

I reflected on the past two weeks of impressions. Words... phrases. *He was the best pastor this neck 'o the woods ever saw. Such a noble and sacrificing man....Never be another'n like'im. Oh, Lord, bless our young Pastor Crenshaw. He's just a young man, after all, and inexperienced – he's got a lot to learn. Help him, dear Lord.* I'd flinched on that one, but Kirk had laughed it all off.

"Penny for your thoughts." He said, glancing at me.

"Oh," I tried to smile, failed and gave up. "Just thinking about how insensitive church folk can be sometimes."

He was silent for long moments. "I don't think they mean to be."

I shrugged, distinctly shamed. "I know. But they are, nevertheless."

"How?"

"Well, they're nice in most ways except –"

"Mama-aaa!" Toby wailed in my ear.

I whirled about. "What *is* it, Toby?" My goodness, I sounded like a *shrew*.

"Kwissie push me."

"I did not." I caught her in her scuttle from the *hump*-attack spot. I frowned disapproval as she settled into the far corner.

"Krissie, you know better."

"Sorry, Mama," she murmured.

"Tell *Toby* you're sorry."

"Sorry, Toby," murmured Krissie with sagging conviction as her brother's mien turned smug.

I turned back to face the front when Kirk prodded me, "What were you going to say, Janeece? You were saying 'except –'"

I'd lost my fizz to share. Only I'd opened a keg of grubs for Kirk to explore. "Oh...it's just the way they *compare* you with Pastor Hanson." I didn't have to say the obvious: *in uncomplimentary ways.*

He laughed. A hearty belly laugh.

I peered at him, a bit aggravated. "I don't see anything funny about it." Kirk could be so out-of-left-field when I least expected it. Exploding when I laughed at him but sliding into denial when the flock behaved poorly.

"Mamaaa!" Toby wailed in my ear again, swiveling my torso to about-face.

"*What is it this time,* Toby?" I fairly shrieked and my son recoiled in fear, making me feel like a witch with whiskers.

"Kwissie p-pinch me." His lower lip jutted out below tear-flooded eyes.

Krissie sat primly in her appointed corner, eyes downcast. "Krissie, did you pinch Toby?"

Silence lengthened. "Well, *did* you?"

The long lashes lifted to expose limpid, sky-blue lagoons of vulnerability. "He made a face at me, Mama," she murmured in near-whisper.

"Did not," countered Toby, his face mutinous.

"You *did*," Krissie's small voice raised a notch in desperation and her gaze darted back and forth from her brother to me, gauging his denial's credibility-impact. "You know you did, Toby. You stuck your tongue out at me."

Toby glared at her, vised to his perch with the aggression of a gladiator.

My stomach throbbed. "Krissie," I said wearily, "you know to ignore facial expressions. That means a spanking." I turned to face the front again, wondering if her sentence was just. After all, Krissie was only six years old herself. Ignore the deliberate insult of a *tongue* poking at her? Especially when it belonged to a little person who had – through birth order – dethroned her from her *hump*?

I wondered if I required too much of my good-natured little girl, who still couldn't see well out the car window while en route. Her lack of guile rendered her defenseless, detectable, while Heather could maneuver a mock war in complete secrecy.

I felt Toby tug slightly at my sleeve. "Yes, Toby?"

"You n-not gon' pank Kwissie, are you?" Blue pools of compassion turned to peer at watery-eyed, downcast Krissie, huddled in her corner.

I sighed. As usual, Toby's tender heart overrode any disagreement between him and his sibling. I tried to look stern. "Do you think Krissie deserves a spanking for pinching you?"

His towhead swung from side to side, bumping my shoulder. "I-it din't hurt," he insisted. "I-I don' want Kwissie get a 'panking."

"Are you sorry you pinched Toby, Krissie?"

"Yes, ma'am." Krissie snuffled with sincere remorse, then a choked, "I'm sorry, Toby."

"All right. I don't feel you need a spanking since you've obviously learned your lesson."

Kirk wheeled into our little parking space and the children spilled from the car to change into play clothes. Kirk reached out and gently seized my arm as I turned to emerge.

His gaze began soberly, "I know how you feel, honey," he murmured, then, in the depths of Atlantic-green, a small pin-point of light began to grow and grow until it filled his eyes with such warmth that I felt myself blush. "I know my Neecy like the back of my hand. But believe me, there's no cause to be concerned about the folks at Possum Creek."

I narrowed my eyes at him. "How can you say that when all they've done is eulogize the former pastor in your first two weeks of pastorship? Not, 'what a wonderful sermon, Pastor Crenshaw,' but 'Pastor Hanson was the best preacher ever was.' I don't appreciate their lack of-of *manners.*"

"Listen, Sweetheart," his tone was gentle, "don't you know that if they loved that aging, ailing man with such devotion, they'll eventually grow to love me – us – the same way?"

I doubted *that,* but I didn't have the heart to squash Kirk's faith.

"Pastor Hanson didn't earn their love overnight." He slid from the car seat and leaned his head back down to look me in the eye. "It took some time. Just as it will with me. But the capacity to love is there. Don't ever forget that."

The new Kirk, I realized in that moment, was a guy I really liked. It was a great feeling to have him encouraging *me* to be patient. Mymymy, how times were changing.

I hung onto that thought during the following months. Months during which Babs, my mama's old pal, contacted and lost her battle with pneumonia – but not before Kirk rushed to her sickbed to pray the sinner's prayer with her. Grandma Whitman died suddenly of heart failure, followed by an already ailing Grandpa Whitman by five months. Daddy was heart-broken and I did all I could to console him, sitting with him, holding his hand through the long nights of both Grandma's and then Grandpa's wakes. My father's need stirred my heart. There was, in his loss, a desperation that smote and shifted me into a nurturing role toward Daddy that would forever after endure.

In those first weeks at Possum Creek, Mrs. McKonna missed few chances to exhort Pastor Hanson. Bewildered, I prayed and soul-searched to come to terms with something beyond my scope of experience.

No longer could I simply walk away from unpleasantness. So I commenced developing my *preacher's-wife smile*, vintage Mona Lisa, that covered awkward situations and inappropriate responses and though it did not always disarm the perpetrator of effrontery, it masked my discomfort.

I wondered, at times, what they really were – my feelings. They were definitely changing. Slowly, I was beginning to look past issues and see faces, to *feel* the hard callused hands that gripped mine in greeting Sunday after Sunday. Nuances crept into uncultured salutations, flavoring them, altering my first impressions.

My stomach ailments eased up.

Brown paper pokes began to sprout in the vestibule after services, bearing anything from a scratch-made chocolate cake to fresh eggs, garden-picked vegetables in season, and later, in winter months, potatoes and yams, onions, canned succotash, home-made jellies and jams and even sides of cured ham.

Two months into Kirk's pastorship, I learned a valuable lesson: looks can deceive. A disgruntled looking Mrs. McKonna paused on the church steps and looked past my husband to peer through small wire specks at me, taking long moments for her huffing breath to catch up to her stillness. I grew tense waiting for something to happen.

"Say," she said, "I know it's hard goin' home to cook every Sunday after driving so far."

"Well, I –" The astute black eyes peered unblinking into my flustered, flushed face – made so by the fact that up until today, I'd been like a fly on the ceiling to her, ignored.

Unexpectedly, the old crinkled face softened. "Ah, I know how it is. You don't have to tell me how it runs you ragged with young'uns this age. Had three o'my own, don'cha know?" The black eyes instantly disappeared into the folds of her smiling face.

I gaped for a long moment, astonished, then flashed my preacher's wife smile.

"Anyway," a veined plump hand reached out to gently touch my arm, "I'd be pleased to have you and your family over to lunch next Sunday after church. That is, if this preacher here don't have any objections." She peered sternly at him.

Kirk grinned, a Howdy-Doody version. "No, Ma'am. No objections a'tall."

A deep chuckle shook the woman's ample frame. "Good. I'll be expectin' you."

I watched her waddle away and then looked up into the clear sky beyond the evergreen range. *Wonders never cease.*

The Sabbath lunches became a weekly thing, saving our family three hours round-trip on the road since Ma McKonna insisted we lay over at her house for the evening service. Ma, as she mandated we call her, discovered she and Krissie shared an affinity for cats, gave Heather scores of books she'd had since her girlhood and doted on Toby, who would climb onto her lap in a blink and snuggle against her plump softness to doze on lazy Sunday afternoons.

I grew to love her old house – pure country rusticity that smelled quaintly of wood smoke, floor wax and baked goodies – whose arms embraced you at the front door with welcome and acceptance. On warm days, Ma McKonna would raise all the windows and we'd enjoy the potpourri of heather and honey-suckle in soft, cooling breezes.

After wonderfully filling, tasty meals, we'd wash dishes, a sweet conversational time during which I learned of her loneliness as a widow with an empty nest.

Sometimes, Kirk took the kids over to play at the church's little playground – one he'd initiated, then rolled up his sleeves and built – while he studied and prayed there in one of the Sunday School rooms. He paced as he prayed and the solitary church setting helped free his mind of clutter.

During one intimate evening, Kirk divulged, "The reason I don't go around my family is – it pulls me down." We sat at our kitchen table drinking coffee after putting the kids to bed. "I know that sounds terrible but – it's true." He shrugged with a dismal helplessness dulling his sea mist eyes.

"And there I thought I was marrying into this big wonderful family and we'd live together happily ever after." I hoped it would come off as teasing, knowing it never did. Not for me. Kirk took everything I said seriously, still does. Yet when he vents, he insists he's teasing and when I don't believe him, says, "you just don't have a sense of humor, Neecy."

I long ago realized I couldn't beat Kirk in verbal sparring.

I couldn't squash down the disappointment that Kirk chose to exile himself from his family because by doing so, he denied me access to them. Me, who bonds so easily and so completely, who wants to take every new friend home and take care of them. How much *more* I cared for his family right from the beginning. After we married, he always had excuses not to socialize, mainly 'no time' with work and schooling and now, the ministry.

Tonight, I got the truth. What I'd suspected for some time now. He held himself aloof because, pure and simple, he *wanted* to. Oh, there were reasons – the unhappy childhood memories – but the bottom line was he wanted to be free of them. In particular, from the bad memories they triggered. A part of me understood and sympathized. The other part warred against the fact of Kirk's ability to isolate himself so decisively and succinctly.

It disturbed my calm waters.

Those two years at Possum Creek sped by, banking up sundry memories that jolt and ebb and flow till this day. Of Mr. Branson getting so confused with the *new-fangled* Daylight Savings Time that he arrived at church two hours early, hopping mad at the government for telling him what to do and with Kirk for messing him up good by going along with it.

Kirk handled him with sterling diplomacy, agreeing with him wholeheartedly before leading him into a perception that began to adjust him to the notion of progress. Of Toby, perceiving my love of pretty roses, presenting me with a bouquet he'd picked, during prayer, from the back of Mrs. Davis's bowed Sunday-go-meeting hat. Of the time when Kirk, just before service, went to fill communion cups for the scheduled ritual, finding the grape juice bottle empty – depleted by Krissie and Toby during one of their rainy-indoor playtimes. Of our first death, sweet Uncle Huey Dodge, a deaf man who'd relied on the kindness of a church family for home and hearth, who'd out-given everybody in love. Our first wedding – Jeannie Morgan and Clarence Jenkins doing vows in the packed out sanctuary and later, receiving guests in Ma McKonna's cleared out sitting room, surrounded by folding tables straining with homemade reception goodies and centerpieced with vibrant blossom's from Ma's own little backyard garden.

By the end of that first year, sentiments toward the present pastor did an abrupt upswing. The Christmas program, directed by the pastor's wife, crowned those first months with a rare mixture of solemn pageantry and not so solemn asides. Ten-year-old Luke Turner, during his first solo, *It Came Upon A Midnight Clear*, burst into stage-fright tears and bawled the entire song, never missing a word. Bessie Tillman, between scurrying scene changes, tripped and fell into the manger scene, upending Mary, Baby Jesus and the three Wise-Men all in one sweep and sending Jake Lester's pet pig Baby-face squealing down the aisle, her lamb's wool costume headpiece a'flapping, setting off Tom Turner's donkey Hoss, who kicked up a ruckus before relieving his nervous bladder right there before the world and splattering Krissie's beautiful white angel costume I'd stayed up nights creating. Toby, one of the little shepherds, tried his best to catch Baby-face, but the pig moved faster than sound, displacing legs, feet and anything in his escape path. Then, suddenly, I saw the porky lamb barreling toward me and without thinking, tackled her with what grace I could muster – absolutely none – and with the help of the Three Kings of Orient, who'd been halfway down the center aisle when the first prop crashed, we wrapped Baby-Face in Baby-Jesus' blanket and delivered her to her red-faced, sweating master.

That the cast and congregation wordlessly set everything aright and proceeded to consummate a befitting dramatization of the Holy Night said something I could not give voice to and shall forever remain a wonder to me.

My clan met at our house that Yule season. We all pushed back thoughts that our time of living within walking distance of each other was drawing to a close. Soon, with Kirk's graduation and ordination, my family would relocate, a fact I'd begun to accept. And to my astonishment, even Chuck and his wife Teresa and their two-year old daughter Patrice AKA Poogie, showed up the day before Christmas Eve, bunking in our kids' room while we threw down early gift sleeping bags for the smaller kids and let out the folding sofa for Heather, who disdained the little ones' exuberance at "camping out" near the small open fireplace.

Chuck launched in to some Andy Griffith monologues for the kids. Within minutes, they were laughing and acting the fool with him. I was astonished at this upbeat comedic side to my brother. Before long, all three of my kids encircled him on the floor where he held court, plastered as close to him as possible.

On Christmas Eve, MawMaw, Papa, Uncle Gabe and Jean arrived for the day. My Johnny Mathis Christmas album played *I'll Be Home for Christmas* on the stereo, Kirk's gift to me the year before. They bore presents that joined the others under the tree and, at least for a few hours, Daddy and my grandparents stumbled upon an unspoken truce. Whether it was the Yuletide spirit or sentimentality, I didn't rationalize their fragile affability. Late that afternoon, Callie, on a holiday visit with her folks, dropped by to say hello.

"You look wonderful, Callie." I pulled her into my bedroom, the only place offering any measure of privacy, where we hugged and hugged, laughing and on the verge of tears.

"I can't believe you're *here,*" I gushed, gaping at her in amazement. She'd had her dark hair cropped in a tousled Audrey Hepburn-chicness. "You're prettier than ever. And just look at how *thin* you are." I gazed woefully down at my abdomen, rounded from three childbirths, and then at her concave stomach and stuck my tongue out at her.

Callie preened dramatically. "Well, honey chile, Ah jus' can't *help* it."

Giggling like silly adolescents, we plopped down on the bed for a quick catch up chat. "How's Rog?" I asked, so excited to be talking to her I could hardly sit still.

"Rog and I are divorced," Callie said, examining her Holiday-Red nails, shrugging, then looking me straight in the eye. "For three years now."

"Thr —" I blinked at the suddenness of the idea but mostly what hit me was that she'd not felt moved to share with me an item so massive. Something inside me diminished in that second, a thing so keenly emotional it was physical. It changed the way things stood between Callie and me.

The thing that stung was that I had not stepped back. Callie had.

Would the pattern remain so for life?

We joined the family where Callie dazzled for a few more brief moments before leaving.

"Why, Trish," hands on hips, Callie surveyed her from head to toe, "You look great. How on Earth did you lose all that weight?"

Trish dead-panned, "Simple, Cal. It's called starvation." They hugged hugely, laughing and complimenting one another. I was glad for the intermezzo separating me from Callie, distancing me from the pitiful truth of our *deep* friendship. I watched my sister with a new appreciation of family. At nineteen, Trish had blossomed into a real beauty with her silken tumble of chestnut hair and eyes the color of stormy blue skies. She'd also developed a sweet self-deprecating wit at which I marveled, considering it was my *least* attribute. I could write amusing anecdotes till the swallows return to Capistrano but wit did not, nor does it now, glide smoothly over my tongue.

After Callie left, we migrated to the kitchen for sandwiches of leftover baked ham and enormous slices of Papa's Icebox Fruitcake he'd brought along to share. MawMaw settled her bulk in the chair facing Chuck across my dinette table, to which I'd added both leaves for more space.

Daddy loomed uncertainly in the doorway while everybody else bustled about making themselves at home. He and Chuck hadn't spoken more than a dozen words to each other during the day so the tension from him was thick enough to slice. Uneasiness rippled through me and I rushed past him to get another chair. "Here, Daddy, take a load off." I was relieved when he stiffly complied.

Kirk, absolutely rapt with Yule cheer, kissed me soundly – one that promised *more later* – and tucked our Polaroid camera under his arm. "We're smack outta film, Neecy. The kids and

I are gonna try and find a drug store open and buy some. You okay without me for a while?"

"Sure," I grinned and watched them exit and pile into the car

"Why doncha go with us, Uncle Chuck?" Toby yelled, fairly bouncing because Santa poised *ready-to-go* on the evening horizon.

"See ya when you get back, buddyroe," Chuck winked at him.

I thrilled at the love Kirk showed the children, always a hands-on Dad, taking them with him on his numerous treks if at all possible, glorying in the liveliness that tired me so from day to day.

"Neecy," Anne appeared at my elbow as I sliced more ham, "where're your apple pies?"

"Oh my –" I shook my head. "I forgot them. They're on top of the refrigerator, wrapped in foil." In a blink, she had them on the counter and sliced into equal portions.

Trish got busy pouring coffee and seeing everybody had cream and sugar. I was passing out the pie when I saw MawMaw's lips quiver and her chin wobble. My hand shook when I sat hers before her, knowing she would not touch it because of the empty space vacated by Dad at the table.

"Daddy?" I called out, an edge of hysteria in my voice. "Your pie's ready."

Anne slipped from the kitchen and I could hear her low voice, then Daddy's from the other room. Trish tried to make conversation to cover what I knew transpired. "MawMaw," she said with forced cheer, "I'm attending Spartanburg Methodist College this year."

MawMaw looked up at her with watery eyes so full of pain it took my breath. "You are?" she managed to croak.

"Um hm," Trish courageously continued. "That's where Kirk's going. It's close enough for me to come home on weekends sometimes."

"And she's a cheerleader, too," I threw in, proud beyond words of Trish's accomplishments.

"That's good," MawMaw barely articulated past lips trembling so violently they threatened to obliterate her lined face. My stomach knotted tighter and I saw, from the corner of my eye, Gabe rise and leave the kitchen, followed by Jean.

Trish prattled on while I went into my bedroom to check on Anne's progress with Daddy. Anne sat on the bed facing Daddy, who was as deeply planted in my little platform rocker as an ancient oak and whose nostrils flared in regal effrontery.

"Leave me alone, Anne," he stated in his most authoritative *back off* and defiantly plopped my latest *Good Housekeeping* magazine onto the highly waxed pine floor.

"I can't *believe* you're doing this, Joe Whitman," Anne practically hissed at him, which only added fuel to the fire burning in Daddy's blue-gray, glaring orbs.

I didn't know until she brushed against my elbow that MawMaw had entered the room and even as I frantically seized her elbow to pivot and aim her back to the kitchen, she began to speak the words that changed the cold war to all-out war.

"I'm gonna leave, Joe," she said with great difficulty, barely making herself heard and Dad, already incensed by Anne's *audacity* as he called it, glared at his former mother-in-law with not one whit of compassion. I couldn't see how anybody could see MawMaw cry and not feel *something*. Only thing I saw in Daddy's eyes was contempt.

"Don't leave, MawMaw." I heard the desperation in my voice and felt Daddy's hackles rise even more. "Please," I pleaded, knowing all along Daddy considered it the ultimate insult.

"Stay, Maude," Anne rose and approached MawMaw, who already moved her head from side to side.

"I can't," MawMaw choked, her chin caving, "I can't stay where I'm not wanted."

"But MawMaw – this is *my* house." I tried to take her clenched, cold little fingers in mine – and though she let me, she wasn't truly *there*, barely heard my fervent declaration, "You *know* you're welcome in my home."

"I know you want me, Neecy," she gave my fingers one lame squeeze, never looking at me. Lord, I wasn't even *there* as far as she was concerned. The old familiar helplessness snaked through me as the drama spun on, leaving me standing beside the road.

"It's Joe," Anne turned to glare at Daddy. "Why can't you behave yourself, Joe?"

Daddy sprang to his feet and toed off with his wife. "Why can't you just *shut up?*"

MawMaw, perhaps a tad more armed with Anne in her corner, pulled her hand from mine and addressed Daddy, "You don't want to be around me and Dan, do you, Joe? You just as well admit it, Joe." Her little chin, lifted ever so slightly, only looked more pathetic to me in its grief-dance.

Daddy's fierce gaze ricocheted from Anne to MawMaw and my breath caught in my throat. *No no no, don't, Daddy!* I felt the tidal wave coming, words shattering and irrevocably crashing upon those I loved.

Daddy's eyes narrowed in defiance. "Yeah, you got that right, Maude." The coldness in his voice slapped me up the side of my head. "I *don't* want to be around you."

"Joe!" Anne's reprimand was sharp, succinct. "That's just plain *mean.*"

"She *asked,*" Daddy reminded her.

"Daddy!" "Joe –" Anne and I protested in unison.

"Leave 'im alone," Chuck bellowed from the doorway. "Maude started the whole thing long time ago. Couldn't keep her danged mouth shut."

MawMaw's shock, at hearing her grandson calling her by her *name* – the ultimate insult – shattered the atmosphere. She turned and staggered from the room, her rotund little figure desolate and slow moving in its determination to escape.

"MawMaw!" I trailed her but had to step aside as Papa, his sweet clown's face sober and pale as death, helped her into her worn brown winter coat. I gathered her quivering form into my arms, hearing Anne and Daddy at it again and wept with her, knowing this would put a pall on all her memories of being in my home at Christmas. I turned to hug Gabe and Jean and little Sherry just awakening from her nap.

"Keep your chin up," Gabe whispered in my ear as we embraced.

I stared into my uncle's kind face and saw my own pain mirrored there. I slowly nodded and dashed to gather presents I'd painstakingly wrapped for each of them and pressed them into their hands.

"Bye, MawMaw," I called as they drove off. I went back inside and saw the gifts they'd placed for us under the tree and seeing one for Daddy from MawMaw, burst into fresh tears wondering *why* there could be no peace.

Chuck sauntered into the living room, watching me with detachment. It lashed out at me, his indifference.

"How could you treat her that way?" It flew out of my mouth and I suddenly didn't care.

Chuck looked at me. "How could *you* take sides with her?"

"Sides?" I narrowed my gaze at him. "*Sides?* What is it with you?" He was a stranger to me, this brother of mine. "Calling her *Maude*. You crushed her, Chuck."

He shoved his hands into his pockets and leaned indolently into the doorjamb, but his nostrils, so like Daddy's, flared. "What about Daddy? *Maude* tried to poison his kids against him and for that, I have no use for her."

The words splashed like ice water in my face. I blinked and fought to catch a deep breath. What had happened to my family? Anne and Daddy emerged from the bedroom, still exchanging heated words. "I can't believe you wouldn't even sit in the kitchen, Joe. It wouldn't've hurt you to come off it and try to be nice for one day."

He glowered at her. "Well, believe it. If I can't sit where I danged well please, I'll go home." Which he proceeded to do by slamming out the front door, but not before pinning me with his *you've jumped camp again* glare. I knew Dad was as ticked off as he'd ever been because I'd heard him cuss underneath his breath, which he hadn't done for a long spell. I felt fresh tears cropping up and swallowed them back. Anne looked at me with helpless fury. Then her gaze softened.

"I'm sorry, Neecy," she said gently touching my arm. She shot Chuck a disappointed look but said nothing, and I knew in that moment, she feared my brother's wrath as much as I did.

"Not your fault," I croaked, watching her trail Daddy, swiped my eyes and returned to the kitchen where Trish huddled in a chair, pale and silent as a little mouse hiding from a tomcat.

"Sorry, Sis," she said in her soft voice. "Wish I could have done more to prevent all that."

"Nobody could." I sat down heavily opposite her, looking over the uneaten apple pie and fruitcake and brimming cups of tepid coffee. "I don't understand," I whispered, tears instantly puddling again. "Why does there have to be so much hatred?"

Trish was silent for long moments as tears riveted pathways down my cheeks. Then I noticed her eyes, though sympathetic, were dry. "You're lucky," I said.

She looked a bit surprised at my flat statement. Then clarity dawned. "It's not that I don't love MawMaw and Papa," she said gently. "It's just that they haven't been around for the past few years. They just – didn't come around. I hardly know them."

"I wonder why." Sarcasm fit me poorly, but I was tired of hurting and felt a little anger was in order. "I've heard Daddy telling you they don't care about you. They do, Trish."

She smiled a sad little smile. "I'm sure they do – in their own way. It's just that – they've not been there for me, you know?"

I did. With sudden, startling clarity. If they'd wanted to badly enough, they'd have waded through hell to get to us. We gazed at each other, my sister and I, years older than our life spans, understanding too much too soon of flawed human nature.

"So long, Sis." Chuck appeared in the doorway, did a flippant little fingers to brow salute, his overnight bag in tow. Behind him, Teresa slipped out the front door with a small suitcase. Little Poogie trailed behind, wiping sleepiness from her eyes.

"But Chuck, I thought you were staying till tomorrow – that we'd celebrate together –"

"Nah." He gazed toward the open door as if in deep thought, already miles away.

"Why?" I asked, shaken anew at his slight, and slight it was because he knew how excited I'd been when he'd called to say they were coming. He *knew*.

He scratched his head and looked levelly at me. "Cause I don't like the way you did Dad."

"The w –" My mouth dropped open. "I don't believe I'm hearing right. After all *you've* put Daddy through and –"

"Look, Sis," his palm addressed me in an I-don't-want-to-talk-about-this gesture. "Just because you and Kirk are sorta –" his fingers butterflied hatefully, "*uppity* now he's a *preacher an' all*, you're all at once a do-gooder, a know-it-all. Dad's not done right by me, but Maude was way outta line back there when she slandered him about the way he treated Mama."

"But Chuck, she's your –"

"Hey. I'm outta here."

"What about forgiveness, Chuck?" I threw at him, stalking him to the front door. "About family? What about wiping the slate clean? You know, starting all over? With MawMaw *and* Daddy – you need to straighten up things. There is a –"

He whirled in the open door, nostrils aflare. "What for? Just to get sliced up again? *Hey!* Leopards don't change spots." His gaze narrowed fiercely. "By the way, *Sis*, don't preach at me."

The door banged behind him, leaving me limp and numb and disbelieving. The thing I'd dreaded most had happened. I watched his car spit gravel on the way out and nearly sideswipe our little VW as Kirk and the kids returned. I still stood there, staring at the space into which Chuck's car had disappeared, when Kirk followed the kids across the porch with an Eckerd's bag of film tucked under his arm.

"Uncle Chuck's *gone*," Krissie mumbled miserably, shuffling her feet, looking over her shoulder at the same space I mulled.

"Where was Chuck headed in such an all-fired hurry?" Kirk asked, then gazed around inside the house, brow furrowed. "Where *is* everybody?" He popped open our camera and began to load film, not in the least deterred from celebrating the Yule season with his family as I slid down into a kitchen chair . I looked bleakly at Trish, who sipped coffee and played with an uneaten piece of apple pie.

"Where's Uncle Chuck?" Toby was stricken that the loveable funnyman had disappeared.

"Gone," I said flatly.

He turned and something in his eyes told me he knew what the drama had cost me, even though I fought like the devil trying to hide it. "What happened?" he asked.

I told him, as unemotionally as possible. "Chuck always was a blockhead," I finished dismally, raised my eyebrows at Trish, willing her to save the day with a witty rejoinder.

For once, Trish was fresh out.

"And every time anybody called him 'Toby,' he'd pop back 'I not Toby. I *Sup-er-man.*'" I laughed and glanced at Kirk, who drove in silence, barely sparing a smile at my little yarn.

Silence stretched out into a flat-line, aligning with the car engine's hum. Lordy, I was hungry for adult conversation. For intimacy. I sighed and watched the countryside flow past, motion turning golds, reds and earthtones to heather. Trish was babysitting the kids to give Kirk and me a rare evening out. I devoted myself to protecting his time, to *not* intruding.

So *why*, I wondered, my gaze straying to Kirk's set profile, why didn't he talk to me when he *wasn't* immersed in duty? Like now? "Kirk...," I began.

"I know."

He did? A dissonant chord struck inside me. If he did, then why – ?

"Honey," he hesitated, seeming to grapple. "Look – I'm in school all week, listening to fascinating lectures, talking to interesting people. People who really have something to say. And then I come home and all you have to talk about is –" He shrugged, looking uneasy.

"About the kids," I finished his sentence lamely. A pain, deep, deep inside me stirred and then churned. I'd forgotten how blunt Kirk could be. How brutal. Oh, not intentionally and not often, but when the i's were dotted and all the t's crossed, it came out that way.

I tightly laced my fingers together and took a deep, steadying breath, telling myself that what Kirk said was, at times, true – *You're too sensitive, Neecy* – that the same sort of things that bounced off him attacked me like a vicious flesh-eating virus, working from the inside out.

Kirk's bored with me. Since he'd begun college nearly four years ago, his horizon had broadened beyond hearth and home. *Has he outgrown me?* The thought flashed like a camera's shutter, freezing me inside. I typed and edited his term papers and English assignments so I knew how much knowledge he'd assimilated, leaving me behind, intellectually, in a cloud of dust.

"It's true," I said in a remarkably even voice, "I really don't have any...outside interests. Staying home with the children, I'm rather limited in my contacts." I hoped the sarcasm and incredible pain didn't come through and was relieved when I felt him relax.

As usual, I'd left the house in a hurry and didn't take time to check my appearance. I pulled out my compact and after applying lipstick with my trembling hands, I watched my husband from beneath lowered lashes. His expression was so self-possessed it angered me.

Why? I couldn't accuse Kirk of arrogance. That wasn't it. Rather, the poor farm boy had evolved into an assured, educated man who wouldn't allow anything between himself and success. His conversation, what little he showered on me, *sizzled* with resolutions for the future.

I'd always admired his zeal and determination, hadn't I? Even when I felt sometimes like an onlooker, an inconsequential thing batted about like a wad of paper in the path of a tornado. Why did his stony profile now set off some alarm deep inside me?

Maybe, I pondered, because that infrequent, ruthless expression transforms his familiar features into the impenetrable mask of a stranger. One I feared.

I latched my unseeing focus on the road and, as usual, blamed my *wounded* attitude on *stinking thinking*. Kirk was determined to change his life. I recalled the alcoholic-hell from whence he came and decreed myself glad for him. And, most importantly, I knew Kirk loved me, reassured me daily that he did.

So what is my problem?

But I knew. I feared that the cold stranger might emerge, the man hidden inside him, the callous, brutal one capable of – God only knew *what*.

That's ridiculous. Kirk loves me, would lay down his life for me.

"*...days talking with interesting people. People who really have something to say.*"

In a heartbeat, a slow, burning resolution began to build in me, underlined with my perfectionist's strength of will. Yes, by now, Kirk's psychology savvy had designated me to that compulsive clump of humanity who *must* oversee life's details while Kirk's segment supervises the big picture. At least, we complement each other, I now consoled myself.

College: I will go to college. Some way. It wasn't altogether a matter of pride prodding me. It was, I recognized with a curious sadness, a thing of survival.

Survival. I must survive. And suddenly, desperately, I realized I didn't even know *what.*

Kirk's final year at Spartanburg Methodist crested the horizon that following autumn. Trish enrolled there as a sophomore. My witty, beautiful sister found herself surrounded by male admirers and for the second year, made the cheerleading squad. I studied piano on campus once a week, driving in with Kirk and visiting with Trish in the dorm between her classes. I was as proud of her svelte figure as she but more proud of her inner beauty that – freed from Daddy and Anne's quarrelsome atmosphere – burst through like sunshine.

Kirk's father died suddenly of a heart attack that fall. His passing barely caused a ripple in Kirk's activities. A sad testimony for a Dad to leave, I thought. Could have been so different.

Kirk fully supported my notion of college, as well as further music studies. With the shortage of pianists in church settings, we agreed that I should at least qualify as stand-in musician. But my fulltime college studies would have to wait until after his graduation.

Lizzie Freeman, Possum Creek's pianist, died suddenly of a brain aneurysm. Beyond our grief lay the need to fill her non-paying position because nothing kills a church service like a labored *a cappella* hymn. Actually, Lizzie couldn't have read a note of music on a boxcar, but what she lacked in technique she made up for in enthusiasm. Never mind that she was hard of hearing, played too loud and every song sounded the same, you got entertained just watching Lizzie's fingers flying all over that keyboard with her gray tendrils springing free of hairpins, looking like she was at a party all the time. We missed her plucky spirit dreadfully.

"You can do it," Kirk insisted when I panicked at playing for congregational singing. "Actually, Neecy, you're the only one in the church who can read music." Of which I was well aware. I was also aware nobody else had Lizzie's gift of playing by ear or her audacity to try. Now, for the very first time, I esteemed Lizzie's spunk.

I groaned. "I'll try, honey. Accompanying a congregation isn't like sitting at the piano at home, you know, so don't expect too much."

The following Sunday, nervous as Ma McKonna's neurotic cat, I took the vacant piano bench and commenced to play before service began. Hands shaking, I made it through *Abide With Me*, in memory of Lizzie, *What A Friend We Have in Jesus* and *Rock of Ages* – all simply because I'd played them so often I could almost do them without music. Surprisingly, the congregationals proved easier. I felt less on display and more a team member as Jake Lester led singing in his slightly off-key way that, months earlier, nearly made my perfectionist-ear curl in on itself. Lately, I'd determined to hear less dissonance and more devotion. Today, I adored the man's booming cater-wauling – augmented by emotion – because it covered up my fumbles and misses.

Everybody *loved* me and thought I was right up there with Liberace. I knew better. By now, Heather, eight, already played in piano recitals, much more talented than I ever hoped to be, soaking up instruction like a thirsty sponge and mastering pieces after two or three brief sittings. Even so, I was more advanced than she at that stage and was stuck on the piano bench for the duration of Kirk's pastorate.

Spring was in the air, inspiring Kirk to leave the church's double doors open that Sunday morning. Sunshine spilled over the small foyer and up the crimson aisle, ushering in a bouquet of wildflowers fragrance that hung lazily over the drowsy flock.

At eleven-ten, Kirk entered the pulpit. From the piano bench, I saw Ma's dog Sugar, a big golden Retriever, sitting on his haunches in the doorway, his tongue lolling happily out the side of his mouth. Sug was the lovingest dog on God's Earth but usually got only as far as the steps in reaching his goal: to get inside the church.

Today, Sugar faced no obstacles. Softly playing the offertory hymn, *How Great Thou Art*, I couldn't watch his progress for fear of missing a note and the building falling in on me. On the last chord, I glimpsed Sug, prostrate, at the end of Jake Lester's pew, Jake's dangling fingers lazily stroking golden fur.

Kirk arose from his pastoral seat and approached the pulpit, not having yet spotted the visitor. "Shall we stand for prayer?" Everyone arose and he began to pray. I peeked at Sug, now strolling ecstatically down the aisle, stumbling over his big clumsy feet, gazing adoringly at all the people who weekly greeted and petted him outside. "And Father, we thank thee for all —"

Kirk's prayer stretched long and Sug ventured onto the lower tier prefacing the pulpit, in full view of the flock, sat on his haunches, tongue lolling happily and then, as if inspired, rolled over on his back, legs in the air, as in surrender.

"Amen. You may be seated. The sermon today is taken from the Book of Matthew."

Laughter began to ripple through the flock, drowning out the riffling of turning pages. Kirk's brow knitted in confusion.

"Psst." I got his attention from the front pew and nodded toward our canine interloper.

"Ahhh," Kirk's composure slid a notch amid the rising rumble of laughter. "Brothers Jake and Leroy, would you assist me in removing our friend from the pulpit?"

The three men commenced to pick up Sug, who mysteriously evolved into jointless mush, slithering from their grasps into a lifeless golden mound on the carpet. It took two more men and changing their tactics to gently drag Sug's dead weight down the aisle to remove his bulk from the worship service. There wasn't a dry eye in the church by the time Kirk returned, flushed and sweating, to deliver his message.

Kirk vows, to this day, that the solemnity to deliver that sermon was the most difficult he ever achieved.

"Trish! You here?" I stuck my head in the dorm room, a messy chamber except for Trish's corner, where she studied, denimed legs pretzeled, on her small bed. She bounded up to hug me and then Anne, who'd gotten Ruthie, her sister, to baby sit Dale, and had driven down with us to visit Trish.

"I've missed you, Trish." Anne's spontaneous declaration warmed me and I thought how the separation had worked wonders with their relationship. It transported them from Daddy's censor to freedom, an ingredient that works magic.

Another thing that worked magic was Anne's spiritual conversion, right after Trish returned home. Daddy's came a few miserable weeks later, after which he threw away his Chesterfields, stopped his cussing and never looked back.

Folks speak of miracles mostly in physical terms. To me, the greatest miracle of all is a life changed by the supernatural power of the Almighty.

The visit that day took us all over campus, where Trish showed us off to friends. During lunch in the cafeteria, we met a guy named Gene, with whom Trish batted quips and whose Alfalfa-twig and outrageous wit seemed to intrigue my not-easily-impressed sis. Like Kirk, he was a ministerial student. I liked him instantly and suspected I would see Gene Tucker again.

Back in the dorm room, we began our goodbyes, hugging like no tomorrow, when Anne took both Trish's hands in hers, looked her in the eye and said, "Trish, I've prayed much about – what I'm about to say." She took a deep steadying breath, her sky-blue eyes stricken. "I wish I could go back and do things different with you. I wish I'd seen your needs like I do now – it took knowing Jesus to open my eyes to *truth*," her voice cracked, but she steadied herself and continued. "And I'm so, so sorry. I hope you – and Neecy – can find it in your hearts to forgive me. If I could, I'd go back and undo it all. But I can't." Enormous grief labored her words. "It wasn't intentional – I've always loved you, Trish. I'm so ashamed to admit this – but I was jealous because your Daddy was so protective over you. He made me feel sorta – I don't know…like he didn't trust me to do right by you. Then I got mad. It wasn't you. I loved you, Trish. I just didn't know how to show.…" She swallowed several times. "When you cried, it scared me because I didn't know how to – ." Her composure dissolved into silent weeping.

Trish flung her arms around Anne, unable to say a word and they hugged like two clinging to a buoy in a raging sea.

Tears of wonder filled my eyes and when they finally stepped away from each other, wiping away tears, I stepped up to my stepmother and hugged her fiercely, knowing the courage of her gesture. The humility. The *love* behind it.

And my faith in humanity took an abrupt upward swing.

"What's she wearing?" Krissie whispered as I took my front-pew seat between her and Toby after playing the offertory hymn *And Can it Be.*

"It's an African native costume." I referred to the colorful clothing worn by our visiting messenger from Sierra Leone, who now stood before the congregation to speak. Her presentation was as colorful as her garb, drawing her audience from quiet little Possum Creek to lush tropical jungles and faraway villages, where she served as a medical missionary. Her stories of exotic illnesses and miraculous interventions drew rapt attention. At the end of the service, when Kirk appealed for the customary love offering, Krissie finally stirred.

After the closing prayer, as everyone milled around, she looked at me. "Mama, I want to be a missionary."

"Oh?" Her countenance had never been more solemn.

"Mm hm." She nodded decisively and raced off to speak to the lady doctor, who took inordinate interest in Krissie's newfound focus.

Toby's fingers slipped inside mine. "Mama?"

I looked down into huge blue pools of excitement. "Yes, Toby?"

"I wanna be a mish-nair, too."

I suppressed a grin. "You do?"

Later, en route home, I felt a tap on my shoulder. "What is it, Toby?"

He poked his head between the seats, cupped small hands around my ear and whispered, "What's a *mish-nair?*"

"Pastor's college graduation's just a month away," Ma McKonna pronounced in her abrupt way. My hand paused on the plate I was about to scrape following our delicious lunch of Ma's chicken and dumplings. I decided not to mention Kirk's appointment with denominational officials the next Thursday. I vigorously tackled the soiled plate as if to scrape away a niggling suspicion playing on my mind: *a change is about to take place.*

"Ahh, Ma," I said, stretching my arm across her rounded shoulders as she washed a plate at the sink, "what would I do without you?"

She chuckled, blushing with pleasure. "Oh, Law, you'd make out."

Drying the plate, I wondered in that lovely moment when honeysuckle breezes wafted through the open window how I could leave Possum Creek and its salt of the earth folk. I closed my eyes. No. God wouldn't do that to me, just when I'd learned to love them as my own.

God wouldn't do that to me.

June sunlight washed the dinner-on-the-grounds celebration of Pastor Crenshaw's college graduation. It was also a farewell feast. Jake Lester and Zeb Branson had built long wooden tables to stretch out beneath a cove of shady elms flanking the front lawn. White sheets served as table cloths and that they smelled faintly of moth balls did nothing to inhibit the flock's appetite.

"Nobody cooks like country women," Kirk decreed as soon as he said the blessing and turned the kids loose to fill their plates from mountains of fried chicken, potato salad, fluffy biscuits, cornbread, vegetables, cakes and pastries that challenged any county fair exhibition, and to wash it all down, vats of iced tea and lemonade.

Later, while Kirk and Archie Wells got a game of baseball going for the boys, Agnes Beech and I gathered the girls for tamer games of Farmer-In-The-Dell and London Bridge. Other ladies joined in once things got going and I realized I hadn't seen Heather since lunch.

I pulled Krissie aside. "Where's Heather?"

She shrugged. "I don't know. I'll go find her." Her patent leather shoes kicked up huffs of dust as she disappeared around the corner of the church.

I turned back to the activities and began to sing, "London Bridge is falling down...."

Moments later, I felt a tug at my sleeve. Krissie guided my head down, cupped her small hands and whispered into my ear. "Oh dear." I groaned. "Are you sure?"

Eyes wide, Krissie nodded vigorously.

"Agnes, will you take charge, please?" I followed Krissie around back to the leaning, weathered outhouse. Inside I found Heather, in tears.

"It'll be all right, honey. Come on," I coaxed gently. "Nobody will know. You can sit with Ma McKonna. I'll tell everybody you're not feeling well."

Heather snorted weakly. "*That's* certainly true."

"Then," I stretched forth my hand, "come with me."

Heather stepped forward and hesitantly took my hand and I knew how difficult it was for my little independent nine-year-old to trust her destiny to me. She took a few steps alongside me, then spotted Krissie standing in the clearing, watching us anxiously.

Heather's heels dug in. "*Nuh uh.* I can't, Mama."

"Oh Heather...."

My heart wrenched when tears tumbled from her lower lids and streaked a path down over her pale freckles and she croaked, "Krissie might tell. Or the wind might blow –"

I gathered her in my arms. "Honey...Krissie won't tell. And if you sit quietly, no one will be the wiser."

Krissie approached, oozing with sympathy. "Come on, Heather," she pleaded, blue eyes pools of compassion. "I'll sit with you."

For once, Heather linked fingers when Krissie offered hers, and hand-in-hand, they settled down near Ma McKonna. Reassured, I returned to the game activities and was soon absorbed into the squeals and excitement of recreation.

Near the end of the afternoon, I noticed Krissie playing with the little Wells girl. "Where's Heather?" I asked. Krissie took my hand to tug me to privacy.

"She's in the car," my little woman-child whispered, who had in her fourth year, cried after me for a solid week when I dropped her and Heather off at kindergarten classes. I fretted until Miss Peggy assured me Krissie was adjusting 'just fine.' Now, at seven, she seemed willing to take the weight of the world on her small shoulders. Mymymy, how I could *read* her.

"Has she been there all this time?" I asked, dreading the answer.

"Uh huh. I tried to get her to stay. But you know Heather." From anybody else, it would have sounded barbed. From Krissie, it was utterly guileless.

"Yes." I smiled at her. "I know Heather."

I found Heather huddled in her corner of the VW's back-seat, climbed in front and turned to her. "Was this necessary, honey? I mean – isolating yourself?"

Heather looked up from her gloom with horrified eyes. "Mama, I'd just *die* if anybody ever finds out I lost my panties in that old toilet hole."

"How did it happen?" I asked, determined to remain solemn.

Heather rolled her eyes, her favorite mannerism these days. "They fell off when I climbed up on the crazy seat. Right down in that *stupid* hole." Her small round face looked so tragic my heart sailed straight to her. "Crazy ol' toilet," she grumbled and dropped her head.

I reached between the seats and took her limp hand in mine. "I'm sorry your day was spoiled, darling."

Heather shuffled and mumbled, "That's okay."

"No. It was a bad break for you. Now, I'll go try to hurry Daddy up and we'll get you home soon. Okay?" The bowed chestnut head nodded.

When I returned to the churchyard, Kirk was addressing the silent flock.

"...this past year and a half has been one of the most en-riching periods of our lives, mine and Neecy's. You've been more than a family to us. You've taken in a green, unlearned Bible student and embraced him as Pastor. You'll never know how much this means to me – how it's boosted me to keep on keeping on." He looked around till his eyes met mine, then ges-tured me to his side, where one arm circled my waist. "As you know, we'll be leaving here in a few days. Where? We aren't yet certain. It will be hard – the separation from you folks. But this one thing I know." His voice softened to husky silk. "With this woman at my side, I can make it. She's God's gift to me – a dream wife for the past four years." He gazed into my eyes, as solemn as I'd ever seen him. "I could never, *ever* have done it without her."

Unexpectedly, he lowered his head and kissed me on the lips. A gasp rippled through the teary-eyed gathering and then a spatter of applause that erupted into a thunderous ovation of hoots and hollers: *Yeaahh, Neecy!* And so it went until, blushing, I looked around see Krissie applauding and yelling to the top of her lungs, the little red face split by a gap-toothed grin. Toby stood beside her, dirty as a ragamuffin from Indian wrestling the Oglesby boy, gaping slack-jawed from Krissie to me, trying to figure out what in blazes was going on.

Heather! "Come on, Kirk," I whispered urgently, tugging him along with me.

"What's your hurry?" He glanced over his shoulder at the flock, who now stood like puzzled statues, watching us as we trudged to our little VW, Krissie and Toby trailing behind.

"Sorry, honey," I stopped, turned to peer at the precious faces and blew them a kiss. "I love ya'll!" I called, waving, and experienced the warm, warm kick of reciprocation when grins, blown kisses and loving yells erupted.

"Everything okay, Neecy?" Kirk took hold of my hand, his gaze trying to read my body language when I gazed back over my shoulder at my little girl huddled in her corner of the car.

Irritation and hysterics battled. *Everything okay? he asks. Changes...kid's heartaches...separations...*my world tilted again.

I looked at him then and my head rolled back in laughter. "Is it *ever?*"

At his bewildered expression, I threaded my arm through his and tugged him toward the car. "C'mon, honey, let's get this show on the road. Tomorrow's another day."

CHAPTER SEVEN

Trish and Gene's wedding was the family event of the decade, held at Chapowee Methodist Church with Kirk – *drop dead* handsome in clergical robe – officiating and Pastor Cheshire assisting. Our small home church packed out until we set extra chairs along back and side walls. It was a beautiful ceremony, during which I, matron of honor, wept quietly as my little sister became a woman before my eyes.

Beside ring bearer Toby stood my little sister Lynette – our little *caboose*, as Dad called her, springing up unexpectedly as Anne approached mid-life. Of course, Anne was elated and after Daddy moaned over it a spell, he perked up and decided to celebrate the tiny one's arrival, only a year after Toby's appearance. Today, the four- and five-year-old duo were on their best behavior in small white tux and long daffodil-yellow dress.

"Get everything moved in?" I asked, hugging Trish at the reception. Gene's present pastorate moved them fifty miles away, near the North Carolina state line.

She waved at guests. "Real country, Sis," she said. "Like *Podunk*. But I love the people."

"Least you don't have to be fully dressed to walk out on the porch for the newspaper."

Trish winked and flashed her dimples. "Your kids *love* it from what I hear."

"What's *not* to love with highway-to-highway asphalt church property that adjoins the parsonage yard? It's a hangout playground for every kid within a mile-and-a-half radius. Oh! Don't forget the basketball goals near the youth building." I snorted. "Course the kids love it. I don't see them till supper. Even nighttime doesn't drive them in – night lights and all."

Trish crossed her eyes and bucked her teeth. "Duh! What means *night lights*?"

I sniggered. Trish's abode *was* in the sticks where, if you struck a match, it would be seen for miles about. "Still," I sighed, "I love your quiet little setting."

"Tell you what," she deadpanned. "I'll trade places. Just say when. Anyway," she gently cuffed me on the shoulder, "you're hardly ever home these days, *school gal.*"

"Yeah," Cole, my not-so-little brother at fourteen, appeared at my elbow. "How you likin' college, Sis?" His long arms snaked around my shoulders.

"Love it, honey." I hugged him soundly, this strapping six-foot-two *baby* of mine. Till this day, I refer to Cole as "my baby" and he simply smiles that warm, warm smile of his that reaches to his gray-blue eyes, turning them into shimmery half-moons. Anne's smile. Warm, rich auburn highlights his chestnut hair and he's one of the most adorable hunks of family I have.

"You going to Hopewell Community College?" he asked. I nodded, moved, as usual, to see him. Immediately, his current girlfriend whisked him away.

"I feel a little guilty, sometimes, I enjoy it so much, Trish," I confessed.

"You shouldn't," Trish quickly took my hand. "You deserve this, Neecy. Don't you worry your sweet head over those kids." She grinned wickedly. "They're *glad* for the space."

"Yeah. Toby loves kindergarten. Rules the roost, quote Miss Alta. Wish my little Krissie were as resilient."

"She still down?"

"'Fraid so. Kirk and I talked with all four of her teachers about matters and – I sense Krissie's got them pegged right."

Trish's mouth flat lined and her eyes turned a rare stormy gray. "How *dare* they."

"Yeah – they all have a militant mentality – like the school is somehow *special* and *above* the ordinary, you know? We – Kirk and I, put the kids in private Christian School because we thought they *would* get emotional and spiritual nurturing. Krissie's become a casualty. Poor thing. She's so – defenseless, Trish – wants to please so badly and now, instead of *one* teacher, she has *four* to please. It's all too, too much for her."

More wedding guests swept in. I started to move away, but Trish surreptitiously took my arm as she bade others good-bye. "Don't leave, Sis," she hugged me again. "We've got to catch up. I miss seeing you all along."

"Me, too."

"Oh Heather," she called, "come here, honey."

Heather, who adored her Aunt Trish, rushed over, looking much more mature than her twelve years. Nearly as tall as me, she'd filled out quite nicely while her face elongated into an attractive oval that framed astonishing sea-green eyes set below burnished chestnut hair that could have, curled, rivaled that of the new Charlie's Angel star Farrah Fawcett. Of course, Heather wanted hers perfectly straight. Heaven *forbid* she look different than any other twelve-year-old on Planet Earth in 1971.

Trish hugged her warmly. "You played beautifully today, Heather. I'm so *proud* of you." I felt so *undergirded* by her love for my child, whom she'd helped me raise in those early years. Trish, who baked cakes to celebrate each family member's birthday when *I* couldn't even *remember* all the birthdays. Who followed Heather's musical progress with as much zeal as I, asking for a *recital* during visits, settling back in a La-Z-Boy, truly listening.

"Where's Krissie?" Trish asked suddenly. "I haven't seen her since before the ceremony." Heather went to get her and soon returned, where Trish and Gene still greeted lagging guests.

Krissie, ten, had evolved from the cherubic stage into a thinness that bordered skinny, looking wonderfully chic in the long sunny-yellow junior bridesmaid dress. Still flaxen-haired with eyes the color of a clear summer day, she was bypassing the awkward stage. At least outwardly.

"Now," Trish took her petite hands, drawing her close for an intimate exchange, "What's this I hear about you calling yourself a *dummy?*"

"We-ell," she divulged quietly, blushing furiously, "sometimes, I *feel* like a dummy –"

"Say! That's my *niece* you're talking about there, *Kiddo.*" Trish rolled her eyes devilishly down at Krissie, "talk about *dummy*, you shoulda seen me when I –"

I turned away to search out Kirk, entrusting my girls to my sister. Trish, dear Trish, whose gift it is to enter another's world, to blend as comfortably with a two-year-old as one ninety, never requiring one to leave their turf.

Hers is an entirely selfless existence. Already, Krissie's battered little spirit buoyed.

I'd recently looked over her assignments and found them difficult for *me*, a college student and felt angry that such responsibility be heaped on Krissie's small shoulders. "They don't like me, Mama," she said with dead certainty.

"Why do you think they don't like you?" I asked, *understanding.*

"'Cause when I raise my hand to answer the things I *do* know, they ignore me. They *never* call on me in class." Her wounded gaze tore at my heart.

At the next PTA meeting, Kirk and I had made a point of talking with each teacher to relay Krissie's insecurities. Each expressed concern, but I'd not yet seen a dramatic turnaround in my daughter's self-image. The bruising left her feeling unlovable.

"You're a bright little girl, honey," I reassured her afterward.

Krissie, being Krissie, never talked back. She was too kind and respectful to overtly disagree, but I could see it in the deep blue lagoons: she didn't believe me.

❖ ❖ ❖ ❖ ❖ ❖

Hopewell Methodist Church sported many musicians, which pleased me immensely because, finally, I could be a regular church person. Well, almost. Thanks to those of the latest flock, I now knew I would never, in ecclesiastia, be just a *person*. Here, as in other churches, I perceived that many regarded me as an *appendage* of my dear husband, Kirk.

Hopewell's personality – oh yes, churches *do* have personalities – differed from Possum Creek's in that while the latter kept Kirk humble at first, making him earn their respect, Hopewell cheered him in with something like a hero's welcome, leaving me behind in a puff of perfume-bouquet, reverting back to the invisible fly on the ceiling.

I felt distinctly jerked around. No Ma McKonna lurked on the sidelines here, waiting it out to see if I was genuine. Nobody seemed to care one way or another when it came to the pastor's wife. Their set-in-motion lives easily accommodated the new pastor, who fit neatly into the recently vacated puzzle space. I suspected that to squeeze me in would somehow throw their smooth life flow off course.

Not so different from me, BP – before the pastorate.

I learned another connotation term – PK. Preacher's Kids. Nobody had a problem with Krissie. Sweet little Krissie with open face and innocence, whose gentleness and reaching-outness touched anybody with a pulse, had no problems. Heather, too, with a new maturity and talent and just plain brilliance, had little difficulty beyond feeling stereotyped as that *nice preacher's daughter,* which, she admitted later, made her want to do something publicly obscene at times, something so outrageous and scandalous that the flock would see *her*, really *see* her.

Now Toby, he was another matter. Precious little Toby – with his shocking tow-thatch of hair, perpetually nosy gray-blue orbs, *busy-busy* hands and feet – had a rare propensity to rattle nerves.

"Let me take him home for *one* week," *teased* Brother Holmes, an old retired minister who'd settled in at Hopewell Methodist, "and I'd straighten him out for you." The white haired geyser's jaw-splitting grin was undermined by a purely malevolent gleam behind watery, mud-colored eyes.

Yeah, right! I resurrected my Pastor-wife's smile. While Toby was, I conceded, perpetual motion and racket, he was a good boy. Like Krissie, his affliction was not of choice but of genetics, his being boundless effervescence, like Kirk's – Krissie's being a gentle vulnerability, from her mother's pool. Trouble was, few of the flock took the time or trouble to get past Toby's liveliness to glimpse the generous little fellow who was unerringly polite and helpful in all things.

Until Jessica Montgomery burst on the scene. My one regret is that we had but one year with this stoical woman whose affliction – a lovely brain-damaged daughter named Deborah – redefined *blessing* to me. A widower, Jessica had decided to retire from teaching in Hopewell to be near her ailing ninety-year-old mother, who was now deceased.

The church service had just begun when a commotion commenced outside in the foyer. A loud raucous voice boomed, *"No way! Shut up,* Mama! You *stupid."*

Kirk didn't miss a beat in his commentary, but I saw puzzlement brush his features.

"Reading from Matthew nineteen, verses thirteen and fourteen: 'Then were there brought unto him little children, that he should put his hands on them and pray: and the disciples rebuked him...."

Cr-rash. The sanctuary doors burst open and in a flash, a young woman appeared halfway up the aisle, where she rooted, twisting the bangs of her shorn pecan-brown hair, gazing curiously about her at the sea of strange faces. "*Ma-Ma-a-a!*" she bellowed at the top of her lungs in a voice not unlike a hoarse, low-pitched trumpet.

Crrraa-ash burst the doors again, ushering in a handsome middle-aged woman who, though hastening, carried herself with queenly dignity. "Deborah, come with me," she commanded in a gentle yet firm tone. Deborah, spiraling her twig and peering about, didn't resist when the woman took her hand and tugged her toward a back pew. There, amid the still, shocked silence, the two women settled on a seat.

At least, the older woman settled. Deborah began to mumble and fidget.

Kirk, master of denial, quickly resumed his message, his mellow voice riding shotgun over the corncob rough bellowing, "*Stop, Mama. No way.*"

"Deborah," came the even, genteel reply, "we're in church now. Let's sit quietly."

"I'm *hungry,*" was Deborah's final roar. The mumbling ebbed away.

Kirk, unruffled, lifted his hand, "'But Jesus said, suffer little children, and forbid them not to come unto me: for of such is the kingdom of heaven.'"

Jessica and Deborah had entered our lives.

Hopewell Community College presented me a bright new frontier. It also filled hours made lonely by Kirk's duty-absences and the children's schooling. With Toby in kindergarten, my nest sat unoccupied until mid-afternoon. Second semester had me on campus until five, thus throwing me into a tailspin over what to do with my rambunctious lad.

Jessica Montgomery approached me in the vestibule between Sunday School and Worship Service. "I'll be most happy to watch after Toby while you're in school, Janeece," she informed me.

I shifted my feet on the burgundy vestibule carpet and stared at her, puzzled. "How – ?"

"I overheard the Pastor discussing it with Mr. Hardy, the Lay Leader. Am I correct in assuming you need someone to care for Toby between the hours of twelve and five?"

"Ahh – yes. But you have your hands full with –"

"Quite full, but I believe I can rout out space for a small tyke." She waited for my response with a dignity unparalleled in my pastor's wife experience, maintaining a fidget-free silence.

I blinked and cleared my throat, unfamiliar with such up-frontness in the South's heartland, where genteel beating-around-the-bush prevails. "I won't be able to pay much but –"

"Pay? I would not require payment to mind Toby, Janeece. Shall I begin Tuesday? I have to take Deborah in for a checkup with her doctor that morning. After that, I'll be free to pick him up at his school."

"Actually, Mrs. Montgomery –"

"Please call me Jessica."

"Jessica – the girls get home about three thirty to see after him."

She looked at me down her well-shaped nose and I glimpsed the beauty of her prime. Seventyish, she still cut a striking figure with her full, short-cropped salt and pepper waves, olive complexion and clear whiskey colored eyes. "Are you saying you want me to pick him up and then drop him off at your house after the girls get home?"

"Well – uh, if you're sure it's not too much –"

"All right. I'll pick Toby up Tuesday at twelve o'clock if you'll just write down directions to his school."

Her succinct decisiveness, I learned, was what gave Jessica the edge on life. She was not a shoot-from-the-hip person, merely intuitive, seasoned with a wisdom that astounded me. Deborah's affliction, I'd learned by now, resulted from the un-diagnosed RH blood factor during her birth. By the time it was discovered and transfusions administered, the infant's brain was severely damage. Jessica did not bear more children because her husband died in an accident when Deborah was only two.

Fortunately, Jessica's widowed mother helped with her granddaughter during those years, enabling Jessica to teach until her retirement some years back. Deborah's favorite activities were watching cartoons, drawing and coloring pictures. Her least favorite things were crying babies, rowdy youngsters and arguments of any kind.

"Deborah reacts emotionally to things we only *want* to react to," Jessica once explained. "Her colorful language, she picks up from her comrades at Flatland Skills, with whom she works three days a week. Since she has no inhibitions, she just simply has a go at it. She does okay if things move smoothly, but if anything unexpected happens, she *reacts.*" She chuckled, leaving the *reacts* open-ended.

After she departed with directions in hand, I had second thoughts. Toby and Deborah?

Deborah's tolerance for noise is non-existent. I rolled my eyes upward, then squeezed them shut. And Toby is *clamor* seeking opportunity. Oh, well, I squared my shoulders and took my front pew seat, Jessica seemed confident things would work out so I would simply release them into her capable hands. Then breathe a fervent prayer.

During our Hopewell Church days, the phone rang incessantly and Kirk's motto was to 'be instant in season and out of season" with emphasis on *instant.* He vanished with sleight-of-hand ease to serve the flock. At times, I felt the old stirring of placelessness but attributed it to my being so busy and constantly en route from one study to another. The busy-ness, I think, kept me from dwelling on the notion that Kirk was distancing more from me. Bottom line: his springy step said he was reaching a pinnacle that I, alone, could not give him.

I convinced myself I had a choice, that I could *demand* Kirk's time and attention should I need it. I think on some level, I feared delving too deeply. On occasion, Kirk acknowledged that he placed his ministry before family.

"I don't mean to, Neecy," he said on one rare night at home, after the children were in bed. "It's just that – if I'm not there when someone needs me, I will have let them down."

"True," I admitted, "folks don't usually call unless there's a real need."

So, I sent him on his way with blessings and took care of the homefront, warmly content that he was a true man of God.

And though I hungered for more of him, I knew that in the final crush, if ever – God forbid – it came down to a choice, Kirk would choose me.

I knocked on Jessica's pristine white front door. From within the modest ranch-brick structure, quietness smote me. Presently, I heard brisk footsteps and the door swung open.

"Come in, Janeece," Jessica smiled and stepped back, pulling me inside with the momentum of her warmth. "Deborah and Toby are out back on the patio having some refreshments. It's been such a nice, sunny day, I thought they'd enjoy a picnic outside." She talked as she walked, focused and purposeful and with a grace that made me feel klutzy. "Here," she pulled out a patio chair for me to join my son and his friend, "Have some cookies and lemonade."

Toby sprang to his feet, then remembering Deborah's propensity to react to undue stimuli, slowly took her hand and asked very nicely, "would you like to go exploring with me? I heard something in that bush over there. It might be a big –" Mentally checking himself again, Toby shrugged, "just a little old bird or somethin'. Wanna look?"

Deborah looked blankly at him for a long moment and then, seeing his curiosity peaking, got awkwardly to her feet, shook loose of his small hand and, twisting her twig of hair, trailed him to Jessica's tiny evergreen garden.

"They're getting along well," said Jessica, looking pleased.

"Thank you," I said without forethought.

She gazed at me. "For what?"

"For taking on my little rambunctious guy."

Jessica reared back and laughed, a sound that rolled from her like stringed alto arpeggios. Once loose, her mirth was as unfettered as her decorum. "Janeece – think about what you just said." She peered at me and cut loose again with laughter.

"No way!" Deborah bellowed from where Toby crouched over shrubbery, his stick probing and separating leaves. She rocked from one foot to the other in her baggy jeans and big loose blouse – she abhorred garments hugging her skin – holding her bang-twig, scowling at Toby, fighting her own burgeoning inquisitiveness.

"Look, Deborah," Toby squealed, then immediately lowered his voice, "look, will ya?"

Deborah slid one sensibly shoed foot forward and stretched her lean body to view Toby's discovery, a green frog that leaped from obscurity, then frantically away from the two voyeurs.

Toby punctuated his belly laugh with three somersaults.

Deborah flung back her head, arched her back and poked out her lips into a huge donut that emitted excited huffs of soundless glee. *"Huhhh! Huhhh! Huhhh!"* Red-faced, she lumbered about in zigzagging circles, shaking and flailing her hands in the air as though freeing them of some invisible, burning liquid. She *spewed* energy and what I recognized as joy. This was Deborah's celebration, this silent ritual of exuberance.

It moved me profoundly, bringing both tears and laughter.

Jessica and I looked at each other through mists of wonder.

The unlikely pair: Toby and Deborah, actually taming each other. Who'd have ever thought it? And gazing at my friend Jessica, who found humor and joy in a life that limited her horizons, I felt ashamed of every complaint I'd ever uttered.

The phone rang. It was Mollie Pleasant, Callie's mother. "I got a letter from Callie today," she said. "You asked me to get with you when I heard from her."

Mollie went on to tell me that Callie was divorcing her current husband Joe, number three, whose ready-made family of three children had unexpectedly delighted my old buddy. Unfortunately, Joe's drinking brought out his darker side and Callie had sustained much abuse before throwing in the towel. I thanked Mollie for calling and hung up, reeling.

Callie – abused? I had to sit down.

What had happened to my spirited friend who called all the shots?

I'd gleaned from mutual friends that Callie had, through the years, developed a drinking problem. She'd always seemed so – smart. Yet, Callie's insatiable quest for thrills had always overrun reason. I felt a stirring of anger. At her. At *it*, the demon that drove her. In the next heartbeat, an incredible sadness swallowed it up.

Ours had been a unique closeness, Callie's and mine. Polar opposites, we'd posed no threat one to the other and when we shared, it was wholeheartedly and with love unconditional.

And with the next breath, I knew I still felt that way about my friend. I loved her. Period. Didn't matter what she'd done: she was still *Callie.*

I rummaged for my stationery and began to write her a letter. I poured out my concern and care, relating to our younger days and my talk with her mother. I poured out my aspirations for her well-being and her spiritual safety. Tears dripped onto the pages and by the time I finished and sealed the envelope, I felt drained.

I felt peace.

A festive Farewell Service packed out the sanctuary. Wonderful food smells wafted from the fellowship hall, where the gathering would convene for a covered dish luncheon. I looked around. Heather sat with the pre-teens and Toby with Jessica and Deborah. I occupied my front-pew seat, growing more misty-eyed by the moment because, despite the less than affectionate start for me at Hopewell Methodist Church, I'd bonded to this flock as surely as to the one at Possum Creek. Time *can* heal most things, I'd learned during those long months there. Just love folks and give them time: they'll come around.

Krissie quietly slipped into the seat beside me, followed by her carrot-topped friend Sandy. My little shadow, I thought. Krissie always opted to be near me and I found myself, at times, nudging her to reach out to others her age, to assert herself into their circles, but shyness held her back. How I understood. I reached for her hand and squeezed it, a thing that would have mortified Heather before her friends.

Heather. I covertly watched my oldest swapping notes with pals, avoiding my gaze, like she didn't know me. Two sides of the coin she was: one side a stranger who detested me, the other, a misty-eyed woman-child who, in rare, private times, told me how wonderful I was, how beautiful. I smiled and faced the front again, thinking how she'd never admit it to her peers, even under torture. Thinking, too, how nothing I did came off *right* in her estimation. I'd slid from being her whole world to being a big fat zero. It was as though she'd launched off to Teen-Planet where nobody spoke my language and only barely acknowledged my alien-existence. But everybody with teens told me it was only a phase. I wished it would zip by more quickly. I missed my daughter.

Andrea Smith finished her solo selection, one of Kirk's favorites, *Beulah Land,*

and I thought of how fortunate Hopewell was with several trained pianists, singers and musicians. I thought of how Andrea, proper, *musically accurate* Andrea, was offended when, at a chain-gang prison service, one inmate had asked her to sing *Just a Little Talk with Jesus* and she'd told him she couldn't sing such a song. Such an undignified, *irreverent* composition went against her conscience.

Dear, dear, I now imagined how that inmate must have felt in the face of such snobbery. Why, Lizzie would have shook the rafters with her rendition and had 'em dancing in the aisles.

I checked the program. The final presentation was a processional with flags, escorting Kirk from the sanctuary to the place of honor in the fellowship hall. The organ rumbled and the piano chimed strains of Charles Wesley's *O For A Thousand Tongues to sing my great redeemer's praise,* and majestic banners swept past, borne by a color guard consisting of church elders.

"Ahh, Crap!" Deborah bellowed, springing to her feet and charging down the aisle, her red face rampant with mutiny.

"Deborah, come back," Jessica commanded and with Toby shadowing her, pursued.

"Deborah," Toby wailed, scuttling past Jessica, "Don't be scared."

"Stupid! Stupid! —" came Deborah's foghorn-trumpet howl as she collided with elder Ben Johnson, who, flag and all, went crashing into a pew, knocking Doris Hepplehoff's new hat askew and drawing a screech of either pain or shock from deacon Silas Tate, who mostly napped through services.

Deborah froze mid-aisle, except for fingers twisting her twig, her mien one of scowled bewilderment.

"It's okay," Toby took her hand and patted it. "Don't be afraid."

"I'm hungry!" howled Deborah, her nose slightly sniffing the aromatic smells. "I wanna eat."

"Shhh." Jessica took her daughter's other arm and along with Toby, tugged her through the double doors into the vestibule. No real damage was done other than to Ben's dignity, which recovered rather quickly. Doris set her hat aright, and Silas roused for lunch.

And more than at any other time, I felt truly at home there.

PART TWO
1973-74

CHAPTER EIGHT
"A time to Die...A time to Mourn."

Moving to coastal Solomon, South Carolina, brought re-freshing change for the family, though at first, Heather insisted upon calling the lovely rural setting *Purgatory.*

"Poor baby," I wrapped my arms around her, dodging movers who scuttled past toting boxes stuffed with Crenshaw paraphernalia, sliding them into empty spaces around walls still smelling of fresh lumber and paint. The recently built, pristine manse was a bonus to the sudden offer of conference officials to shift us to a bigger harvest field. An *opportunity,* they said, height-ening my wariness.

Toby and Krissie romped outside – out of the workers' way – lickety-splitting to examine the ancient cemetery beyond the lovely brick church with its white steeple, investigating with a child's clarity the mysteries of what lay beneath those flat-tened, verdant mounds towered over by headstones bearing cryptic inscriptions. Some marble finishes, dulled by mildew, revealed hazy pictures of the departed. What Toby could not decipher, Krissie patiently read and explained.

The parsonage, a gracious sprawling brick ranch, came fully furnished and offered the Crenshaws the distinction of be-ing its very first occupants. Until now, an older town dwelling had housed Solomon Methodist's clergy. Our old hodge-podge furniture went into storage, but my resilience ran out when I re-fused to part with the rich cherrywood four-poster upon which two of our children were conceived.

"Okay," I told the children, "you each get a room of your own. Go pick it out," and laughed when they scattered like startled flies in three directions. I proceeded to place folded sleepwear in drawers, bracing myself for the usual calamity, but surprisingly, peace prevailed. My instincts – as to which room fit whom – panned out. Heather, of course, got first dibs, but the two younger harbored no opposition. Glory be! Already, I could see the influence of the tranquil environment.

Mid-afternoon, Kirk, in gray coveralls, came up behind me, as I stretched clothes on hangers for our his-and-hers walk-in closets and pressed himself to me. I dropped the garment and turned into the familiarity of his arms, a haven amid disorder. And we embraced for long moments, soaking from one another solace and ongoing oneness, augmented among virtual strangers.

"Honey?" Kirk lifted his face, the sharp planes and angles softened by an atypical vulnerability. "Did I make the right decision – coming here?"

I peered at him, mystified by his sudden qualms. Rarely did my husband look backward. He could have stayed on at Hopewell for another term. This two hundred-plus mile transfer had been his decision – a quick one at that, given the fact that annual Conference sat upon us as he weighed his choices. His. Because, as in most major resolutions, I acquiesced to Kirk. A simple matter of trusting his logic.

"After all," I'd told him when he asked my opinion and I knew what he wanted – needed – to hear, "you're the one who stands up there in the pulpit, looks them in the eye, feels their pulse. It has to be your decision when to leave one flock and embrace another."

The move, so sudden, *blurred* with a ridiculously haphazard twenty-four hour period of packing and loading moving vans, manned by low-country, new-flock men who snatched boxes literally from beneath my hands and open drawers and slapped them onto the porch where, under my glazed direction, they loaded valuables and tossed away trash.

Tearful farewells abounded on the asphalt parking lot, underscored with Deborah's bewildered scowl, pacing, and "*No way!*" while Toby trailed and patted her resisting arm, muttering, "we'll come and see you, Deb. It'll be all right"... while Jessica and I fueled her agitation by having one good breakdown, unbridled cry on each other's shoulders. While Krissie and Sandy vowed solemnly to write each other every single day and Heather, with friends, joined by arms tangled and cleaving, bodies heaving in grief at parting.....

Was it only last night? I gazed into Kirk's weary face, so dear. So needy. And I smiled, stretched up for a long kiss and said, "Of course, it was the right decision."

❖ ❖ ❖ ❖ ❖ ❖

"Git outta my face!" bellowed a distinctly angry male voice from outside. "It's *my* furn'ture, I tell ya."

I thanked the departing church ladies, who'd earlier slipped quietly into the kitchen with steaming bowls and a succulent baked ham garnished with pineapple and cherries and within an hour, fed us and cleaned up.

What *was* all that racket about coming from the front yard?

I dashed to the front door and peered outside where moving vans hovered on the busy front lawn, gilded golden by nightlights. My gaze combed workers who, for the first time today, appeared frozen and mute, peering at two men who stood, toed-off, glaring at each other.

"I spoke for that bedroom furn'ture nigh on two years back," the tall, lanky red-haired male named Homer Beauregard bellowed.

The other one, Fred Chastain, who seemed older, shook his salt-and-pepper head. "Can't help dat. Clancy, he be in charge o'parsonage stuff." His stance was quiet and firm and his dialect thick low-country. "He said it's mine since I put down da deposit on it ovuh a year ago, case it ever got sold. Since Miz Crenshaw don't wanna use it, it's *mine.*"

In a flash, the carrot-top man advanced with white, clenched fists to within an inch of his opponent's nose. "*A twenty dollar deposit? I don't think so,*" he roared.

"Hey!" Kirk stepped between the two men. "Say fellas, can't we sit down and discuss this without all the anger?" This in his most engaging, conciliatory manner. "I mean, –"

"Hey, preachuh," Fred turned abruptly to Kirk, "You best stay outta family bid'ness 'round heah." He lightly cuffed Kirk's shoulder in good ol' boy fashion. "Dat's da best advice ah can give ya. Do dat, you stay outta trouble."

"Yeah." Homer Beauregard grunted assent. "He's not shootin' you a line. Solomon Methodist's a tight, family church. You best remember – family? They stick together. Hey?"

"Thanks," Kirk replied evenly, his expression shuttered. "I'll remember that."

Kirk left the men to their dissension, which within moments rose to pitch again.

Disbelieving, I quickly turned away and fled to the clutter of my room, which I attacked with new vigor, closing my ears to the furor beyond the new walls. *Where's Christian charity?* Is there no place for pastoral counsel when family gets out of line? *What*, I asked myself as I savagely stuffed wadded paper into a garbage bag, *have we gotten ourselves into?*

"Cousins?" I gaped at Kirk across the breakfast table the next morning. "First cousins?"

"Yep," he replied, crunching into toast. "Seems they've been feuding all through the years. Over some land – they're all big landowners, by the way, as are most of these folk."

"Did they settle the dispute last night?"

Kirk chuckled, elbows on table, nursing his coffee mug in both big hands. "Nah." He blew on the steaming brew and his gaze moved past me to the double windows that framed a breathtaking view of the evergreen forest backed up to church property.

And I knew. That smiling half-moon glimmer of green said a part of him enjoyed the near-to-blows adventure.

The next six months will forever stand out in my memory as a time of supreme joy. Loosed from fast-paced inner-city hubbub and exposure, our family rediscovered one another. Granted, the forced seclusion at first did not lay well with the youngsters, but, predictably, without a playmate-smorgasbord, the two youngest siblings established a camaraderie that led to previously unheard-of, *creative* diversions. Late afternoons found them riding bikes until classroom-accumulated restlessness was spent. Then came quieter pastimes, when Krissie patiently taught Toby games, such as Parcheesi, Password and Old Maid Cards.

Kirk was – well, Kirk was gone most of the time. Pastoring, I knew, so I carried on.

Teenage Heather discovered a new world of peers surprisingly as appealing as her former ones. Added to this was the pleasure of her very own *space*, luxury for a private girl whose former cramped quarters forced her to share her bed.

"They're your rooms to decorate as you please," I said during the first week, "so go to it."

Krissie's room was the brightest and perhaps most engaging in the parsonage, a study of pastel yellow and gold accessories that splashed against soft antique white walls and rested on plush pale moss-green carpet that invited toes to dig in. In this near lackadaisical atmosphere, her industriousness leaped to my attention. All day, while I cleaned and organized kitchen and bathrooms, I'd see her zip by, in and out of her quarters with cleaning supplies and vacuum. And pride, warm and sweet, oozed through me. Surreptitious peeks revealed Krissie's closet, drawers and shelves organized fastidiously enough to pass military inspection

When, I wondered with considerable awe, *did this metamorphosis take place? Why she's as diligent and responsible as an adult.* And I decided it was Providential, this oasis in which I found myself, this timeless bubble that halted and allowed me to see, really *see,* all the good in my life.

At 3:10 a.m. I jerked upright in bed. Toby's scream hauled me to my unsteady feet and down the hall-length to his pecan-paneled room. His muffled yells augmented into terror. I gazed wild-eyed into the darkness, searching for him. Kirk, on my heels, flipped on the overhead light, exposing the rumpled, empty bed and myriad sports decals attached to his walls with enough Scotch-tape to complete a season's gift-wrapping.

"Mama-a-a!"

I pivoted to my right and peered through the closet door, a mere three feet to the left of his bedroom entrance. Huddled there, pale face plastered to the corner, hands splayed over cheeks, Toby sobbed.

I peeled him loose and wrapped my arms around him.

"What happened, Toby?" Kirk asked gently.

"I – I couldn't find the *bathro-o-om.*"

Disoriented, he'd taken the wrong door and couldn't find his way out.

Heather met us in the hall as I guided him to the bathroom, looking surprisingly sympathetic and I thought again how our cohesion, our dependence on one another was blossoming into something rare and precious.

Newton-John's *Let Me Be There* blared from the portable record player.

"Well – what do you think?" Krissie stood back to display her room in its final splendor.

"Very nice." My gaze roamed appreciatively over her neatly arranged dresser, fragrant with talc and cologne – to the highly polished furniture, immaculate closet and shelves. A gigantic new poster sang to me from one spacious wall.

"How do you like it, Mom?"

She noticed my attention riveted to the huge freckled-faced, splitting grin of Pipi Longstocking, carrot-red pigtails "startled" straight out over each ear – as a tiny brown shrieking monkey, long tail draped around one pigtail, perched on the heroine's shoulder.

"Do you think it's cute?" The *vulnerability* behind that query ambushed me. Right then, at that precise moment, my opinion stood between her and desolation.

"I think it's darling." The truth. "Where did you get it?"

Her instant smile revealed perfect teeth and restored confidence. "Ordered it at school."

Something burgeoned inside me, a warm thing strung with silk and velvet and sweet-smelling orchids. It had to do with the fact that she'd bypassed lesser wholesome choices for this. A small thing, yet I'd never felt more proud of my daughter than in that moment.

In the following days, I desperately sought to de-clutter my quarters. Clutter, to me, connotes chaos and my mind spontaneously lines up with it. One day, as I tried to make sense of the jumble, I paused at Heather's door to gaze longingly, admiring her organizational skill and wondered how on earth she arranged neatly and attractively on her dresser the following: a wooden treasure chest jewelry box, three photos, a large decorative green bottle, owl salt-pepper shakers, hair spray, Kleenex tissues, two stuffed animals, three bottles of cologne, an assortment of nail polish (eight to be exact), ranging from colorless to primrose, and a beautiful daisy petal bordered cosmetic mirror, a Christmas gift from Krissie.

Her bedside radio, on duty most off-school, awake hours, played *The Most Beautiful Girl In the World.*

Curiously, I entered the sophisticated pewter gray-paneled room accented with greens and melon. In true peer-style, she'd added, literally, wall-to-wall posters featuring "First Love," Snoopy and "Love Story." Her door sported first-place ribbons from small talent contests, an Indianapolis 500 pennant (Kirk's gift after a ministerial convention in the city), a gigantic greeting card that read "Jesus Loves You!" from a friend. Last – most definitely not least – screamed a door-sized poster of Mick Jagger.

Through the years, I've tried but never accomplished with paraphernalia what my daughter did so effortlessly. But, at least in those days and in that particular arena, Toby became my soulmate, for no matter how often we neatly arranged his toy box, which fit comfortably into his spacious closet, within weeks the contents would mysteriously evolve into a jumbled disaster area.

Days later, I found myself recruited into the Church's War Department, a thing I'd vowed would *not* happen. As soon as Kirk proudly divulged my musical training, the small choir waylaid me, pleading with me to take them on. The current director, Donna, merely stood facing them, hymnal in hand, and got them going on key. She, too, quite fervently wanted change. And despite my wish to remain low profile, my heart responded to their longing to rise above mediocre.

The first rehearsal convinced me that Heather must, absolutely *must*, be my accompanist. Betsy, the sixtyish, spinster pianist, read music, but somehow, no matter how vigorously I launched the choir, we all ended up marching to Betsy's lethargic cadence. I kept reminding myself this arrangement was Ted Smith, *not* Sousa, and the distinction simply *had* to be made. The perfectionist me caved in after two attempts at *"Wonderful Grace of Jesus"* drooped and dragged worse than Grandpa's old plough through rocky terrain.

"I have a suggestion," I said in my most pleasant "let's get our heads together" voice. "If you would agree to Heather's being my accompanist, I'll accept the position. I'm going to be doing some quite difficult special arrangements and Heather and I can work at home on these, saving much time –"

"B-but," Betsy sputtered indignantly from her piano bench, "*I* can play those arrangements."

"Oh my, Betsy," I turned to her, all sympathy, "these are quite advanced and I don't feel right about heaping this sort of thing on you."

"But –" she blinked several times behind thick lens as magenta splotched her plump cheeks, her back turning ramrod stiff, "I can learn them. I don't *mind*."

"That wouldn't be fair," I insisted. "Heather is accustomed to playing these arrangements and – this would only be for the choir specials, mind you. Betsy, you would still play for all other congregational singing. That won't change."

She stared at me, only mildly mollified. Everyone else ignored her pouting to fling arms wide to welcome the Crenshaw duo aboard.

I had a moment's consternation about her family ties in the church. The choir was but a small fraction of the Solomon Methodist's membership, but were they Bessie's *kin*?

Family sticks together, echoed Homer's admonition.

Only *I* heard the distant blast of cannons and recognized the battlefield.

Solomon's Charlestonian setting beguiled the dreamer-me. Everything within the tropical framework sparked my imagination and aesthetic leanings and I found myself doing things for the sheer sake of doing. One free afternoon, Kirk and I impulsively drove the kids to Kiawah Beach. He swam with them as I settled onto a folding lounge chair with an unopened Pat Conroy novel while listening to Heather's little portable radio blast *Bennie and the Jets.*

"Like fish," Kirk said proudly, drying off, watching Toby and Krissie splash as he settled beside me in his lounge chair. We recalled Toby's terror in YMCA swim-survival classes during the sixties and how, distanced by a ceiling-high glass window, I'd near panicked when my son teetered on the edge of a twelve-foot high diving board and his instructor pushed him off. Krissie had quickly resumed the role of mentor and protector, swallowing her fears to pioneer the way, while Toby toddled along, shadowing her every move.

Today at Kiawah Beach, I watched with pride as they fearlessly tackled surf and sand. Krissie, my tan, platinum-haired mermaid...Toby, a bristle-topped otter gliding effortlessly through the water. My gaze drifted to Heather, lying on a blanket, lifeless as a seashell, toasting to nutty bronze beside Dixie, her friend from the church clan.

Kirk clasped my hand in his.

That golden summer epitomized the old proverb, *"time flies when you're having fun."* Kirk and I were a team. Solomon Methodist Church flourished. Kirk was proud that my choir grew until the loft bulged and began plans to expand the sanctuary. The choir members rhapsodized over hearing themselves sing four-part harmony. Heather graced the accompaniments with mind-staggering mastery. Soon, invitations poured in for the Solomon Choir to appear at religious and civic functions. In the process, I sought out solo voices for specials.

One day, my phone rang and it was Donna Huntly, the former choir-leader who now sang first soprano. "Ms. Crenshaw," she said in her abrupt, succinct way, "I feel a need to tell you how I feel about the way you're handling things."

Dread pitched my pulse into syncopation, but I managed a cautious, "Yes?"

"My brother Charlie and I have been coming to this church all our lives. Now, you're giving solos to newcomers – overlooking me and Charlie. Charlie loves to sing and he's hurt that you haven't picked him to do specials." She stopped as abruptly as she'd begun and just as strongly. "I just wanted you to know how we feel," she tacked on, as in *"t-t-that's all folks."*

Disbelief washed over me – *me, the* soft-peddler, challenged by double-barreled *blatant* boorishness. Crude razor-y edges and all. As Kirk would say, welcome to the *real* world....

"Donna –" I took courage from my calm voice, "I really don't know what to say."

"Well," she staccatoed, "I just wanted you to know."

"I'm sorry you've been hurt. I truly am. And I assure you that I'll give the matter much thought and prayer."

"Thank you." *Click.*

I stood for long moments staring unseeing at the receiver. I immediately dialed Kaye, Charlie's wife and Donna's sister-in-law. Kaye, too, sang alto in my choir and we'd established a warm camaraderie. I needed an objective playback so I relayed the phone conversation to her.

And besides, Kaye wasn't *blood* kin to the family clan. In-laws didn't always count.

Kaye snorted. "Neecy, that's pure *Donna.* She's outspoken and makes me mad as blazes at times. You can't let her get to you. Charlie hasn't said a thing. This is all her doing."

I hung up, feeling only mildly reassured. I recalled other hurts I'd glossed over, in particular those of Betsy, the church pianist. I encouraged myself that *that* particular crisis had eased.

Betsy actually was the last surviving member of her particular family clan at Solomon, leaving her with no one to dissent with her. Learning that had a peculiar effect on me: it made my heart more tender toward her.

The spinster had, over time, warmed toward me. And I knew compromise had been the catalyst that gave me Heather, yet allowed Betsy to keep her church-pianist position. *This,* I ventured, *is no different.* I bowed my head and prayed over the new clash. Part of me felt shredded. Yet – I was suddenly able to see Donna, the little girl, crying out for validation. It changed my feelings.

Another revelation stunned me: *perfection is good but not more important than people.*

In that moment, the resolution came to me.

"Donna," I said off-handedly at the next choir rehearsal, "I'd like you and Charlie to do this duet special for the Homecoming Service. We'll work out the harmony during rehearsals. Think you can handle it?"

A five-hundred watt smile broke over her face. "Yes *Ma'am.*"

"With this setup, you can't afford *not* to go to Coastal Carolina College," Kirk jokingly remarked. I'd just won a musical scholarship and would be singing with the college choral group. I decided to enroll full-time since the school was only a twenty-minute drive away.

Kirk came up to me at the sink where I washed dishes and slid his arms around me, turning me, dripping hands and all, into his embrace. We kissed, slowly and deeply, knowing the kids romped outside while Heather hibernated in her room, phone to ear. Hand in hand, we went into our bedroom, closed the door and quietly locked it.

Our lovemaking was, as always, passionate and unhurried. Our incredible chemistry was the 'glue,' to quote Kirk, that made all the hardships of matrimony fade. Afterward, Kirk showered, dressed and departed to do visitation.

I decided to take a walk down the white sandy lane that wound through the cemetery near the church. From a distance, my gaze captured a beautiful scene framed by a frothy blue-white sky and washed with golden sunshine: Krissie and Toby biked over flat verdant lawn, at peace with life and one another. Heather, I knew, was enjoying her privacy. Kirk was out about his Father's business.

I passed the church, my sneakered feet mincing pearly sand, my heart keening toward our dwelling. *"Home."* My lips formed the word and I smiled, remembering how I'd dreaded leaving Chapowee. Now, I knew – home is anywhere God puts us.

Tall pines aglow with tropical sunlight drew my gaze upward. The November climate was pleasantly warm and the air smelled of spring. My heart swelled with gratitude.

This is fulfillment. "Thank you, Lord," I cried aloud. "How can one heart *contain* so much happiness?"

Oh, had I only known what lay ahead, I'd have gloried even more in those moments.

Toby waxed well at Solomon Elementary while Krissie remained mum on her school activities. Heather breezed through middle school. My first semester at Coastal whizzed by, transporting me to senior status and the Dean's list.

My phone rang one afternoon. "Mrs. Crenshaw?"

"Yes?"

"I'm Mrs. Carter, Krissie's teacher. Are you free to talk right now?"

She went on to say that Krissie remained shy and reluctant to join in classroom discussions. I explained to her what had happened the past year and how my daughter's little spirit had been beaten down.

"Oh-h. That explains it all. Thank you, Mrs. Crenshaw. This helps me more than you can know." I liked Mrs. Carter instantly. Something in me relaxed about Krissie. She was now in good hands.

The heavy stage curtain opened to reveal Coastal Carolina College's Chorale in long red skirts, white ruffled blouses, and guys in black tux. First faces I spotted in the school's auditorium belonged to Krissie, Heather and Toby, who sat with their dad. During my *Winter Wonderland* solo, my children's awed gazes reached out and touched me. Afterward, they all rushed backstage to throw their arms around me. Kirk kissed me soundly before the whole world and I felt Heaven descend for those short moments.

The holidays passed in a flurry. Christmas Eve began at five a.m. when Krissie and Toby dashed to the den to find their presents beneath the seven-foot live fir decorated with ornaments collected through the years, each bearing sentimental significance. Heather trailed them, and soon, unable to sleep because of the joyful ruckus, Kirk and I slid from bed to join them. We celebrated with a huge brunch then loaded our car for the four-hour upstate trip.

We sang Christmas songs on the long drive to Daddy and Anne's, harmonizing and improvising special arrangements with even Toby participating. Once at our destination, Krissie and Dale immediately paired off to wrap gifts, then distribute them around the mill village to my brother's friends. Only months apart in age, they enjoyed the same music, movies, foods, and shared dreams, aspirations and secrets. Heather rode with Cole to see his current girlfriend while Dad and Kirk lounged about watching ballgames or going for their male bonding drives. Toby played outside with neighbor kids, leaving Anne and me in peace and quiet to sort out festive meal menus.

I yearned briefly for wonderful shared Yule celebrations at MawMaw and Papa's before Mama died. I rarely saw them anymore. That grief had diminished with time spoke harshly to me. Therein lay the thorn: intimacy a casualty. A spasm of loss seized me and I fought resentment that my loved ones had sacrificed our bond in their quest for an elusive dignity. *I hope it was worth it,* I mulled, then let go, refusing to let it spoil my holiday.

The day after Christmas, Trish took the kids to see *The Sound Of Music* at a local movie theater. Krissie and Dale came home singing "*Doe, a deer...*" and other selections from the film. All too quickly, leave-taking arrived. I missed my folks, but home was now Solomon and I keened to be there. We arrived home near nightfall and the kids rushed to their Christmas loot.

Krissie and Toby sprawled on the den floor, listening to Krissie's new Harvest King record *Dancing in the Moonlight*, creating dialogue and drama with Krissie's Barbie doll, who entertained Toby's GI Joe in her Country Home. I'd been careful to buy wardrobe for both dolls so Toby could join her in the dressing game without getting teased. A new Parcheesi game replaced their old one. Dixie, Heather's pal, dropped by to munch goodies and retreat to Heather's bedroom to exchange gifts, then rhapsodize over *what*, I was never certain.

Heather's wardrobe of seventies' wisp and billow burgeoned from her holiday stash, as did Krissie's, whose flared-jeans and clog-shoes accented her thinness.

"Look, Mama," Krissie said that night as I stood at my dresser brushing my hair, "I'm nearly as tall as you." She stepped before me, backing against me until her head just barely reached the underside of my chin. We gazed in the mirror and in her delicate features I glimpsed a younger me. "Think Daddy would cut my hair?" she asked.

I ran my fingers through her long, thick blond thatch. "Do you really want to?" I asked, surprised. "It's so pretty like this...."

"I want a shag cut," she said decisively.

The next day, Kirk whipped out his barber shears and snipped away. When he finished, I nearly wept. She was so cute – a teeny bopper whose chin length hair lay softly in waves that hugged her small oval face and framed enormous blue eyes. *She'll be a real beauty soon,* I decided.

"Say," Heather circled her. "I like that. I want one, too."

We all laughed and Heather's long locks fell next to Krissie's on the earthtone carpet. "Wait!" Krissie dashed to get a plastic bag. "Don't throw the hair away. I'm gonna save mine."

"Not me," Heather declared as her sister scooped up blonde tendrils and stuffed them in the plastic zip-lock bag. "I'm glad to get rid of mine."

Both girls insisted I get mine 'shagged,' too. I complied, happy for a carefree 'do.'

"Now, we're triplets," Krissie giggled and the three of us preened before my dresser mirror, admiring our matching hair-cuts. I hugged them close, astonished that though my two girls did not strongly resemble each other, both bore a striking like-ness to me.

"I'm jealous," Heather pouted good-naturedly, pulled her new sweater tight across her chest and scowled, "Krissie's got boobs already and I don't." A half-truth since the younger sister was beginning to bud.

"Least you don't look like a toothpick," Krissie generously offered.

"You keep eating those deviled-egg sandwiches every day after school and you won't brag about being skinny long," Heather shot back, fluffing her chestnut hair for the mirror.

"Krissie's not *skinny,*" Toby piped from the den.

"Who asked you, *Tubby*?" Heather shot back, striking a model's pose.

"Kids," Kirk warned on the way out the door, shoving arms into his suit coat.

"He's not *Tubby,*" Krissie's back stiffened and her hands rolled into tight little fists.

"Hey," Heather grinned at her sister's ire, "can't blame 'im if Aunt Josie insists on feeding him half the food in the school lunchroom."

It was true. Toby *had* fluffed up in recent months be-cause our church secretary Josephine Beauregard served as his school's dietician. I knew I should say something to the love-able grandmother about instructing all the servers to overload

Toby's plate, but I simply couldn't face another confrontation at that precise moment.

Fact was, *no* time seemed appropriate to start another war.

Working with the college choral group stretched me to new musical expanse. My sight-reading took an overhaul when I became first-soprano section leader. Everyone depended on me to shuttle them into each new melody and cadence so I pushed myself to be ever ready. Our upcoming spring concert would feature songs from the *Sound Of Music.*

"Wow, Mama!" Krissie's eyes shimmered at my news. "*You're* going to sing Julie Andrew's song –" and she commenced to sing the words in an exaggerated falsetto and vibrato, '*the hills are ali-i-ive – with the sound of mu-u-si-ic....*'

I joined in and we ended up laughing and clowning. Heather, too, was impressed that her ol' mom had the solo. "I've got lots of work to do," I injected, buoyed by the attention.

"Aww, you'll nail it," Heather reassured me on her way out for a drive with Dixie, Charlie and Kaye's daughter, who was now in her first year at Coastal.

And suddenly, I realized I really *had* found something I could do well – something that *fit*. Something that filled in during Kirk's increasing absences. *Music.*

My studies soon consumed me, but it was wonderful and exhilarating and liberating. The old fears and psyche shadows receded as though they never were. My creative itch was being scratched and with it came freedom. From the past. And most importantly, from *me*, my own worst critic. Amid swift eventfulness, with no time to reason, I began to grasp *me* for who I was.

Another phenomena occurred. My spiritual awareness heightened. Loosed from constant introspection, I looked outward and perceived brilliant horizons. So I carved out a devotion time with the children, immediately after dinner in the evenings, when Kirk did hospital and home visitation. I'd decided I couldn't rely on him to lead in that area. The years were passing too swiftly so I must do it myself.

One evening was especially intimate."Let's start bringing prayer needs each evening," I suggested to the children. "One can always use help in some area." I felt it might sharpen their introspection and broaden their thoughtfulness. I was right.

The very next evening, Krissie said, "Mama, there's a black girl in my class I want us to pray for. Her name is Joanne and she's so sweet. I feel so-o-o sorry for her...."

Racism doesn't exist in our home and I said, "Why, honey?"

Her sincerity and depth stirred me as she told of Joanne's deprivation and poverty. "The kids don't have anything to do with her." We prayed for Joanne and I suggested she befriend the girl. "Go out of your way to make her feel good about herself." She nodded solemnly.

Heather's concerns encompassed peers who teetered between doing right and diving into the seventies"'anything goes' abyss. We grew closer during those hours before an open crackling fire, sharing not only scripture and wisdom but exposing hearts and souls to one another.

"I did what you said," Krissie tucked her leg up under her on the sofa several nights later, her face surreal in firelight's golden glow. "I've been playing with Joanne. She's really a nice girl – a real friend."

I was so proud I could have bawled. "That's wonderful, honey."

"I wish I could see Deborah," Toby said wistfully of his eternally young friend left behind in Hopewell. "I miss her."

"We'll invite Deborah and her mother to visit soon," I suggested.

"Yeah!" Toby bounced up and down on his side of the sofa, stirring dust until Heather, seated next to him, sneezed. But she didn't yell at him as she once would have.

Little things. But they made a profound difference in our lives.

School demands soon had me peddling uphill as fast as I could. The perfectionist me wanted to be a straight-A student while the mother-me balanced my act. Yet, when I found myself embroiled in term papers and reading assignments, I felt mired in timeless quicksand. The minutes zipped away before I reached my daily goals.

"Mama," Krissie cleared her throat, standing in my bedroom doorway one evening, "listen to my story –"

"I'm sorry," I fairly shouted at her from my bed, where I sat propped amid littered notes and books. "Do I look free to listen to *anything* right now, Krissie? I've got to finish this reading and I'm so tired I already can't see straight."

"But this is tomorrow's –"

"No!" I gazed helplessly at her as emotional teeth ripped and jerked me back and forth. "Honey, I – *can't.* I'm sorry. I just don't have any time left. You'll do fine."

She quietly backed out the door and closed it. I felt rotten but knew I had little choice if I wanted to finish my assignment. Krissie's composition *would* be fine, I assured myself. My not listening this one time wouldn't make or break her.

The next afternoon, Heather entertained us on the piano with a new song, *The Entertainer.* Toby goofed around with silly dance steps, cracking me up. "Yeah, Heather!" I clapped at the number's finish "that's *wonderful,* honey. I've got such *talented* chirrun."

I stretched back in the easy chair. "Mama?" I felt a tug on my sleeve. "I need to talk to you, Mama," Krissie said, very softly.

She looked a mite pale. "Okay, honey." I followed her to her room where she purposefully shut her door then joined me to sit pretzel-legged on her bed.

"Is something wrong?" I asked gently after she hesitated and began picking at her yellow chenille bedspread, her gaze riveted to its texture.

I watched her lips begin to tremble and her small chin cave in. "I don't feel like anybody loves me," she murmured in a choked voice.

My breath caught in my throat and refused to progress for long moments. "Oh, *honey,*" I exhaled forcefully. "I love you with all my heart. Why do you feel that way?" *I knew. Oh, God, suddenly, I knew.*

I watched, horrified, as tears rolled down her cheeks. "Cause nobody pays me any attention." She shrugged but still gazed at her small fingers, picking, picking at the chenille tufts.

"A-and I'm not smart and talented like Heather and not funny like Toby a-and – I'm *stupid* and –"

In one movement, I gathered her into my arms and across my lap where I cuddled her as though she were one instead of eleven. "Ahh, sweetie, if you only *knew* how precious you are to me. And Daddy. And Toby and Heather."

"Not Heather...she doesn't like me, sometimes." The words floated out as guileless as an angel's song.

"But she does, Krissie. She's just –"

"She's just Heather," wise little Krissie finished. "And I s'pose she does like me at times." She gazed up at me with red swollen eyes just beginning to hope again. "She just needs to grow up a little more, huh, Mom?"

I nodded and smiled, thankful for her openness and forgiving spirit. Oh, how I regretted having pushed her needs aside. But this was today.

"I don't know if I want to be a missionary anymore, Mama," she said softly. "I want to have lots and lots of kids and I don't think kids would like growing up in Africa."

"Mmm. Probably not."

She sat up to face me again and I sensed the conversation was not over. "I don't know what's wrong with me. Mom, how does it feel to be in love?" Her lips began to wobble again as her eyes, pooling, gazed into mine, trusting me for wisdom.

"Why do you ask, honey?"

Her hands flailed the air helplessly. "All I can think about is Johnny, Johnny, *Johnny.*" The tears this time flowed copiously.

Aha. "Tell me about him." I reached to gently brush away the tears, knowing Johnny's family attended Solomon Methodist Church and owned the skating rink where all the kids, including mine, congregated on Saturday nights. Krissie shared with me her crush on the cute Williams boy and how he'd sorta left her dangling. A new thing for my pretty little blonde whose romantic notions were just being stirred. Her *hormones*, as well, I suspected.

"C'mon," I stood and held out my hand.

"Where we going?" Krissie asked, already lacing fingers with me.

"For a walk." Usually, I walked alone, seeking my blasted solitude. Today, I wanted my daughter with me. The stroll along the sun-washed white path was silent as, arms around each other, Krissie and I shared a sweet time of simply being together. Words weren't needed.

"Well, I'll tell you one thing for sure," I broke the silence as warm breezes kissed our cheeks.

"What?" The sweet face turned up to me.

"There are more fish in the sea besides Johnny Williams."

Something flickered in the blue depths that warmed me. Then she grinned. "Yup."

The next evening, the two of us prepared dinner together. "Let me peel potatoes," Krissie pleaded.

"Your hands are too small to handle this knife, honey," I insisted. "But I'll cut them into strips and you can dice them. Okay?"

That worked. "Thanks, sug, for folding the laundry." *And sweeping the pine needles scattered across the back lawn into neat, tidy piles and all the other little things you do without being told.*

Her face glowed. "I knew you'd be tired when you got in from school."

I chuckled. "*That* I was."

A moment of silence except for the *swump, swump* of knife dicing potato, then, "I think Johnny likes Sherry Snow."

"Hmmm." I raised an eyebrow at her. "He doesn't *know* what he's missing."

She grinned, then pressed her shoulder to mine conspirationally. "There are more than one fish in the sea, huh, Mom?"

"I'm concerned about Heather." I sat facing Kirk in the den during a rare one-on-one with him. "She's spending too much time with Jaclyn Beauregard, who's already eighteen. I smell cigarette smoke on her occasionally and I know how girls are at Heather's age. They want to try things."

Kirk's antennae rose. That his daughter-vigilance never relaxed was the thorn in our oldest child's side. Their shared genetic assertiveness created some unpleasant confrontations, but when things slid past my range of effectiveness, I passed them on to Kirk. Most of the time, that checked Heather before she backed me into a corner.

"Have you seen anything —"

"No. No – Heather's too smart to get caught. Jaclyn is, too. She's polite and all that but, there's something about Heather's hero-worship of her that alarms me. Heather's so vulnerable right now."

"Well," Kirk stood and reached for his suit coat, "we'll just have to keep our eyes open."

Dale Evans sat at the piano centering the outdoor stage of downtown Charleston's Marion Square, taking part in the Sunday afternoon Spiritual Celebration. The concert, featuring Dale, Andre Crouche and Children of the Day, drew scores of low-country people, now thickly planted on blankets spread from corner to corner of the grassy music arena.

We'd piled into the VW after a quick lunch to drive to the festivities, allowing Heather, after much pleading, to ride with Dixie Tessner and other Solomon Methodist teens.

"Only," Kirk stipulated, "if you follow me. Stay within range in case you have car trouble."

Heather rolled her eyes after Kirk turned away but was pleased not to be 'scrunched up' between Krissie and Toby en route there. I knew she, along with everybody else, anticipated hearing and seeing Andre perform.

Yet, two hours into the celebration, the star performer's plane still had not arrived. Dale, gracious as ever, returned to the podium to continue her ministry. Seven-year-old Toby people-watched as parents, on adjoining blankets, bottle-fed babies and shushed active toddlers. Heather lounged with her peers. Krissie sat huddled against my side, beginning to shiver in the late afternoon breeze.

"Cold, honey?" I asked, putting my arm around her. She nodded her shag-cropped head.

Kirk volunteered to take her to the car for a sweater, happy, I was certain, for an excuse to stir around a bit. Stillness has always made my husband antsy. I watched them track their way, hand-in-hand, through pallet mazes, dodging elbows and feet until they disappeared into the parking area. I smiled, pondering Krissie's mother-hen ways...and her aspirations to cook and clean alongside me.

She was my shadow. Heather avoided me like strep. Go figure.

Dale Evans' voice pulled me from my reverie. "You'll just have to put up with me for a bit longer," she informed the crowd in her folksy way. With one eye on her and one on the reappearance of Kirk and Krissie, I heard Dale's account of her thirteen-year-old daughter's death in an accident. "The church bus carrying her and other teens home from a gift-bearing mission to an orphanage crashed, killing her on impact."

Kirk and Krissie quietly resettled themselves beside me as a hushed silence fell over the audience. Krissie snuggled close and I slid my arm around her thin, jacket-clad shoulders.

Dale paused to compose herself and in that moment, even the babies rested and toddlers grew still, their gazes glued to the platform silhouetted against gray-blue, primrose-veined sky. A coastal breeze, bearing earth's fecund, winter fragrance stirred softly.

"Until then, I'd had an acute aversion to death. But at the funeral home, God took my hand and led me every breath, every step of the way." She went on to share Debbie-vignettes, spiced with the girl's vitality and sweetness. Dale's parting comments moistened all eyes. "It is not given to us to understand everything that happens on this earthly vale of tears, but someday, if we trust the Lord explicitly, He will make all things plain. Christ did not promise one easy way for the Christian, but He promised *peace in the hard way.*"

Dale waved and made her exit amid a roar of applause.

My gaze swept over Krissie and Toby, then sought out Heather's animated features in the sea of young faces. Dale's account left me a bit troubled. If this could happen to Dale Evans, the perfect mom, then who was safe?

My self-assurance began to wilt, to lose substance. I didn't like the feeling.

You worry too much, Neecy. Kirk's litany echoed. It was true. I *did* fret too much.

I pushed away the unsettling emotions. *Each case is unique.* Faith in maternal mindfulness recoagulated. Godly vigilance could and *would* ward off harm.

"Andre's plane still has not arrived," the loudspeakers blared.

"We've gotta go," Kirk murmured, motioning to the teen group. "We'll be late for evening church service if we don't leave now." They nodded while gathering blankets and paraphernalia for the forty-five minute drive to Solomon.

There, I caught up with Heather on the church lawn and walked with her up the portico steps. "Can't *believe* we didn't get to hear *Andre Crouche*," she groaned as we entered the church. "A wasted trip."

"No," I slid my arm around her shoulders, where, these days, she was more inclined to accept it, "nothing is *wasted* in the spiritual realm. Don't ever forget that."

Her fingers slid into mine and the soft reply just barely reached me. "True."

And I thanked God for where He'd brought us.

CHAPTER NINE

The following Thursday dawned golden and unseason-ably warm, even by coastal standards. January 31, 1974 was so perfect, like Spring, my favorite season. Years later, I look back and still feel the peaceful ambience of it. I've been told that the eye of a hurricane is that quiet and tranquil.

That morning was – I now know – the pinnacle of my life.

I worked on a college English theme while Kirk, in gray coveralls, worked on our balky VW. That afternoon, he stopped long enough to collect the kids from school as I continued typing.

Krissie and Heather breezed in the door and I stretched my stiff back.

"Where's Daddy?" I asked over my shoulder. "And Toby?"

I heard Heather's bedroom door close behind her. *Into her lair, my lovely one goes... When she'll come out, nobody knows.*

It's not personal, I reminded myself.

"Ahh, he's on the carport, working on the car. And Toby's with him," Krissie informed me as she put two eggs on to boil and poured a tall glass of iced tea, a ritual now for her as she fought to put on weight. Also ritual was record music blaring from her room, Harvest Kings' tinkling rendition of *"Dancing in the Moonlight."*

"Could you turn it down a tad, Krissie?" I called, frowning at the text staring back at me, challenging my concentration. I simply *had* to finish the darned paper today.

Immediately, the noise softened and I relaxed as she re-turned to the kitchen to fix a fat deviled egg sandwich to munch, then thoughtfully move to the den to eat, giving me solitude for my task. She only broke silence once, to tell me, "Grandma called last night and said a little girl named Tammy was kid-napped from a laundromat this week. They found her body in a river today. Grandma said for me to be careful and not talk to strangers."

"Good advice," I said, warmed by Anne's call. True to her word, she had done everything in her power to make up to Trish for those wasted years. "Grandma's smart. And she loves you like I do." I resumed typing.

A little after three, Jaclyn Beauregard sauntered in, trailed by her younger brother, Zach. I barely looked up as they brushed past me to visit with the girls. Husky little Zach, twelve and 'fudgy' as Trish would say, with Indian dark hair, eyes and features, migrated toward Krissie, whom he saw at school, church and Hopewell Skateland Rink. Skating was their topic today.

"Man," outgoing Zach gushed, "that Toby can skate good for a little kid." Then he began singing, *"Hey! Did you happen to see the most beautiful girl in the world?"* a song played repeatedly at Skateland. Krissie sang along, blushing a little but obviously enjoying Zach's uninhibitedness.

I smiled, glad Toby was hanging out with his Dad, watching him mechanic, asking endless questions. He wouldn't cotton to being called a 'little kid.' I again receded into the aura of my essay theme, whose subject was Heather's growing pains.

"Can Heather go home with me for awhile?"

I blinked at the intrusion and gazed up into Jaclyn Beauregard's strong, dark features, ones that matched her assertiveness. "I – ahh – no, I don't think so, Jaclyn." Six months had not given me enough time to know these people that well. I knew I'd come across as standoffish, not a good thing with Kirk's parishioners, but I couldn't help it.

"Please?" she clasped her hands together, as in *beg*. And charm.

I frowned, fortifying myself. My gut said 'no.' "I'm sorry, honey. But I think not."

Heather appeared behind another oak dinette chair, facing me. "Why not, Mama?" she challenged, though affably. "We have choir practice at six so she's coming back this way."

"Go ask your Dad." Kirk would recognize my distress signal and issue a firm 'no.' I was astounded when moments later, they reappeared.

"It's okay with him if it is with you," Heather ventured. "See? I told you you're too protective." *"...and you smother me,"* she'd accused just days ago.

Was I? Being too protective? Smothery? I remembered my Dad's heavy-handed control and nearly shuddered. Still –

"I don't think so." I began typing again, hoping to dispense them. "Besides, you haven't cleaned your rooms." I went back to pecking as they scattered, again battling the snobbery I whiffed in me.

Within minutes, they were back. "Now can she go?" the undaunted Jaclyn asked. "We cleaned their rooms."

"Aww, Mama," Krissie now joined the circle around the table, hooking her thin elbows over the chair back. "C'mon. Why doncha let her go?"

I gazed at her, moved. She, the overlooked, the *uninvited*, pleaded Heather's cause.

An idea flashed. Without forethought, I said, "Only if Krissie can go, too."

They'll be safer together. Krissie would spread her wings and at the same time, with her little sis along, Heather wouldn't be apt to misbehave.

The older girls looked at each other as in "what now?" Then they shrugged in unison. "Sure," Jaclyn said.

"Neat!" Zach quipped, grinning broadly at Krissie, whose blue eyes rounded in surprise.

Suddenly, second thoughts ambushed me. *Krissie*, a homebody, *may not want to go*. She was too polite to refuse and chance offending the Beauregards.

"Of course, you have homework to do, Krissie." I offered her a graceful way out. Her consistent studying *had* brought her grades up.

"I'll help her," Zach Beauregard chirped, beside himself with bliss, and I only then sensed his crush on my middle child.

"I'll do homework there." Krissie's joy was gaining momentum. "We took the Achievement Tests today at school, Mama." She then added quietly, "I think I did okay."

"That's great, honey." Then beneath my breath, "Sure you want to go?"

Her countenance brightened. "Yeah, Mama."

My doubts vanished at her happy face. "Okay." I sighed and returned to my work.

"I'll go change my top. This one's too hot. Ya'll wait for me!" Krissie cried and scampered off to her room to shed the red sweater for a cooler top to match her flared jeans. The day had warmed up during the morning until now, midafternoon, the outdoors beckoned.

Settling back down to my typing, I fought niggling little misgivings. I reassured myself again that together, the girls would be safer. Levelheaded Krissie would safeguard Heather's good behavior. More relaxed about the whole thing, I proceeded with my paper and only glanced up when the four of them filed past me as they left.

Heather kissed my cheek, "Thanks, Mama."

"Bye, Mama!" I glimpsed Krissie's hummingbird departure over my shoulder. *Still afraid they'll leave her.*

"Bye, honey," I called as Zach sprinted out the back door last.

I sat very still, staring blankly at the typewriter and felt a strange compulsion to call over my shoulder. "Hey! Be *good!*" I glanced at the clock. It was three-thirty.

"We will," came Zach's faraway cry. "We always are!"

Toby played outside while I finished my paper and cooked a quick supper of grilled pork chops, rice, gravy, peas and fluffy buttermilk biscuits. The aroma was wonderful, reminding me that Krissie loved pork chops and Heather always *oohed* and *ah-hed* over hot biscuits and my homemade strawberry jam.

I'll call them to come home.

At four-thirty, I moved to the phone, then stopped, my hand mid-motion. They'd only been gone little over an hour. *"I told you you're too protective, Mama."*

Am I? I lowered my hand. *But Krissie loves pork chops.* I aided and abetted her weight-gain efforts, which were beginning to fluff up her small hips in an attractive way. I lifted the receiver again.

Choir practice is at six. That's only an hour and a half away. I put the phone down, feeling selfish. It was unreasonable of me to ask Jaclyn to drive the distance twice in less than an hour. At the same time, since I had no intention of allowing a repetition of today's subtle coercion, I'd allow the girls to make an afternoon of it. It would have to last for a long spell.

Toby and I ate together. Kirk had driven into town to find needed repair parts. We finished our meal just as the Volkswagen pulled into the carport next to the kitchen.

I cleared the table, put away the food to heat up later and resumed work on my paper.

At five-fifteen, Kirk burst into the house. "Come on, Neecy!" He yanked off his oily coveralls in three swift movements.

"What?" I froze, recoiling from something in his voice, dreading I knew not what.

"The kids are gone," he gasped, his green eyes wild. "Something's happened to them! Come on."

My bare feet remained riveted to the floor. My mind swirled. "What – who's gone?" My words sounded far away. The earth tilted at a grotesque angle. I swayed and caught hold of the counter's edge.

"Janeece!" Kirk implored frantically at my lack of response. "Get dressed quickly. We've *got to find them!*"

Jaclyn appeared in the doorway. I tried not to read her pale face.

Then Larry, Jaclyn's older married brother who attended Solomon Methodist Church, appeared, his white face registering shock. He moved toward me...he and Jaclyn were both talking at once.

"Krissie and Zach went for a walk and we can't find them."

Panic seized me. "What do you mean, you can't find them?" I steeled myself not to become hysterical. They'd probably wandered off somewhere. *There's hope.*

I shook my head wildly, "But Krissie doesn't do things like that. She's so care –"

Larry's pasty features loomed before me. "Mrs. Crenshaw, they were walking on the trestle. A train came through – they radioed back to the caboose that they'd hit two kids."

"Oh-h-h, Mama –" Heather moaned from the doorway, her eyes stark with horror.

"Oh, God...." I groaned and turned away. *This can't be happening. It's a bad dream. That's all. It has to be.* I turned to escape – God wouldn't let this happen. He *wouldn't.*

"Janeece!" Kirk's commanding voice cut into my stupor. "Get dressed. *We have to find them.*"

In that moment, a terrible vision flashed before me, of faceless kids in the muddy river that runs beneath the trestle, drowning....

No! I blinked. No! Another memory zapped in like lightening – only last year I'd insisted that Hopewell Church fence in the parsonage yard, to protect our children from railway tracks that bordered the property.

How could I have let down my guard? I didn't even know the Beauregards lived near the railroad. *Dear Jesus....*

I stumbled to the bedroom and with trembling hands, tore off the loose robe I'd earlier donned to type and cook in and somehow managed to hurriedly dress in slacks and pullover. Kirk and I dashed out the door and into the car to speed the two miles to the Beauregard home where our girls had been visiting.

Kirk drove, his knuckles white against the steering wheel, moaning, "Not our little Krissie...Oh, Neecy, how did it happen?"

His words fed a sunless atmosphere, eluding me.

Woodenly, I turned my head to gaze at him. He was crying. Kirk, who rarely cried.

Why wasn't I crying? Why did I feel so – dead? Slowly, I began to realize that my body registered no sensation whatsoever, like I'd guzzled novocaine, went swimming in it. Kirk and I had always met each crisis head-on.

I stared at him. He was dealing with *it*, the phantasmal thing that evaded me. I clung to the detachment. Dry-eyed. I experienced a sense of shrinking, shriveling within myself. *Diminishing.*

Our VW whipped onto the Beauregard's property that bordered the railroad, near a deserted old depot building. Today, paralyzed railway cars littered the horizon and blocked our view of the trestle, a half-mile, straight shot distance from the Beauregard's front lawn. Pulling as close to the bridge as possible, Kirk bounded from the car and commenced running toward the hidden scene of the accident.

I climbed heavily from the car and began to wander, in no particular direction...away from people, from the horrible train, from *me*. My legs and feet grew more leaden with each laborious step. The phrase *"something has happened"* kept knocking around in my brain, trying to get a foothold. I desperately embraced the compartmentalization that now isolated me from a drama that grew and burgeoned on my dark periphery.

My shock-blurred gaze combed the endless trainload of piggybacked trucks that hid from me the thing trying to swamp me – to *destroy me.*

Something has happened – happened – happened....

Words bleeped through my bleak numbness only to gel, unheeded, then dissolve into the nothingness surrounding me. A sense of helplessness began to steal into my nebulous consciousness...heavy and thick and smothery.

Faces invaded my space as I floated there, suspended, unaware of earth's floor beneath me or her atmosphere or sound beyond, cocooned in merciful oblivion. Arms embraced me, words drifted around me. Eyes conveyed pity, horror and compassion – emotions that bounced off my shield of nonpresence. I tried to speak, but my tongue would not react, nor would my limbs carry me away from them. My arms would not lift to return embraces.

I wished them away.

Vaguely, like the roof's *drip, drip, drip* after a heavy rain, *"something has happened"* imprinted itself, against my will, forcing my awareness that this tragedy was, somehow, *mine.* Again, zombie-like, I rebelled, somehow turning away, distancing myself further from those who *knew.* From the words hovering there, waiting to obliterate me.

Yet, an overriding certainty emerged. I faced an agonizing decision. I stood with my back to them – to *it,* when unexpectedly, Dale Evan's words pierced my darkness: *"God took my hand and led me into that funeral home – me who'd always had an aversion to death – and He helped me...helped me...that beautiful mangled flesh was only a shell of my Debbie. She'd already gone to be with the Lord."*

"Oh, Dale," I moaned. "I didn't realize –" Was it only four days earlier that I'd sat on that blanket and listened with my ears but not my heart? *Now, I stand where you stood. One of my children is – I can't even acknowledge which one, can't put a face to 'it.'*

How can I bear it?

Never, before or since, have I felt such humility as at that moment. Self-sufficiency crumbled, shriveled away. Mortality seemed imminent, so complete was the chastening. I would have, at that precise heartbeat, welcomed it. I stood beyond self-loathing, teetering between cataclysm and the dizzying black void clutching at me.

I took a deep breath. Blew it out. *Hang in there* coaxed my survival instinct.

How can I? flesh and blood groaned. Death's black chasm yawned, pulling, pulling me toward its edge. Then I realized, I *wanted* to die. *How could I have let it happen?*

Lean on me, whispered the presence I'd listened to all through the years. *You didn't know that formulas don't always work.*

Then realization struck me like a thunderbolt. *You prepared me for this moment four days ago, didn't you? You knew.*

I took a deep, shuddering breath. *Oh, Lord – it will be so hard.*

Here. Take my hand. I'm here.

I really don't have any other choice.

I then uttered the most difficult petition of my life: "Help me to realize what's happened, God... and to accept it. And Lord," I set my eyes toward Heaven, "give me strength. And courage. Especially *courage.*"

Then a force within pushed me slowly, ever so slowly back to that hazy intangible thing called reality. That day, as I turned to leave the scene of tragedy, God heard my cry of surrender. *It* took form. A face emerged, precious and indescribably sweet. From deep within, grief gushed forth, riding the essence that was my Krissie.

Tears came. Painfully. Slowly at first, then copiously. But just as the well sprang forth, as pain engulfed me, I saw Krissie, smiling, enfolded ever so gently in Jesus' strong arms, ascending upward until they disappeared into frothy white clouds.

Kirk returned, anguish ravaging his features. My darling, who'd held out hope until the last moment, embraced me. "She's with the Lord," he sobbed.

"I know." Over his shoulder, I glimpsed the ambulance departing, with the small covered form visible through the window. Again, reality hit like a sheet of lightning.

Dear God, Krissie. I didn't even hold you in my arms one last time.

As if hearing me, Kirk lifted his head and gazed into my eyes, revealing his tortured soul. "At least, you were spared," he said hoarsely, "seeing her lying on the cold ground – alone. Oh

God!" He threw back his head and screamed in anguish. "She died all *alone on that cold ground."*

On the ground.

My knees buckled and he caught hold, helping me to stand. "You mean –" I whispered, "she wasn't –"

"No, she wasn't on the tracks." He shook his head as tears dripped from his cheeks. "Thank God, she wasn't mutilated. They found her lying on the sand bar, where she fell from the ramp. There were no injuries except the blow to her head. Near her ear. You can't even tell –" He broke down again for long moments, then lifted his tear-streaked face, his watery eyes tortured. "She was only a few steps from safety."

"Oh God...." *Why, Krissie? You, who wouldn't even close the bathroom door completely for fear of getting trapped inside. How did it happen?*

"Zach?" I croaked.

Kirk shook his head, then fought for control. "He's under the train." Zach's body wouldn't be retrieved until the train – steel wheels now brake-flattened on one side – was moved. A difficult task because of the wobbly movement on the steel trestle structure, a thing, we later learned that had caused the train crew some tense, terrified moments before everything jerked to a final halt.

We embraced again, sharing sorrow uncoveted.

My perfect world, as I knew it, would never again be.

Heather slipped her hand in mine and we walked together to the Beauregard dwelling. Clancy Beauregard, Zach's father, sat on the front steps of the big wraparound porch weeping inconsolably. His wife Norene stood on the porch with members of the Beauregard clan encircling her, all familiar faces from church. Clancy arose as I approached and I embraced him.

"Aww, *Law,* Mrs. Crenshaw," he said brokenly, "I'm so sorry. I feel responsible. Your children visiting our home and something like this happening."

My heart wrenched. "Please don't feel this way. I don't blame anybody. If your children had been visiting *us,* something could have happened."

I sat down beside Clancy and felt Heather lower herself next to me. Kirk now spoke with Norene, whose Cherokee

Indian stoicism held her erect and dry-eyed, only ashen features betraying her suffering. Her black eyes met mine and without a sound, we communicated maternal torment.

My mind began to formulate snatches of coherent thoughts, like a distorted kaleidoscope....*Krissie's gone! Oh, dear God, it can't be....I've got to call Daddy and Anne...How did it happen?... Trish. I want to see Trish...Krissie – my sweet little girl. How can it be? You've always been the cautious one...I've failed you...I should have kept you under my wing. Why, oh, why didn't I realize something like this could happen?...I don't deserve to live.*

I kept pushing it away – the guilt, knowing I couldn't cope, knowing I had to survive for the sake of Kirk and the children.

In my weakest time, I was called upon to be my strongest.

On the silent drive home, my heart continued to break into a billion tiny pieces, like an atom, splitting and dividing, on and on. Several cars already lined the parsonage drive when we arrived. Kaye Tessner met me at the door and embraced me, speaking gently to me, her gray eyes deep pools of teary compassion, but I comprehended nothing of what she said.

Other familiar faces encouraged us as Kirk and I made our way to the privacy of Krissie's room. There, we shut the door behind us. Kirk dropped to his knees beside her bed and great sounds of grief erupted from him, loud unrestrained mourning as I've never heard before nor since. I sat on the other side of her mattress, weeping softly, holding her pillow to my face, inhaling her scent, disappointed that well-meaning friends had already cleaned her room and were now laundering her last worn garments. They meant well, but I felt deprived that her existence was not allowed to continue for a bit longer.

Kirk's weeping finally subsided and he raised his head to look at me, tears dripping from his face. "Neecy – I can't go on. I can't live with this."

The plea in his voice smote me as he buried his face in her chenille spread and began to weep again. I closed my eyes and groped for strength. Krissie's face appeared before me and in her eyes was a message: *Trust.* She'd always leaned on me and believed I could do anything.

I shoved away the guilt and clung to *her* image of me. I would be what she expected and I would preserve her memory with dignity and fortitude. This was my last gift to her. For the first time, something from which to *give* sparked to life inside me, splitting off from the raw, bleeding me and filled my mouth with soothing words.

"We'll get through this, Kirk. I loved Krissie as much as a mother can love a child. I carried her in my womb for nine months, nursed her at my breast and cared for her. She was my little companion, so much like me we didn't even have to speak to communicate. "But, honey, we have two other children who need us. And God will guide us, one minute at a time...a day at a time. We'll take it just like that – one day at a time. Don't look backward or ahead right now, honey. We'll just have to accept God's help for right now – this minute."

Kirk wiped his eyes, embraced me and hand-in-hand, we walked through the door together to face friends who'd taken time to come and share in our sorrow.

The next week still blurs in my memory...*Zach's funeral held the following day because, due to the condition of his body, he could not be embalmed...Dad and Anne* beside me, Dad crying with me in the wee hours, holding me, murmuring "I wish I could take this pain for you, honey"...*Trish,* upon arrival embracing me and whispering, "When I got the news, I dropped to my knees. I *saw* Krissie – going up into the clouds and *Jesus was holding her!*" and I said "*me, too*" and we gazed through tears at each other in joyful wonder and *her husband Gene,* inconsolable at first, raising his wet face, saying "*I should be comforting you instead of you comforting me*" and my reply, "*you are comforting us, by sharing our grief...Toby's* quiet detachment from everything...Kirk wanting to conduct the funeral and my gentle insistence that *he himself* needed ministering, adding, "*Heather, Toby and I need you beside us*"...Mrs. Carter, Krissie's teacher's words to me "*You are so brave, Mrs. Crenshaw*" and me thinking "*you just don't know what I'm feeling inside*"...

Amid the hazy recall, the next two days stand out with crystal clarity. I wanted to select Krissie's burial gown. Kaye Tessner called several children's boutiques to describe what I wanted. She located a shop in a nearby town that had three or four selections, which fit the description nicely, then drove me there mid-afternoon.

One of the dresses was perfect, a soft feminine white, spattered with tiny red Swiss dots, featuring a high lace collar and long lace-trimmed sleeves. A fitted bodice joined the long full skirt with a dainty red waistband, from which identical, slender red bands ran up over each shoulder, giving the impression of a peppermint pinafore. Mid-way, it hit me: *This will be the last time I'll get to deck out my little girl....*I swallowed back tears and gave close, close attention. I would not relinquish this precious homage.

I asked Mr. Jones, the funeral director, to arrange with the florist to keep a fresh long-stemmed red rose in her hand until the time of burial. Later that afternoon, Kirk took my hand and we walked to the cemetery to select Krissie's resting-place. "Someday," I said, "we'll move back upstate and – I know the wise thing is to bury her there. But Kirk," I gazed at him, "I can't part with her."

"I know," he murmured. "Neither can I."

Then, I saw it. The perfect spot. A lovely grassy slope beneath the regal oak tree with its softly swaying shawl of Spanish moss. "Here she can remain close to us." Kirk looked at me strangely. "What?" I whispered.

Tears gathered along his lower red rims. "This is the exact spot I chose – in the event I died while here at Solomon. This was where I wanted to be buried."

The following day, we made the solemn pilgrimage to the funeral home. Then I saw her. How beautiful she was. So *heartbreaking beautiful*. New pain lanced me, hurt as I'd never known existed...the flawless complexion...the fine, *delicate* bone structure of the sweet face.

That little face. So peaceful. So innocent. I took her small hand in mine and kissed the cool soft cheek. "Ohh, Krissie," I whispered, "I'm so sorry. Mama's *so sorry*. Please forgive me for allowing this to happen. I've failed you." I began to weep – for her, for the life ended too soon.

In the background, I heard a man crying brokenly. It was Kirk.

Toby stood near me, peering into the casket with a glazed expression on his small round face. "She looks like she's asleep, doesn't she, Mama?" he whispered.

"She is, Toby," I murmured, pulling him into my embrace.

Heather slowly approached the quiet little form. She stood there for a long time, holding her sister's hand, touching her hair, her face. She turned to me and burst into tears, "I love her so, Mama...and I *never told her!* Oh, Mama —" I wept with her, knowing her remorse.

She leaned over and kissed the dear face. "Oh, Krissie," she sobbed, *"I love you so."*

I chose a funeral service that befitted our daughter's extraordinary tenure on earth, selecting only those who loved her to participate. Krissie's still-fresh trust in me gave rise to purpose, one that blazed and spurred my mind and limbs to do what needed to be done to ensure her earthly departure be one of honor. We asked Trish's husband Gene to officiate, with Pastor Cheshire assisting. Both adored Krissie. Gene, though feeling he'd not hold up well, consented when he saw how much it meant to us.

I chose Krissie's favorite songs and asked Julian Grimsley, a dear friend from the college choral group, to sing the joyful selections.

"But Mrs. Crenshaw," Dixie Tessner sobbed when I asked her to play other Krissie-favorites on the organ, "I don't t-think I can do it. Krissie was s-so special – I *feel so close to her."*

"Exactly," I replied. "That's why it has to be you. Your love will shine through as you play. God will help you. Together, we can all get through this."

Moment's later, Heather slipped her hand into mine and joined me in my room for a short private interim. When the door closed behind us, she turned to face me and grasped my hands in hers. Her fingers were icy. I rubbed them gently. Her eyes, tear-filled, beseeched me in some way. "Mama," she swallowed back a sob, "I was so afraid...."

"Of what, honey?" I put my arms around her and pulled her to me as she burst into tears.

"Th-that you and Daddy would b-blame me. I should have been watching out for her a-and —"

I closed my eyes and swallowed back a bubble of alarm. "Oh, Heather, Heather." I blinked back tears. "We don't blame you, sweetheart. We don't blame anybody. Please —" I held her back and gazed into her eyes, "don't *ever*, for one instant, blame yourself. Promise?"

She gulped and nodded and I held her close. Her weeping began to subside and, with it, the quivering. Poor baby. What a load she'd carried.

Not until I felt calmness overtake her did I release her and return to greet guests. I watched her rejoin her peers, whose vigilance sustained her through this lowest point of her short life. *I'm glad I got through to her.* In no way was her sister's death her fault.

It was *mine*.

I awoke early the morning of the funeral, having slept very little, if any. That was the most difficult time, when sleep's co-coon vanished, when I suffered raw reality. Loss tidal-waved and battered us into each other's arms, Kirk and I, to sob out our sorrow together until we could arise and face going on. This would continue for days, weeks and months to come. But this morning, we knew: we must say goodbye to our flesh and blood Krissie...*our Krissie.*

Dear God, how could we reconcile to such an irreconcilable situation? To never see her face again?

How?

Kirk joined Dad for coffee at the kitchen table just as MawMaw and Papa arrived.

"We had to come," MawMaw's mouth wobbled on the raspy words. "She was so sweet. Papa always got her to giggling —" I nodded as she and Papa silently wept. We had visited them, on occasion, during the years. And they had, sporadically, popped in for weekends, as well. Not as often as I'd have liked, but Kirk and I had made sure the children knew their great-grandparents. I hugged them both, thankful for their presence. They joined Kirk and Dad at the table and for once, their relationship to my father didn't matter.

I walked out onto the tiled front porch with its white columns.

Alone. I needed time with God.

The air was mild, the sun rising as though nothing unusual had transpired in the past forty-eight hours. I gazed up into the clear blue sky and shivered despite solar's golden warmth. I tried to pray. Words would not come. Only memories...Krissie trying on Heather's make-up and adult beauty filtering through – *Oh God! She won't ever grow up.*... And with each surge of memory, pain's dark chasm snarled and deepened.

I need you, God. You said you'd be here. The accusation was listless and weary. Desperate. *Pray. I need to pray.*... What? How? No thoughts formed – the need was too vast. Beyond articulation.

The next time I opened my mouth, language I'd never before heard issued forth in a flow as rich and smooth as nectar and I knew from whence it came and from whom because a supernatural strength began to enter me that lifted me above human debilitation and with it came courage and calmness I had encountered only once previously.

Six years earlier, my Aunt Mary, Daddy's older Pentecostal sister, took me into the privacy of her bedroom during a family gathering and insisted on praying for my migraine and me.

Aunt Mary was the most flamboyantly religious person I'd ever known, marching to a drumbeat so far out I was embarrassed at times to acknowledge her as kin. Yet I loved her and refused to join in when her Bible Belt, hard-shell Baptist and Methodist siblings lightly poked fun at her unorthodox stance. Underdogs always draw my sympathy, Mary being no exception. But that day, I groaned and sank down onto her red bedspread, determined to humor her then swallow three aspirin and get the heck out of there.

I tried not to recoil when she lowered her hand on my bowed, *throbbing* head.

"Lord," she commenced praying softly, "heal this headache."

Oh Lord, let her finish soon. This head is a lost cause.

Aunt Mary stopped for a long moment, then hissed, "You're a *liar* Satan! Get outta here, you scum. You're not gonna cheat Neecy out of what God's got for 'er. Ya hear? *Scat!*"

Goosebumps scattered over me and my mind stopped thinking.

"Now, Lord," said Aunt Mary in her that's-taken-care-of way, "heal Neecy from the top of her head to the soles of her feet."

She removed her hand from my head and immediately a force, like a solid slab of lumber, slammed into my crown and moved slowly, slowly down my body, not missing an atom, synchronized and level, in smooth sustained passage until it reached my feet.

At the tips of my toes, it stopped.

My eyes popped open and I marveled at the *rightness* of what I felt. It began to move back up my ankles, calves, over my hips up my torso, shoulders and reached the base of my skull, where the wildfire, knotted pain threatened to rupture into a cerebral hemorrhage. Then, in two heartbeats, perhaps three, the phantom-slab hoisted the infirmity out my crown, tumbling my head forward with relief. I reached up to grope for proof that I still had a head.

"It's gone, Aunt Mary." I gazed at her, astonished. "It's gone!" I sprang to my feet and strode about grinning, then *laughing* and bubbling with joy and the certainty of a holy presence.

Aunt Mary smiled. Suddenly, she didn't look peculiar. She looked intelligent and saintly and compassionate. "Neecy," she said softly, extending her palm, "God's not through yet. My hand is still warm." She placed it on my head again. "Now, Lord, fill Neecy with your Spirit." Again, she stepped back.

An invisible gate flung open above me. I felt it with every fiber of my being and something like a vacuum drew my gaze, my hands, my arms, the whole of me upward, upward in mystical expectancy until I no longer felt the floor beneath me and I was alone in a golden realm with this incredible energy.

Quietness settled over my new realm, so silent that a faint brush against crystal would sound as cymbals and the tug grew more powerful and complex, with the open window a two-way channel, hurtling us together: Me and IT. What IT was, I still didn't know except that it was Holy and good and I wanted it more than I'd ever wanted anything in my life. Anticipation and joy crescendoed like harp arpeggios as my upstretched fingertips connected with it. From it, something quite like honey began to pour over me and into me until I felt submerged and floating, filled with a calm serenity that surpassed anything I'd ever encountered. It was a warm, warm thing that permeated everything ME: the physical, emotional and spiritual.

"I am here." I felt the words. My eyes popped open, my gaze still drawn upward. The aura above had no face, only brilliance and soothing warmth and peace and in that instant, it touched my throat. A physical touch from invisible fingers, at the base of my tongue – much as the phantom-slab, only now localized in that tiny speech area. And my tongue, of its own volition, began to move quite freely. I felt no fear. Calmly, my gaze sought and glimpsed Aunt Mary's serene face through the ivory mist. She nodded and smiled. *"Give Him your voice," she said softly. And I did.*

Today, the same melodious utterances spilled from my throat and lips as had gushed forth that day following the miraculous migraine-healing, accompanied by the same incredible tranquility and strength. And I knew, as before, the source.

The Comforter.

God had, after all, kept His promise.

After a quick shower, I dressed, then asked Anne to accompany me to the funeral home. This morning was to be my time alone with my daughter and I wanted every moment to count. Never before nor since has my mind had such clarity. Decisions came without hesitation.

A fresh long-stemmed red rose replaced yesterday's. I carefully placed the discarded one in tissue, hoping to dry and treat it. *How I wanted to keep it.* I brushed her hair and the thick blonde tendrils curled softly toward her face. How many times I'd performed this act, knowing every contour of the precious little head.

I touched each familiar feature...soft, slightly tilted nose, smooth forehead with high, perfectly arched brows, long lashes fanning over satiny, finely contoured cheeks with a tiny beauty mark just to the right of her nose. Just above the short feminine chin, beautiful full lips suggested a pink rosebud. I leaned to gently kiss them and to nestle my cheek against hers for one last time. It felt cool, yet soft as velvet, and held not a trace of strangeness and I realized death did not alter the fact of *her*. She was forever Krissie. My Krissie.

How I cherish those last moments of solitude with my daughter.

Anne hovered nearby, not in the least intrusive, weeping, wrestling with her own grief. She drove me back to the parsonage around noon, where driveway and lawn bulged with upstate cars. I was astonished that over a hundred friends and relatives made the five-hour trek.

Honoring our wishes, Krissie's send-off to Heaven couldn't have been more celebratory. Even Gene, after a moment's breakdown, gave a happy eulogy that brought both laughter and tears to the packed gathering, which, after filling all pews and standing lined around sanctuary walls, spilled over into Sunday School rooms to listen over the intercom.

Julian's medley of Krissie favorites was punctuated by the silent weeping of school classmates – her honorary escort – and teenagers who'd adored the shy, friendly Krissie, as well as youth who'd played and worshipped with the happy little blonde. Then, Pastor Cheshire, now aging and a bit stooped, shared marvelous little anecdotes from Krissie's and Heather's early romps and then comforted us with favorite, sustaining Bible verses.

Hand-in-hand, Kirk and I led the entourage from the sanctuary, across the verdant lawn to the white sandy path that led to a newly opened gravesite. We heard the organ playing familiar strains from *Safe in the Arms of Jesus*. Warm succor flushed through me, and I couldn't help but smile.

What a babysitter.

"Neecy?"

I swiped away tears and turned from the mound of flowers covering the new resting-place. The crowd now scattered and meandered about, distinctly reluctant to disperse. In the lingering, I felt profound love. The voice addressing me was familiar –

I squinted up into familiar features. The eyes, half-mooned, clued me.

"Moose?"

Huge arms folded me into a bear hug and I felt the big-boned, six-footer begin to tremble violently. "I-I'm so s-sorry, Neecy –" He burst into weeping, his arms squeezing me.

I snuffled along with him as he rode the waves, patting his shoulder and rocking to and fro, until the trembling subsided. I disentangled myself and gazed up into his face, now elongated somewhat because he was at least fifty pounds lighter than I'd ever seen him.

"Moose McElrath. My goodness – how did you know?"

"Saw it in the paper – 'bout the accident."

I knew accounts of the tragedy were in upstate papers, as well as local ones. "You came all this way down –"

"I'm in Charleston now – in the Air Force. Been in for the last ten years. Just got transferred here four months ago." He pulled out a white handkerchief and blew his nose soundly, then refolded and returned it to his hind pocket. "Didn't know ya'll was down here till I saw the newspaper headlines. God, Neecy –" His eyes puddled again and he looked off, biting his bottom lip till it turned white.

I took his hand, still big with fingers like sausages. I felt the calluses on their tips and squeezed them. "Ah, Moose. Your coming is so – *special.*" He shuffled his feet, still gazing off, blinking rapidly. "Have you spoken to Kirk yet?"

"Naw." He snuffled loudly, shrugged his wide shoulders, and shifted from one foot to the other. "He's tied up with folks who've drove so far, I thought I'd wait till –"

"Crap." I took his arm firmly and pulled him along through the gathering to where Kirk stood, his face haggard and intent as he grappled to focus on Pastor Cheshire's kind words.

Both men turned at our approach. "Look who's here, Kirk."

Kirk peered for a moment then exhaled audibly. "Oh my goodness, *Moose.*" Then they were hugging and Moose let loose again, crying brokenly. Kirk silently wept with our old friend, allowing Moose's grief to buttress his own.

We insisted Moose return to the parsonage with us and stay awhile. The house swelled with relatives, friends and church folk, but the atmosphere was appropriately subdued. Betty, Kirk's mom, had driven down that day with Mitzi and Randolph Scott for the funeral. Kirk, drawn in so many directions at once, spent little time with his mother and siblings, but I hugged Betty – still gaunt and haunt-eyed in widowhood – and thanked her for being there for Kirk.

Trish and Anne moved quietly in the background, answering the phone and exchanging pleasantries with guests. Later, church ladies brought covered dishes and served dinner to the remaining family and upstate visitors. Kirk talked quietly with Moose as I said endless goodbyes at the door and in the driveway.

MawMaw and Papa hugged me bye just as dusk settled over the sandhills. "Be careful," I cautioned because MawMaw had divulged that Papa now suffered from a bit of night blindness.

"Aww," Papa's beefy hand flicked away my concern, "I can see all right. Don't you worry none, Neecy."

For once, MawMaw held her tongue and didn't argue the point. Teary-eyed, she waved until they were out of sight. I went back inside where I trekked to the bathroom and while relieving myself, spied Krissie's pink toothbrush lying on the vanity, again experiencing the *wham* of loss, of her absence. *My little shadow....* I quickly returned to the den, where my gaze sought Heather, who huddled in the dining room with Dixie and Jaclyn Beauregard, who'd dropped by after the services. Jaclyn rose and came to hug me and lingered in my embrace for long moments as we shared our common sorrow. I said soothing words to her, knowing how she had adored her brother Zach and knowing how difficult this time was for her family.

Then I returned to the den, lowering myself beside Kirk on the harvest brown sofa and immediately felt Toby plop down next to me. I smiled at him and he snuggled against me. *He's tired.* I'd seen little of him during the past two days, except glimpses coming and going. He mostly played outside with church kids except for sporadic little interludes, like now. He'd shown little to no reaction to what was happening. I figured that, inevitably, he would grieve.

"Moose tells me he's got something going with a pretty young thing," Kirk said quietly, winking at Moose, who blushed but shot me his half-mooned-eyes grin.

"Oh? Who?" I asked, curious. "From here?"

Moose looked away for a long moment, the smile fading. "Ahh – she's not from here, but she lives here now."

"Where does she work?" Kirk asked, as nosy as I.

"She – ah – she's kinda in show business," Moose replied, looking distinctly uncomfortable.

"We-e-ell," I slanted him an impressed look, "A singer? Actress?"

"Uhh," Moose's neck turkeyed and his shoulders rolled over a couple of times, as if his shirt was too tight. "She's – actually," he resolutely looked me in the eye, "she's a dancer."

"Aha." That gave me pause. What exactly was my friend Moose getting into?

"So how long have you been here?" Kirk promptly switched subjects and Toby whispered in my ear that he would like a piece of Betsy Clemmon's Texas Chocolate Cake.

As I made my escape from Moose's news and sliced my son's fudgy portion of dessert, I experienced mixed emotions. I was relieved that Toby lent me continuity during this time but was puzzled at his non-involvement in what was going on around him.

I tried to eat a small piece of the cake, but it turned to sawdust in my mouth. Toby's plate was clean when he rushed off to greet Bobby Clemmons, whose parents Fred and Betsy talked quietly with Dad and Anne before heading my way. Trish offered me coffee, which I accepted to make her feel better. I glanced again at Toby, who took his friend's hand and eagerly tugged him to his room to show him something.

I sighed. *He's so young. Will he remember her?*

Will I remember her? Fear spliced through me and propelled me to my feet. What a thought – of course, I wouldn't forget Krissie. I took my cup to the sink and began vigorously washing it and searching for others to assault. "Sis," Trish's hand gently grasped my shoulder. "Don't. Come sit down."

She knew. My sister knew that, when cornered, I always attacked clutter.

Woodenly, I allowed her to lead me away from the sink but not from the idea now gyrating in my head. *Krissie, Krissie...why did you have to go and die?*

Oh God, I could have prevented it. Aww, Krissie – you were perfectly content to stay home with me and I was busy and I sent you away....

I sent you to your death, like a little lamb to the slaughter.

It's all my fault.

"Come on, honey," Kirk coaxed, "It'll do you good. Moose wants us to meet Roxie. It's all he talks about." He sat down beside me on the sofa and tweaked my chin. "It'd be fun."

I stared dully at him, with my feet curled up under me and an unopened magazine on my lap. "I don't feel like it. Okay, Kirk?" Rarely had I ever denied my husband's requests, until recently. "I'm sure *Roxie* is a barrel of laughs but —" I cut him a weary, wry glance.

"Neecy," Kirk scolded softly. "That doesn't even *sound* like you."

I looked away, slightly repentant but too numb to appreciate fully any wisdom at that precise moment. Roxie was an 'exotic' dancer, quote Moose — who, by trying to upgrade his girl's status from 'burlesque' to 'exotic' only worsened it.

"She doesn't sound like Moose's type, much less *mine.*" I laid my head back and closed my eyes, giving in to the apathy swathing me day and night, draining me, leaving me limp and uncaring of life, exhausted by late afternoon by living, emotionally, *years* in the space of short hours. A week and a half had passed since my family and friends departed, leaving us to fend on our own. And with their departure, my initial drive, fueled by Krissie's faith in me, fizzled.

Finality set in. And with it, a permeating indifference to living. The degree of apathy changed hourly. The *enormity* of loss rose sharply by the moment. One moment, I was amused at something silly Toby said, the next, dissolving into sobs.

I thought again of the irony: just when folks think you got it all together and leave you alone, reality sets in. Even Kirk had his church duties and the kids, school. I couldn't yet face returning to classes at Coastal. A refrain ran over and over in my head: *Nobody needs me.*

Krissie always needed me. More pain. Will it never end?

"Neecy, look at me," Kirk's finger gently guided my chin around and I opened my eyes. "Don't forget where I was when God rescued me. He can do the same for Roxie. For Moose. For anybody, in fact. But you know that." He gently brushed my hair from my forehead. "This is not like you."

It wasn't. I sighed and shook his finger loose. "I know," my voice was dull, flat. "Tell Moose we'll go."

The next night, Saturday, we drove into Charleston to dine at Bessinger's.

"Man," Moose crowed, "this barbecue's great, doncha think, Roxie?"

The redhead slid her agog suitor a seductive, amber appraisal.

"Yeah," she droned lazily. "Marvelous, Moose. Just mar-ve-lous." Her appraisal skipped me and lit on Kirk, who seemed too busy cutting his chicken to notice.

"Where are you from originally?" I asked her politely, try-ing not to gape at her low-cut, clingy sweater and abundant cleavage set above a wasp waistline and softly rounded hips fas-tened to Rockettes-long legs.

She tore her gaze loose from Kirk and focused on me as though I'd just walked in. "Oh – all over. My daddy, he was in the Army, ya know?" Then she tore into her food like she hadn't eaten in days, saying little for the remainder of the meal.

Kirk and Moose reminisced and for the first time in days, I felt myself lifted from the dark here and now and transported back to *when*. The guys reminisced about a ruckus during our Senior Prom, when Kirk had sailed to a drunken Moose's aid, after Moose had gotten into a fight outside the school with tres-passing Grey High rivals. My pal Callie had seen the whole thing, jumping and screaming obscenities at the interlopers till she nearly got herself arrested, along with Moose, the five ri-vals, Kirk and Hugh Nighthawk. That was the only thorn Kirk sustained in an otherwise honorable fight, during which he was ambushed and held down by two of the rivals while another beat him senseless – Nighthawk had rushed in and in Cal's words, "Beat the crap outta all of 'em."

"Remember ol' Nighthawk jumpin' in that night you got beat up on and –"

"No." Kirk grinned and tried to change the subject. "I don't remember."

"Fortunately," I inserted, "the thing was over by the time the police arrived and everybody had scattered."

"It was really ol' Hugh Nighthawk who done saved your tail," Moose insisted, then guffawed, *knowing* Kirk hated

Nighthawk's guts after the half-Cherokee Indian had put the make on me. I *still* believe, all these years later, that if he'd had his rathers, Kirk would rather have served time than be saved by Nighthawk.

That may seem ungrateful to some and perhaps it is but that's Kirk and on his priority list, except when dealing with family, nobility doesn't rank all that high.

"C'mon, Kirk," Moose prodded good-naturedly, "'fess up."

Kirk laughed, but I saw the fire flicker in his eyes as he glanced my way. "On second thought, I *do* remember Nighthawk jumping in. Poor guy," Kirk shook his head. "That boy's face looked like a swelled up prune next day."

"Almost as bad as yours," Moose reminded him.

I laughed and it sounded foreign – Kirk glanced at me and I thought of all the times he would have gotten angry at me laughing at his expense. Tonight, he didn't.

Krissie would want me to laugh.

So do I, breathed that presence I felt at all times now. Not ever in-my-face. But *there.* I existed on two planes. On the one level, I remained raw and torn, frustrated and deprived, clawing my way through each moment, while higher, on the spiritual rung, a strange compelling peace enveloped me. Amid all this was an 'okay' to deal with the human aspects of my psyche, permission to seek answers that would give my troubled mind solace. This presence carried me, like a swaddled babe at times, spanning the black abyss of hopelessness, nursing me through nights when defenses took flight and I awakened on a sob and curled into a fetal knot, weeping my devastation.

"Neecy, I don't know how you put up with this guy," Moose teased, "he was always tighter'n a drill sergeant. Now he's a preacher, he's *really* on a high horse."

Again, laughter spilled from me and I marveled that it was in me.

"Now, Moose," Kirk leaned forward on his elbows and grew serious. "You know you need to be in church." Then he grinned that crooked grin of his, a rare one that disarmed even the most cynical personalities. "Can't be running with a heathen, now can we, Neecy?" He laid his arm across the back of my chair and winked at me. I rustled up a passable nod, my fleeting response to humor having evaporated.

My emotions remained jumbled. Perhaps I would survive, I thought while staring dully at Moose. Didn't time heal all wounds?

I picked up my iced tea and made a pretense of sipping. But did I truly want to go on? One moment apathy swooped as a listless black crow perched on my shoulder, filtering into my spirit a *don't care* that pinned me to sofa, lounge, chair or bed, staring at life with unseeing eyes until Kirk nudged me to do something with him. The next, it came as a raging black bull with red eyes and smoking nostrils, that pawed the earth and insisted that I *must* die. Go join Krissie. Then, Toby or Heather would tug at my sleeve and pull me back.

I was needed, though briefly and sporadically. *Need*: the catalyst that tethered me to earth.

"Okay," Moose turkey necked and nodded vigorously. "Me and Roxie'll see ya'll in church tomorrow, won't we, sug?"

And though Roxie rolled her eyes and half-heartedly agreed, I couldn't help but be lifted by our pal's exuberance. Again, my mouth pulled into a genuine smile and despite its heaviness, my heart lifted just a bit at the possibility of two changed lives.

It was a beginning.

"Hello?" I wondered who would be calling at five a.m., though Kirk and I had already awoken and wept together.

"Neecy? This is Callie."

"Lord help us – Callie? Is it really you?"

"Last time I looked. Naw – this isn't the time to joke. Listen, Neecy – I didn't know about Krissie till Mama called me. I was out of town when she tried to let me know."

"Oh, Callie –" My words choked off. Her voice, so dear and familiar, melted away any constraint I'd acquired in the wee early hours.

"I'm so sorry I wasn't with you, Neecy—Oh, *God*." She began to wail and cry and I was amazed at the depth of her caring, again struck with the sense of a change in her and for long moments, we mourned together. "I-I'm not doing this good, am I?" she croaked.

"Yes, you are, Callie," I snuffled, "the best." Then, "I wish you'd been here with me, too. But I understand."

"There's something else, Neecy. Lots of things have changed in my life – your letter started it, remember? But it took this thing with Krissie to push me to where I needed to be. And – I need to ask a favor of you."

"Anything."

"Can I come stay with you a few days? I've got to get outta here."

"My door is already open."

She arrived barely six hours later, announcing that she'd already been packed when she called. "I'm not going to impose on you and Kirk at a time like this," she insisted while hugging me. "I'm going to get a place –"

"Don't be silly," I reared back to gaze at her. "Of course, you'll stay here."

"Tonight," Callie insisted, shucking off her red wool coat. "Tomorrow, I'll go apartment hunting."

"Apartment – are you planning to move here?" I asked, my heart almost doing a leap. *Almost.*

"If it's where God wants me," she said matter-of-factly, looking me straight in the eye.

God? A word that had never, *ever*, in my experience, appeared in Callie's vocabulary?

"I got saved recently. But don't look too close," she huffed a laugh. "I'm still under construction."

"Oh, Cal," I grabbed her and held on for dear life, laughing and crying all at once.

"I know, I *know*," Callie quipped and snuffled, squeezing me. "Who'd have ever thunk it?"

"Where's – Jim?" I asked, uncertain.

"Jack. Number four is now history. After him, I decided I don't need a man." Her words were firm but surprisingly gentle. "I'm not bitter, Neecy," she shrugged. "Brought most of it on myself. Not to excuse his cruelty, mind you. But once I got my life on track, he really turned mean. I prayed about it and then, filed for divorce."

"How does he feel now? I mean –"

"Aw," she waved it away with her well-manicured hand, "he's okay about the divorce. After the initial shock, he sorta got spooked by the change in me. Know what I mean? Jack – well, he likes to party and drink and have never-ending fun and laughs. He didn't figure on losing his party girl." She crossed her eyes and lolled her tongue out the side of her mouth.

I laughed and then she laughed and it felt good. I took her by the arm and led her to Heather's room, where she would sleep. Knowing intuitively that being bunked in Krissie's old room might bother Callie, Heather had thoughtfully volunteered to sleep there.

"Let's eat supper and then, you can tell me all about it."

"How would you like a job in the church?" Kirk asked Callie between bites of a chicken casserole Donna Huntly had dropped by. We'd located Callie a small, inexpensive apartment in downtown Solomon, near the park, the day after she arrived. Now, a day later, she needed a livelihood.

"You serious?" she paused, fork midair, then put it down.

"The church secretary, Tillie Dawson, is on maternity leave and I hear from reliable sources that she's not planning to return. Betsy is grumbling about having to fill-in for her. So, I need somebody desperately." He shrugged and raised his brow. I still marveled at his change of heart toward my old pal. But the spiritual Kirk had a pastor's heart and anybody who tried at all in those days, he was there to help

Callie's mouth worked but no sound came forth for a long moment. Then, she cleared her throat and I saw the moistness in her chocolate eyes. "Thank you, Kirk."

"You didn't even ask how much it pays," Kirk reminded her, grinning.

"Don't matter. God will provide." Hers were not maudlin' words but an affirmation.

During our long conversations since her arrival, Callie had told of praying for guidance, desperate to escape Jack Farentino's sadistic grasp. She didn't feel she could go home and burden her mom, who had her own battles with an increasingly alcoholic husband. "I'd be jumping from one frying pan into another," she said flatly. "Anyway, Mama can handle her own woes better than she can mine. She's one hundred per cent maternal. I can't unload on her. I'm letting her down easy, saying Jack and I are just separated, to see how we feel about each other. I haven't told her the whole story. Probably won't, either."

"Anyway," she continued, "I was praying about where to go and Mama called. She told me about Krissie and immediately, my heart was drawn this way. I packed my clothes, then called you, Neecy, and as soon as I heard your voice, I *knew.*"

Callie had been right. I needed her. She needed me. And the church.

I marveled daily at how love, pure and simple, kept me – *us* – going in this minute by minute trek.

Toby jumped up from the table and sprinted to the back door, then, remembering, turned and muttered, "s'cuse me," and banged out the door. I arose and peered through the window at him climbing on his bike to disappear toward the white path. During the past days, Toby's face still gave no indication that he felt the enormity of what had happened.

Will he forget her? The old familiar fear pierced my haze of pain. I honestly didn't know what to say to him and when I tried – something always stopped me.

"Mom?" Heather stuck her head around the hall entrance, "can you help me hem these slacks?"

"Sure, honey."

We sat on Krissie's bed, our hangout place together, and reminisced about happy times as I stitched the bell-bottom trouser legs to accommodate Heather's less than statuesque height. Actually, her five-foot-four is normal, but alongside Callie and Roxie, she felt like a, quote, "stunted dwarf."

"You're lovely," I insisted. "Perfect."

"Aww," Heather protested, blushing, "Mamas always say that."

"Maybe so. But to me –" I looked her in the eye, "you are."

My hands stilled when I saw the tears in her blue eyes. I lay the sewing aside and held out my arms. "Come here."

She moved into them and snuggled to my bosom, silently shedding tears. I felt her heartbeat as she nestled there. My throat closed and throbbed. The pulse was so miraculous – so *profound* in that moment. *Life. Precious life.*

"Mama," Heather said hoarsely, pulling away and looking sadly at me. "I know you miss Krissie. But Mama –" She took both my hands in hers and her lips trembled, "you *still have us.*"

The words tumbled so straight from her heart they pierced my soul like a bullet. And I knew, in that moment, it was not selfishness or irreverence toward her sister but a need to be *validated.* Like me at her age, she was trapped in a dark drama, one not asked for nor deserved. One over which she had no control, that had reduced her to a *non-person.*

Dear God, give me the right words.

"I'm so thankful to have you, sweetheart." I squeezed her fingers. "Right now, I'm consumed with grief. I'm sorry. I can't change that. Time will help. In the meantime, I want you to know this: God divided my heart into equal compartments and each one is reserved for you, Toby and Krissie. I love you differently but equally. No matter what happens, that space is *yours.* Forever."

I resolved in that moment that I would henceforth attempt to shield her a bit more from the grimness surrounding her.

We embraced and lay there on Krissie's bed for a long, long time.

Callie slid into the secretary's role as effortlessly as an otter into water and every bit as gracefully. To me, she was still beautiful, despite her nose, slightly crooked since being broken – compliments of Jack – and the small scars on her neck and arm where he cut her. The nose alteration made her look – interesting. Anyway, that's what I kept telling her, though I don't think she fully believed me. Modest but fashionably fitted clothing replaced her minis and snug sweaters, while she traded her Farah Fawcett mane for a modest but luxurious shag style. She was determined to be a credit to Kirk and the church. But first, quote Callie, to the Almighty.

Her coming to Solomon was a balm to me and when she moved into her apartment, I missed her. When she and Moose reunited, it was a hoot of all hoots.

"What happened to you, Moosey?" she eyed him up and down just before we sat down to dine at Bessingers. "Some other little pig been beatin' you to the trough?"

Moose explained that a bad case of flu had started the weight decline, after which he simply flowed with less food. With his weight down, he qualified to join the Air Force. "Found out I felt better not stuffin' everythin' 'at didn't move into my mouth," he declared, then gazed adoringly at Roxie, who maintained her all-male vigilance like a trooper. "B'sides, if I hadn't 'a slimmed down, Roxie wouldn't 'a give me a tumble, would you, Roxie?"

"Huh *uh*. Not on your life, precious," she droned in her nasal way, never looking at Moose, who didn't seem to notice or care. Just being in her presence sustained him in some way I'd not yet divined.

Callie cocked one brow at me but kept her mouth shut. She was slowly acquiring the art of discretion.

"You and I could've danced on the table *naked* and she'd never have noticed," she commented later in the ladies' room on Roxie's fetish with the opposite sex. "What's got into Moose? Don't he even *notice* she eyeballs every man in the place except *him?* I thought he had more sense. Course, Moosey *does* bring home a good paycheck, which could account for her sacrificial offering of self."

She rolled her eyes heavenward. "Forgive me, Lord," she muttered without remorse.

"Well, she's coming to church with Moose at least," I said. "There's always hope."

"I'm glad you didn't say *faith*. In this case, I'd sure have to dig for it."

"You need to get back in school, honey. It's been nearly two weeks since – Well, you need to get out of the house."

I gazed unseeing out our rain-spattered bedroom window, toward the cemetery. I still hadn't gotten past the nightly head count mothers do. I tried not to agonize that her grave was wet and cold.

Kirk thrust his hands into his pockets. "I've been meaning to talk to you, Neecy. Your Dad's worried about you. When they visited last weekend, he said he's concerned you spend so much of your time at the graveside."

I whirled about to face my husband. "How dare you or anybody tell me *how* to grieve, Kirk Crenshaw. Do I tell you how? Huh?"

Kirk's shock at my outburst registered in his face. "No, you don't. Your Dad is just worried about you."

"Well, Daddy can just get over it." Anger caused me to tremble and brought tears to my eyes. "I walk in the cemetery every day, for goodness sake. I did before Krissie's death and I still do. It's my favorite quiet place to take a blanket and to sit and write under that shade tree. It's my meditation place. And yes! I do want to be close to my daughter right now, okay? That doesn't make me a nut case."

How dare they!

I started to leave then turned again. "And I'll go back to school when I doggone well please."

Kirk remained in the bedroom for a long time before approaching me in the den, where, because of the weather, I was forced to remain indoors and stare at the television screen, unseeing, while Toby watched afternoon cartoons.

The phone rang. Woodenly, I answered it. "Hello."

"Mrs. Crenshaw, this is Mrs. Carter, Krissie's teacher. I've got something I think you'd like to have." Her voice quavered with emotion. "Remember the little girl named Joanne, Krissie's classmate? She was the black student Krissie befriended. I noticed her playing with Joanne often before her accident."

"Yes. I remember." Kirk kissed my cheek and his concerned eyes lingered on me before I forced a smile to reassure him. I heard him quietly close the door behind him on his way out.

"I asked the class to write an essay entitled 'The Person I Admire the Most' and Joanne wrote about Krissie." She began to weep softly. "I'm sorry. I didn't mean to call and upset you, but you've just got to read this. You'd just have to know Joanne – who didn't, before Krissie, trust or open up to anybody. She's been abused and –"

I listened to her snuffle and wiped my own tears away. "I'd love to have it."

"Another thing, Mrs. Crenshaw. The Achievement Test Scores just came back today."

I think I did okay on the test today, Mama.

"Her score was quite high," Mrs. Carter stated with audible pride.

"Krissie was a bright little girl."

I dozed the next morning after Kirk left to take Toby and Heather to school. Usually, he did hospital visitation after dropping them off at respective locations, leaving me alone for long spells, some of the most difficult to span so I tried to delay starting the day as long as possible. I heard the back door open.

Eyes closed, I listened to footsteps falling heavily down our green shag-carpeted hall.

A weight fell across me, jolting me to full wakefulness.

My hand touched Kirk's head, pressed to my bosom. His arms grasped me and his body shook violently. *He's crying.*

"Oh Neecy," he wailed. "*I miss her so-o-o.*"

I stroked his head and felt fresh tears scald my red lids, swollen from earlier weeping. "I know, honey. I know," I murmured, realizing he'd been holding all this in during recent days, only allowing the early morning valve release and then going about his day as though nothing were any different. Doing his denial thing. But denial had run out this morning.

In the midst of the squall, he sprang to his feet and dashed across the hall into Krissie's room. I heard rummaging in her drawers and presently return with the clear plastic zip-lock bag bearing our daughter's thick, glossy wheat-blonde tendrils she'd so painstakingly gathered from the carpet to save. He clutched them to his chest and fell across me again.

Kirk cried until drained and limp. "I was listening to the cassette of the Carpenters music," he said hoarsely, "the one Krissie liked, that we play every morning on the way to school." He gulped back a fresh sob. "That song – *We've Only Just Begun*...I can still hear her singing along with it. How am I ever going to make it through this?"

I hugged him to me, soothing and stroking his brow, wanting more than anything to ease his pain but knowing I could not. Some things aren't fixable. Some things we all must walk through.

"Y'know," I said softly, "I once thought my faith would insulate me from this kind of anguish. But it doesn't. I think the more spiritual we are, the more vulnerable we are to truly *feeling* things. Death hits us as hard as anyone."

Kirk stirred and gazed up at me. "The Bible doesn't say we won't grieve. It says we won't grieve as those who have no hope. Even Jesus wept when Lazarus died."

We lay together in silence for long moments, absorbing that, absorbing each other, our affinity spiraling to new depths.

I sighed deeply as Kirk raised up on his elbow, still inclining himself across my midriff, "It's amazing what well-meaning folks say to me right now. Pearl Stone said, 'God knows best. He takes the best to come live with Him in heaven, don't you know? *Cliches.*" I huffed a sad laugh. "I'll never again utter those glib responses to somebody's heartache. Those who've gone through losing a child are the ones who don't say a thing except 'I know what you're going through. I'm sorry' or they just simply hold you and weep with you. Worst of all, some folks think we're past the worst in a few days and begin to avoid talking about Krissie altogether."

Kirk reached to brush hair from my temple and said gently. "I love you, Janeece Crenshaw. Sometimes, your wisdom astounds me."

I gazed at him, my love surging so, it could have washed us out to sea.

Kirk slowly shook his head, solemn as I'd ever seen him. "What if we'd never *connected?*"

I smiled. "But we did."

His answering smile soon faded as great tears puddled his tired lids. "Oh Neecy," he said hoarsely, "if only I hadn't moved us down here. We could have stayed on at Hopewell for years to come. And Krissie would be alive. It's all –"

"Kirk," I put my fingers over his lips. "Stop doing this to yourself. I could have discouraged the notion of relocating. I didn't."

He pulled my hand away and laced his fingers through mine. "Another thing – if I hadn't been working on that blasted car the day of the accident, I'd not have sent the kids back to you. I'd have said 'no, you can't visit today.' Deep down, I *knew* you wanted me to intervene but I was so aggravated with missing tools and trying to find the right parts."

"You were doing what you had to do, honey. That's you. You take care of us. Stop beating yourself up over it. Here," I reached to the bedside table and handed him the essay Mrs. Carter had personally dropped by the previous afternoon..

"It's written by Joanna. Remember the little girl I told you Krissie befriended at school?"

He read it aloud: *"The Person Who I Admire the Most...I admire Krissie Crenshaw the most of all people because she was the most prittiest girl of all. She was a very sweet girl who did everything her mother or father told her to do. I would like to be like her because she was so nice to everybody and she had many friends in her class. I would like to be like her because she was a cristian and when I die I would not have to worry about going to heaven because I would know I was going there. I would like to be like Krissie because she went to church every time there was services. I wish I could have been her because she was loved by everybody. She was my best friend in the whole world. Joanna Coggins."*

"Some tribute," he said softly, his eyes moist.

"Her life *did* count," I said.

We embraced and kissed before Kirk took his leave. I watched from my reclining position on the bed as he disappeared to do his Father's bidding. How on earth could he feel responsible for Krissie's death?

It was, after all, *my* fault.

"And we want you to sing at our wedding, Neecy," Moose announced, grinning so big his eyes disappeared into the folds of his cheeks and brow. I forced my preacher's wife smile. I'd deal with my feelings later. Right now, I needed to be there for Moose.

"Of course," I said and hugged him, then waited until Roxie finished embracing Kirk, who seemed not at all disturbed that his pal was being railroaded. Rather, he grabbed Moose for a celebratory bear hug while I tentatively embraced the lovely fiancée, whose exuberance had waned by the time I reached her. She smelled heavenly. *Chanel No. 5*, I surmised, another expensive gift from Moose, no doubt. And she was beautiful, as usual, an effortless thing with her full auburn hair that tumbled loose and wild, *a la* Farah Fawcett, and enormous, exotic tawny-gold eyes that tilted in feline perfection. Her seafoam outfit today was no less sexy because of its more demure cut.

"*Some females are cursed with beauty,*" sniped Callie during one of her Roxie-assessments. "*I've seen man-eaters, but this gal takes the prize.*"

"She's one of God's creatures, Cal," I'd reminded her – I fear more from duty than conviction. I struggled to cut Roxie some slack and tried not to judge what could actually be a slight personality conflict twixt her and Cal. Roxie was, after all, attending church now.

"Well, we better take off to shop for a ring," Moose took Roxie's limp hand, still grinning like he'd just won the Publisher's Clearing House Sweepstakes. "April 20. Mark it on your calendar, Kirk. We want it done right, man."

"Sure thing, Moose," Kirk called, waving from the doorway.

Toby rushed past me, on his way outside again. Again.

Amid the blurred coming and going of loving, caring condolence-bearers, Toby still seemed set apart from the grim drama taking place around him. My curiosity rose and I went to the kitchen window to watch him. His play activity had changed recently, from solitary excursions on biking and trekking over nearby terrain to a role that required a shovel.

Annoyance pierced me today as I watched him, shovel gripped tightly, head for our property's back corner, actually a low-country sand hill with marshy sod in places. His area of interest sloped away and downward, out of sight from the kitchen window. For days now, his backyard toil had continued and I now wondered what make-believe fantasy held him captive.

At first, his solitary activity didn't seem extraordinary, since Toby now had no steady playmate. But when he continued to trudge over the hill, day in, day out, I'd asked him, "What's going on?"

"It's a surprise," he'd informed me matter-of-factly. Toby had always been the fun-seeking adventurer of the family. Now, quite frankly, his enthusiasm stirred my anger. After all, he never mentioned Krissie. I certainly didn't expect him to anguish as I did, but it didn't seem right somehow that he ignored her absence.

Kirk kissed me goodbye and took off to do visitation.

I showered and dressed. My hair was still damp when the doorbell rang.

"I brought you a cake," Donna Huntly's moist eyes belied her flat way of expression. "I know Toby likes them."

"Where *is* Toby?" Eddie, Donna's nine-year-old, asked. I pointed him in Toby's direction and visited with Donna for an hour or so. Today, Donna's rather curt personality didn't seem important. Her kind gesture and countenance revealed a bigger heart than I'd ever guessed.

When the Huntleys departed, Toby waved goodbye to Eddie from the hill, then returned to his play. I called him in for lunch, during which he gobbled down a ham and cheese sandwich in record time. Kirk called to say he'd grab a burger at Sally's Grill. When I returned to the table, Toby said, "s'cuse me."

"Toby, don't you want a piece of Donna's chocolate cake?" I asked as he dashed to the door.

"Later," he replied and slammed out the back door.

I rushed to the door and flung it open. "What's going on?" I called to his retreating backside, more irritated than ever at his preoccupation.

"You'll see, Mom," he yelled, disappearing over the hill.

I wanted to be alone. *Clung* to solitude. It had something to do with survival. *What?* I'd not yet discovered.

"Please, honey," Kirk slid his arms around me from behind as I stood gazing at the hilltop beyond which Toby continued to migrate, "do it for me?"

School. Second semester was now in full swing. Classes. All that seemed eons ago.

"Neecy? Will you?" he persisted softly.

I took a deep, ragged breath. What choice did I have? He was right. "Okay."

Callie hugged me. "You've made the right decision, Neece. School is what you need."

I'd walked out to the church later that afternoon, where she prepared the Sunday Bulletin for the following day's morning service. Hers was the small office through which one gained entrance to the pastor's larger, more masculine study with its leather sofa and chairs, greenery and endless book shelves.

"Those are the last copies," she said, shuffling and stacking them neatly on her desk.

"You work so hard, Cal."

"This job is a piece of cake compared to my last one in car sales, Neecy."

"I know Kirk appreciates all you do. Says you've taken lots of pressure off him."

"Good." She drew up to her full height, adjusting the belt of her tailored slacks and gazed around, looking for loose ends. Satisfied, she said, "Well, I'll be off."

I walked her to her car, a beat up gray hatchback Honda,which astounded me because the old Cal would have sold her soul for a Continental and designer fashions. Nothing but the best. This new Callie cared little for material gain. Her flip-coin side proved as passionate as its opposite one.

The next day at church, Moose had Roxie showing off her diamond, a rock big as the tip of my pointer finger. I squashed down my aversion to what I perceived as her shallowness and hugged her. "It's lovely, Roxie."

For the first time, I felt a response. She squeezed me back. "Thanks, Neecy." Maybe I'd misjudged character this time. My heart began to open up a mite.

After service, Kirk invited Callie, Moose and Roxie to join us at a local restaurant featuring seafood where we had a wonderful meal. Afterward, everyone hung out at the parsonage, laughing and reminiscing the entire afternoon away.

"My goodness," Kirk looked at his wristwatch, "Only an hour till evening service."

We all walked to the church for an uplifting, serene time together, then returned to the house and raided the refrigerator and ate leftovers and sandwiches of all varieties. The pantry still bore soft drinks and chips brought in by folks days earlier during the funeral gathering.

I hugged our friends goodnight as they left, hating to see them go.

With the last one gone, I closed the door and locked it, then followed Kirk down the hall. At its end, I glimpsed Krissie's bed through the open doorway and my heart lurched. We had not closed her room off, had allowed it to remain an integral part of our living. Not a shrine, simply a place in which to relax and remember the good times and as Kirk disappeared into our room, a collage of Krissie-snapshots strobed through my head: *Krissie raking the perpetual carpet of brown pine needles into tidy little heaps...standing framed in her doorway, dressed in large loop costume earrings, Mom's high heels and long sleeved blouse caught up and Gypsy-tied under her small bosom, and a pair of last summer's shorts – until she gets my startled attention, erupts into giggles and goes clonking off down the hall, exaggerating the swing of her narrow hips...Krissie clowning, making rubber faces for small children....*

I froze in my tracks gazing at the room's stillness, absorbing its silence and Krissie's *non-being.* Her absence clawed at my flesh and bones and my soul cried for a glimpse, a touch from her. My mind had, most of that day, taken other directions, had somehow ventured from *now,* across some invisible bridge that transported me to a place timeless and survival-friendly.

A place where memory slept.

In that moment, reality hit so forcefully I nearly fell to my knees.

I paid the price of the afternoon's lapse, however unconscious and however *needed.* By pushing it away, I'd set myself up. The stark cruelty of death shredded me again.

I went into the room, lay on her bed and cried silently, pressing my face into her pillow, inhaling her lingering fragrance, wrapping bereftness about me like a cloak, so that soon, I felt the blessed apathy creep over me. Sorrow replaced the searing anguish.

And I wondered, *Will the pain ever stop?*

Looking back now, I'm glad I did not have the answer to that.

CHAPTER TEN

"Come on, Neece," Kirk turned me from the sink and handed me a towel. "Dry your hands and ride with me on home visitation this morning."

I dried my hands without argument, running on automatic, knowing he wanted me out of the house for good reasons. After a restless night, permeated with nightmares of searching for my daughter, I was ready to cooperate.

"Just a minute." From my closet I grabbed the cloak-sweater, a seventies mainstay, threw it over my flared jeans and gossamery hip length blouse and hastily finger brushed my shag-do as I joined him at the door. On the drive, I absent-mindedly glossed my lips from one of Heather's cast-off tubes.

Our first stop was to see Tillie Dawson and her four-day-old daughter, Raquel, an adorable little replica of her mom, from her pixie thatch of ebony down to her tiny pink toes. Tillie already moved agilely about, reminding me of a Disney flea with big amber eyes framed by sooty lashes thick enough to dust furniture with.

"Do you miss the office?" I asked Tillie as I nuzzled Raquel's sweet jowls and delicious talcum-powdered neck.

"No." Tillie burst into irrepressible, non-apologetic giggles. "Sorry, Pastor," she slapped petite fingers over her lips in mock horror, then slid them up to peek through them. "I cannot tell a lie."

Kirk rumbled with laughter. "That's okay, Tillie. I'm *tough.*"

"Enjoy your baby," I said, shifting Raquel to my shoulder and caressing her swaddled, old woman's back. "They're not this little very long before –"

"They change," Kirk finished my sentence, I think because he saw the sadness returning to my eyes and I sense, was afraid of where the conversation was going.

"I know," Tillie bunny-wiggled her nose, "like *Toby.*" She adored our son, doted on him, in fact, and so, her remark was truly funny for its honesty.

From a flea-market, elephant-shaped bowl, Tillie fed us home-baked chocolate chip cookies, "compliments of Mama," she confessed, eyes rounded tragically, "definitely not *my* creation. Sorry, I don't have coffee made, Pastor." Seeing Kirk's relief, she burst into her brand of laughter, sorta like a donkey's jerky bray. Tillie's reputation as a cook was as tarnished as any I'd ever witnessed, as was her taste for funky clothing and off-the-beaten-path home decor. All of which, quote Tillie, *proved* hubby Rick's love for her was gen-u-ine. What Kirk missed in the office was her upbeat humor that refused to let anything heavy set down where she happened to be. Yet, he admitted, Callie possessed some of those same qualities.

Our next stop was Ralph and Sarah Beauregard's ranch-brick home. Sarah was, as her husband Ralph was prone to admit, a mite *peculiar* at times. Subject to moods and temper. So I made it a practice to walk softly around her and keep practiced up on my pastor's wife smile.

Fact was, everybody walked on egg shells around Sarah.

Today, Sarah's mood was conciliatory, even warm, no doubt because of our recent loss.

I gazed forlornly at Kirk's back as he ambled on ahead to the den to speak to Ralph, who watched The Price Is Right almost as faithfully as he attended Solomon Methodist services, while Sarah hugged me and expressed condolences again.

"Wait here just a minute," her brown mules swished together as she disappeared into the kitchen, leaving me standing in her living room that boasted of Victorian influence with its wingback sofa and matching chairs and whose air smelled faintly of mothballs. When she returned, her small ebony eyes glimmered with ebullience below beauty parlor blackened and frizzed hair. Her small, slightly hooked nose, set above thin, hard-set lips, lent her a mildly sinister look.

Today, however, the ruby-red mouth smiled as she approached, gripping two glass Mason canning jars in her hands. And my heavy heart lifted a mite as she stopped, almost touching me, gazing up from her short stature – even beside my five-three – to whisper, "these are crowder peas."

"Oh," I smiled and spontaneously reached for them, "How sweet –"

"No." I felt the cold glass abruptly withdraw from my fingertips. Her brows drew together as she stage-whispered, "these are for *him.*"

My face refused to accommodate my pastor's wife smile, so I simply nodded and awkwardly clasped my hands together while my heart plunged to its former lackluster status. *No problem*, I thought, knowing Sarah's propensity for obtuseness. I trailed her as she entered the den and ceremoniously presented the pastor with her gift while Ralph hugged me hugely and complimented me on my 'sweetness,' and I marveled at the *opposites-attract* chemistry as he plied me with concerned queries as to the Crenshaw's well-being during that difficult time.

All the while, Sarah tittered and fawned over Kirk's effusive delight at receiving his "favorite" country food.

I had the last silent laugh, however, at her territorial presentation, knowing that therein lay her reward: the pastor's recognition. From that moment on, the peas were mine to do with as I doggoned well pleased. I'd long ago decided to regard insensitive parishioners like Sarah as weaker vessels and love them anyway.

I vowed anew to do just that. Even if it killed me.

The next morning, I returned to school and sat through the nine o'clock Government Class in a stupor, its normalcy augmenting the emotional distance between me and students who flanked me on all sides, breathing the same air, laughing and joking about last week's test and Friday's rock concert, reminding me their worlds remained intact while mine was irrevocably altered. My limbs didn't seem to belong to my body, whose lungs refused to pump out completely my shallow intake of air.

Everything was the same except me. The last five minutes seemed forever as I choked back dark pathos. The bell rang and I sloughed like a druggie toward my next class.

Suddenly, mid-stride, without warning, grief, like an angry volcano, roiled and surged upward, *upward*. I ducked blindly into the empty ladies' room, slammed my books on a bookshelf, where I planted my elbows and cradled my head, then erupted into convulsive weeping. It rode out on a crashing tidal wave, violent and unrestrained.

"Is there anything I can do to help?" a lady, who appeared from nowhere, asked.

I lifted my head, tears dripping from my cheeks and gazed into her kind eyes, feeling as stripped and emotionally naked as I'd ever felt in my entire life. Sorrow so completely consumed me in that moment, it smothered embarrassment or fear of rejection.

"I'm grieving," I croaked. "I lost my little girl two weeks ago in an accident. The one on the trestle – in Solomon." Recognition flashed across her stricken features and she simply wrapped her arms around me and wept with me. She could have been an older student or a staff member. I'd never seen her before nor have I since, but I shall never forget her compassion and I am convinced she was divinely placed that morning.

Again, I experienced that dual-plane existence, one of hellish torment, the other of holy favor. Somewhere in all the fog, I acknowledged anew that *love* – from everybody sent the Crenshaw's way – kept us going.

I immediately made the decision to drop those college courses requiring memory and recall, such as mathematics, my old nemesis. So I spoke individually with my professors, who each in turn, waved away my apologies for copious tears and proceeded to mourn with me. No advice. No profound words of wisdom. Drying their eyes, each urged me to take as long as I needed to recover and assured me they would work to get me through the remainder of the semester.

As I left the campus and drove home, *aloneness* embraced me like downy swaddling.

Now, I knew the *why*.

It was a haven from the outside, where people untouched by tragedy reminded me I was no longer one of them.

Daily letters arrived from Dad, nurturing me with colorful anecdotes of my carefree childhood and teen years and offered me moments of respite from *now*. They acquainted me with a mellower father, a product, I quickly gleaned, of our mutual tragedy. Through the years, his heart keened more and more toward hearth and Anne and when, without fail, Anne's little yellow VW pulled into our parsonage drive each Friday night, I knew the extent of Dad's generosity in loosening her to sail like a porpoise to my side.

Sometimes, Dale came with Anne and my little sister Lynette; sometimes, he stayed home to assuage Dad's loneliness. Cole, now dating, opted to stay home. My youngest brother, already turned twelve, spent much time at Krissie's graveside.

"He's having a hard time coming to grips, Neecy," Anne told me on her third weekend journey to Solomon. "He cries a lot and can't understand why it happened. You know they spent a lot of time together, listening to music and talking about sweethearts and sharing secrets –"

"They were best friends." I stared dully at Spanish moss dancing in the gentle February breeze, apathy still mercifully shielding me for long moments at a time. It ceased in a heart-beat and my eyes pooled with tears. "My greatest heartbreak, Anne, is that I'll never see the *woman*, Krissie." I gazed at her blurred features. "You know how she loved babies. She'll never experience holding her very own baby – or romance, for that matter. Oh *God – there's so much she won't experience.*"

Anne moved to my side and put her arms around me, rubbing my back gently. We'd walked out to the graveside, hand in hand, and I knew it was okay to grieve. Anne was so *there* for me and I knew beyond doubt that her grief was as profound as her wisdom and sensitivity. Where Dad conveyed compassion through pen and paper from a distance, Anne showed up weekly on my doorstep, sleeves rolled up for a full weekend of hands-on care.

So apathy-steeped was I at first, I only vaguely noted her arrival, but as weeks passed, then months and her trek persisted, I found myself standing at the door, awaiting her appearance. It was always my call. If I wanted to talk, Anne listened. If I wanted to be silent, she walked or drove me places in contemplative quietness. She continually touched me, physically, holding my hand, hugging me, linking arms as we walked, rubbing my arm or back gently, knowing instinctively the healing in that contact. My stepmother never studied a course in psychology but she was and remains the most intuitive, kind-hearted woman I know.

Today, I needed to rail against the injustice of Krissie's death and she murmured soothing assent and nodded understanding, tears riveting her fair cheeks and turning her periwinkle-blue eyes puffy and red.

"Oh Anne," I sat down on the blanket spread beneath the tree, "I miss her *so.*"

"I do, too, Neecy. It still doesn't seem real."

Perhaps the greatest of Anne's gifts was that, through the years, she never stopped referring to Krissie as a part of now, providing the continuity denied by so many others. Without words, she *saw* inside me. She loved me still. Unconditionally.

Her long weekly pilgrimage to my door would continue for several months.

"Janeece!" came a chorus of shouts as the college choral group flocked to hug and welcome me on my first day back. Their love enveloped me like great, soft wings, and their "*We need you, Janeece. We're so glad you're back!*" said in at least a dozen different ways penetrated my world of foggy passiveness. On one level, I knew they could go on without me, yet, their avowals were not to patronize but to *give* of themselves to me. On another level, I realized somehow, corporately, they knew the magic, life-giving word was *need.* And in that moment in time, they wanted more than anything to help shoulder my grief. It was a phenomenon repeated over and over on that long, long climb from the valley.

Soon, strains from the *Sound of Music* filled the air and I faced another staggering challenge. Preparation for the big Spring Concert had been launched before the accident. Two ensemble numbers on the program featured my voice and I felt the crunch of responsibility. Three weeks earlier that opportunity thrilled me. Now, it was torturous because for me, singing must come from the heart – is joyful.

Today, I felt leaden and mechanical. Every time we sang, "*do, a deer, a female deer – Re, a drop of golden sun,*" the next phrase choked me until no sound issued forth. The intrinsic sweetness of the words "*Me...a name I call myself*" encapsulated the childlike essence of Krissie. How she'd loved that music. My mind's eye glimpsed her face during the recent December Christmas Concert, upturned rapturously to listen to Mom's Winter Wonderland solo. And though still part child, she stood poised on the brink of the womanhood glimmering in her cerulean gaze.

I could not control my mind's eye because a hundred, two hundred times a day, tiny reminders flashed images before me: the slender blonde girl in English Class with enormous blue eyes and soft voice...*Krissie would have looked like her in years to come...* the empty chair at the kitchen table...*Krissie smacking her lips, "Oh boy! Pork chops and gravy!"*

Each memory jolted and left me trembling and keening to see and touch my child.

Dr. Reinebach, our choral conductor, would, each time I broke down, sensitively avert his gaze and proceed as if everything were normal. The hour left me shaken and limp and when the dismissal bell sounded, I bolted for the door.

Guilt sat heavily upon me this morning. Along with the grief, it seemed insurmountable. I headed for Dr. Jordess's office.

Psychology had, from the beginning of my scholastic jaunt, beckoned, secondary only to English. I'd taken every psych elective permitted and now, in my senior year, found myself a minor immersed in a mainstream of senior psych majors, tutored primarily by bespeckled Dr. Reese Jordess.

Rather short and squat, his wispy nut-colored hair was vintage *Julius Caesar,* minus the ivy-vine headband. He paced incessantly, chain-smoking as he lectured, surprisingly light-footed given his thickness. I imagined all that nicotine vapor had enlarged and shaded the nostrils of a blunt nose that always sounded as if it were recovering from an eruption of sneezes.

At first, I'd considered his precise movements posturing, convinced he reeked of pomposity. But humor lurked behind mud-colored eyes and rode Cupid's bow lips that perpetually twitched before bursting into laughter. It was a frequent occurrence during lectures, one that, at first, confused me as I tried to classify *why* the mirth and *who* the man behind the thick glasses really was. Now, familiarity and hindsight determined his humor unfailingly appropriate and his crispness to be conviction and decisiveness.

Today, he didn't smoke but listened to me pour out my guts, weeping and crying aloud my damning secret.

"I-it's my fault she died." My confession rode out on a hoarse whimper as I fisted my hands against my mouth to stop its wretched wobbling and wailing, not from embarrassment but from desperation to *unload* and weeping prevented that. I'd waited until this moment to face up to the thing. "I – I don't want to live at times. Honestly – I truly want *to die.*"

"Janeece," Dr. Jordess said gently, "you're reacting normally to your situation. Any time a child dies, parents inevitably blame themselves in some way. Even in cases where a child dies of a rare, incurable disease, parents are known to say '*if only I'd taken better care of him – not exposed him to certain elements... he'd have been stronger and wouldn't have contacted this.*' "

Something inside me, coiled and tightened by guilt during recent days, started to slowly unwind as his words sank in.

"You see, Janeece – what really bothers people, parents in particular, is facing the fact that *we do not control circumstances.*" His sonorous laugh spilled over and today, I understood – it punctuated absurdity. "We *humans* don't like to deal with that. We want to believe we have a handle on everything."

Realization rippled like soft light over a dark ocean during instant replays of the former smug Janeece Crenshaw spiraling to the bottom of the *helpless sinkhole*. In my self-recrimination, according to Dr. Jordess, I'd discounted all the variables at play.

"Five minutes earlier or later," his stocky tweed shoulders shrugged, "the kids would've had their adventure and gone home unharmed. Thing is, you didn't know, Janeece. Sure, if you had, you'd have kept her home. Heck, hindsight is always great to have. But we never have that during decisions."

Another wave of liability struck me from left field. "But I should have thought about –"

"You wanted her to have a good time, didn't you? Wasn't that your motive?"

I pondered for a long moment, being brutally honest... then nodded. I *had* back-pedaled after suggesting she go, had, in fact, tried to dissuade her, gave her a reason not to go. When she'd persisted, truly wanting the outing, I'd seen how much it pleasured her to be included. I *had* wanted Krissie to have fun. In the end, that had been the deciding point in allowing her to go that ill-fated afternoon.

"You had her best interests at heart, Janeece. Don't ever forget that."

He peered at me through thick lenses that augmented his tawny-hued concern. "Write down your feelings, Janeece," he said succinctly. "Keeping a journal will help you heal. It won't be overnight. But eventually – you'll want to live again."

Thus began my in-earnest preoccupation with rhetoric, one I'd laid aside in recent days. For three years, I would pour heart and soul onto paper, words to purge, analyze, shape and define the emerging *me*. Never would I recover my former trust of self nor shake entirely free of accountability, not when pondering my fateful suggestion that Krissie join the others that day.

But Dr. Jordess' counsel marked a pivoting point in my grief.

It enabled me to begin to forgive myself.

The following week, Jessica and Deborah Montgomery visited us for a wild wonderful weekend, during which the kids took Deborah to Skateland, where loud music and the rumble of skate wheels drowned out Toby's friend's outbursts. Kirk and I relaxed at home with Jessica, absorbing her sympathy and wisdom like thirsty sponges. The twenty-four hour visit passed all too swiftly, save the sleeping hours, when Deborah, being in strange surroundings, wandered about at times, mumbling and – despite Jessica's harried attempts to quiet her – keeping everybody awake.

Except Toby, who, exhausted from his bucket-toting labors, slept through it all.

While I wandered in the melancholy wilderness, Kirk threw himself into pastoral duties with unprecedented fervor. Heather had her friends and activities and youthful resilience to cushion the grimness of loss. Toby – well, Toby simply kept on sprinting over that darned hill every minute of his free time.

Then, one day, I was folding laundry when he burst into my room.

"Mama! It's ready!" His blue eyes danced with excitement. He grabbed my hand, pulling me from the laundry, through the hall, out the door, his grin stretching wider and wider.

"Wait till you see it!" He continued to tug me up the hill, down the slope, then right to the digging site.

I stopped dead in my tracks. My mouth fell open in wonder. He looked up at me, beaming with pride. "I made it for Krissie."

There before my eyes was a miniature pond. A small bridge of stacked split logs formed a crude ramp, big enough for one to walk right out to the center of the water.

From atop a tall pole on the shallow shore flapped a white banner. Meticulously printed in Toby's neat handwriting, it read: **KRISSIE-SOLOMON POND.**

"Well, Mama, what do you think about it?" He gazed expectantly at me.

I was so choked I couldn't say anything. Emotions invaded, pummeled me. Grief, pride love, admiration...*shame.* How could I have questioned Toby's depth of love for Krissie? I felt like sinking into the marsh and never coming up.

Suddenly, I understood why I'd not been able to talk with him about it: God was telling me to entrust Toby into his capable hands.

I swallowed audibly and groped for words. "I think it's a very sweet gesture. Krissie could be so proud to know that you built this in her honor."

Oh, so proud.

Later that night, Toby called me to his room, and as he dressed for bed, I sat beside him. The warmth of the shared afternoon lingered.

"Mama, you know why I built that pond, don't you?" As he tugged off his sock, I noticed the grubby, callused little hands.

"I think so, honey, but why don't you tell me anyway?"

"Well – I just had to do something, y'know – *big.*" Blue eyes turned up to my face. And that's when I saw the sorrow in their depths. And the dark shadows beneath them.

"She didn't have much of a life, did she?"

My heart lurched. "What do you mean?"

"Eleven years isn't long to live, is it?" He grimaced as he pulled off his other sock. "That's why I couldn't just do a – dime thing. I wanted to do a – a *dollar* thing." He grew still for a long moment, reflecting solemnly on that. "I think she knows, Mom."

I nodded, too choked to speak, grasping his second-grade logic. Such was his love for his sister.

And I knew in that moment that of all the tributes, Krissie's very, very favorite was his.

"I can't believe she had the gall to say that." Kirk paced around the den, stopped, shoved his fingers through his hair and gazed helplessly at me. His four o'clock appointment with Sarah Beauregard had left him in tatters.

I sat planted on the sofa, Psych books and notes littering my lap. "Let me get this right —" I shook my head. "She actually asked 'what's happened to you, Pastor? You've *changed?*'"

"Verbatim." Kirk plopped down in the easy chair next to the big open fireplace, which was seldom lit because of the warm coastal climate. He gazed past me through the window, unseeing. "I told her, 'Sarah, you must remember I recently lost a daughter.'" His tortured gaze met mine. "What do they want? *Blood?*"

"I know," I murmured. Kirk had given his all and it wasn't enough.

He gave a bitter little snort. "Course, I've changed. Who *wouldn't* change under the circumstances?" His emerald gaze held mine. "Don't we have a right to grieve, Neecy? Tell me that. Don't we?"

I sighed and lay my book aside. "Not everybody feels that way, Kirk. You've got to consider the source. Sarah's always been less than sensitive. Even her husband says so. Most folk here are very sympathetic and are allowing us space." I didn't add that I felt deprived, living so far from family and close friends, while the Beauregard clan had each other for daily support.

"Maybe it's *me,*" said Kirk. "I sense most of the church people don't really think we need the time to — well, the Beauregard clan is still grieving Zach, as they should be. But — few seem to understand when *I'm* quiet and need time out. When I don't read minds and divine needs. Unspoken ones at that. Would you believe that Grandma Beauregard's in the hospital? And she's mad as a wet hen because I haven't visited her?"

"When did she go?" I asked, astounded that we hadn't been informed. She seemed healthy as a kangaroo despite her eighty-five years. "Why didn't somebody call us?"

"My question exactly. Ralph heard her complaining, realized nobody'd notified me, then called me. I immediately phoned to apologize and reassure her I'd be there Johnny on the spot. She's still miffed. Said, quote, *it's your business to keep up with these things. You know we've just gone through Zach's death.'* "

My mouth fell open. Kirk's nostrils flared and he nodded. "Exactly."

He slouched in his seat, looking for all the world like Toby. But today, it wasn't humorous. Reality, again, was unkind. Three-dimensional truth slapped me upside the head. Wasn't Krissie's death significant to these people? Didn't they realize that we, too, *felt?*

Resentment shot through me. "I was visiting Grandma Beau just days ago and she had the nerve to say that though Krissie hadn't, quote, really been pretty, she was sweet. 'Pretty is as pretty does,' she told me, as though her remark wasn't offensive."

Our gazes locked in indignation. "She went on to say how 'attractive' her grandson, Zach, had been. And he was. But in our eyes, so was Krissie."

Our lovely Krissie, poised betwixt adolescent awkwardness and stunning beauty, to have someone define her so. What was it my Grandma Whitman always said? Blood's thicker'n water. Folks always cut lots of slack for blood kin.

"What's wrong with Grandma Beau?" I asked, turning loose of resentment.

"X-rays. Her stomachache proved to be a simple case of gastritis. But they're doing other tests."

Kirk's face slowly emptied as he gazed unseeing at the floor for long moments before decisively rising and striding from the room.

"Where you going?" I called after him.

"To the hospital." The back door slammed..

And I knew that though Kirk's *denial* was alive and well, it didn't seem at his beck and call now as in the past. For once, I found myself wishing for a bit of it.

CHAPTER ELEVEN
"A Time to Heal."

Guilt persisted. It struck with vicious precision, scattering what peace I'd managed to scrounge amid desolation. My head reminded me of Dr. Jordess' counsel, that I'd had Krissie's best interests in mind when I sent her to her death. Logically, I knew that was true.

My heart said something else entirely.

"Neecy," Kirk held out the phone to me several weeks after the accident, "this is Mr. Greene, the conductor on the train. He wants to talk to –"

"No –" I backed away, shaking my head. I wanted no details.

"Please, Neecy," Kirk's eyes pleaded with me, "he wants to say –"

"I'm sorry – I can't." I spun around and fled the room.

The unknown terrified me. I had nightmares that Krissie had been mutilated from the waist down. So I avoided any mention of specifics except with Kirk.

"She only had one injury," he kept insisting, "here." He'd point to that spot behind his left ear.

But what if no one had told *him?* Cynicism persisted. That my fears had no true basis didn't stop them. In the earliest nightmares, I was Krissie, frozen before the roaring train whose whistle shrilled as its mammoth spotlight swirled, *swirled toward me....* I would awake suddenly, jackknifed in bed, heart pounding and breath shallow, *feeling* her terror and pain in death's jaws.

In those dark pre-dawn hours, the maternal-me screamed out against the monstrous visions. *Those trusting blue eyes....* My arms ached to hold my little girl, to soothe and comfort her.

But I'd *failed her.*

I prayed.

God heard.

Seemed every time reality became too much, something would happen to balance out flesh and spirit. On an upstate visit to Dad and Anne's, we stayed up late, talking and simply loving one another. The next morning, Kirk arose early and went with Dad on one of their male-bonding drives. Still tired,

I decided to lie back down while Anne went to the grocery store. I soon drifted off to sleep.

I began to dream. Yet – I knew right away this was no ordinary dream. I saw Krissie moving toward me...not actually walking, more like gliding. She was smiling. The vision was so crystal clear, the blue in her eyes glimmered and her teeth sparkled like sunshine spattered snow.

"Please, God," I breathed a prayer, "let me hold her, *feel* her."

Then she was in my arms and I embraced her in a warm snug hug, closing my eyes and thanking God for the privilege.

Presently, she moved back, just enough that I looked directly into her eyes and pure gratification shot straight to my heart, then filled me to overflowing. Suddenly, her features were aglow and this luminous glow extended beyond her face, forming a halo effect, encircling her entire upper body.

Ahh, the sweet smile.

Krissie began to talk, chatter-box fast, as though trying to cram as much into our time as possible...."*I didn't have trouble – you know, with breathing. It wasn't like that at all, Mama!*"

Thank God. "But Krissie," I moaned, "if I'd only kept you home that day – "

"*Mama, you can't go on feeling this way. It was my time, don't you see?*"

"No," I groaned, "you'd still be alive if – "

"*Please, Mama, don't.*" The smile softened and the eyes turned so compassionate it made my breath hitch. "*I love you so and I don't want you to feel bad. I made the choices that day, not you. Promise me you'll stop blaming yourself.*" How *mature* she talked.

I began to weep. "*Promise?*" Her head tilted slightly and the smile charmed.

"Yes, honey. I promise."

"*Good. Now we'll both have peace.*" The emphatic words and unwavering smile began to reassure me. She continued to talk of comforting, happy things while the brilliance of her features grew ever brighter until she disappeared behind it.

I struggled to see her, the desire so great I nearly wept aloud and once more, she emerged through the glow. I drank in the sight of the joyful face, radiant with love.

The soft glow grew and shimmered again, until the sight of her quickly diminished from view. Power, like a pleasant electrical jolt, surged through my body.

Jubilation opened my mouth to thank God for the vision. The words that poured from me were in that now familiar, yet unknown rhetoric, a flowing, beautiful language. And as I hovered there in the trance zone, between sleep and wakefulness, a deep male voice, like many waters, thundered, *"Let this be a sign unto you. This is from God."*

In the next breath, I was fully awake, sitting upright, flooded with a curious warmth and supreme comfort.

Beyond any doubt the future would offer, beyond all cynicism hovering behind darkness, I knew I had two visitors: My child, who, in her own words, revealed she had not suffered in her final moments and absolved me of guilt, and *the* comforter: the Holy Spirit.

"Callie, stay and eat supper with us," I coaxed as she gathered her purse from under her desk and when she hesitated, I threw in, "I'm frying chicken."

'Aw, oka-ay," she laughed and slung her purse strap over her padded shoulder. "You know I can't resist your chicken, Neece."

"Yup." And I couldn't resist having her around to talk to.

I'd gone from not wanting to talk to a desperation to vent. And few could hang in there with me. Only Anne and Callie. Not even Kirk. He could for short treks but not for the long haul. It was Anne who took me to talk with the rescuers who'd found Krissie's lifeless form on the riverbank, whom I'd asked, "was there any pulse? Did anyone try to resuscitate her?" Anne who held me and wept with me when the answer was 'no, we didn't feel it was safe to move her.' It was Callie who called Mr. Jones, the funeral home director and handed me the phone to ask, "Did Krissie sustain any injuries other than the head wound?" And when he answered, "no, Mrs. Crenshaw, Krissie never knew what hit her. Her death was instantaneous," Callie held me and silently celebrated with me that it had been so.

Kirk fought his own battles. His strategy was to snub and ignore the fact of. Mine was to probe, dissect and analyze until it neutralized to *bearable*. Neither tactic superceded the other. Ours became an unspoken respect for the other's method.

Today, I needed Cal. And so she dined with us and afterward, when Kirk and Heather departed to the convalescent home with the Tree of Life Youth Group for their monthly service, she stayed to visit for a while longer.

"How's my boy?" Callie asked a listless Toby, plopping beside him on the sofa and giving him a warm hug. "Mom said you came home early from school today. What's wrong?"

"My tummy hurt," Toby murmured, watching the television with dull eyes.

"His teacher said he complained of not feeling well and appeared tired and inattentive," I explained. "She called us to come pick him up."

"Heather okay?" Callie kicked off her heels and curled long bronze legs under her.

"She cries a lot. Oh, not in front of us, but I see her red eyes. And during the night, she crawls in bed beside me and sleeps there until morning. Other times, she'll disappear for hours and I find her in Krissie's room, dressing Krissie's Barbie dolls or looking at her pictures."

Then there were the times I'd find her sitting quietly near her sister's grave, under the shade of the graceful oak. I understood her need for solitude and granted it.

"Mama," Toby arose and motioned me to follow him to his room, where he stretched out on his bed, then curled over on his side into fetal position.

"I dream about Krissie, Mama," he said softly, staring morosely at nothing. "She always came over to speak to me at recess. I miss her." A tear slid down across his freckled nose.

This had been Krissie's last year of elementary school. She'd bubbled with anticipation when speaking of junior high next fall.

"Mama – I feel kinda...you know – funny."

"About what?" I suspected his feelings related to last night's dream of Krissie.

"Well...I wish I could go to Heaven and be with her."
Bingo.

"But – God isn't ready for you to go now, Toby," I explained gently. "Only those picked carefully by God, like Krissie and Zach, are privileged to go to Heaven so early in life. We don't always understand why He calls some so soon but – your time will come later. God still has things for you to do here."

He solemnly nodded his head. How he missed his little mother-hen sister. But he still believed God knew best. My faith had been tossed about like a rag doll in a pit bull's jaws, at times barely coming out intact. Yet – Toby's held firm. I tenderly laced my fingers with his.

A little child shall lead them.

I sat there beside him, holding his limp hand, until his lids drooped in slumber.

"Let's have another baby, Janeece." Kirk moved to stand behind me at the sink and slid his strong arms around me as I drained the water out and wiped the surface dry.

This wasn't a new topic. Had been batted around for days, in fact. Initially, I'd not thought Kirk would persevere, that his urge to procreate, as other phases of grief, would pass. But when Heather and Toby joined him in his persuasion efforts, I began to slowly relent. First, I had to neutralize the obstacle between conception and me: apprehension.

Complications during and following Toby's birth still haunted me. A possible recurrence of allergic drug reactions, muscle problems and resultant post-partum depression spooked me. But I'd been thinking more and more about Lamaze, the new natural childbirth procedure I'd used eruditely during my three previous labors. The process would eliminate scary threats.

I turned into Kirk's arms and gazed up at him, allowing the image of procreation to stir anticipation within me. "If you'll locate a Lamaze clinic within traveling distance, I'll do it."

Kirk's gratitude glimmered from green depths for a long moment before he reverently took my face in his hands and kissed me "Thank you, honey."

Two days later, Sunday, Tillie Dawson ambushed to me as I entered the church sanctuary. "I've found a Lamaze clinic, Neecy," she bubbled, gripping my hands so tightly my fingers tingled. "Doctor Jennings does Lamaze at Summerville Medical Center." I didn't mind that Kirk had incorporated others to search out a solution. Was, in fact, glad. Because now, I felt a surge of something closer to joy than I'd felt in weeks.

Another sentiment regenerated: *anticipation.* Sometime in the wee hours, I'd lain awake thinking about Krissie's maternal leanings, so obvious in her love of babies and her ability to calm unruly children with softly spoken words and a smile. Few little ones could resist her charm.

"You're a natural born mother, Krissie." How many times I'd told her that and seen her beaming response. How I'd looked forward to sharing her joy of motherhood. *So much left undone....*

"Mama, I don't know if I want to be a missionary anymore. I want lots and lots of kids and kids might not like growing up in Africa."

In those twilight hours, a higher wisdom came to me: a new life would fill our family's need to love and be loved. And while Krissie could not be replaced, the small life brought forth could, in a sense, replace the child she was not privileged to bear.

This would not only be our child: It would also be Krissie's baby.

Insemination posed no problem. Within six weeks, I bore symptoms of pregnancy. On one level, I exulted in bearing this new life, my focus trance-like in purpose, moving through the initial nausea that racked me round the clock, never complaining, glorying in it because the chemical change would, eventually, deliver a babe into my arms to hold and croon to. The craving to love and be loved leaped into being and was as instinctive as my next breath. It burned in my bosom.

On another level entirely, I remained as gaunt and numb as the day Krissie left us. The zombie-me neutralized all anxieties in tandem with childbearing. A strange coupling it was, the Zombie and the Zealot, one at which, in retrospect, I've marveled. This mystical coalition, in the end, carted me to fruition.

While the Zombie remained the *in control* part of my psyche, the Zealot posed a whole new set of quandaries. During fecundation, my hormones soared and raged and demanded *touch and feel.* My skin screamed for Kirk's slightest brush of flesh, a desire that, previously, would have delighted him. Only now, breeding complete, his libido took a nosedive.

"It's not you, Neecy. I desire you more than ever," he whispered to me time after time, tears glimmering in the silver glow of night. "Grief has affected me, too. Only thing is – I can't perform and you can." He would hold me then, not realizing that just the touch of his skin sent me into spirals of clawing *want*.

When I'd groan and pull myself from his grasp, his tortured, "I'm so *sorry*, honey," cut straight into my heart.

I understood. But perception did not assuage the piercing, gnawing sexual hunger inside me for the next nine months, and there were times, in the wee hours, when war raged over *which* was the more responsible for my silent tears: sorrow or desire.

Our friends Callie and Moose joined the church choir and I was delighted to discover that Cal was a marvelous contralto soprano. Her strong voice supported the soprano section so well the females fairly preened over their new sound. And while Moose's baritone wasn't as forceful as Callie's, it helped drown out Nick Clemmon's off-key caterwauling.

Nick – my inheritance – was of the family clan who believed fully in blood being thicker'n water. Asking him to leave was tantamount to treason. I wasn't about to challenge them on it.

So before my choir did special selections, I asked God to sorta adjust the electronic and human sound systems so only harmony was heard. A tall request, even for the Almighty. But I persisted, clutching the hem of his garment, at times certain I was dragged along behind Him wailing and pleading while He moved ahead to see to more critical issues. He took pity on me and, apparently, blocked out *some* of the dissonance because invitations to perform at numerous civic and church functions continued to pour in.

Then, before Sunday afternoon Homecoming festivities at nearby Pleasant Brook Baptist Church, God answered my SOS in another way. "What is it, Nick?" I asked, concerned about his pale, distressful face.

"I'm sorry – but I can't help you today. His golden eyes were as mournful as a cocker spaniel's. "I got laryngitis," he announced in a squeaky croak. "I can't sing a *lick!*"

"I'm sorry, too, Nick," I said, surprised that I meant it. "Tell you what," I leaned close and whispered, "Come on with us and just move your lips while we sing."

His face brightened. "Think we'll fool 'em?"

"I'm sure we will."

We did.

Sarah Beauregard planted herself before me in the vestibule as parishioners swept past to speak to the robed pastor outside on the white sun-washed portico. I had not been swift or smart enough to dodge the encounter and so, resigned myself with lips stretched into my pastor's wife smile.

Sarah's rheumatic, scarlet-tipped talons seized my wrist as she inclined herself forward until her nose almost met mine and my torso instinctively curved away. Beady eyes glittered, belying her softly spoken words, "You know, Miz Crenshaw, this baby you're carrying won't take the place of Krissie."

My smile instantly dissolved and my gaze narrowed. "I never entertained the thought that Krissie could be replaced."

Her black gaze slanted, as in skeptical and as in disparage. "And it might not be a girl – I know you're hoping for one. I'd just *hate* to see you disappointed."

Anger, pure and blazing white, shot through me. Why, she'd be *delighted* to see me disappointed, over *anything*. I wrenched my wrist free, stepped back and spoke so fervently the words came out on a *hiss*. "Of all people, *I know* my Krissie could never be replaced." I took a deep breath, opened my mouth to say *"How dare you!"* then clamped it shut. No use causing a scene, especially when several folk, seeing my stricken features, had slowed to eavesdrop.

I considered my Christian position and the scriptural *woe* unto those who caused a little one to stumble. I'd long ago suspected that most converts freeze into that *little one* phase for an interminable length of time. Few advanced to maturity until donkey-kicked by the devil so many times they figured – *duh!* – it's wise to climb on up. I stepped back, composed my features into a sickly mime of patience and managed a passable exit line. "Thank you for your – *concern*. Please, excuse me," I said, then abruptly turned and hightailed a distance between myself and the bearer of angst.

I was halfway across the church lawn, aimed for the parsonage, when Kaye Tessner caught my sleeve. "Neecy – wait up," she huffed breathlessly from her sprint.

I stopped and turned to face her, barely controlling my tears of indignation and hurt.

"I heard everything," Kaye said and took me in her arms. "That ol' *biddy*," she growled. "I just knew she was up to something, waylaying you like that."

I clamped my teeth together to stem threatening tears. I would *not* allow that woman to reduce me to blubbering. "I'm okay," I gave her a wobbly smile, "But thanks, Kaye."

"Hey," she narrowed her silvery-gray eyes, "if she says anything else like that to you, just let me know. I'll straighten her out." All the while, her slender nurse's fingers gently rubbed my arms and her porcelain features, framed by loose mahogany curls, looked absolutely angelic to me in that moment.

"Hey, Neecy!" Callie swaggered comically up to us. "How about our choir special, huh! Did we pin that number or *what?*" She first gave me a big *five*, then Kaye.

"*You* nailed it, Callie," Kaye captured her hand and held onto it knowing by now that Cal slipped away as gustily as she came on. "You should make a tape. You're *good*, girl."

"Aww, go on." Callie pulled her hand loose, shuffled her feet and looked away.

"I can't believe you're blushing." I laughed and hugged her. "You should, you know."

"What?" Callie's gaze kicked back to mine, chocolate eyes wide.

"Cut a tape."

"*Stop it*, you two!" She turned on her heel and retreated, shaking her loosely waved ebony mane, muttering, "quit that." I had to grin at Cal, the ol' hooligan's newfound modesty.

"*Chicken!*" I yelled after her, drawing some curious looks from stragglers but for once, didn't care. I was having fun and it felt good.

"What?" she shot me a slit-eyed appraisal over her shoulder.

"Fried," I called nonchalantly, hugged Kaye 'bye' and turned for home.

I heard Cal's footsteps fall in with mine. "Thanks for the invitation."

I linked my arm to hers, sliding into our yoke of familiarity. To heck with Sarah's sorry-placed banality.

"You're welcome."

I'd known pregnancy's hormonal terrain would stretch my equanimity, but knowledge did not prepare me for the abruptness with which it came. Within weeks, surging chemical highs and lows jerked me around like MawMaw's first agitator washing machine, churning my mood from serenity to ballistic in a moment's span. And yet, the tiny ember nestling inside my womb fed my will to get on with the future. Not every second and not on every level, but the conscious-me finally grabbed a fragile lifeline.

Overall, everybody was pleased that Kirk and I expected another addition to our family. Outside Sarah's insensitive remark, only my father appeared apprehensive. It surfaced during a visit.

"I can't *believe* you actually shut down that shop of yours," I shrieked and flung myself into his arms when he showed up with Anne on my doorsteps one Friday night. "Law, what's gon' happen?"

"They'll wait on me. Least, most of 'em will," he kissed the top of my head as I squeezed his lanky ribcage and blissfully shut my eyes. "Anyway, they know all about what you've gone through and I'd been telling them I was planning on sneaking off one weekend."

"C'mon in, I'm cooking supper – hope you can eat spaghetti, Daddy." It wasn't his favorite entree by a long shot. He was a bona-fide meat and potatoes man, my Dad, actually light on the meat and long on veggies. Mainly because it lay easier on his sensitive stomach, a trait passed on to at least half his kids.

"Long as it don't have too much hot stuff in it, else it'll bother my stomach."

"No hot stuff a'tall. Only a speck of Worcestershire sauce." A couple tablespoons. "I don't tolerate chili powder too much myself, you know." Lordy, talk about two peas in a pod. I was a mite uneasy with all the similarities surfacing. "Especially now."

He drew himself up to his slender six-foot-one and peered down at me. "You all right?"

His concern sorta ruffled my insulation. Ordinarily, it would've been comforting, but now, it bordered on prying. And censor.

"Daddy, you don't seem too happy about the baby," I mumbled, turning away to stir the sauce, fighting the danged angst that hovered like a vulture over a still warm carcass.

"I'm just worried about *you*, Neecy, is all. You're not real strong right now and –" he shrugged and gave a lop-sided Daddy rendition of a pained grin, "you know me. I worry because you've always been a bit frail." He put his arm around my shoulder as I stood at my stove, adding a bit more salt and garlic powder, wanting to bristle at his claim but knowing any illusion of a pink-cheeked, robust self-image had been blown to smithereens by a host of allergies from hay fever to hives.

Still... "I'm not *that* fragile, Daddy. I've already had three kids, you know." My words were gentle, yet firm.

"I know. I know. In some ways, Neecy, you're one of the strongest people I know. The bravest. But – you'll always be my little girl, honey. And I want you to know that I'm tickled as can be about the new baby." He gazed solemnly at me. "You know that, don't you?" he asked gently.

I nodded, emotions swirling like snowflakes in a blizzard... the little girl inside me trying to override the woman planted at the helm.

He patted my shoulder and gave me a Walter Matthau no-nonsense appraisal. "Just take care o' yourself, y'hear?"

I could handle that. "Yep." I hugged him hugely until Lynette tackled me around my thickening waist for her portion of hugs. My baby sis' russet tendrils and periwinkle eyes were so *Anne* it took my breath. "Law, chile, you're growing up. What a heartbreaker you're gon' be."

"Can I play with Krissie's Barbies?" she asked, knowing that should she ask, she could get my last nickel.

"Sure, Sweetheart." I took off down the hall to pull the toys from Krissie's top closet shelf. I couldn't bear to part with them. Just the week before, Kaye Tessner had offered to help me pack up Krissie's things.

"I can't, Kaye." I'd fought the urge to explain myself, but the misery must have shone through.

"Hey, honey, I'm sorry." Kaye hugged me. "I understand. I just thought you might – well, some folks say it's easier if you get rid of the reminders. What do they know?"

"There *is* no *easier*, Kaye. Trust me."

Kaye nodded, pushed a limp hair strand from my cheek and smiled. She was so sweet. So understanding. And she'd been there for me every waking hour. That day, she took me to eat at Pete's Drive-In, where we scarfed down our favorite grilled chicken livers – with sweet coleslaw and golden crisp fries – a friendship ritual that barred any mention of a cholesterol payday up ahead.

"Sure you're not trying to make me fat?" I teased.

Kay didn't smile. "You still got a way to go to filling out those hollow cheeks, Neece."

I sighed and ate another fry. I did look gaunt, even to myself. Despite my expanding waistline.

Tonight, Daddy's presence secured me as nothing else recent had. Cole lounged with Heather in her room, quietly sharing peer experiences, while Toby and Lynette dubbed voices for dolls vacationing in Barbie's two-story Dream Country Home. Dale, quieter than usual, hung out with us 'old' folks, usually within my elbow distance. I knew he missed Krissie dreadfully and while I was not her, I was his closest connection to her. We all hugged and touched spontaneously, healing one another with affection.

On Saturday, we piled into cars and drove into Charleston to dine at Bessinger's Buffet. whose specialty is a wonderful barbecue hash. There, we ran into Moose, Roxie and Callie. Singing in the choir together had forged a tentative bond between the two females, while their statuesque-ness fashioned yet another. There, all similarity ended. A good thing, too, because too much would have caused a nuclear clash. As it was, they tolerated each other. So, understandably, I was delighted to see them together and insisted long tables be joined to seat them with our party, which, with the addition, now numbered an even dozen.

When I went for seconds of the sinfully rich sweet potato soufflé – Bessingers' has the silkiest I've ever spooned into my mouth – Callie shadowed me and whispered, "Have you heard Sarah's latest gossip?"

I turned to gaze at her, my heart doing a spiral dive. "No. What?" Curiosity only slightly overrode dread.

"Says Tillie's husband Rick is running around."

"Oh, no. Please don't say that." My pulse shot into syncopation. I dolloped a spoonful of yams onto my plate. "But – you can't believe everything Sarah says." It came out weak because while I could attest to Sarah's being a cocklebur in the seat of one's pants, her truthfulness bordered on brutal.

"She told me it came straight from the horse's mouth." Callie slanted me a dubious look. "*Whoever* the horse is, I can't say."

"You didn't ask?" *Now why did I say that?* Cal's black eyes sparkled.

"Nah." She brushed past me to get some rice and hash gravy. "I didn't give her the satisfaction."

Oh Lord. What were we dealing with here? Tillie was such a – precious, *kind* person. A bit zany, true. But – *Stop it, Janice Crenshaw.* Do-not-believe-gossip. A husband as good as Rick Dawson would never do such a thing. I loaded up on just a tiny second portion of zesty smoked barbecue pork and resolutely put the thing behind me.

Sunday morning at the Crenshaws was an old Marx Brother's movie, while bathroom use was musical chairs and hot water *obsolete* by the time my nausea subsided enough for me to stagger into the shower. Cool water tingled over my ever-hot skin, bringing me around and finally, refreshing me. Strangely, all that went on inside and around me during those days sorta bypassed my brain. I couldn't then and still do not, years later, understand the invisible bubble that enclosed me or the segmentation that rewired me so I became someone entirely different.

One part of conscious-me stood aside while the physical-me hung my head over the toilet bowl to vomit up my insides. For once, my delicate, oh-so-sensitive mind overrode my body.

At times, I look back and yearn for that plane of existence. But it doesn't come by a snap of the finger nor upon meditating and the price for it was too, too great.

At that time, however, it saved my sanity and gained me a new start. A new dawn.

That, I decided, was to be my baby's name.

Dawn.

"Heavenly Father...hear us as we pray...here at thine altar, on our wedding day...."

The song, a prayer, floated effortlessly from Callie's mouth. Her rich contralto soothed and convinced me that Moose's marbles just might still be intact. Roxie, a virginal dream in white – if one's gaze didn't stray below her mini-skirt hem – actually looked at him as she vowed to "love and to cherish you from this day forward." I wanted so much to believe she spoke the truth.

My solo "If" was done between the prayer and ring vows.

Poor Moose cried through the whole thing, obviously daft over his 'pretty thang.' I still couldn't get a clear read from the new Mrs. McElrath but decided since she was now Moose's other half, I'd just have to get past any misgivings. She had, after all, attended church regularly for months and should, in her new status, be considered family. Anything less would be an affront to Moose, something Kirk and I would avoid at all costs.

The following weeks propelled me swiftly toward the college choral Spring Concert. Ensemble rehearsals, coupled with Solomon Methodist Church's upcoming Easter Cantata, kept me too busy to dwell for long intervals on our family's loss. Both musical presentations required one hundred percent, snapping into play the perfectionism seed burrowed deep inside me – one that needed only purpose to explode into a living, panting being – one whose force astounded me at times. It kept me busy. It kept me from thinking too much.

Kirk seemed as driven as I. At night, we both slid from Zealot to Zombie, collapsing into bed to drown in exhaustion. "I never dream," my husband told me one morning as we lay in each other's arms after I relayed the Technicolor scenes I'd moved through during sleep.

He sighed sadly. "I wish I *could* see Krissie in dreams. I envy you...."

"Don't. The searching part leaves me – gutted." In that instant, I envied his cocoon that kept unpleasantness at bay.

Seemed denial – or numbing-out – was second nature to Kirk. A perpetually accessible thing that needed no summons. How could two people, who shared a bed and children, be so different?

Old-fashioned Sunday brought out hitched-wagons, a rainbow of long gingham costumes, top hats, string-ties and enough kids' overalls to blast Oshkosh stock to Mars.

"Oh my –" I snatched little Raquel from her mama and snuggled her beneath the hood of her bonnet, kissing her fat little jowls. "You look just like your Mommy," I cooed. And she did.

"Hey – don't let Rick hear that," Tillie gave her jerky, donkey-bray laugh. "He says he *did* have a small hand in getting her here."

"Course he did." I glanced around and saw Rick's handsome blonde head towering above kinfolk scattered over the church lawn. He looked grand in his long black coat and Abe Lincoln hat. *Thank God*, I silently prayed for the umpteenth time, Sarah's gossip held no water.

Tillie's Hershey eyes sparkled as she leaned to cup her hand and whisper loudly in my ear, scattering goosebumps over me, "I tell Rick her little butt is *exactly* like his. You oughta see that big ol' grin spread over his face!" She reared back to gauge my reaction, gurgling all the time. "Oh!" her fringed eyes rounded, "I've got a surprise for you."

"Hey, Mama! C'mere!" Tillie called to Zelda Diggers, who was the antithesis of her sprightly daughter. Tall and lumbering of gait, Zelda's dull clay-colored eyes and flat expression gave no hint that she'd parented Tillie Dawson. As she plodded toward us, her long brown skirt and sunbonnet reminded me of a boxy-pup tent. I blinked away the uncomplimentary image, feeling guilty and instantly froze my features into my preacher's wife smile because, for some reason, I did not feel comfortable around Zelda Diggers. Despite Tillie's abounding adoration of the woman and her unfailing efforts to get her mom to accommodate the preacher's family, Zelda remained distant.

Tillie hugged her hugely then gushed. "Did you do one of your carrot cakes that Neecy likes so much, Mama?"

I cringed at the blatant expectancy but quickly covered by giving Raquel a loving shift of hip-position.

"Naw," Zelda's bonnet flopped in the breeze, revealing stubbornly straight apricot-tinted bangs above her plain, unfeeling features, "I done a Mississippi mud cake." I saw Tillie's face fall. I averted my gaze. Without another word, Zelda pried Raquel from my arms and retreated to her husband, who huddled with relatives across the lawn.

I mentally shook my head, wondering again how this quiet, rather handsome man was ever attracted to such an uncomely, surly woman. Alton Driggers' genetic legacy to Tillie was all that stood between her and stark homeliness. There, his bequest ended. I've yet to determine the source of Tillie's warmth and charisma and unflappable spirit.

Zelda was – as Tillie and I both knew – well aware of my allergy to her walnut-loaded treat, had been since I'd broken out in hives after ingesting two slices following a homecoming feast.

But, hey! I'd long ago accepted that the world did not revolve around Janeece Whitman Crenshaw. Had not, in fact, ever expected it to. I just hated to see my little peacenik friend's efforts so callously elbowed aside.

Tillie's thick lashes blinked a couple of times before she screwed up her mouth and looked at me, clearly apologetic. "I made an egg custard for you, Neecy?" She steepled her clasped hands to her flat bosom in supplication.

I burst out laughing. "Thank you, Tillie."

"You're probably the only one brave enough to sample –"

"Don't forget Toby," I reminded her.

Her irrepressible giggles spilled over the day like warm Pepsi fizz. "Toby rarely turns down *any* desserts, regardless of their source, *Neecy!*" She playfully poked a finger in my rib.

"That's beside the point, my star second-soprano." I looped arms with her and headed for the choir room, mildly surprised – no, *pleased* that I'd finally begun to develop a thicker hide.

In late April, Possum Creek Methodist Church called Kirk to assist in Ma McKonna's funeral. We made the long sad pilgrimage to Oconee County, the four of us, and wept with those to whom we would forever remain bonded by experiences both euphoric and devastating. Years later, I still marvel at love's adhesive force between flock and clergy family.

The following week, out of the blue, I got a call from Chuck. My brother spoke as though we'd not been estranged over the year – though he had shown up at Krissie's funeral. I hadn't heard from him since. Strange, what with all that was happening to me, it didn't matter. I'd ceased needing Chuck. He knew I was pregnant, via Anne during a recent phone call, when he'd divulged that he and Teresa had separated. More and more, Anne was *Mama* to us all. I reassured him my pregnancy was progressing normally and then he dropped a bombshell.

"I got diabetes, Sis," he said as though relating the weather.

"Oh no, Chuck...dear Lord. How bad?"

"I'm on insulin shots. But, hey! That's okay. I've learned how to give 'em myself. Nothing to it." Above all things, like his sister, Chuck hated pity.

Strobe images flashed through my head of the disease's destructive path – Mama's early death, Uncle Gabe's health struggles.... But at that precise moment, my brother needed encouragement and support.

"You're tough, Chuck. You'll be okay." *Please God.*

"Got that right, Sis."

"Does Dad know?"

"Nah. No use in setting everybody off. Hey – I'll be off these shots in no time."

"Sure you will. Thanks for being here when Krissie died. It was comforting."

"You okay?" Fatherhood had focused Chuck in miraculous ways.

"I have my moments." I sighed. "Quite a few of them, in fact. But staying busy helps."

"Yeah. That helps. Listen –" Another moment of silence. "If you need me, just call. I might not be able to travel because of my job, but I'm as near as your phone. Okay?"

"I might just take you up on that. Love you, Chuck."

"Yeah. Me, too."

We hung up and I reflected on Chuck's recent legal separation from Teresa, whom I'd never really gotten to know. I'd always wondered if she really loved Chuck. Her aloofness – somewhat like Roxie's – troubled me. Whatever had happened, my tight-mouthed brother wasn't about to reveal. He had visiting rights with Poogie, as he called his adolescent daughter Patrice, who now lived in upstate Greenville with her mother. Which was why, according to Chuck, he'd moved there as well.

"Changing jobs was nothing. I'd'a moved heaven and earth to be near Poogie. Not much left for me without my little girl," he'd revealed during one of his rare somber moments. Now, to be hit with diabetes. I shook my head and dove into straightening up the den, sorting out papers and notes and stacking textbooks, trying to come to grips with yet another loved one's unkind fate.

How *much* I understood his grief for his child. My sorrow merged with his and I found myself outside, cresting the back lawn's hill, heart racing to my sacred spot of solace. There, I hugged the tall pole whose banner still swayed under a balmy breeze. Toby's labors, though slowed, still kept the pond rippling with six to eight inches of water.

Tears streaked my cheeks and dripped from my chin.

Oh, God – *please help my brother.*

"I'm nervous," Tillie squeezed my arm with icy fingers and did a little bouncing jig as the choir filed into the loft, making her robe vibrate comically. I put my arms around her, listening for Kirk's cue to begin the Easter Cantata.

"Tillie – your solo is the most beautiful song on the program and –"

"That doesn't help at *all, Neecy,"* she whispered, brown eyes round as donuts and nearly as big.

"Okay, just open your mouth and let 'er fly when your time comes. Just be Tillie." I dramatically pressed my hand to her forehead, squeezed my eyes shut, threw back my head and said, "*O-o-oh*, Lord – give Tillie courage! *Ye-es and hallelujah!* She needs it! Amen."

A gusty giggle trailed her as she filed into the front row.

Kirk's voice, beyond the heavy crimson velvet curtain, ceased and I took my place on the choir loft's low platform, checked the score on my music stand and picked up my small baton, a newly acquired thing. In the past, I'd done quite well without one. I'd learned in Music Theory 102 to imagine that water dripped from my fingertips as my hand, an extension of a fluid wrist, beat out time. But I'd gone along with Kirk's advice to use it and had only recently learned of Sarah Beauregard's suggestion to Kirk that I would appear more proficient with a wand.

Anything to please, I always said, trying this time not to begrudge compromise.

Tonight, I rapped on the stand to bring my choristers to attention. The curtains behind me silently parted to reveal the white and purple robed chorale standing at adrenaline-charged alertness, eyeing me like hawks ready to swoop in on prey. I silently prayed a quick imploration that Nick's exuberance not exceed the team's volume and that Tillie would blink and expel that hypnotized glassy-stare.

Aw, heck, I raised my baton and both arms, *it's all yours, God.*

Down came the baton and Heather's fingers flew over the piano keys in a classical introduction to *Crown Him with Many Crowns.* Dixie's thundering organ accompaniment added majesty and pageantry to the old hymn as the choir sang the first two verses with somber dignity, then, to everybody's delight, launched into the third with syncopated contemporary swing. The mood lightened and by song's end, had toes tapping and heads bobbing in time. The program continued with Charlie Tessner's solo *Were You There When they Crucified my Lord?* I winked at Donna, whose pride in her brother bypassed deadpan features to shine through her eyes. Next came a medley of *Blessed Redeemer*, *Near the Cross* and *Glory to His Name.* By now, we were warmed up and going strong. Anointed, Aunt Mary would declare.

Tillie moved to stand beside Callie and Moose for the trio selection *Because He Lives.* I saw her hand tremble as she took the microphone and when our gazes met, I gave her a big smile. She straightened and began singing in a clear smooth voice, "God sent his so-o-n, they called him Je-e-sus...." On the chorus, Callie's alto and Moose's tenor mellowed out the melody and drew tears. On the last verse, the entire choir joined in and...

What was that sound? I angled my right ear and – *oh no! Nick.*

Nick's rust-gray head was tossed back in euphoric abandon and his caterwauling grew louder and louder... *"And then as death, gives way to vi-ic-tory...I'll see the lights of glo-o-ry and I know He li-ives!"*

Tillie's startled chocolate orbs implored me, *"Do something!"*

I gazed up to Heaven. *Lord, please.....*

Nick gazed up to Heaven, too, and burst into tears, falling gloriously silent as tears riveted his lined cheeks. The last chorus swelled in praise to our celebrated Lord and my weak knees flexed and set themselves for the big finale, which recapped the beginning – a majestic, rousing rendition of *Crown Him with Many Crowns.* By now, Nick boo-hooed as unrestrained as he sang and my baton did battle for preeminence, its tip a fanning, dancing lariat whose circumference grew and grew until, stunned, I watched it fly through the air and hit Moose smack in the face. I only missed two beats before my fingertips flung imaginary water all over the rostrum, while Tillie burst into giggles and the entire choir sang with grins as wide as possum road-kill.

The baton mysteriously disappeared the very next day.

Friday of the following week marked the college choral group's Spring Concert. I was surprised when, on the evening of our performance, I was nearly as excited as my singing peers.

Toby's interest in another baby was becoming – well, a bit strained. Oh, he'd not resisted the idea at first, had sorta flowed with Heather's enthusiasm. But as time passed, his excitement waned. I sensed he did not like to discuss this little stranger who would, in a few months time, usurp his cozy *family baby* rank.

Heather, on the other hand, was beside herself with joy, pampering me shamelessly, massaging my back, legs and feet with lotion. Dawn's first movements were celebrated with tears of elation while my teenage daughter's fingertips gently pressed and probed. And as my abdomen rounded and swelled until I no longer saw my toes, Heather gave me pedicures, painting my toenails bright, sassy colors.

In July, Toby's sole comment was, "You're getting kinda fat, aren't you, Mom?"

I hugged him every chance I got and spent time with him, hoping to dispel any hovering insecurities. In late July, we vacationed in the mountains of North Carolina. At six a.m. on the second day, I awoke and surveyed from my hotel window a golden sun slowly climb up over the purple Smoky Mountain range. I'd thought this change of scenery would make me forget.

It didn't. Tears puddled, then coursed down my cheeks. *Ahh, Krissie...I miss you so.*

I felt Kirk's arms slide around me from behind. His cheek pressed against mine and our tears mingled. We shared silent moments of memory before Toby bounded from the other bedroom, ready for some adventure.

"We gon' go to Ghost Town?" he asked, plundering an Oreo Cookie bag.

I wiped my cheeks and turned. "After lunch. The park doesn't open till threeish."

Toby gazed at me dubiously. "You not throwin' up, are you, Mama?"

"No." My smile reassured him his fun was not thwarted.

Heather and Dixie, her buddy, roused from their comatose slumber only after Kirk lured them with promises of the grandest breakfast of a lifetime at nearby Ma's Restaurant. A meal of sausage gravy and buttermilk biscuits launched us on a tour of Maggie Valley gift shops. In one, I bought an oversized T-shirt emblazoned with mountain flowers for Callie. Kirk selected Moose a book of Redneck Jokes, then suggested I pick out something for Roxie. I finally settled on a little cedar jewelry box. I wanted to buy something for Kaye Tessner, but Kirk frowned.

"You can't do for one church member what you can't for all, honey." We'd already established that our lifelong pals did not fit neatly into the 'church-folk' slot.

"I know." I sighed, wishing life were different but knowing it simply could not be.

"Hey," Kirk slapped another five dollar bill into Heather's extended palm, "that's *it*. I can't fork out for everybody and his cousin, Heather. You're gonna have to limit the gifts to a couple of friends. Okay?" We'd also decided to cut the kids some slack along the way, since their childhood was tied up almost exclusively with 'church folk'.

Heather nodded as she turned away. She half-heartedly rolled her eyes but trudged on ahead with Dixie to the next shop, fully aware of her father's generosity.

Kirk draped his arm around me as we trailed the girls and Toby, who loped along people-gaping.

"I saw Brad Chisholm last week." Kirk said off-handedly. Brad was a local attorney with whom we'd discussed a lawsuit against Coastal Railway. I'd felt strongly that had there been a stop-gate at the trestle entrance, Krissie's tragedy would not have happened. Still did.

"I still resent Homer Beauregard's interference," I said, feeling my hackles begin to rise.

Kirk's hand tightened on my shoulder as we walked. "I know. But – many of these folks do have family who work for Coastal."

"*Heaven help us*," I hissed sarcastically. "I *know*. The *clan* has spoken." I resented that Homer Beauregard didn't hesitate for a moment to appeal to the pastor to not sue because of longtime family ties with the railroad. I hated then and still do the fact that folk will put pastors under bondage they wouldn't dare impose on themselves or anyone else. A sort of spiritual blackmail. A *prove yourself* thing. It wasn't *Homer's* child who'd been lured onto a seemingly innocuous ramp, then slaughtered.

I closed my eyes for a moment, then breathed deeply. "If Krissie had seen anything that said *STOP-Danger*, especially with a gate forcing her to crawl under, she'd *never* have gotten on that ramp. Why – she wouldn't even completely shut the bathroom door for fear it would stick and entrap her. You know that, Kirk."

"I know. It's not fair," Kirk said quietly. "But I *do* have an obligation to the flock. And – money won't bring Krissie back."

"No," I said, "but insisting that Coastal put up those gates would ensure no one else's child would get trapped like Krissie and Zach did."

"Well, it's too late to rehash it. We settled with the railroad."

"For a pittance. What's ten thousand dollars in the face of our Krissie's death? *Nothing.* Not counting potential tragedies as a result of the railroad's neglect to install those gates."

"I agree. But it's out of our hands now, honey. As Brad said, we didn't have the resources to fight Coastal. They have the finances and the lawyers to fight spending what it takes to install those gates everywhere. It boils down to money. According to Brad, if we'd sued, the case would be tied up in litigation till Jesus comes and nothing would be accomplished anyway. We never had a chance."

It was true. Besides, I didn't want Coastal Railway's money. What I wanted couldn't be had.

I wanted Krissie.

I took the next semester off. Kirk and I began Lamaze classes at Summerville Medical Center in October. Up until then, I'd mostly seen my midwife Marjorie Wellon, a young married woman, whose intuitive care and knowledge amazed and calmed me. Now, Dr. Jennings added a touch of paternal care by seeing me every other visit.

With extra time on my hands during Heather and Toby's school hours, I busied myself with projects. Since Krissie's death, the importance of family photos shot right up there beside oxygen. I purchased endless bound albums and filled them from boxes stacked on closet shelves. One featured Krissie, another, Heather and another, Toby. I meticulously labeled and filed them. Once done, I immediately searched for something else to consume my time.

And my mind.

My body thickened and slowed, limiting my busy-ness. Then agony set in. My abdominal muscles gave way and pressure from the baby caused excruciating cramps and pain in my back and legs. I was bedridden most of the time. Other times, I only managed to get to the bathroom by crawling. Kirk begged me to let him carry me. I explained that it wouldn't help. I had to let the baby's weight – lodged against my sciatic nerve – drop forward to relieve teeth gnashing when I moved. This could only be accomplished by crawling on all fours.

When I went in for check-ups, Marjorie met me at the car with a wheelchair.

My hormones were still crazy and my moodiness settled down to 'low' melancholy and 'high' melancholy. Only difference being that I could function a bit more with the high. Weepiness plunged me from high to low in a wink. Yet – it was an automatic process, a chemical entity not connected to my thinking.

Pregnancy was but another reminder of Krissie. I grew desperate to reach a place of refuge, one that *"time will help"* had promised. Where the terrible longing would abate to bearable. Seemed the only thing time did was to separate me from my child's *being* and torment me with her *non-being*. A deep, deep part of me wailed at the inhumane deprivation.

Another part of me thanked God for what I had left.

For at least a month after our warm bedtime talk, Toby daily carried water to Krissie's pond, as soft sand rather quickly soaked it up. Of course, I knew this could not continue indefinitely. As his 'do something' grief phase ebbed, Krissie's little pond eventually dried up. Toby moved on to yet other healing and acceptance stages.

For months, I allowed the banner and the rough-hewn bridge to remain on our yard's secluded back corner. I couldn't bring myself to part with it. Rain faded the letters and the wood began to crumble, but the message remained alive. Time passed, and it continued to comfort me.

Late one warm October afternoon, during a short respite from the horrible muscle spasms, I stood on the ramp in the silence. And then birdsong penetrated my haze, sweetly transporting me to a plane of peace. I knew in that moment that though Toby's grief was not always as visible, his tribute to Krissie surpassed all others. I knew also that his gift extended to me.

If Toby could turn loose, so could I. A soft breeze ruffled my hair and drew my damp face upward. I looked beyond the tall pines into frothy white clouds and infinite blue.

I realized this visit to the pond would be my last.

Because I knew what Toby, with a child's simplicity, already knew: in the Lord, we never truly lose someone we love. Their essence remains forever in our hearts.

I placed a hand over the growing mound inside me. *This is your baby, my sweet daughter.*

I blew a kiss and whispered. "I love you, Krissie." I turned and walked away.

PART THREE
1975-80

CHAPTER TWELVE

Dawn's birth created a royal Crenshaw stir. On the drive home from the hospital, my swaddled infant swished to and fro, the prize in Heather and Toby's tug-of-war. Kirk kept sliding me warm glances. "Thank God, you got through the delivery okay, honey," he said so quietly only I heard him.

I knew he referred to the moment in the labor room when I'd whispered to him that I felt my heart had nearly stopped during the last contraction. I still remembered how his face, already pale, had blanched even more when he took both my hands in his and squeezed them, tears shimmering in his eyes.

"I wanna hold 'er, Mama," Toby wailed at yet another Heather victory.

"Why don't you pass her up here to me, Heather?" I asked wearily, taking charge of the newborn for the remainder of the drive.

Home never looked more beautiful nor smelled more heavenly of nourishment.

"The church ladies prepared lunch today," Kirk announced as we entered the foyer.

"Mmm." I inhaled appreciatively. "I'm as hungry as –"

In a flash, Heather snatched the baby from my grasp and bounded down the hall. Her door slammed, followed by a solid *click*. Toby's eyes narrowed in comprehension and he flew into delayed reaction.

For the next hour, while Kirk and I enjoyed a delicious lunch, Toby banged on Heather's door, shrieking that she relinquish her 'hostage.'

Heather, being Heather, took her own sweet time getting acquainted with her little sis.

Coastal springtime, when azaleas in raging colors invade the lowland, provided a high for me that year. At five months, plump little Dawn's dark thatch was irresistible to my fingers and nose. Her arrival reinstated our former sibling quota, but with Krissie's vibrant, loving personality missing, the whole complexion of our family had shifted. Not augmented or diminished. Just different. It took some getting used to.

"Now I know why God makes women mothers in their younger years, Kaye," I told my friend during our weekly drive-in feast of grilled chicken livers. We sat in her car, windows lowered. "Energy level, between ages eighteen and thirty-two years, sinks like a concrete-weighted Mafia hit."

"You're by no means *older.*" Kaye *tch-tchded* and fed Dawn – ensconced in infant seat between us – a bite of French fry, then chortled at the wrinkled little pug nose and reemergence of mushed potato.

"True," I conceded, catching Dawn's drooly reject in a napkin. "But some experiences propel folks past their actual years."

I was, emotionally, infinitely older than in early 1974.

"Kaye," I looked at her through sudden tears, "Krissie's vacancy in my heart will always be."

"I know." Her steady gaze moistened.

"But now – the baby's crooked grins and belly laughs make me smile. There are hurts to soothe and a little one's needs that keep me too busy to think."

My little one's loud burp intruded upon the moment's solemnity.

"See?" I spread my hands and we burst into laughter.

"By the way," Kaye's face sobered. "I'm worried about Tillie."

Kaye confirmed what I'd noticed in recent months. "I know. There's something not quite – right lately."

"Exactly."

Tillie's exuberance had fizzled. During choir activities, she seemed somewhere else. And though she didn't exactly avoid me, she no longer reached out. So out of character.

"I'll give her a call," I promised. "Right away."

"Rick wants me to get a job." Tillie's voice, an octave below her usual squeaky pitch, sounded as though coming from a damaged tape. "And, Neecy – I don't want to leave Raquel."

"Then don't." My fingers gripped the receiver tighter as I sought the right words. "There are ways to get around moms working."

"That's what I tell Rick."

A long silence ensued. I cautioned myself that a thin line exists between friendly concern and unsolicited advice. *I must not allow passion to loosen my tongue too much.* Were the Dawsons having money problems? Rick's position with a local Southern Bell Company seemed to meet their financial needs.

"Tillie – are you okay? I mean, is your health all ri –"

"Oh, yeah. You know me – Mighty Mouse. I bounce off the walls." A sigh. "I don't know – Rick says I have too much time on my hands. To *think.*" Her little chortle lacked its usual lilt. "Imagine – *me* thinking. Oh, well – I do call him at work more often than I should. But it's usually about Raquel doing something cute or a wasp outside stings her or –" Her voice trailed off.

The words were forced – not from the spontaneous Tillie I knew. She seemed somehow vulnerable and I knew I must not coerce Tillie to say things she did not want to say. I also knew that the most sticky situation on God's earth is a marital conflict and the greatest fallout occurs after an outsider interferes.

"Tell you what, Tillie. Every day, I'll pray that your and Rick's discord be resolved."

Tillie exhaled a palpable sigh of relief. "Thanks, Neecy."

Months passed *"Like those strobe lights,"* Kirk liked to say. Events swooshed past with blinding swiftness...Dawn's first birthday, whose party was *the* event of the year... Heather's piano recital – I was always *there* to hold her icy hands before the performance – that left me breathless and weeping tears of pride. I fed her aspiration for a college music degree...Toby's fascination with football and his concern that his plumpness might deter his quarterback aspirations...Moose's 'retirement' from the Air Force for 'health reasons'...Tillie was gone behind those sunken eyes, simply not there. I opened my mouth to ask questions—then closed it. Somehow, I knew she needed space. Maybe it was the way she embraced normalcy, the way her giggles masked a fragility I now glimpsed...Ed Pleasant, Callie's

Dad, passed away...Kirk's mom's death from a major stroke. Poor Betty...my brother Chuck's disappointment that insulin shots remained paramount to his health and his joy that his estranged wife Teresa moved back in order to take care of him, though I suspected she was more interested in Chuck's Social Security checks than his health.

Lord, forgive me.

Dreams of searching, at times, invaded my peace and grief would linger into the morning hours, only to dissolve when the round little angelic face smiled up at me and chubby fingers tugged at my arm. "C'mo, Mommy. Go bye-bye."

Leaving sorrow behind, we walked together into the beautiful outdoors and marveled together at her discoveries; a tiny purple blossom peeking through fading autumn grass or a huge pine cone.

I thought back to Sarah Beauregard's prophecy that I must *not* expect a Krissie lookalike. And so, I had promised the Maker that – regardless of gender or genetic pool – I would be thankful. Kirk agreed, knowing as I did that chances of a like gender/genetic blend was nil.

We did not count on God's mysterious ways.

Dawn had appeared on the scene a tiny pink cherub. Dark thick hair did its own thing.

And then it happened.

Before our eyes, a wonder unfolded...dark hair slowly turned blonde...then curled...smokey-gray eyes turned the blue of a clear sky...pink complexion turned olive...the budding personality displayed gentleness and sensitivity...*Mommy got a boo-boo? I kiss it, Mommy*...tiny voice rising in song with perfect pitch.

Coincidence?

Not.

The Maker did exactly what folks said He wouldn't do. Go figure. One thing emerged from all that transpired: folks cannot program the Almighty.

In fact, I've grown to distrust *anybody* who feels they have it all figured out.

"Where are you, Krissie?" I searched the school playground as children scattered. The bell was ringing...Krissie disappeared into the forest, black and white saddle oxfords flashing as she ran, blonde hair trailing...the bell clanged louder and louder....

"Neecy," Kirk stirred beside me. "The doorbell's ringing."

I squinted at the bedside clock. "It's four o'clock. Who could it be?"

Kirk sprang to his feet and grabbed his robe on his way to answer the persistent summons. Presently, I heard the door open and low voices that rose and fell with emotion. I crept from bed and moved to the door to hear better. A man's voice...familiar...weeping.

A man weeping. What's wrong? Yet – I dared not intrude. Confidentiality was paramount to trust in the pastor-flock relationship. Frequently, the troubled party sought nurturing from both pastor and wife. Other times, pastor's wife was succinctly excluded. It was not my decision.

I quietly closed the door and crawled back into my warm bed.

Next time my lids cracked, sunlight lay over the soft green bedspread and wrapped my hand. I looked at the pillow beside me, whose head-indention declared Kirk's absence. Then I remembered the early a.m. mystery visitor. I yawned, stretched and remembered, too, that this was Saturday.

I smelled coffee as I spanned the hallway, glimpsing Heather's belly-down form sprawled on her bed, then Toby's rapt focus as, in the den, he watched Scooby-Doo. "Where's Daddy?" he asked, gaze never veering from the screen.

"I don't know." I moved Toby's cereal bowl from coffee table to sink and washed it, then poured myself a cup of coffee. As I searched in the fridge for milk, the back door opened.

It was Kirk, as haggard and exhausted as I'd ever seen him.

"Bad, huh?" I poured him a cup of coffee as he sank into the chair opposite mine. I purposefully didn't probe, knowing he'd talk if it was appropriate.

Kirk took a long drink. Kirk drinks, I sip. I waited. "Want some breakfast?"

"No. Thanks." He stared at his cup, still nestled between big hands. Suddenly, he looked at me, a look that pierced straight to my heart. "Rick Dawson came by this morning."

"It was him?" Dread swamped me.

"He –" Kirk shifted tiredly and set his cup down. "Tillie caught him with another woman."

"Oh, my – God help us!" Tears gathered. Poor Tillie. No wonder she'd –

"Let's go in the living room," Kirk suggested, casting a glance at Toby, who remained transfixed, chuckling suddenly at Scooby-Doo's cowardly capers.

We settled on the couch. My hand went to my bosom, where my heart thruumped a heavy syncopated cadence. "Oh, Kirk. Say it isn't so."

His face was grave. "I'm afraid it is, honey. Rick told Tillie he was going out of town on business. She went along with his story, apparently aware of something. Anyway – he met this woman at the Star Motel in Charleston. They were in bed to-gether and Tillie walked in on them."

"Dear Lord." I wiped tears from my cheeks and snuffled. "How did she get in? I mean –"

"She apparently told the clerk she was to join her husband, who was in room 101, and she wanted to surprise him."

"How did she track him down?" I was gaining a new re-spect for Tillie's intellect.

"She'd found a match packet from that motel in one of Rick's shirt pockets. Seems that was their meeting place when this woman came into town."

"Where did he meet her?" I groped for the Kleenex box on the end table.

"On a Charleston job. She works in one of the sales offices there. Rick installed phones there when they first opened."

"That far back, huh?"

"Couple of years."

"It gets worse." I shivered and hugged myself. "Why were you – where did you go?"

"Rick asked me to go talk to Tillie. He's devastated that she's so – shredded by the whole thing. He wants her back."

I looked at Kirk. Astounded. "Oh, really?"

Kirk ignored my sarcasm. "Well – you've got to realize a crisis like this many times yanks a person back to reality. Rick's been living in a – fantasy world, his own words, for all this time.

Seeing Tillie's face when she rushed in to find them together...
well, it's tearing him up."

"No joke," I said flatly and crossed my arms, wanting to
beat up on Rick.

Kirk sighed. "That's not like you, honey." It was sad, the
statement.

"I know." I blinked back tears. "Give me a little time, huh?
It's just – Tillie adores him. Rick could do no wrong. And now
– what's she going to do, Kirk?"

"I went over to talk with her. Rick was with me. She barely
looked at me. Or him. She just looked – dead. I'm truly concerned about her, Neecy. I tried to help her see that it is possible
to forgive and go on. That Rick wants – needs her forgiveness.
He cried and pleaded with her to not leave him. Said he'd make
it up to her if she'd just give him a chance. I've never seen a
man more desperate."

"What did she say?"

"Nothing much. When I left, Rick was still pleading with
her for mercy." He looked at me then and I saw the misery in
the green depths, the caring, the helplessness. I slid over, put
my arms around him and drew his head down to rest on my
shoulder.

"You're a good man, Kirk Crenshaw."

Toby stuck his head in the door. "What's for lunch, Mom?"

A familiar gray Chevrolet sat in our drive as we drove in.
Our family had eaten an early dinner at Bessingers, needing
that time together. A pall jaded the day for Kirk and me, one
we'd tried to hide from Heather and Toby. Somehow, we'd
succeeded.

Until now. I drew in my breath and watched Zelda and
Alton Diggers emerge from their car. "Go in the house," I told
Heather and Toby as Kirk braked the car then got out.

"Why?" Toby gazed at the Diggers, knowing them to be
church folks and wanting to socialize with Tillie's parents who,
to Toby, had to be nice if related to his pal.

"Because I said so." I spoke more sharply than intended.
But I'd seen Zelda's 'planted' stance, which, according to Tillie,
meant 'ready for war.' But then, for Zelda, that was normal. I

decided that I'd best serve Kirk by getting our children out of hearing range so I shooed them quickly inside. Heather looked pompously over her shoulder at me, as in "back off." But she didn't say anything. That, I could handle.

I got busy fluffing cushions and emptying the dishwasher. From the bedroom window, I spied the intense palaver... Zelda's hands-on-hip stance, her red face, Alton's silent stiffness —

Poor Kirk. Despite his composed features, I spied the bleakness underlying them.

Please...please make her shut up. I hurried back to the kitchen so he wouldn't think I was eavesdropping. The front door opened and closed quietly. His footsteps, usually a crisp clicking stride, now sloughed. I turned from the sink. He sank — literally — against the doorjamb. Hands dangled limply at his sides. And his face — like an animal shot between the eyes, ready to fall.

"Kirk?" I moved to him. "What happened?"

He blinked then cleared his throat. "They said I was of the Devil." Pain flickered in his eyes. "Said I told Tillie to ignore Rick's philandering ways. She's twisting my words."

"*What?*" My mouth dropped open. Then closed in a tight line. "How *dare* they!"

That seemed to spark a little life into him. He straightened and moved to sit on the living room sofa. I followed him. "Zelda said I should be shot for telling Tillie to forgive that — I won't repeat what she called Rick. Said a decent man would've sympathized with Tillie, not tried to talk her into staying with an adulterer and fornicator."

I plopped down beside him. "Oh, Kirk."

He sighed deeply, his eyes unseeing. Sad. "I tried to tell them that God's word instructs us to forgive." His shoulders shrugged. "Else — how can God forgive us?"

"That's what He says," I agreed. I wanted to take him into my arms to soothe and heal but knew not to. Not yet. Hurt ran too deep for him to receive my comfort. Kirk battled alone. Oh, he wanted me there. Heard my soothing words. And I knew they helped. Some. But in the arena, he did his own hand-to-hand combat. Since childhood, this was so.

At times, Kirk didn't even seem to trust the Almighty to handle his fights.

Immediately, I pushed away those traitorous thoughts.

The phone rang and I went to answer. It was Rick.

Kirk took the phone from me. "Yes, Rick. They were here." A long silence. "No – I haven't heard from Tillie. Zelda says she and Raquel are staying with them for the time being."

Another long silence, then, "I certainly will. And Rick – hang in there. I'll be praying for you, okay? Yeah – sure thing. Bye."

I took the phone from his limp hand and hung it up.

He stared out the window, elbows on the kitchen table, fingers steepled to his mouth. I poured him a fresh cup of coffee and sat opposite him to sip my iced tea.

I saw desolation slowly seep away. "I know what the Bible says about love," Kirk spoke to himself, as well as to me. This was his recovery time. "Zelda's opinion of what decency is is beside the point. I have to check against what God's word says. And it says a marriage not only can but *should* be able to with-stand outside attacks against it."

"Kirk, your advice was right on target. Most people *want* to hear that their marriage can be saved." I watched him relax more by the moment. His *denial* strength began to kick in.

I was beginning to suspect that denial and faith *could* overlap.

"Anyway," I reached for his hand and squeezed it, "Zelda's well known around here for her harsh nature." I grinned. "Rivaled only by the infamous Sarah Beauregard."

Kirk's smile started in his eyes and spread to his entire face. "Yeah. Nobody's going to listen to either of those two busybodies."

"Can I hold Dawnie, ple-ease Mrs. Crenshaw?" Twelve-year-old Cindy Stone held out her hands to Dawn, who sat astride my hip, decked out in her new blue calico dress and bon-net. We wore matching outfits for the annual Old-Fashioned Sunday. I stood on Solomon Methodist's white-columned por-tico, reluctant to join the folks milling about the lush church grounds. I recalled last years' warm, friendly atmosphere. A real family feeling.

Today, it was a family thing again – only this time, I was not *family*. In recent weeks, folks had begun to distance themselves from the Crenshaws. Subtle things. Averted eyes. Pretending not to hear when I spoke. Kirk had, characteristically, tuned it out. Today, the coldness was a tangible thing, leaving me limp with confusion.

Callie had summed it up. "Zelda's doings. She's an expert at twisting words and throwing them back at you entirely differ-ent than they started out. She's managed to get most of her part of the clan to believe Kirk's morals are so loose he's giving out immoral advice. Hey, you and I both know this crazy redneck mentality on 'sticking together.'"

"Yeah," I'd agreed. "As MawMaw's old radio song goes, *Slap 'er down agin', Maw... Slap 'er down agin, We don't want our neighbors talkin' bout our kin.*"

I hated to think church folks could believe such nonsense, but when it came to loyalties – especially at Solomon Methodist – kin stuck together. Oh, there were a few exceptions but not enough to deflect considerable damage when someone like Zelda set her bead.

Today, the clan's coldness was a grim statement to that effect.

"Please?" Cindy persisted, her eyes twinkling at Dawnie, who leaned toward her, reaching.

"Sure," I smiled and handed her over. From the corner of my eye, I saw Cindy's mom Lucille Stone come out of the vestibule.

"Mama!" Joannie rushed to her mother. "Isn't she cute?" She proudly thrust out her blonde, bonneted prize. "Here! Wanna hold her?"

I folded my hands and held my breath. Red-haired Lucille's chin rose two, three notches and her nostrils flared as though smelling something foul. Her pale nutmeg gaze flickered from Dawnie to me and back, not lighting on either, like an angry cornered animal ready to snarl.

"Mama?" Cindy looked bewildered. "Don't you wanna hold her?"

Lucille's russet head did a brisk, negative nod and she was gone in a heartbeat. I watched her march to join her Clemmons kin clustered around Homer Clemmons' horse and wagon. First cousins of Zelda Diggers, most of them.

Her daughter stared after her with the same befuddlement I felt inside.

"Cindy," I forced a smile. "I think I'll take Dawnie home for a nap."

"Aww," Cindy reluctantly relinquished her little friend. "Bye, Dawnie."

"Janeece," Kaye Tessner caught me as I turned to leave. "Where you going? It's time to eat."

"I —" I swallowed back the bubble of hurt and forced a wide smile. "Dawn's tired. I'm going to lay her down for her nap at the house." I turned and hightailed it home, feeling Kaye staring after me.

"Want me to fix you a plate?" she called.

Sweet Kaye…but I shouldn't vent to her. She was, by marriage, of the kinship. It wouldn't be fair to drag her in.

"No," I hollered back and kept walking.

Inside the parsonage, I tried to swallow the enormous, heavy weight lodged in my chest, wishing Callie were here today. She'd gone to visit her mother. Mollie's health had suffered since Ed's fatal heart attack and Callie liked to check on her every three to four weeks.

I put Dawn into her crib, went into my bedroom and closed the door. Only then did I allow the tears to fall. Recent snubs and slights rushed and swarmed me like killer bees, beating and stinging me into incoherent sobs and spasms of grief. I'd suppressed them, the memories...*cold, disdainful faces freezing me on my Sunday morning processional from pulpit entrance to choir platform...mocking, cruel smirks when I faced the congregation to sing choir solos...my greeting smile freezing as backs turned to me....*

Grief.

I'd ignored the meanness toward me. Today, the ugly thing loosed itself upon my baby. How could I ignore that?

An innocent baby.

God? What can I do?

I can't pull Kirk down by complaining. "It'll pass," he'd say. Would it?

I wept until I heard the last of the mules and wagons pull out. Until the late afternoon sun began to fade. Still, I wept.

"Janeece?" I heard Kirk call out as he came in.

I snuffled soundly then pretended sleep.

Tillie missed choir practice the next five Thursday nights. I'd caught on that Zelda Diggers' ill will toward Kirk extended to me when I called her house and asked to speak to Tillie. She hung up on me. So, I kept praying Tillie would contact me.

It was on the sixth Thursday night of Tillie's absence that Moose staggered into the choir loft's back row and plopped down, looking like a fugitive from Hell. He'd been looking less than swooft for months, since he'd chosen to not re-up in the Air Force, but tonight, his glassy-eyed gauntness alarmed me. I'd been so engrossed with Tillie's dilemma I'd missed Moose's swift decline. I knew he'd taken morning and evening jobs to make ends meet. He'd had to miss some practices and Sunday services because of revolving work schedules. I rushed over to him and whispered, "Moose, what's wrong?"

He looked at me as if I had two noses. "Nothin'."

Callie moved to stand beside me, scowling at him. "You look ghastly," she whispered.

He reared back and gave her a mock glare. "Thanks a *lot,* Cal."

"Anytime, pal." Callie gave him an in-depth, slant-eyed assessment. "*Sshheezz.*"

I touched his shoulder, keeping my voice down as others filed into the loft, laughing and talking. Thank God the choir, so far, did not seem affected by the cold war fallout. And despite Tillie's no-shows, I wasn't convinced her heart had changed toward me.

"Ahh, Moose. I know you're working your tail off at two jobs, trying to make ends meet. But –"

"Three." Moose's thick fingers inserted themselves between us.

"You're crazy, Moose," Callie snorted. "You got a death wish or somethin'?"

"Roxie needs things, Cal –" He suddenly switched to address me, seeing Callie's lack of sympathy for Roxie. "You know, like clothes and new shoes." His eyes half-mooned suddenly.

"Woman's gotta be pampered some, Neecy. That apartment we live in is a real dump and I need to —"

Callie's disgusted snort signaled her retreat and I noticed everybody heading for their appointed seats.

"I know." I patted Moose's arm and gave him a sympathetic smile. "Please, just take care of yourself. Okay?"

"Shore, Neecy." The eyes dissolved behind his grin and he reached up to pat my hand on his shoulder. "You know me. Strong as a danged moose."

I went to the podium, fighting my disgust with Roxie's demands. I arranged my music, silently miming Kirk's brush-aside manner, his "that's Moose's problem. He's gotta decide things for himself." But, for me, they were only words. I closed my eyes for a long moment, struggling for composure. *Tillie... Moose...rejection...*everything crashing, crashing, *crushing my spirit as one would a roach bug.*

Tears gathered behind my closed lids and I heard the silence settle in. Felt the curiosity. Or was it concern? At this point, I didn't know. Did it matter?

Pray. The command was succinct.

"Stand, please." My steady voice belied the inner turmoil. "Charlie, lead us in prayer, please." I reminded myself that Kaye's spouse – of the clan – remained loyal to me. Others, perhaps a third, of the clan did as well. But the scowling, palpating disapproval of those dissenting ones served to erode joy and spontaneity.

Charlie Tessner rose. "Lord...please meet us at the point of our need tonight. And – especially endow Janeece with an extra portion of strength because you know how much her work here blesses us and all those around. Thank you. Amen."

"*...especially endow Janeece....*"

I opened my eyes and smiled, buoyed for the moment. For now, that was enough. "Let us begin...."

Our family's weekly Saturday night eat-out at Bessinger's BBQ Restaurant now included Callie, Moose and Roxie. After Moose's choir loft admission that he felt pressure to pamper Roxie, Callie barely concealed her disgust for "Sweet Thang."

"Need to go?" I politely asked Roxie as Cal and I excused ourselves from the table.

"Huh uh," she droned and leaned her face into her hands to hang on to every word of Kirk's funny golf stories. That she managed to always seat herself beside him was funny to me. Not to Callie, whose eyebrows shot up higher each time Roxie plunked herself next to my husband. I'd teased Kirk about her little crush at first. But he always looked disappointed in me, saying Roxie was simply childlike and anyway, she loved Moose. That statement, at times, strained my imagination, but I always repented and gave her the benefit of a doubt.

Actually, I had to admit Roxie *had* changed. Compared to earlier courtship times, she now seemed to, at least, acknowledge Moose.

"She's changed, Cal," I insisted, yet not fully believing it myself.

"She's a *slut*, Neecy. Moose deserves better."

"Cal, you're gonna have to hide your feelings more," I gently coaxed as we made our way to the ladies' room.

"I can't help it," Callie hissed. "She's a—a…"

"Don't say it. Please, Cal, try to keep peace." The bathroom was occupied so we stood outside the door, waiting. "You know how bad things are for us right now anyway – what with Zelda's grievances and all."

Callie's ebony eyes flashed fire. "That woman's an old biddy. And you *know* I could say worse. Lots and lots worse."

I laughed and gave her rigid, crossed arms a playful smack. "Do I *ever* know how *charitable* that term is? From *you*, who at one time could have turned this air *blue*."

"Darned right." Callie raised her chin and stared at the wall as though she wanted to take it apart.

I gently elbowed her in the ribs. "Know what you and I used to say, '*sticks and stones may break my bones, but words can never harm me*,'" I singsonged to lighten her up.

Her frown loosened and her lips curled up at the corners. "Yeah. You're right."

An elderly lady emerged from the enclosure, smiled at me and washed her hands.

Callie went into the stall and I felt relief that I'd humored her into letting go of anger.

Now, I just had to convince *me*.

That Christmas, Dad, Anne and the kids drove down to spend the holidays with us.

"To play with Punkin'," Dad cooed at Dawn, who climbed all over him, lavishing him with hugs and wet kisses and tugging him hither and yon to explore all her domain. He loved it.

Anne got, quote, 'leftovers.' She giggled and gooched Dawn into hysteria every chance she got. Trish and Gene came down the day after Christmas to spend a couple of days.

"When are *you* going to have us one?" Daddy kidded his baby girl. Trish didn't laugh, hadn't for a long time. Daddy sobered and hugged her tightly. "Sorry, honey. I forgot."

"It's okay," Trish kissed his cheek. "I'm used to it. Gene's family is merciless with their jokes." She shrugged and mugged. "I'm doing all I kin, but it jus' ain't working, ya'll. Anyway," she did a funny clown's waddle across the room to pull Dawn from Anne's lap, "I gots my own baby *ri'chere!*"

Dawn giggled and scrooched up to Trish, enjoying every little squeeze and smooch.

"C'mon, Lynnette," Toby called on his way to the back door, "let's go ride bikes."

My sister rose from my lap, where she still occasionally sat, even though her feet now touched the floor. Our affection remained spontaneous and relaxed.

"Coats!" I called, because though milder than upstate, lowland weather still chilled.

"You get more handsome every time I see you, Cole." I patted the vacant seat beside me on the den sofa. "Come sit next to a good-looking woman." He grinned and planted himself next to me. Heather soon plunked down beside him.

Dale, now fourteen, sat on my other side and browsed through photo albums, pausing at Krissie's pictures. He did this every time he came. Afterward, he would hold my hand for long spells as the entire clan talked back and forth, carrying on several conversations simultaneously.

Sometime during the afternoon, the front doorbell rang. Anne answered it. "It's Moose".

"Tell him to come in and join us," I called.

"He wants to talk to Kirk."

Kirk went outside just as we all gathered around the piano. Heather played and we sang everything we knew from *Oh Bury Me Not On the Lone Prairie* to Dawnie's current favorite *Itsy Bitsy Spider.* Then Toby and Lynette came in with red noses and cheeks that had them looking like painted wooden nutcracker soldiers.

"Do *Delta Dawn!*" Toby requested. Heather immediately modulated into the country tune and while we adults fumbled our way through the unfamiliar lyrics, the younger ones nailed every word, grinning ear-to-ear with shameless pride. The next tune, *Sentimental Journey*, provided payback time. Daddy's rich baritone gave life to the melody, with Heather and Cole's alto and mine and Trish's second- oprano smoothly blending into a passable imitation of the 40's Modernaires.

"Sing something *we* can sing, too," Toby whined after we finished.

"Yeah," Lynette chimed in.

After a mad, Three-Stooges' huddle, we plunged into a rousing rendition of *You Ain't Nothin' But a Hound Dog* that would've done Elvis proud. Halfway through, the phone rang.

I rushed to answer it.

"Chuck! It's so – so good to hear your voice."

"What's all that racket there?"

I laughed. "Us. The whole family's here. Except you."

"Except me, huh?"

"Yeh." Long moments passed as the rock'n roll beat wound down. "We miss you, you know."

"Yeh? Well, I'd a come if I'd been able, Neecy. I mean that."

"Kidney infection no better?"

"Nah. But you can't keep a good man down long, ain't that right, Teresa?" He laughed and I heard Teresa's low response in the background.

"How is Teresa?" I asked out of politeness.

"She's doin' great. Come'ere, Teresa, Neecy wants to say 'hey' to you."

I clenched my teeth, knowing in my gut she wouldn't give Chuck – or me – the satisfaction. His hand muffled the mouthpiece, then, "Ahh – she's frying steak and can't leave it but says to say 'hey' to everybody."

I'll bet.

"Sure will. How's Poogie?" He put adolescent Poogie on the line, who, in turn, awkwardly shifted the brunt of conversation to me. A sweet girl, Poogie knew little of us and I felt her uncertainty. "Love you, Poogie," I said from my heart.

"Me, too." Muffled mouthpiece. "Here's Daddy."

"Chuck? Wouldn't you like to speak to Daddy?"

"Mmm-nah. That's okay. He sounds busy."

"He won't mind." I turned to get Dad's attention. "Da –"

"Don't interrupt him, Sis. Let 'im sing. I'll be going now, hear? Give everybody my love."

I closed my eyes and took a deep breath, exhaling disappointment. *Why?* "I will. And Chuck – take care of yourself. Bye."

"Who was that, Mama?" Heather asked over her shoulder as she pulled a southern gospel hymnbook from a pile of music. I knew she wanted to hear from Ralph Stevens, a boy she'd recently begun to like.

"It was Chuck." I saw her eyes cloud, then Dad's face fall. I added quickly, "He said give everybody his love. He's not well."

I went on to explain Chuck's kidney crisis, seeing Dad's hurt turn to alarm."I wish he'd call and let us know what's going on," Dad murmured, but absent was the characteristic anger.

I didn't know which was worse, seeing him angry or worried. I quickly decided *worried* was better.

"He'll be okay," I insisted, "You know Chuck. Strong as an ox, to hear him tell it."

Dad's face relaxed a mite. "Yeh. That kind of attitude carries folks a long way toward healing." He thumbed through the songbook, pressed back the pages and set it on the piano. "Heather, let's do this one. You sing alto, Trish, and you do second soprano, Neecy. Rest of you do what you want to."

"C'mon, help us out, Anne," I coaxed, knowing she wouldn't.

"I'll just listen and hum along." Dawnie, having gone full circle, crawled into her lap again. Anne's voice was wonderful for lulling babies. Period.

"Anne and I'll pay ya'll back in Heaven," Kirk liked to say. "I believe we who can't carry a tune here will be soloists up there." Actually, Kirk's voice wasn't bad when bolstered by others around him.

I wondered again what was taking Kirk so long outside. He and Moose must have gone out to the church office to talk. What was too urgent that it couldn't wait until we didn't have company?

After *Each Step I Take*, *Mansion On the Hilltop* and *Wait till You See Me In My New Home,* we declared ourselves starved and raided the leftovers, lowland chicken bog, pork barbecue, baked beans, coleslaw, potato salad and Anne's special macaroni pie.

"Don't you want to wait on Kirk?" Anne asked as we started to be seated.

"Sit down." I laughed. "If I waited on Kirk to get away from pastoral duties, I'm afraid we'd go hungry half the time. By the way, *Heather* made the Mississippi mud cake."

"*Yeh, Heather!*" They applauded and she rose and took a bow. From across the table, her eyes twinkled to me a silent message of love.

My heart swelled with gratitude.

Life, I thought, doesn't get any better than this.

The parsonage was dark and silent when Kirk finally came in. He quietly undressed and slipped into his side of the bed.

"Honey?" I turned to him. "Is something wrong?"

I couldn't see his face in the dark as he lay facing me. Only shadows. The silence stretched out. "Kirk?"

"No." The word was clipped. Underlined with tension. "Nothing's wrong."

"Is Moose – okay?"

Kirk gave a long shuddering sigh. "Moose spoke to me in confidence."

"Okay." That was that. Kirk's pastoral confidences were sacred.

"It's – nothing to worry about…" He turned his back to me, then reached back to pat me. "Go to sleep."

Deep, deep inside I knew.

Kirk had not told me the truth.

The afterglow of my family's visit *poofed* within a day of their leave-taking. Tillie Dawson was hospitalized with an overdose of valium and though Kirk was not barred from Tillie's hospital room, Zelda, who treated him like the lowest form of vermin, distinctly discouraged any ministrations from him.

On second thought, make that *next* to the lowest form – *that*, Zelda reserved for son-in-law Rick.

I know because I was there, having insisted upon tagging along to catch a glimpse of my friend. The room was empty when we arrived so we made our way to her bedside. My heart lurched when I saw her, a sheet-draped skeleton more dead than alive, whose eyes sunk like dark caves in the small face. What lingered of the vibrant girl I'd known wouldn't cast a shadow beneath a bright afternoon sun.

I crouched behind Kirk when Zelda came bounding into the room. "She's asleep. Not s'posed to be disturbed."

"Mama?" The apparition on the bed stirred the tiniest bit. "Please...."

"What is it, honey?" Zelda rushed to the bedside and hovered.

Tillie's little mouth worked to emit sound. Her lids cracked to reveal mere slivers of white.

"See?" Zelda cast a glower at Kirk. And for once, I was glad she didn't consider me significant enough to acknowledge. "She's not up to company."

A frail, pale hand slowly trembled its way from the white sheet folds to clutch Zelda's arm. "I need – prayer," Tillie whispered.

"But, sugar," Zelda gripped the skinny fingers, "I don't th _"

Kirk's stubbornness kicked in and he stepped up beside Zelda and leaned to speak to Tillie. "Of course, we'll pray with you, Tillie." He turned to me. "Join us, Janeece." His courage transferred itself to me as we joined hands and took hold of Tillie's limp, icy ones. Kirk tossed Zelda a brief 'join us?' glance and, when she did not respond, proceeded.

Rick walked in on the *amen*. Zelda glared at him.

"She's my wife, Zelda." Rick shook hands with Kirk, hugged me and planted himself next to Tillie's bed, all in a matter of seconds.

Zelda lumbered to his side and leaned nearly nose to nose with him. "Not for much longer if I can help it." Her voice reminded me of Ma Kettle in her most mettlesome moments.

Rick's gaze didn't waver. "Don't you think that's for Tillie to decide, Zelda?" he asked quietly.

Zelda snorted and gestured toward the bed. "Now, don't she look like she's fit to make any kind of decision?"

"Mama," Tillie struggled to speak. "Don't...."

"Okay, honey-bun." Zelda's big hand roughly patted the prone skeleton. I winced. "Mama won't let him harass you. Now you git out, Rick Dawson."

"Let's go, Neecy," Kirk took my arm, his features closed. But I saw the flare of his nostrils, the barest revelation that he'd like to stuff Zelda's mouth with dirty socks. "Hang in there, Rick." His nod to Zelda was terse. "Good day, Zelda."

"Humph."

As we left, we heard Rick's quiet response.

"Now, you can like it or lump it, Zelda. I don't care. But I'm *not leaving my wife.*"

❖ ❖ ❖ ❖ ❖ ❖

Three days later, my phone rang. It was Tillie.

"I've missed you, Neecy." Her voice was reed thin, like a weak kitten's *meow.*

"Oh, Tillie, you just don't know how I've wanted to see you and help you...."

"I know." A long sigh. "Neecy, I told Rick to bring me home from the hospital. Mama's pitching a fit, but I don't care. Well – I *do*... but she's just gotta get over it."

Tears rolled down my cheeks. I swiped at them. "You okay, Tillie? I mean – the last time I saw you, you looked like death warmed over."

"I'm getting there, Neecy. I just lost it there for awhile. Always said I'd never be able to live with an unfaithful man." She huffed a little hoarse laugh, then burst into tears. "I-I didn't know how hard it is to stop loving, Neecy, till –"

"Listen, Tillie. All that stuff's past now. I'm proud that you've decided to hold your marriage together."

Tillie snuffled. "I just wanted to say thanks. Yours and Kirk's hospital visit – and prayer – was a real turning point for me. I just wanted to know."

"Thanks, Tillie. Now, you just get yourself well and get back to singing, darlin'. The choir jus' *ain't the same* without you. Y'hear?"

Tillie giggled. "I *hear* you, girl." My heart soared.

"Thanks for the coffee, Neecy," Cal kissed my cheek, "I gotta run. Promised Mama I'd call her."

"Call her here."

"Naw. I need to shampoo my hair anyway."

After she left, I checked on Dawnie, who'd fallen asleep playing, using her 'bankie' as a pillow on her carpeted floor. I lay her in her bed, covered and kissed her and returned to the den, where Toby's cartoons blasted away.

"Toby? Would you listen for Dawn while I take a short walk?"

"Sure, Mom."

I strolled to the cemetery, knowing I would find Heather there.

"Hey, sweetheart," I said softly. She looked up at me from her little plaid pallet beneath the oak and lay her book aside. She smiled and it took my breath, for it was both sweet and sad. Auburn silk framed the lovely face that had seen too much – too soon.

"Sit with me, Mama." She patted a spot and I joined her. We gazed at each other in wordless affection.

"You know, Heather," I said gently, "we have our share of mother-daughter climaxes. But – times like this makes me think of porpoises who bump folks along from one threat to another, keeping them afloat." I took her hand. "These sweet moments are like that. They rescue us from deep, troubled water...keep us focused on what's important." I squeezed her hand. "What's important is that we love each other."

"Oh, Mama," suddenly, she crumpled into tears. Heather, who seldom cried.

"What's wrong, honey?"

"I don't understand, Mama." She gazed at me imploringly. "I know Ralph likes me," tears riveted her cheeks. "But his family has heard so much ugly gossip about us. *Darn* that nasty old Zelda and her big mouth. They – Ralph's family – just can't believe we're what we are. They don't approve of him dating me."

"Ohh, baby." My heart lurched. How *could* they? The Stevens family didn't even know us personally. They attended the Episcopal Church in town and had only heard the mud-slinging stuff via the gossip channel. And the *stuff* was mainly innuendoes.

"It's n-not *fair,* Mama! We haven't done anything wrong. Know what they said about Dad? Steve told me they said Daddy is a Bible-thumping, jack-leg preacher from the back-woods." She drew her knees up, buried her head on them and bawled like little Dawn.

Anger machine-gunned through me. What *lies.* What malicious vilification. And from so-called Christians, in whose hands Kirk, at one time, would have entrusted his life. Kirk's sermons *had* changed in recent months. How could he bury a child and *not* change? But *Bible-thumping, backwoods preacher?* No. Since Krissie's death, his speaking had become more eloquent. If anything, it had prompted more soul-searching.

Was that the sore spot? Had Kirk's mellowed entreaties offended some traditional, stiff-necked parishioners who didn't want to be blown from their comfort zone? But wasn't that what sermons were supposed to do? To instruct and challenge and exhort? If not, why even have church?

I rubbed Heather's shoulder, feeling as helpless as I'd ever felt in my life.

When the wails subsided, I held her in my arms. "I know it's tough, baby." *Why do my children have to get hurt?* "But try to remember what Ephesians 6:12 tells us...we wrestle not against flesh and blood, but against principalities, against powers, against the rulers of darkness of this age, against spiritual hosts of wickedness....'

"In other words," Heather gazed at me with red swollen eyes, "the Devil."

"Exactly. We just have to remind ourselves from time to time what it's all about."

She furrowed her head against my shoulder. "I know." A long silence. "Thanks, Mama."

"Mama!" Toby called from the distant parsonage back-door. "Dawn's awake!"

I sighed and stirred but Heather said, "He'll be okay with her for a few minutes."

Toby yelled again. "*Ma-a-ma! She's pooped!*"

Heather burst into giggles and stood. "C'mon, Mama." She took my hand and hoisted me up. "We'd better go rescue the little *wimp.*"

Moose came by that afternoon to visit. Alone. I washed dishes at the sink, giving him and Kirk time to themselves. In the open kitchen-den area, I heard snatches of their quiet conversation. Moose mentioned Roxanne getting off from work soon – she'd taken a job at the Seven-Eleven, insisting that despite Moose's sometimes triple-shift jobs, they still didn't have enough money to make ends meet. I couldn't quite figure out what *ends* meant in her vocabulary, but I suspected it had to do with her *ends of the earth* demands for costly things.

When he departed, I hugged him at the door and noticed he seemed inordinately preoccupied. "How'd you get off this afternoon?" I asked.

He shrugged and looked away. "Told 'em I was sick. No other way." He left then, without another word.

"What's going on?" I asked Kirk, who'd disappeared behind the newspaper.

"What do you mean?" he asked brusquely, lowering the paper and pinning me with a look I'd not seen in a long time. For years, in fact. His *back off* one, reserved for last ditch offensive maneuvers.

"Oh," I shrugged, "everybody seems so –"

"Drop it, Neecy." Up came the paper. "You're seeing things that aren't there."

The warmth – lingering from my time with Heather – evaporated, replaced by socked-in-the-stomach indignation. "I –" I took a deep breath, weighed my odds of coming out unscathed, then clamped my lips together. I went back to work, determined that it wasn't that important, whatever transpired. Nor were his condescending words.

I banged dishes as I emptied the dishwasher, furiously wiped counters and vacuumed the carpet.

Kirk's attack on my intellect wasn't important enough to get upset over.

It *wasn't*.

Moose looked fine that Thursday night at choir practice. In fact, he and Kirk spent some time in the pastoral office that afternoon. So, I relaxed.

Kirk, however, remained untalkative. He functioned well enough that no one, outside me, noticed. I'd shared Heather's angst about the gossip with him and thought perhaps that might have brought on this contemplative lapse. When I probed, he remained adamant that he was *fine*.

"Quit worrying, Neecy. I've just got some things on my mind. No big deal."

Recognizing the bite in his tone, I did the only thing I could. I backed off.

I returned to college. Sweet Mrs. Autry, white-haired little widow whose only son and family were of our flock, was ecstatic to baby-sit Dawn. She devoted those days to enjoying my child as though she, herself, had spawned her.

Weeks passed, then months. Thanksgiving, Christmas flew by, a time when Chuck's gaunt, skinny appearance shocked me speechless, then sent me scurrying for cover to cry my eyes out. His bravado and distancing from Daddy never wavered. Too soon, family departed...Azaleas painted the world vivid... faded...then died.

College graduation came and went with the usual family fanfare. I framed my Fine Arts Degree and hung it on my den wall, where it remained, only occasionally reminding me of my desperate quest to justify my existence.

Once, the framed certificate would have been my life's summit, one from which I evolved into an illustrious teacher, then significant human being, in that order. *Once.* Eons ago.

Before I realized I would trade all I was and am for just one day with Krissie. Before I regarded my children my most notable accomplishment in this crazy thing called life.

That realization altered the yardstick thing with me. I no longer felt I had to go out into the world to prove anything to Kirk. Or to myself. My roots belonged in the home.

The gossip wilted. Heather began to see Ralph Stevens, whose parents finally relented that, just perhaps, the defamation of the Methodist pastor had been unjustified. Ralph was a nice boy whose ambition was to become a medical doctor, like his father, the town's general practitioner. Some of the church folk grew warmer toward the Crenshaw family. Others did not.

I welcomed the truce – such as it was.

Because one thing was certain: none of the clan would ever leave Solomon Methodist Church.

Any adjustments would be ours.

CHAPTER THIRTEEN

Something about Kirk's demeanor raised my antenna. I couldn't quite finger the underlying tension in him. It just *was.* Eighteen years with him had finely tuned my radar so that it missed little. But then, life with Kirk, as I said before, was a roller-coaster odyssey and by now, I'd begun to regard such as normal.

Kirk's pulpit manner remained mellow and his messages focused on saving the lost. As a result, non-clan folks now added to the Solomon flock. Rising attendance, plus Tillie's return to church and choir, served to boost morale and a slow, steady recovery from past problems. Oh, there were some who didn't welcome newcomers, but overall, the scales began to slowly tip in Kirk's favor. Even Zelda and Alton Diggers' frostiness seemed to thaw a tad.

One day, my brother called.

"I'm on dialysis, Sis," Chuck talked as though he were at a party.

I nearly dropped the phone. "Chuck! Why didn't you let us know? I knew the kidney problems were bad but –"

"It's no big *deal,* I *tell* ya. I have to go to the hospital every Monday, Wednesday and Friday for treatments."

"Do they hurt, Chuck?"

"Nah. A breeze."

Dialysis. The last resort. *Dear God.*

"Have you talked to the doctor about a transplant, Chuck?"

"Yeah. Gotta wait till they do a long series of tests to see if I'm a candidate."

"Oh, Chuck...."

"Don't worry, Sis. I'll be okay."

"I know. But – is there anything I can do?"

"Naw. Teresa's working two jobs now since I can't work. Not easy on her, I know. I hate sitting around while she's out working her butt off, y'know?"

"You can't help being sick, Chuck."

A long silence. Then a huff. "I wish Teresa felt that way."

I felt my second wave of alarm. Chuck's health had slipped more than I'd realized in the past couple of years. Before, he'd never revealed anything of this nature to me. *He must be desperate.*

"Chuck? I'll be praying for you every day, y'hear?" My throat was closing up and I swallowed hard. "You know I love you, don't you?"

"Yeah, Sis." His voice, suddenly weary, wrung me limp. "I know."

"Please, promise me, Chuck, that you'll hang in there."

He laughed suddenly, sounding more like my brother. "Like a hair in a biscuit! You know me —"

"Yeah, yeah, I know, strong as an ox."

The glowing Sabbath sunrise hinted of a wonderful Easter. First indication otherwise was my splitting ragweed season headache and cough, plus Moose's empty choir seat. He'd only last week quit two of his jobs after vowing he had everything "all worked out." Roxie didn't appear too happy about it, but he seemed determined to follow through. Appeared, in fact, calmer than I'd seen him since teen years.

Problem was, today he had a choir special solo. Near to a migraine — not counting a bronchitis bout — I rushed to ask Charlie Tessner to fill in and sing *Because He Lives*. He happily complied.

Kirk's message today was especially poignant with appeal. At its conclusion, he said, "Consider how the grave only held our Savior a brief time — on the third day he arose." Tears filled his eyes and instantly, mine moistened. A hushed silence fell over the sanctuary as he slowly walked the length of the platform and back, a dignified trek to regroup himself.

He swallowed several times before continuing, his wonderful hands gripping the sides of the podium. Snuffles rippled across the congregation, and I knew Kirk's rare emotional lapse impacted others, as well.

"I can't help but remember my daughter Krissie today." He smiled tenderly. "How, on that last Easter, she got up at the crack of dawn to attend the outdoor sunrise service with me."

I recalled that morning, too. The rest of us less hardy Crenshaws burrowed beneath covers as the two of them banged out the door to join other zealous early risers gathered beneath a purple-draped, weathered cross, flanked by two others.

"I asked Krissie to lead us in prayer," he said huskily and blinked back tears. "She did, in her sweet simple way, praying for everybody standing there and those who weren't." His lips trembled, then stilled. "She prayed for 'Daddy.'"

Kirk's eyes shimmered as they looked past us, upward, to a distant place.

His voice, velvet and gravel, vibrated over me. "When Krissie died – the Lord took an anchor from my soul and cast it over into eternity."

My breath caught on a sob. I felt Toby's hand slide into mine and he tipped up his face to solemnly watch me. On my opposite side, Heather's hand lifted to swipe at her tears, while the other gripped my arm.

Kirk looked directly at me and in that look bore all his soul. "Heaven is more precious than ever. I must make it there – I *must.*" His eyes closed. "Let us pray."

I gazed at him, my beautiful robed specimen of manhood, whose humility and grace smote me in a powerful new way. Desperation augmented his magnificence. In that moment, he personified everything male that is pure and noble and good.

At two a.m. the jangling woke me. Kirk stirred beside me as I groped in the dark for the phone. "Yes?" I croaked.

"Neece? I need to speak to Kirk!"

"Roxie?" I cracked one eye, then closed it against the lingering headache. "What's wrong?"

"It's Moose – he's gone. I'm worried to death."

Kirk raised up on his elbow in the dark. "What is it?"

I handed him the phone and grappled for the headache medication on the bedside table.

As the conversation proceeded, alarm set in. I gathered Roxie had not seen Moose since early Sunday morning when he'd gone to buy a paper at the corner Seven-Eleven.

"No," Kirk said quietly – too quietly. I gauged his emotional turmoil. A solid ten. "No, Moose doesn't do things like this, Roxie. Look –" He glanced at the quartz bedside clock. "Try to lie down and rest a bit. There's got to be an explanation."

I could hear Roxie's frantic voice rising and falling in sync with my wildly throbbing heart and head pain.

"Yeah, Roxie. I'll call you back."

Kirk slid from bed and pulled on his robe. "Try to rest, Janeece. Probably something simple like Moose getting a wild hair and going upstate to visit Pearl, his stepma. He's had a lot on him lately." He leaned to kiss the top of my head. "Let me take care of all this. No use in us both losing a night's sleep. Head still hurting?" I nodded and he kissed me again, this time on the lips. "Rest."

I did doze off after the medicine kicked in. When I opened my eyes again, the sun was up and Kirk's indention next to me empty. I glanced around and saw his robe carelessly tossed over the foot of the bed and his shoes missing from their space. Apprehension sliced through me and I sprang to my feet. I rushed down the hall to the kids' rooms, then to the kitchen, where empty silence told me they'd already gone to school. I heaved a heavy sigh and fought guilt. Heather was now the official school chauffeur. I felt badly that I'd slept through everything.

Least my headache's gone. Never mind the drug hangover. It beat pain. I dropped onto the sofa and propped my bare feet on the coffee table.

The front door opened softly, then closed. Kirk stopped when he saw me. "You okay, honey? Headache gone?"

"Yeah. Moose show up yet?" He would, I felt certain. Moose was too danged in love with Roxie to simply disappear.

"No." Kirk sat down in the easy chair facing me. His eyes were so sad it took my breath. "I don't think he will, Neecy."

My pulse skipped into syncopation. "Why?"

He gazed long and hard at me, as if weighing something. "All those talks we had, he confided some things to me that – well, leads me to believe he wanted out."

"Out?"

"Of here. Everything." Kirk shrugged, a jerky, tense movement.

"What—"

"Please…honey," he rolled his neck as though it were in a noose. "No questions. That's all I feel free to share."

The following days blurred with near lethal potions of panic, Roxie's hysteria, phone calls from upstate, phone calls *to* upstate, church folk dropping by to commiserate – Moose was quite popular with his big doofus grin – speculations, tears and Roxie's constant *needs*.

To us, church folk were *family* and when something happened to one of them, Kirk and I felt the impact as forcefully as genetic kin. In Moose's case, lifelong ties intensified that bond.

I tried to understand Roxie's desperation. What I didn't always understand was her clinging to my husband like a newborn monkey to its mother. But I smushed my reaction and prayed extra hard that Moose would turn up and it would all go away.

Besides, Kirk needed me as he had at no other time. With Krissie's death, we'd reached out to one another, almost exclusively, save our other children. This time, Roxie's anguish inserted itself between us, emotionally and physically. I kept telling myself she had no one else upon which to lean.

Callie's view was less charitable. "Listen Neecy – she chooses *not* to be comforted by us mere females." She sat on the edge of the sofa, hands clenched together between her denimed knees. Despite tousled hair and makeup-less face, she maintained the Gardner glamour and mystique. She slashed me a dark gaze, then threw up her hands. "*Okay, okay.* So I'm heartless." She sat back, savagely crossed her legs and hugged her ribcage.

We gazed at each other, leashed together by history and memories....

I snuffled loudly and met Cal's gaze head-on. "He'll be back."

"Is that faith or presumption?" Her testy rejoinder didn't fool me for a second. Her chocolate eyes shimmered.

"Neither. It's hope."

Her lips trembled. "I know."

Kirk slammed in the front door and abruptly braked when he saw us sitting there pale and teary eyed. The starch left him and he plopped into the nearest easy chair. I noticed his fingers trembled as he steepled them to lips set in a brooding face. Anger was beginning to replace the stunned countenance.

It wouldn't be Kirk if it didn't.

"The police think finding his car in Raleigh, North Carolina, is a bad omen." His words came out staccato and spiked. "Say that direction wasn't where Moose would have gone."

"That's what I thought," I said. "He'd have gone upstate or – somewhere familiar."

"I still think he just took a hike," Kirk insisted bleakly.

That evening, Cal stayed over for supper. We needed each other and she needed us, the Crenshaws. Halfway through the meal, the doorbell pealed, then again and again, nonstop.

"I'll get it." Heather rushed to the front foyer.

"He's not coming back!" Roxie burst into the parsonage, weeping and clutching a letter.

We jumped to our feet while Toby ogled the hysterical female.

"Roxie –" I hurried to calm her, but she sidestepped me and threw herself into Kirk's awkward arms. He gazed frantically at me over her head, as in 'do something.'

I shrugged helplessly. Short of prying her loose with a crowbar, I had no plan of action.

"Please, Roxie," I laid my hand on her arm and attempted to pull her into an embrace. No go. She merely dug in deeper.

"Let me help you," I coaxed and shot Callie an SOS look. She came over and half-heartedly did the pry attempt, but we ended up wilted together, frantic about Moose.

Roxie's auburn head turned from side to side. "M-Moose is *gone.*" She tilted her head and gazed up into Kirk's astonished features. Tears dripped off her chin and I felt the first tug of pity.

And fear. "What do you mean – he's gone?"

Kirk forcefully pried her away and held her at arm's length. "W – what's going on, Roxie?" His brow furrowed and his eyes blazed. She began to bawl again and he gently shook her by the shoulders. "Tell me," his voice softened. "Tell me what happened."

Together, we took Roxie to the sofa and settled her shaking body there as she wept and howled. "H-he *said* he'd '*worked things out.'* Do you think he would actually – " One hand covered her red lips while the other shoved the crinkled paper at Kirk.

I quickly grabbed some tissues and pressed them into her hands. I watched the blood drain from Kirk's face until his lips looked blue.

"Kirk!" I cried. "For Heaven's sake – what's it say?"

Only the eyes moved in his zombie pale face. "It's a private letter to Roxie."

"Then why –" I stopped. I was going to ask why she let him see it and nobody else.

But I knew. Pastoral privilege. Pastoral confidence.

He cleared his throat, patted Roxie's shoulder and settled himself in his La-Z-Boy, a safe distance away.

Distance. That summed him up perfectly. He was in another land, deliberating. If brains had sound, the clamor of his would have drowned the revving of jets. As it was, I sensed his frustration. Not by his facial expression, that was gone. Not by his eyes. Those were flat. I can't explain it. I just somehow knew he faced agonizing decisions.

It's perhaps good I didn't know. I don't know. Maybe I could have prevented some of what happened next. Maybe not. I'll never know. Because I said nothing that day.

I trusted Kirk to do the right thing.

CHAPTER FOURTEEN

"What's wrong, Anne?" I gripped the phone, unaccustomed to the tension in my stepmother's voice.

"I just got a call from Teresa. Chuck's in bad shape. Seems his dialysis's not helping him as it should and – complications are setting in." The last phrase quivered across the wires.

My big brother swam before my eyes. I blinked back tears. "I'm going to be with him."

"Me, too." I heard her relief. Anne and I linked tighter and tighter as years sped by.

"I'm glad they've moved into the Greenville area," Anne said. "We can be with him more. Do you think Kirk and the kids will come with you?"

"Not Kirk. The world would stop if he didn't occupy that pulpit Sunday. Anyway, everybody's been down since Moose left. Bet he doesn't realize how much everyone loves him. So Kirk's needed here, especially now." I failed to quip *especially by Roxie*. Anyway, I felt guilty thinking that way.

I quickly scanned pros and cons of Heather and Toby making the trip.

"They're out of school and both goofy over their fun-loving Uncle Chuck. Heather can get Dixie to fill in for her at the piano."

"How about the choir –"

"I'll just dispense with choir specials in the face of this family emergency. Charlie Tessner can do a fair job of getting the congregation started on key." I chuckled. "They'll appreciate me all the more when I get back."

Anne laughed. "Don't you *know* it?"

Abruptly, humor took flight. "I'll call you when we leave," I said.

Heather and Toby packed in record time. Kirk helped us pile luggage into our family Chevrolet sedan trunk.

It was when I turned to hug him that I felt it again. I gazed deeply into green depths. Searching. I found nothing. The shutters were in place. Why? Only when Kirk was troubled did they close. I hugged him again and felt his strong arms tighten around me. His kiss was Kirk. I relaxed.

"You okay?" I asked quietly. Kirk's initial anger over Moose's disappearance had – with weeks passing and no leads – leveled into what I read as resignation.

"Do you think he's okay?" I asked Kirk.

"Probably." Kirk looked away and shrugged limply. "I hope so, honey."

So did I. So did Cal. "Hard to believe," she insisted, "that Moose would voluntarily leave his *sweet thang.*"

Roxie, too, seemed to accept Moose's absence. Her gauntness convinced me she'd truly loved Moose. Callie wasn't as sold on it but at least gave Sweet Thang the benefit of a doubt.

Now, gazing into Kirk's face, I had a sense of us standing on a bubble that could at any minute go *splattt* and send us tumbling into an abyss. Raw fear struck a chord somewhere deep in me. I quickly attributed my angst to our long running trauma with Moose.

And Kirk's features daily set in marble. I repeated, "You okay?"

My husband's lips spread slowly into a smile that twinkled his eyes. "Sure I am." Immediately, the smile fell from a face momentarily unguarded. Dark circles beneath tired eyes revealed worry and strain. "Give Chuck my love and tell him I'm praying for him."

"I will." One more tight hug and I climbed in the car.

My last glimpse of him in the rearview mirror was him standing hands in pockets, gazing unseeing into the distance.

My brother's deteriorated appearance kicked me hard. It jerked me around till I was dizzy and crazy.

Oxygen tubes hooked to his straight, perfect nose, above usually firm Fabian lips. But today, near comatose lethargy made them hang slack. His stillness screamed and cursed at me. The reality of suffering took a momentary stranglehold on my faith in God's mercy

Then his eyes opened. And beyond blurred blue, past pain and misery, I saw Chuck.

My brother. My playmate. Friend. Foe. Hero.

The slack lips tightened, stretched wide, wider.... "Hey, Sis!" he croaked and his hands trembled toward me. I dissolved into his arms, a heap of weepy mush. *Oh God!* He was all sharp bones and angles. Where was flesh? I hugged him as tight as I could without crushing his frailness. I hugged him till my lips stopped quivering and could manage a smile. Then and only then did I pull back to look at him.

"You're beautiful, Chuck," I said softly. And he was, despite that he huffed a weak little snort of protest.

"Yeah, *right.*" The words floated as gossamer on a tropical breeze.

Anne's breath caught on a sob. She sat on the opposite side of the hospital bed. Dad at its foot with Trish next to him. Heather and Toby came into view.

"Hey!" Chuck's blonde head raised a fraction as he fought to focus. "My ol' bud, Toby. C'mere lil' feller." I winced as Toby threw himself at his uncle, harboring none of my frailty fears. After a good wallowing embrace, Toby climbed down to share my chair, a tight arrangement to say the least.

"There's my sweetheart," Chuck closed one eye to squint at Heather, who stood uncertainly beside me. "Prettier'n ever."

I looked up at Heather, nudged her gently. "Go ahead."

She fell on Chuck, an uncharacteristic mass of tears and affection, hugging and rocking him from side to side. This time, I didn't flinch. If Chuck survived Toby, he could endure anything. "I love you, Uncle Chuck," she sobbed. I started to worry that Chuck might get the idea we thought he was dying.

He wouldn't be wrong.

After Heather pulled a chair up to join the family circle, Chuck struggled into sitting position, tubes dangling from his head. His eyelids remained half-mast over glazed azure irises. His weak body weaved about like a sheet flapping softly in the wind. Anne's hand slid into his.

"I'm the luckiest guy in the world." His words slurred but lilted with exuberance. "Just *feel* the love in this room, would ya." He wibble-wobbled about, struggling to keep his eyes open. "My loved ones – all here." He huffed a laugh and nearly fell over before Anne caught hold of him and coaxed him to lie down. He meekly complied, rolled over into fetal position and, holding tightly to Anne's hand, tumbled into slumber.

Daddy went outside and I followed. I caught up as he turned a corner down the hall. I took hold of his arm and fell into step.

"Daddy, I —" I saw his wet face. Tears dripped from his cheeks, rolled down his neck.

Daddy weeping...a rare thing, not since Mama's death had he looked so barren, and I realized my own face was now damp.

We walked silently for perhaps twenty minutes, only sounds being snuffles and hiccuping sobs and once, Daddy's impassioned, hoarse, "I love him *so*, Neecy."

"I know, Daddy." I squeezed, patted his arm and snuffled. "I know."

We turned at the elevators and started the trek back. "By the way," I said, "Where's Teresa? And Poogie?"

"Went home for something." Daddy's voice was flat, non-committal. "Anne asked Poogie to stay but —" He shrugged.

"What's with Teresa?" Anger, a propane torch, blasted through me. "We're *family*, for crying out loud. Why couldn't she let Poogie stay with us for the day?"

Daddy turned to me. Desolation ravaged his features. "Honey, Poogie didn't *want* to stay with us."

I gaped at him, trying to assimilate the fact that Chuck's daughter chose not to be around us. Granted, we'd seen little of her through the years, due to Chuck's self-imposed exile. But our rare times together had been warm and affectionate family occasions – times when we'd all stumbled over each other to show *our Poogie* boundless unconditional love.

"It's *her.*" Unannounced, the edict shot from my mouth. Dad's gray lifeless gaze shifted into agreement, and we proceeded down the corridor.

"I can't let myself think about it," Dad said quietly. "I don't want to get a thing about her."

"No." It wouldn't do. While I could get angry and get over it, Daddy couldn't. "We're probably sensing things that aren't really there, anyway." I doubted that but right now, it helped to foster good thoughts. Chuck needed peace about him.

Lord only knew what had made my brother abandon all rationale and marry Teresa.

Teresa. Pretty, distant Teresa with her ever wary, assessing raisin-black gaze, who, for reasons known only to herself, did not like her husband's family. Never, in fact, gave herself a chance to.

For years, I'd sought to melt away her ice husk with warmth, hoping to discover some common ground upon which to build a measure of amiability. Chuck, I quickly learned, was *not* to be that common ground.

Truth was, she didn't like Chuck, either.

We entered the hospital room to find Chuck awake again. "I'm hungry," he said in a slurred near-whisper. "'Bout to starve in here."

Anne leaped to her feet. "I'll get them to bring you something, son." She disappeared out the door in a flash. Again, pure amazement shot through me as I remembered the miraculous transformation of my stepmother years back. *Thanks, Lord.*

Chuck's eyelids seemed to work separately, both trying to lift and failing miserably. I impulsively leaned to hug him. "Love you."

His arms were remarkably strong in their response. "Me, too."

Within minutes, an orderly delivered a turkey sandwich, arranging it on the bedside pulley-tray. Nearly flat of his back, Chuck tucked into the sandwich.

"Hey, Chuck," Dad teased, "You not gonna share your food with your ol' dad?"

"I will if you'll con me something to drink." He winked lazily.

"Now, son," Anne patted his arm gently. "You know they won't give you but just so many liquids. It'll hurt you."

"Aww," Chuck muttered without real conviction, "A little won't hurt."

I wanted to bawl. Chuck, who'd always drank so much of anything – water, tea, coke and later, beer – now sentenced to a mere pittance of daily liquid. But I managed to keep smiling and joshing.

Soon, Chuck was sitting again, for a much longer period. By the end of the day, he was – to my way of thinking – even sounding stronger. At nine-thirty, visiting hours ended and I insisted Anne, Dad and the rest of the family leave and let me spend the night vigil with Chuck.

"You sure you don't want me to stay, too?" Trish asked, making a comical moue of disappointment.

"I'm sure, honey," I laughed, then whispered, "No use both our hubbies sleeping alone." I winked at Gene, who'd been in and out all day, between pastoral obligations.

"'Night, Mama," Heather hugged me, then Toby, just before he zipped out the door with Grandma and Papa Whitman.

Chuck, exhausted from all the visitors, crashed. I quietly opened up the folding chair-bed and scrounged a pillow from the night nurse.

Then I dialed my home number on the bedside phone. It rang. And rang.

I looked at my watch. Ten-twenty. Kirk was at some late event. I didn't realize how tired I was until my head touched the pillow. I sank into instant sleep.

"Sorry I missed you," Kirk said when I called at seven the next morning. I'd gone to the pay phone for privacy, so Chuck wouldn't hear himself being commiserated over. "Roxie called. Swore she was having a nervous breakdown. Cal and I went over to see about her. She really did look terrible." A long sigh. "I had dinner with Kaye and Charlie and sat around and talked 'til late. How's Chuck?"

"You know, I think he's a bit stronger. Pray that it lasts. The infection he got during dialysis attacked his main artery and is causing some heart problems." I took a deep breath and let it out. "More bad news. His doctor came around this morning and called me outside. Said Chuck's dialysis isn't helping like it should. And that he might get better for a while, then get worse. Could go round and round for who knows how long?"

"Oh, no-o-o," Kirk groaned. "I'm sorry, Neecy. But – he's getting better for the moment?"

"Not exactly. The doctor said Chuck will probably go suddenly – a major heart attack when the fluid buildup is too great for his heart to – well, you get the pic –" My voice choked off.

"Neecy? You okay?" Kirk's voice was honey to my spirit, a calming, comforting force.

I gulped back my fears. "I'm okay."

"Look – take care of yourself. *Please?*" A long moment of silence, then a desperate, "And hurry home, honey."

Hurry home. *Chuck needs me.* "I will – as soon as Chuck's out of danger." Please, Kirk, don't pick now to be difficult. *Territorial.*

Another long silence. Static rippled over the wires. "Of course, honey. That's what I meant. You know I understand and want you to be with him during this time, don't you?"

"Sure."

"God – I love you, Neecy." I let that sink in and flood me as Kirk's sweet voice continued, "I'll be praying for him, darling. Tell him that. I've got to scoot. Love you."

"Me, too, Kirk. Bye."

When I got back to the room, Teresa had arrived. I hugged her profusely and searched her features for signs of the grief I felt. But her face was an empty canvas.

"Since Teresa's here, Chuck, I'm going to Dad's to shower and change. I'll be back probably mid-morning, okay? By the way, Kirk said tell you he's praying for you." I leaned to kiss his gaunt cheek. His lips quickly turned to smooch one on my own.

"Love you, Sis," he murmured. "Thanks for staying last night." He gave a pitiful parody of a wink.

"Anytime." I squeezed his hand and turned quickly away, in time to catch something flash between Teresa and Chuck. Her face was almost contorted with distaste just an instant before a curtain lowered over her emotions. "Yeah, Neecy," she muttered, "thanks."

She tossed back her long salon-streaked wheat hair and plopped down into a bedside chair. "I had to work." She gazed steadily at Chuck. "As usual."

Chuck looked pained. "Why do you –"

"It's true." Teresa shrugged lazily and stretched, then yawned, ignoring Chuck's injured, beseeching gaze.

"I hate it that you have to work, honey." Chuck's words slurred slightly, then quavered. "You don't know how hard it is for me to see you work when I all I can do is lie here –"

My heart nearly leaped from my chest, seeing – *feeling* his castration. My golden, manly brother –

Teresa sat there stone-faced, denimed legs crossed, one foot swinging back and forth. Back and forth. Something in me curled and twisted and agonized for my once proud brother.

An instinctive response tumbled from me. "Chuck, you can't *help* being sick. Teresa understands that, don't you, Teresa?" I pivoted to face her, a mute appeal on my face.

She looked at me, long and steady with those unfeeling onyx eyes. For an eternity.

Please, Teresa, my heart cried out. *Throw him a dadgum crumb.*

The black orbs blinked. Once. Twice. Slowly.

She's enjoying this. Help me, Lord, not to *strangle her with my bare hands.* "*Don't* you, Teresa?"

Then I saw it. The glimmer of pure gloating. "Sure, I do, Neecy," she drawled, then examined the scarlet, chipped nails of one hand. "After all, my ol' man was laid up for years before he died. Mama had to work two jobs – just like me. Had it hard, my mama. Yeah, I understand." The foot swung back, forth, back, forth, brisk like the slash of a knife blade.

"By the way," I hauled her from her vicious angst, "Dr. Paulos came by this morning. Said he'd come back mid-morning and catch you up."

She frowned, sliding her features into *sullen.*

I wasn't about to discuss Chuck's walking-on-ice condition in front of him. Better to let Teresa wait and talk to the doctor later. So, I left them for the fresh outdoors that let me breathe and exhale my emotions beneath a sky that wept with me during the thirty-five minute drive to Dad and Anne's house.

There, they were just leaving to go back to the hospital, the whole kabootle of them. I promised to join them as soon as I showered and redressed.

I was back in the Greenville Memorial's rain dampened parking lot by twelve, having wolfed down a bologna sandwich in Anne's kitchen. My interrupted night's rest – hospital noises are the world's loudest – was beginning to thwart my reflexes. Lordy, I missed Kirk.

Inside, Anne leaped to her feet and met me at the door as I arrived. She steered me out of hearing range. "You won't *believe* what Teresa did." Anne's periwinkle blues glittered with fury.

"Oh no." I collapsed against the wall and shut my eyes in dread. Braced myself. "Go ahead. Tell me."

"Dr. Paulos came by and updated her on Chuck's condition – all the things you told me on the phone about his heart problem and all. Well, after you left, she told *Chuck* in detail what the doctor said. That was the first thing Chuck said when we got here – *'Teresa, tell Anne and Daddy what the doctor said to you.'* And she did, *emphasizing 'he'll die suddenly of a massive heart attack.'*"

My breath came in short gasps, hurt. "After I tried so hard to keep him from having to deal with it." My voice slumped as low as my heart. How *could* she? I shot Anne a bleak look. "How's he handling it?"

Anne raised her eyebrows and gave a dubious shrug. "You know *Chuck*. Nothing ever seems to really – *get to him*. You know?"

"Oh, it does. Inside. It gets to him."

Anne nodded sagely, her face ablaze. "It would have to."

Trish came scurrying up the corridor, a round, sweet little flurry of winded and apologetic movement. "Sorry I'm late. Gene and I had a funeral at ten and –" She braked and peered warily at us. "What's wrong?"

As Anne repeated the latest of the Chuck/Teresa saga, Trish's eyes rounded to donuts then slitted to mere strips. "Let's go beat up on her, Sis," she balled her fists, thumbed her nose and danced a couple of steps back and forth. Trish's weight gain through the years had spawned revved-up comic improvisations that rarely failed to crack me up.

Today, I sighed heavily. Sickly. "Wish it were so simple, Trish."

"Then God would get *us*, too." Trish hugged me hugely, hooked arms and we went in together to undergird our brother for battle.

This one, I thought, would rank Chuck's fight with Dad under *Romper Room stuff.*

Chuck's fifth hospital day saw him upright, moving haltingly, pulling along his oxygen tank, of course, but *walking.*

I called Kirk that evening at nine-thirty to rejoice. I *missed* him with an ache. When there was no answer, I decided to call later.

Chuck's room buzzed with family noises and laughter. Only Teresa was absent. And Poogie. I'd learned, by now, that this was standard for Chuck, them not being there. His divulgences were never whiny. Nor did they deprecate. Nor were they freely given. I gleaned just that hint of his loneliness overhearing phone calls and one visitor's conversation with my brother. His disclosures were simply emotionless, cut and dried, this-is-the-way-it-is.

For those *not in the know*, Teresa and Poogie came out smelling like honeysuckle.

I coped by putting my emotions on hold. Shelving them. By loving Chuck extra.

By praying.

"I want to go to Anne's tomorrow and eat Sunday dinner with ya'll," Chuck declared on Saturday afternoon, clutching his scrawny chest, "I'd *die* for her macaroni-cheese pie."

"Your transfer to the Pinehurst Convalescent Home should be completed by five-thirty today," the nurse signing Chuck out said. "You're feeling so much better, I see no reason why you can't go."

Nursing home. The sister-me screamed in protest. In reality, I held no control over Chuck's destiny. Teresa had, quote, *power of attorney over her husband's life decisions.* Seems in this last life-death episode, my sick brother was coerced to sign away his rights to her, a thing that hit me as screwy, but pitting Chuck against Teresa was like tossing a lamb into a cheetah's den.

Though I'd always despised the Chuck/Dad explosions, I now found myself wishing back a spark of that spirit for my brother. Thing that made it so difficult was – I knew it would never again be.

"Sis," Chuck took my hand, seeing my sadness at his relegation to a nursing home. "It's okay." His speech remained sluggish and connect-the-dot. "Y'know, if I was home, Poogie might get up one morning, come into my room and find me sprawled out dead. I wouldn't want that to be her last memory of me – cold and stiff and blue and God only knows what all." He smiled sadly and squeezed my hand, trying and failing to hold his marvelous blue-gray eyes open. "It's for the best."

So I built up his spirit with the promise of a beautiful family day tomorrow at Dad's and Anne's. *Home.* I could see his joy building. I called Kirk later, during the transfer – they allowed Dad and Anne to drive Chuck the short distance to Pinehurst – on the pay phone. Our conversation was brief and I was relieved Kirk didn't command me home immediately. But then, the next day, Sunday, was his busiest. Saturdays were filled with long hours in the church office, where he studied and finalized his Sabbath message. I felt a bit guilty not rushing home, but Kirk seemed preoccupied with home-front things so I didn't address the subject of when.

The nursing home was dismal at best. Pine and Lysol disinfectants battled urine and body odors. Most of the residents were older than Chuck, the majority beyond mobility and meaningful dialogue. My less than joyful reaction to the dark ambience had Teresa's nose rising a notch.

"This is the best I can do," she snapped without apology. "And it's close to where I work so I can come more often." Her current job was waitressing at two restaurants, one a lunch specialty diner, the other a classier dinner restaurant, where, she said, her tips were pretty good.

At least, I consoled myself, *she'll visit Chuck more.*

I called Callie, lonesome suddenly, for home territory.

"Would you check on Mama for me, Neecy?" she asked. "Just a teeny-weeny visit is all I ask."

"Of course, Cal. Hey – thanks for helping Kirk out when Roxie had her nervous breakdown the other night."

Silence. "When you went with him to her apartment?" I reminded her.

More silence. Then. "Ohh." Another long silence. Then, "Hug Mama for me."

Heather and Toby were enjoying leisure with my siblings, Dale, Cole and Lynette. So when I set out to visit Molly Pleasant, they quickly bade me *adieu*, insisting they didn't want to tag along. The short solitude became a blessing.

Strolling along Church Street was wistfully nostalgic. I'd spent most of my time at the hospital, worrying about Chuck's outcome. Now, with him on at least a temporary mend, I dwelled on familiar sights I'd once passed unseeing.

I turned in the direction of Molly's house. I nearly gasped when I saw her. The Molly I knew was gone. Replacing her was a wasted woman with neatly shortened, natural-waved, snow-white hair. Once glowing skin paled against a long ago attractive, bony face. Her tall frame, Callie's birthright, appeared scarecrowish, as if draped in loose gauze. And then she smiled.

Molly Pleasant shone through that smile. Her arms, still strong and loving, drove away the spooked feeling that had begun accumulating from the moment I saw Chuck near death six days ago. We commenced to talk about things past and things now. Animated, Molly began to restore my sense of balance. Of continuity from girlhood days to now. As she talked, I saw more of Callie than I'd ever glimpsed before. Not just physical similarities. Gestures, mannerisms. Strange – the things Callie had run from in our youth, she now embraced and emulated.

"How's Kirk?" Molly asked, with a hint of Callie's exuberant curiosity.

"Great, Molly. Busy – to quote him – as a one-armed-paper-hanger."

Laughter rolled from her. "Sounds like Kirk. I'm so proud of him – of you."

As I departed, she gave me one last, huge bear hug. "Pass that on to Callie," she whispered, moist-eyed.

Later, that evening, I called Kirk, missing him sorely and eaten alive with guilt, knowing I needed to go home, knowing how – though he rarely admitted it – he hated me gone. But Chuck was going to eat Sunday dinner with us. I did so want to be there for the celebration of his remission.

Tomorrow. I promised myself. *Tomorrow*, I would go home.

Anne and I stayed up late that evening and arose early the next morning and cooked until church time. Daddy departed at ten to pick up Chuck at the nursing home and transport him to the house. Anne sent a warm welcome to Teresa and Poogie to come for lunch, as well. We'd tried calling at Teresa's residence and got no answer. As usual, the family attended Chapowee Methodist where a new pastor preached. Pastor Cheshire, now retired, still attended there.

"Ahhh, Neecy." His British clip had softened through the years, but his affectionate hug remained firm. "It's so good to see you again, my dear girl." He stepped back to survey Heather, who blushed becomingly at his shameless flattery. Sunlight washed his bald crown shiny. I noticed his little hair strip, which barely topped his ears, was now entirely gray.

His stooped frailty smote me, as had Molly Pleasant's. Aging was, I decided, a mixed blessing. It destroyed beauty but kept one alive. And as I watched Pastor Cheshire banter with Toby, I wanted more than anything to preserve him *alive*. And well. All the while aware of my selfish motives – I wanted him around to enrich my family's lives for years to come. Forever, in fact.

We rushed to the house to finalize food preparations. Dad's car already occupied its graveled spot in the small driveway. We lined the curb, spilled from cars and dashed inside, everyone vying to be the first to welcome Chuck, our guest of honor.

Daddy sat planted on the den sofa, granite Walter Matthau.

"Where's Chuck?" Anne asked as we scattered, hunting in bedrooms, nooks....

"He's not here," Daddy called out, somewhat sharply, aborting our search.

"What – ?" We asked in unison, flocking to our bearer of news. Not good news, I gathered from Daddy's pale gravity, from his slightly flared nostrils.

His stony gaze riveted to a far, straight ahead wall. "Teresa left orders that Chuck not be allowed to leave with anybody except her."

"*What?*" I heard myself bellow. "What's her reasoning?"

Now *that* pulled Daddy's lip into an ironic one-sided curl, stopping short of a smile. Nothing else moved in his face. "Said she didn't trust anybody to feed him properly. Afraid it would make him sick after his crisis."

I clenched my hands and stared into Heaven. "Lord – I *can't believe this!*"

For long moments, we stood there, emptied, defeated and infinitely grieved.

"He wanted to come so *badly*," Anne moaned.

The clan erupted into murmurings of misery, amid which Trish and Gene arrived, having fudged a bit of time by ending his sermon early. Their church was thirty-five minutes away.

"C'mon, Neecy," Anne said resolutely, "let's fix Chuck the biggest plate of food he's ever seen and take him a picnic."

That lifted the mood and soon, we'd finished our meal, piled into cars and formed a caravan to Pinehurst Convalescent Home.

Chuck lit up like a thousand candles when we all converged to form a protective wall about him. He ate two plates of macaroni-cheese pie and three pieces of Anne's fried chicken before declaring himself *stuffed*.

I thanked God for my brother's rallying spirit.

And I asked Him to increase my mercy-forgiveness index.

I would be needing it in days to come. Fortunately, I didn't know just *how* much.

Kirk's arms felt so wonderful wrapped tightly around me, shifting and squeezing as though hunting more to consume. His cheeks and lips caressed every inch of my face and neck in the first moments of our greeting. This, of course, after the kids scattered to sniff out home turf and phone friends.

We'd left for home immediately after visiting Chuck, arriving late afternoon, near evening church time. Toby immediately hopped on his bike and sped out the white sandy road that wound through the cemetery, private and perfect for him to blow out restlessness accumulated on the four-hour drive.

Kirk had pulled me into our room, kicked the door shut with his heel and sniffed out *me, his* turf. Now, he gazed into my eyes as though seeing me for the very first time. It took my breath, his passion. Like the young Kirk I'd parked with at Silver Lake. It sent a shiver of excitement over me, mingled with a tinge of apprehension. Of what, I wasn't certain.

"Honey," he said huskily, one big hand brushing hair from my cheek, his green gaze roaming desperately over my features, "Please, don't *ever* be gone from me like that again...for that long."

I pressed my face to his and inhaled, absorbed him. "Okay."

I floated through service that evening, warmed by Kirk's apparent need. A need that fed the benevolent-me, the one who thrived on giving.

"How was Mama?" Callie asked me immediately following the benediction. We stood in the vestibule, near Kirk, who'd kept me within whispering distance since my return. He was talking with Charlie and Kaye Tessner.

"She was beautiful, Callie." I enjoyed seeing her chocolate eyes light up at my compliment. A sincere one. I'd discovered, overnight, that beauty goes way beyond skin or color or shape. Or hair texture. Beauty is spiritual *essence.* Not necessarily religious. Though it can be. I hugged Callie hugely and whispered in her ear, "Your mom said to pass this on to you."

I saw tears in her eyes when I released her. "I didn't mean to make you cry," I said gently.

"It's not − you didn't. I just miss Mama. She's not well. I know you noticed. And things around here haven't −" She took a deep breath and rolled her eyes upward to stem tears, but they gathered anyway, forcing her to step to the foyer table and snatch a tissue from the ever present box there.

"What?" I asked, perplexed. "Things haven't been going right here?"

She took her time wiping away tears and blowing her nose. I noticed the Tessners leaving at the conclusion of Charlie's hilarious golf joke. Kirk, still chuckling, joined us.

I raised my eyebrows at Callie, who seemed deep in thought, faraway.

Kirk, too, watched her. Curiously − concerned, I was certain, that her face was red from tears.

"Well," she straightened her shoulders and face, smiled and hugged me again. "Gotta go. Haven't had dinner."

I grabbed her sleeve as she turned away. "Come home with me and −"

Her head already moved decisively from side to side. "Nope. Thanks, anyway, hon. Gonna go curl up with my kitty cat Ginger, eat a banana and peanut butter sandwich and turn in."

"'Night, ya'll," she tossed over her shoulder on the way out.

"What's wrong with Cal?" Kirk's query was low-key, quiet.

"She's worried about her Mama, is all," I said, wondering if that was *all*.

We were silent on the short walk home. After we snacked and retired to our bedroom, we remained so. Our lovemaking swept me back to when we first married. Fresh and thorough and *right*. A complete giving of ourselves to each other. Afterward, we spooned together, Kirk's arms encircling me like a warm vise.

Could my being away have triggered this – *intensity* in Kirk?

As I drifted off, his plaintive plea floated through my mind...*Please, don't ever leave me like that again...not that long.*

I won't, Kirk. I burrowed my hind parts even cozier against him. *I promise.*

Happiness filled and buoyed me and floated me into twilight. My last conscious thought was a buoyant, fuzzy *Kirk needs me.*

CHAPTER FIFTEEN

The nightmare of Moose's disappearance was a thing we dealt with day by day, minute by minute. Kirk bore the burden of grief heavily. Not only his, but Roxie's as well. Hers was a constant clawing distress that demanded my husband's solace.

Before Chuck's health crisis, I'd barely stayed ahead of the nipping-at-the-heels sensation Roxie generated. Not my heels. Kirk's. My husband's. Before being away, I couldn't put my feelings into words, but since coming back from my brother's bedside, I had no such problem.

"Callie," I said, facing her across her receptionist's desk outside the empty pastor's office, "am I being foolish? For gosh sakes, it's just *Roxie*. Flaky, silly Roxie." I shrugged dismally. "I get these weird butterflies in my stomach when she gets near Kirk. Like —" I took a deep huff of air and blew it out, "like *fear*. Sorta. Jealousy?" I rolled my eyes. "That's stupid, isn't it?"

Callie, solemn and closed-faced until now, sat up straighter and cleared her throat. "No. It's not stupid at all."

I gazed at her. This time, the thing that leaped through me was no mystery. It *was* fear. Callie saw it and tried to soften her features. "That's —" She stopped, gazed at the window for long moments, during which my heart stopped a dozen times before her brown eyes met mine. "Neecy — Roxie is after your husband."

A physical force slammed my midriff, taking my breath. "Cal...why do you say that?" The words seemed to come from afar as emotions pummeled and disjointed me.

Callie started to say something then thought better. She continued to watch me as if weighing something precious. Finally, she said, "Neecy, I just think you need to keep your eye on things. Kirk's up against something potent."

"Potent?" I whispered and was on my feet, as in run.

"Aww, Neecy," she leaped to her feet and rushed around the desk to gather me in her arms. "I don't want to hurt you. Wouldn't hurt you for anything." Then she was shaking, holding me to her like I was a life raft or something. I pushed back and gazed into her face. She was crying.

"Don't, Cal." Don't. *Please don't let it be something I don't want to know.*

"I'm sorry...." She slapped her hands to her face as tears streamed down her lovely cheeks, peering at me over them with enormous chocolate *watering* eyes. Eyes that pitied me. She's *sorry....*

For what? I don't want to know. *Please don't tell me.* Why had my body gone numb? Where was the floor? I didn't know I was weaving till Callie caught hold of me. "Here, sit down, Neecy," she said gently. "Don't pay me any attention." She seated me and rubbed my hands, trying to give them warmth. "You know me, Neecy, ol' motor mouth Cal. Always thinking the worst...."

The worst. What exactly *was the worst?*

"What happened while I was gone, Cal?" I spoke through lifeless lips.

The question seemed to stun her. Her head moved from side to side. "Nothing, Neecy. *Nothing.*" She gripped my shoulders and gave me a gentle shake. "Nothing."

Footsteps. Kirk appeared in the doorway. "Hey. What's up?"

Then he saw me. "What's wrong, honey?" Instantly, he dropped to his knees beside me and took my hands. "You sick?"

His voice was so loving, so concerned, I began to cry, then sob. Quietly, actually, but with such momentum I heaved until nearly blue then came up with a gasp and plunged into the next one. A reflexive thing. One I could not have stopped for the life of me. I was in the grasp of Hell itself. Only Kirk's touch reached my soul. His soft voice. His concern.

Then, I was standing against him, in his arms, my face burrowed into his neck. "What happened?" I heard him ask Callie.

"She asked about Roxie." The statement was flat.

"What about Roxie?" Flat, too.

"Just – she felt Roxie has crossed over a line – that she's chasing you."

Kirk's arms squeezed me tighter as he gazed at Callie. So tightly I couldn't have moved had I tried, which I didn't. As long as my face connected to the warmth of his neck, felt his heartbeat, his energy, smelled his essence, I felt safe. "What did you say to her?" Kirk's question was almost casual. But I felt his tension.

The flailing inside me commenced again.

A long silence. "Look – you need to talk to her, Kirk. It's not my place."

"Your place to *what?*" Was his question a challenge?

I heard Callie move quickly to the door. "Sorry, Kirk. This is your thing." Her footsteps abruptly faded into the sanctuary and out the vestibule. The front door closed firmly.

Thing? I felt the impact of sickening panic building again and stiffened. The arms resisted my pulling away. Held me like a vise. "Stay here, honey," he whispered. "Let me love you."

I relaxed against him because I had no other choice. Kirk was my world.

He held me up until I gained enough strength to walk home with him. There, he gently undressed me and slid into bed beside me, lay touching me, his leg linked protectively with mine.

"Kirk?" I turned my face to his in the darkness. "Is there something between you and Roxie?"

I felt his gaze. "If you mean other than a pastor and flock member, no."

I stared at the ceiling for long moments trying to believe that. Belief did not take. I had to know. Suddenly, I had to know for sure. I sat up in bed, reached to turn on my bedside lamp, then resettled beside him where I could see his face. It looked as miserable as I felt.

Please, Lord, help me.

"Kirk," I said slowly, gathering strength, "I want to know the truth. Is what you told me the truth?'

He gazed at me for long moments as I searched his features for signs of honesty – or dishonesty. What I saw was a man who wanted desperately to help his wife. I could not rely on reading his features because, in crisis, Kirk's shuttered. I had to trust his word.

"Are you telling me the truth."

Something flickered in his eyes. Only a heartbeat movement. Then it was gone.

"Yes," he said firmly. "I'm telling you the truth."

Papa died suddenly the next week of a heart attack. Kirk, the children and I drove to Asheville, to the funeral. Daddy and Anne came, too. MawMaw wept on my shoulder, moaning, "I'm gonna have to depend on you'uns, Neecy. It's gonna be hard without Papa, honey. Please...try to come as much as you can to see me. I need you now."

It broke my heart to lose my jolly-clown, laughing Papa, who'd loved me so much. And it broke my heart to see my feisty little MawMaw so broken. She, the family backbone, now needed *me*. "I won't let you down, MawMaw," I whispered and kissed her wet cheek.

Gabe took Papa's death hard. Because of diabetes, Gabe had not been able to sire children and it was particularly devastating to lose such a significant other as his lively, fun-loving father.

When we went back to MawMaw's after the Pentecostal service and burial, the small house overflowed with church folk and kin. Daddy spoke to MawMaw, took her hand and tried to comfort her. She accepted his words with only a hint of wariness. It warmed me to see them communicate at last. Daddy then cornered me and took my hand. "You okay, Neecy?" he asked softly.

I nodded firmly. "Yes. Why?"

"You look – worried. Are you losing weight?" His gaze swept my features as they had throughout my life, seeing more, sensing more than I wanted.

"I've just been busy. And Papa's death has hit me hard." *Among other things. Things I still face.* Things I'd rather *die* than Daddy find out. I resolutely pushed away the thought.

He put an arm around my shoulder and pulled me up to his side. "I know, honey. You loved him a lot, didn't you?"

I nodded, my eyes puddling. Daddy pulled me into his arms.

It came late. Too late for Papa to know. But not too late for me to know.

Daddy cared.

Sunday morning, I walked out to the church early, before folks began to arrive. Kirk had already gone to study and pray. Toby and Heather had eaten breakfast and were dressing for service. I'd not slept well the night before. Nor had I been able to eat much. Papa's death had taken what little stamina I'd held onto during the Roxie-trauma, leaving me with a nervous stomach and insomnia. A bad case of nerves, actually. And depression. My old nemesis. But I'd get through it, I told myself, hating my weakness.

I mounted the church portico steps, inhaling fresh morning air. I walked over to the end and gazed out at the grave. "Good morning, Krissie," I whispered, then turned my gaze upward to azure infinitude. "Someday, I'll come to you, you know." I closed my eyes for a second, then turned to go in.

That's when I saw it. Roxie's car. The red sports car Moose had worked so hard to pay for. *Moose, where are you?*

What's she doing here this early?

I quietly let myself in. My heart pounded like a bass Congo drum tripped into syncopation. My breath caught in my throat as my feet moved swiftly, soundlessly over the carpeted corridor to Kirk's office. I paused inside Cal's office, at the closed door and listened. Silence.

Then I heard voices. From the kitchen. I moved in that direction like a tracking jungle cat, my breath coming in spurts, not deep enough to sustain life. I stopped and took several deep breaths, hand clutching chest, until I felt oxygen reach my fingertips again, then commenced my trek.

Laughter. I stopped dead. Roxie's trickling laughter. "Kirk, you're too much."

It wasn't what she said. It was the *way* she said his name. As though she *knew* Kirk.

I took two, three more silent steps. Until I could peer around a corner into the dining area. Kirk lounged on the corner of a table, his profile to me. Roxie stood before him, almost between his legs, yet not quite touching him in that instant. Both were grinning from ear to ear, as if at some private joke. Their gazes remained locked, amused. Roxie's next words were so low I couldn't hear. Kirk nodded.

I could stand it no longer. "Kirk?" I barged into the room.

His head turned indolently. Not an eyelash moved to reveal any discomfort. I halted, as though frozen by some invisible force.

"Yes?" His reply was formal. Like I was intruding.

Any peace I'd gained since his avowal the previous week took flight. I stopped and looked coolly at Roxie, who merely gave me a dismissal glance and Kirk a smile as she breezed past me in a new designer outfit of ultra feminine ruffles and flounces that set off every sensuous line of her statuesque shape. In the wake of her departure, I inhaled Channel No. 5. Expensive. Moose's money bought it.

Kirk remained seated on the table, watching me with such ease I wanted to scream at him. Kirk knew. *He knew* how I felt and *still* allowed her access to him. I didn't say a word. I simply let him see my displeasure, then spun and left. I went home, pulled the cover up to my chin and called out to Heather as she started out the door, "I'm sick. Tell Charlie to lead the choir. Put Dawnie in the toddler nursery with Donna."

I knew it would cripple the service, but for once, I didn't have the strength to care. I was too sick to cry. I closed my eyes and sank into momentary numbness.

In that moment, I hated Kirk Prescott for his denial ability. For his duplicity. For his callousness. And I hated myself for loving him.

The tears puddled.

Oh, Krissie, if only I could come to you.

The following days blur in recall. Mask in place, Kirk stepped onto another stage. Everything in the universe adapted to his chameleon shift so smoothly that it missed not a beat.

Everything except me. I'd shifted from *normal* the morning when I saw, felt and heard the simmering intimacy between my husband and this woman who called Kirk *'my pastor'* with emphasis on *'my'*...who drove Moose away as surely as I breathe, by taking, taking, *taking* − sucking the life from him before he disappeared. Just as she now sucked the life from Kirk.

Oh, Kirk didn't acknowledge Roxie's hold over him. In those days, Kirk didn't acknowledge *anything.* The two of us functioned on different planets, spoke different languages.

From there, equalization plunged even lower. Kirk moved as though nothing had altered. I moved as though everything had changed. Like a zombie, yet this time, the zombie had feelings that bled and screamed and pleaded eloquently for help. A plea unheeded. Kirk's denial shot to new zeniths. We spoke to each other, but there was no communication.

Kirk's premise was that Roxie was his best friend's deserted wife. Plus – most significantly – he was her pastor and in her time of grief and rebuilding her life, she needed him.

"How can I not be here for her, Neecy?" had been his reply to my reaction in the church fellowship hall. "We were only talking, for goodness sake."

"What about?" *I have a right to know why she was in your face, oozing, rubbing her sexuality all over you, flaunting and seducing you with her French fragrance, laughing over little things known only to the two of you. Why she'd never let me get to know her on any level, allowing neither Cal nor me to comfort her.*

I have a right to know.

In that last moment of spontaneity, it was, to me, a simple matter of Roxie having jumped a boundary that canceled access to my husband. Not her pastor. *My* husband. I was still naive enough to believe I could call her on it and that Kirk would concede to what *I* felt.

Kirk stared at me as though I'd grown trees on my head, sprouted spiked hooves on my ears. I'd never before questioned Kirk's ethics or faithfulness. Nor had I challenged his pastoral sovereignty or confidentiality.

Kirk's expression puzzled me, made me uncomfortable, insecure. He shook his head and said softly, "Neecy – jealousy is a terrible, terrible thing." He walked away from me that morning without another word. Just *jealousy is a terrible, terrible thing.*

Was that all it was? Me? Jealousy?

My head spun from self-talk. Despite my wish to believe Kirk, I could not turn off my rationale. My rationale did not jive with Kirk's contention – that nothing existed between himself and Roxie. Kirk was ultra gentle with me on other counts in life. Except with the issue of Roxie. I was beginning to think I *did* have mental problems.

To me, she was *the* issue.

Every time I turned around, she was at the church. She'd taken to dropping by the office at all hours of the day. Her reasons were incessant and, to my humiliation and horror, valid. Kirk's expertise with finances and legalese were now my curse. He was simply too brilliant and too male to not show off his genius to the helpless, *flaky*, forsaken Roxie.

That her beauty was perhaps another snag did not elude me for a heartbeat.

"She's driving me up the wall," Callie sniped one day when I walked out to the office to spend time with her. I now dreaded time alone. "Would you believe," she sat back in her chair and clicked her ballpoint pen rapid fire, "she's jealous of *me?* Glares at me when she goes into Kirk's office, then when she comes out, gives me this smug little *'nya nya'* look."

"Why is she jealous of you?" I asked, feeling as sick as I'd ever felt in my life. Like an invisible tiny insect cowered in a torture chamber crammed with Goliath's, all stomping at me, determined to squash me underfoot. *When did Roxie ever arrive at 'jealous?' What gave her the right?*

"Because I try to keep her away from Kirk." Callie's ebony gaze glittered with fury.

"But he won't cooperate with you." My voice was dull and flat. Resigned.

Callie's expression softened. "I think Kirk is thinking like a pastor. Roxie's simply being what she is. What I've always known her to be."

"Same difference." I turned in my chair and gazed out the window at irate black skies.

"Neecy, we've got to trust in God to take care of the outcome."

"Um hmm." I gazed unseeing as the sky erupted and began to weep, splattering and riveluting the window. *Trust in God.... So easy to say. Almost glib.* I knew she was right. But at the moment, I'd lost contact with myself. *Who* would reach out to God?

Am I losing my mind? I took a deep, ragged breath. *So tired. No sleep. Can't eat....*

"You okay, Neecy?" Cal's voice brought me back. She watched me closely. "Look, honey. You need to get that stupid Roxie off your mind. Kirk's too smart to get mixed up with a bimbo like her. Or anybody for that matter. That man loves you."

Her belief in Kirk pierced my fog, made hope flutter.

She smiled at me. I smiled back.

"Yeah," I said, feeling my heart lift for the first time in days.

That night, I initiated sex. Something I rarely did. Oh, I'd always been responsive to my husband's touch. Our passion had not diminished. But for the first time since the Roxie invasion, I felt a surge of confidence that I *was* first in Kirk's life.

"Ahh, darling," Kirk kissed me breathless, then rolled over onto his back, cupped hands under his head and grew still. That was it. As in *do me.* I stared at him, feeling my bubble of buoyancy *splaaatt* and flatten into a cold solid sheet of nothing. I had expected – *something* from Kirk. *Needed* him to give, to resurrect and validate me. Tonight of all nights I needed that. A sudden urge to flee seized me. Leaden, numb, I slid from bed and reached for my robe.

"Where are you going?" Kirk asked quietly.

"Kirk – I," my fingers shook violently as I buttoned my housecoat and slid my feet into slippers. "I need to take a walk. I'm keyed up...I've not had much rest lately and need to clear my head."

"Why?"

I wasn't up to an all out argument or recriminations so I headed for the door. "I just told you."

"You don't know what you're walking out on." His words, so quiet, so enigmatic, so challenging, stopped me dead and stirred my anger.

I whirled around and squinted through the darkness to where he lay, relaxed, flat of his back, waiting to be serviced. Did he actually say that or was my mind playing tricks? I narrowed my gaze at his indolent pose. "What do you mean, Kirk? What *am* I walking out on?"

His still silence sizzled an unspoken message of sexual domination.

Why, you would subjugate me further.

Not in this lifetime, Buster. I spun and dashed from the room, shaking with indignation and hurt. How could he *not* know how I would take that? I strode through the front door and across the lawn. A night light illumined church and parsonage property so I walked briskly within and over its silvery confines, desperate to purge myself of churning, swirling forces that spawned anxiety, shredded nerves, cancelled sleep, destroyed appetite, mocked tears, and pummeled my body into a heap of garbage. That told me I was unloved and unlovable.

I dropped to my knees beneath a tree and dug my fingers into the soft sand. "Oh, God," I moaned. "Please help me." My hands plowed deeper into the bog as tears dripped and added to its moistness. "I-am-so-alone," I whispered through my teeth, not wanting to chance being overheard. By whom? *Who* would overhear? taunted the oozy, black thing that swirled and sucked away at my substance. *Who cares enough?*

I knew. Something deep, deep inside me *knew*. Kirk would not come and find me.

I sat on the ground for a long, long time, staring dully at the starry sky. How far I'd come from that girl who'd believed in true love. Life seemed crushed from me. My limbs resisted movement, but I forced them to carry me into the house and into the kids' bathroom, where I ran a tub of water then crawled in, hoping to cleanse away sand and tension.

"Mom?" Heather came in to use the bathroom, squinting sleepy-eyed at me. She'd been asleep for hours. "You okay?"

"Um hmm." I smiled but failed to fool her.

"I know about Roxie chasing after Dad," Heather said matter-of-factly.

I gazed at her, dry-mouthed and blurry visioned. "Why – how?"

Heather's nose rose a notch and she cast me a sidelong look of disgust. "Anybody would have to be *blind* not to see it. Besides, I've been out to the office when Callie tried to keep her away from Dad. No way, Jose. She's *nuts.*"

My heart lurched. Please, God, protect Heather. But I did so need somebody.... "I thought I was imagining things," I said, hardly recognizing my scratchy, hoarse voice.

My daughter looked at me with wise eyes. "Mom, I'm beginning to think you're the only one around here with any sense a'tall." With that she swooped to plant a solid kiss on my cheek. "'Night, Mama. I love you."

"Love you, too," I whispered as the tears came, too late, thank goodness, for her to witness. I bit my lip until I tasted blood but could not stem the tears until they got good and ready to cease.

Afterward, I crawled into Krissie's bed.

Alone...alone...alone. Only thing worse was being with Kirk, yet *not* being with Kirk.

Where are you, God? I'm frightened. I tried to quote Bible verses but couldn't finish a single one before losing grasp of the words. The slimy, reptilian presence of demonic seducing spirits, different than any I'd before encountered, taunted and slithered and hissed at me and I realized they'd been doing this for days, hours I'd been fighting and driving them back with strength from the Almighty.

Tonight, I could not escape. Through the long black hours, I grew to recognize the smell, touch and sound of them.

Daylight scattered the darkness. Only then did I feel myself loosen to swirl, then plunge into instant, exhausted oblivion.

I awoke with a start, heart palpitating. Sunlight washed the empty house. Disoriented, I gazed blearily about the room, then identified it as Krissie's. *Why am I here?* Then I remembered and the blackness rushed at me, its viciousness incited by time-out. I mentally fought to buttress myself, to stave off the worst.

I glimpsed the blurred bedside clock. Eight-twenty-three. I'd slept two and a half hours, not nearly enough for a seven to eight-hour gal, but it had to do because once awake, I braced myself against an avalanche of adrenaline.

I rolled into sitting position. My head dangled forward and spun for long moments as I sat there, waiting for blood to reach and quicken my extremities. When moments passed and still they remained numb, fear lanced me. My brain toiled while my body vacationed somewhere.

Help! I ignored the inner shriek as I flexed and unflexed my fingers, flailed and rubbed them. I stomped my feet on the floor. Dead. My arms felt nothing when I frisked them. I pushed myself up onto wobbly limbs and discovered I could walk, though unsteadily. I moved clumsily about, holding onto furniture, knowing that doing so generated circulation.

Within moments, sensation began to seep back into me. But rather than soothing awareness, my skin screamed as though on fire. My scalp and face burned from raw nerves. My ears buzzed and hurt and my dry tongue stuck to the roof of my mouth.

Terror gushed upward from my bowels and filled me to bursting. I threw open my mouth, then heard them: *screams*. They went on and on and on. Forever. I felt pain in my throat and wondered who howled in such shrill agony. *Poor thing.* I stumbled against Krissie's oak dresser that still held her toiletries and knick-knacks and caught myself before falling. The cries recommenced, stronger than ever, with such travail I thought my heart would break. I white-knuckled the dresser's edge, my eyes squeezed shut as the ear-splitting shrieks climbed to crescendo.

That's it. I've got to help that person. I lifted my head and found myself gazing into the mirrored sufferer's face.

The screams abruptly ceased. I stared horrified at a person I no longer knew. Enormous, *terrified* eyes burned from dark pits gouged into a pitifully bony, tear-streaked face whose mouth froze into a wide death rictus. My gaze slid down to fingers so frail as to be nearly transparent. Wrinkled clothes hung from a stick-drawn skeleton.

When? How did I ever come to this?

Shame washed over me. I closed my mouth, snatched a tissue and blew my nose, then wiped my wet face dry. Survival took over. Instinct. My last dredge of self-respect snapped to attention and demanded immediate action.

Stripping last night's clothes from my ridiculously skinny frame, I took stock of what was left of me to salvage. My skin still burned and my hands tremored but I could endure that. Had, in fact, before marriage, when Kirk had wanted his 'time out with buddies.' That endurance recall calmed me some. I analyzed where I'd come from all those years ago. By George and by cracky, I'd battled the demons then and won. Insecurities, insomnia, involuntary anorexia, the whole kit and kaboodle..

No one knew of my battles. Not even Daddy suspected their brutality. Neither would they now. I refused to amplify my unloveableness with revealed frailties. By concealing the truth, I may, just *may*, avoid driving everyone from me.

I turned from my ugly reflection and padded to the bathroom. Under the shower, for the first time in days, I succeeded in talking with my maker.

Talking, not listening. "Lord, please help me to be stronger. Please – do something to rid me of Roxie. I don't believe Kirk's guilty of – unfaithfulness. But I don't trust *her* for a minute. So, anything you can do to help me, I'd sure appreciate it. Thanks, Lord."

I rushed to dress and join Callie at the church office, to escape aloneness. I didn't linger to listen to that inner guiding voice.

A big mistake, I would learn much later.

Kirk didn't know about the Pastor Appreciation Day scheduled at Solomon Methodist Church two weeks later. It was a secret thing to honor him. Behind-the-scene plans ran smoothly, due to Callie's administrative skills.

"Just call me *bulldozer*," she snorted when I complimented her, then grabbed me for a huge hug. Roxie had gone low profile, barely showing her face anywhere. Secretly, I was jubilant. So was Callie. Kirk seemed – well, almost normal again. We'd had a heart-to-heart about that night and his cryptic remark.

"You can't pay any attention to me, Neecy, what with Moose's disappearance and all." He shrugged his wide shoulders, looking desolate. "It's still hard to believe he split. Anyway, I don't even *remember* what I was teasing you about that night. Then, when you said you needed to clear your head, I figured you needed time alone for *whatever.*" He'd taken me in his arms and declared huskily, "Just know this, Neecy. I love you with all my heart."

Undercover, I fought my way from trauma's wasteland. Nights still stretched long and food churned in my stomach, but at least, I functioned without it being detected. My rationale continued to argue with the romantic me. Told me I was crazy for believing every word Kirk spoke.

Fact was, I *wanted* to believe him, chose to trust him.

My self-disgust went on hold. I sort of drifted along on autopilot, not dealing with it. At that moment, survival came first. Regaining strength. Health and self-esteem would come later. First things first.

Dad, Anne and family came down for the special service, arriving on Saturday. Of course, with the event being top secret, they didn't tell Kirk the reason. "We need a weekend off," was Dad's sole comment.

On the Sabbath, I dressed Dawn and sent her on ahead with Lynette and Heather to church, then rushed to my room to get ready. "Come with me, Anne," I gestured, "tell me how Chuck's doing."

Anne, already decked out in an alabaster suit, lounged on my bed as I pulled a navy-blue skirt and long-sleeved white blouse from the closet and riffled through my dresser drawer for panty hose without holes.

"He's holding his own, Neecy. You know Chuck – never complains. Doesn't want pity. But –" Anne's eyes moistened, "I can't help it. He breaks my heart sitting around that nursing home with folks old enough to be his grandparents, nobody to talk with – on his level that is. I can see his loneliness when I arrive, before he spots me."

I pulled off my robe and began to thread my leg into the hose. "I wish –"

"*Neecy!*"

I swiveled to look at her, startled. "What?"

Her eyes were stricken, like huge donuts. "Neecy – what's happened to you? You're no bigger round than a toothpick!"

I could have kicked myself for exposing my wasted self to her. Usually, my loose fashions camouflaged it. "It's nothing, Anne. I've just been busy lately and forget to eat, is all."

She gazed unbelieving at me. "You look *sick.*"

"I'm *fine*. You worry too much, Anne." I laughed nervously, covered myself and steered the subject back to Chuck. "Has Teresa been nicer to you and Daddy lately?"

Her brow still furrowed with worry, Anne sat back against the headboard. "Not really. Chuck finally told me what I'd suspected all along. She told him she doesn't like his family. Resents us."

I spun to face her, incensed. "You know why? Because we *love* him. We make it hard for her to convince him he should just go ahead and die."

Anne nodded sadly. "I'm afraid she doesn't want him to linger."

"She only went back to him to get what little money he had left in the bank."

"Well," Anne cut me a wise look, "that's all gone now. Poor boy doesn't have a cent to call his own."

"So she's shoving him at the mortician." I beat my hair with the hair dryer and finger-fluffed it. "Has she allowed him to go home with you for dinner?"

"Not yet. He still wants to. In the worst way. It's hard, seeing him humbled like that."

"I know." I choked on emotion, my mind's eye seeing a magnificent blond Adonis in his youth who had the world on a string and girls at his feet. Whose zest for life exceeded all those in my experience, save Callie's and Kirk's.

Anne and I walked to church across dew-kissed grass, inhaling spring coastal air sweetened by honeysuckle and early azaleas. Inside, I escorted Anne to where Daddy was already seated, reading his Bible to pass time. Naturally antsy, he'd left earlier with the kids. Only two or three early arrivals milled about in the vestibule, including the Prescott and Whitman offspring, who kidded around in subdued tones.

I headed for the office complex in the rear of the church, where my choir robe hung in Kirk's closet, not its usual place, but he'd picked it up at the cleaners for me only yesterday. Callie almost slammed into me. "Come on, Neecy, don't go back there." She took my arm and propelled me back from whence I came.

"But , Cal," I tried to shrug loose as she kept moving, "my choir robe is in Kirk's office."

She stopped abruptly. I could hear her mind churning. Then she raised her hands half-mast. "Okay. I'm going back for it. You stay here. Promise?"

"What's going on, Cal?"

"Stay *here!*" She glared at me for a long moment, her intent to intimidate me.

Her backend vanished promptly. Then my feet began moving, trailing her. Somehow, I *knew.*

My insides, nearly relaxed from earlier ordeals, instantly knotted.

Roxie was on the premises. I *felt* it. The black slime was alive and well.

At the office door, I collided with Callie, whose face turned thunderous. "I *told* you to not come –"

Roxie appeared like sleight of hand, her eyes in feline slits. Kirk on her heels, growled, "Don't do it, Roxie!"

She simply smiled and stepped toe-to-toe with me, slanting me a smug look. "He doesn't want you to know, Neecy. But I think you ought to –"

"Stop it!" Kirk grabbed her shoulders and shook her like a rag doll. Callie pushed me farther inside and slammed the office door to keep the noise down.

"Keep your filthy mouth shut, Roxie," my husband hissed so quietly I flinched. I knew that sign meant he was at the breaking point.

Roxie shot him a look of pure sensual malevolence. "Y'know what, Kirk? You don't have a blasted thing to do with what I say or not say." She turned to face me again and opened her mouth to speak.

"Say one word," Callie pushed me aside and mingled breath with Roxie, "and I'll make you wish you were dead."

Roxie hesitated, then opened her mouth again, "Neecy –"

Callie grabbed Roxie by the hair and slung her against the wall so forcefully, Cal stumbled backward. I reached for her just as Kirk caught her, a breath away from hitting the floor. Roxie slid to the floor soundlessly, pale and disoriented.

"Would somebody please tell me what's going on?" I peered fearfully at them, knowing I didn't want to hear but it was like a keg of worms turned loose. There was, for me, no turning back. "Tell me."

Kirk's eyes when they met mine blazed. "She's trying to destroy everything with lies."

"Lies?" Roxie, sprawled in the floor, gave a small strangled sound of disgust and climbed to her stiletto-heeled feet.

"Shut up!" Callie stepped forth warningly.

"Lies." Kirk turned to Roxie with a look on his face I knew to be throwing down the gauntlet. "Get out of my church and don't show your face here again."

Roxie's face turned ugly. "For now."

She swept past Callie, searing her with a look of disdain. "Before I'm through, you'll both wish you were dead." Then she turned and looked at me with bald contempt. "Let's see – what was your name? Oh yeah – poor, poor *blind* little *Neecy*. You –"

"Lay off her!" Callie shoved violently and Roxie's padded shoulder struck the door with a loud *thud*.

"Get your sorry behind out of here! *Now.*"

I reeled from Roxie's assessment of me, one I myself entertained all too often. Was it accurate?

Roxie got her footing, brushed her short skirt over her hips in a defiant caress and shook the titian mane from her shoulders.

She looked straight at Kirk, whose poker face was unreadable. It annoyed me. It sent fissures of fear through me. "For now," she purred and oozed through the door with much elaborated hip movement.

"Thank God." Callie closed her eyes as the footsteps faded. Then her eyes popped open. "I'd better see her out." She raced to make sure Roxie didn't detour.

Kirk peered at me. "You okay, Neecy?" The query was so tender and caring it caught me off guard, made me dizzy.

I nodded. "You?"

"Yeah. I am now." He shook his shoulders and rolled his head as if to dispel the catastrophe. "I should have done that a long time ago. I just didn't know how – devious she was. Had no idea."

I told you so. Yet I could not, *would not* speak the words because I could not get away from my ethics – would never be able to abandon them. In essence, I treat others as I want to be treated.

Then, his arms held me so desperately, everything fled except the two of us. And I realized that whatever had happened, Kirk was as much victim as I. He helped me into my choir robe and hand-in-hand, we walked to face whatever the day might hold.

My healing was not instantaneous but calm was. In the wake of infernal anarchy, I wallowed in heavenly tranquility.

Pastoral Appreciation Day proceeded without a whiff of what had transpired in Kirk's office that morning.

"What brought it all on?" I asked Callie later that week. For the first couple of days following the explosion, I'd simply floated upon euphoric deliverance, paddling round and round in it like an aimless intoxicated duck. "Why did Roxie go over the edge?"

Callie sat on my sofa after dinner one evening, sipping coffee. Kirk, Heather and Toby were doing their monthly Convalescent Home odyssey, involving that evening the entire Solomon Youth ministry. Alone, Cal and I packed the dishwasher, wiped the counters and curled up across from each other in the cool earth-tone ambience of the den.

Callie nursed her cup in both hands, legs tucked beneath her at an alluring angle that still showed ample calf and ankle, and drew from her brew leisurely. Giving her time to think. These days, the old impulsive, shoot-from-the-hip Cal did not exist.

"She wanted my job." Callie stated matter-of-factly. She placed her cup on the end table and then steepled her fingers to her full lips.

"Your job?"

"Yeah. See – I might be leaving soon."

Whammo! "Cal. No."

"Fraid so, Neecy. Mama's got cancer."

"Dear Lord – no. How long have you known?"

"For a few weeks now."

Hurt washed over me. A flashback to the past when Callie failed to share important things with me. I tried to brush it away. Had to.

As though reading my thoughts, she said, "I didn't say anything because – Neecy, you've been through a lot lately. I didn't want to add to it with my problems."

"Am I that transparent?" I choked on the words, hating my vulnerability.

Callie's smile flashed, showing her even white teeth. "I've known you a long time. Remember?"

That, too, made me uncomfortable, but I hid it by smiling. "Yep. Fraid so. I just hate it that you don't let me help you carry burdens, is all." Then suddenly, I despised myself for whining.

"Sorry," Callie threw up her hands, making me feel guilty. "Thought I was doing the right thing."

"You were saying Roxie wanted your job." I truly thought I was ready to talk about it.

Callie's face clouded. "Did she *ever.*" She wiggled herself into tailor position, ankles crossed before her, more animated. "She got to sneaking in, to eavesdrop on me and Kirk. I told you she was jealous, accused us of having this thing going." She rolled her eyes. "Wishful thinking on her part – thinking if Kirk would hit on me, she had a chance, you know?"

I nodded, feeling my insides begin to churn. Too late, I realized I wasn't as ready to hear Kirk discussed in this context as I'd thought.

"Well," Callie continued, "one day, she overheard me mention I might be leaving soon to take care of Mama and she appeared like a Genie in a bottle – *ta da!* – cutting her eyes at Kirk like a western Geisha, smearing it on like mayonnaise. '*Oh, Kirk, I've been praying for a job like this. Ever since Moose left, I've been crying myself to sleep at night tadatadatada.*' The whole nine yards, baby." Callie said all this through clenched teeth, the chocolate eyes all pupils, now moistened with rage. "I told her 'no way.' That first on the waiting list is Tillie Dawson, who'd love to be back."

Tillie. How little I'd understood when another woman clouded her marriage. I thought I had sympathized, but I'd not had a clue.

Callie's leaving. Despair flushed through me. "When're you going?

"Not until I have to. Soon, however. Mama's going down fast."

Butterflies flapped away inside me. I had to ask. "How did Kirk handle Roxie's demands for your position?"

Callie's brow knitted and she crossed her arms, thinking. "He didn't, really. Left it to me. Like everything else concerning her. It's like – he had to appease her or something. Got to me at times. But...." Her voice trailed off and she glanced at me, as though sensing she'd said too much.

"You've been protecting me, haven't you?" I asked in a flat voice.

Something flashed in her face then vanished. "Both you and Kirk." She slid her feet into slippers and stood. "Gotta run. My bedtime."

"Wait," I stood. "Why did you feel you had to protect Kirk?" Dread pounded my heart like tom-toms.

Callie whirled to face me, eyes ablaze. "Because, I hated to see that floozy destroy what you and Kirk have worked so faithfully to build. Roxie would blow this ministry to confetti without as much as a backward glance." Her features slid into sadness. "You were always the good girl. I was the bad. I've done lots of things wrong in my lifetime." Moisture gathered in her onyx eyes. "I want to do this right. If you two hadn't taken me in and helped me onto the right road, I don't know where I'd have ended up."

She hugged me fiercely. "Thanks, Neecy. I couldn't let Roxie get away with what she was doing. I just couldn't."

My voice caught on a sob. "T-thank you, Cal. I hate to see you go, but I understand."

She gazed at me, humor breaking over her face. "I'm just going home to *bed.*"

I playfully smacked her shoulder. "You know what I mean."

"Yeah. I reckon I do. It'll all work out okay. You'll see."

I waved from the door as her car spun away and then dressed for bed, listening for Kirk and the kids to come in. Propped in bed, I read my Bible verses and thought on Callie's divulgences. With Roxie's threatening presence gone, I realized I could think more clearly, could assimilate truth from fiction – *Or could I?* I had not heard Roxie's lies, thanks to Kirk and Callie's barricade that Sunday to hush her up. How could I judge something I did not know?

Something on the deepest gut-level told me I did not want to know.

Truth was, I wanted my life with Kirk back. The one before Roxie.

I could no longer tune out the litany going round and round in my head since. Was too tired to fight it.

How, exactly, could Roxie destroy us?

CHAPTER SIXTEEN

There were in those post-Roxie days, two of me. Amid a self-diagnosed, self-treated mental breakdown, I grappled for wisdom via past-experiences-survived. Following my daughter's tragedy, I'd splintered into several of me who tackled survival in varied, necessary ways. I sought counsel and took it. There was no easy way to recover, but I tried to heal in as healthy a way as possible.

Now, I faced another scenario entirely. Oh, the devastation of both experiences slashes to the bone and leaves lasting gnarled scars. Difference being that losing Krissie captured the sympathy of the world at large while the hovering scandal transferred to my account shame and secretiveness. *I could see no wholesome way to survive this.* To reveal that my husband – a man of the cloth – had been tempted to stray would compromise my self-worth in such a way as to annihilate me.

It would substantiate my subterranean unlovable-self-image. Oh yes, add *ugly* to unlovable, compliments of Roxie-O. Even now, after all that's happened, I feel a little guilty doing Roxie-sarcasm.

I never liked to denigrate dead people.

It happened the day after my conversation with Callie.

Kirk had gone to the office for a while and the kids were off doing their things, Toby riding his bike, Heather out at the cemetery shade, no doubt.

The phone rang, interrupting my vacuuming. "Hello."

"Janeece –" a woman screeched my name on a frantic note of hysteria. "I know you don't want to talk to me, Janeece. I'm sorry I've hurt you but I need –"

The wind *swooshed* from my lungs and I croaked, "Roxie?"

"Yes. I-is Kirk home?" I heard the plaintive hesitancy.

"Roxie –" I wanted to tell her where she could shove her request, but my inner-guide stopped me. "No, he isn't."

"Please – *please, Janeece.* I need help."

I took a deep breath to calm my trembling. "Did you try his office?" I've *got to be crazy to be talking to her. Okay, Lord, I know, I know.*

"Yes."

"Well, I'll tell him you called when he comes –"

"Oh, *god!*" she wailed on a long breath. "Tell him I need help."

"Okay, okay, Roxie. Calm down. Okay?"

I could hear her harsh strident breathing on the other end. "Please, forgive me?" I heard sobs.

My heart relented. "For what, Roxie?"

Snubbing. "E-everything."

"It's all right, Roxie. Everything will be all right. Is there anything I can do to help?"

"N-no." A fresh burst of sobs. "They're going to do it, Neecy. Tell Kirk *they're going to do it!*"

"Who's going to do *what*, Roxie?" I cried as her terror transferred to me. I felt, smelled, tasted it. "For goodness sake, *tell me!*"

Click. The connection broke. I pushed the button frantically as the front door slammed upon Kirk's arrival. "Hi! Anybody home?" he called good-naturedly, tossing the Solomon Daily Crier on the counter.

"Mama?" yelled Toby. "What's for dinner?"

Kirk's laughter trailed. "Don't you ever think about anythi –" He stopped and gaped at me still holding the receiver. "What's wrong, honey?"

I blinked. Then opened my mouth. Now I knew I was crazy. "Roxie called."

Instantly, his eyes hooded. "And?" His reply was flat.

I swallowed back a bubble of vehemence. "She said to tell you 'they're going to do it.' She sounded hysterical and said she needed help."

I watched color drain from behind Kirk's mask. "I've got to go."

I gazed at him, aware of the plea in that statement. But I could not say it. I could not say, "Go to her, Kirk." It simply wasn't in me.

"It's your decision, Kirk." My lips were wooden. I turned away and switched the vacuum on and began to push, push, push.....

I heard the door slam as Kirk rushed outside to his car. I turned off the machine and moved to watch his – our – car spit sand as it sped from the driveway. Two hours passed, long and tortuous minutes, seconds during which I prepared spaghetti for supper, simply because it required little thought and effort.

Heather sat with me on the sofa after dinner, holding my hand, watching, unseeing Sonny and Cher in living color. She'd asked me where Dad rushed off to and I'd explained the situation to her as truthfully and unemotionally as possible. Her initial thunderclap reaction quickly settled into one of concern for me, her near catatonic mom. She'd believed me when, during past weeks, I'd insisted on Kirk's innocence of sexual duplicity.

"Don't worry, Mama," Heather's voice now soothed my uncertainty. "Daddy's too smart to let somebody like *her* mess up his life."

"I know." I patted her hand reassuringly. Yet, the shock of Kirk's dashing to Roxie's rescue whammied me. I tried to tell myself he was a pastor after all but by now, that rang hollow and mocking. Even sinister. And I felt used and ugly. And incredibly stupid.

"I love you, Mama," Heather laid her head on my shoulder and squeezed my hand.

I kissed her sweet forehead. "I love you, too, bugger."

"Me, too!" Toby landed next to me, burrowing in for his share of hugs.

It hit me suddenly, that this was what Callie had wanted to protect. Us. All us Crenshaws.

I wanted to protect us, too. And I would, by the help of God.

I *would*.

Kirk walked in. His facial mask had not moved, had only turned grayer. His arms hung limply at his sides as his desolate gaze sought and found mine.

"I was too late." His quiet words floated one by one to me, threaded with unreality.

Dread dropped over me like heavy black foam. "What do you mean?" I whispered.

"She's dead." He shrugged.

"How?" My hand flew to my chest.

"Murdered." He turned and shuffled zombie-like down the hall to our room, where the door clicked softly, firmly behind him. I presently heard him throwing up in the bathroom.

God knows, I didn't want Roxie dead, but I felt no great gush of sorrow. Only the sick stupor from being slammed by an eighteen-wheeler with *Death and Betrayal* emblazoned across it. I've since surmised that one's grief-reservoir can only cough up so much before drying for a spell. I'd used mine all up in recent days.

Kirk had found Roxie in her blood-spattered apartment, stabbed repeatedly in the chest and neck. Such a horrible end for someone so young. Such a horrific sight for Kirk to see. He remained pale and shaken for days.

Rumors were the murder was drug-related. A police investigation was launched. Kirk was questioned but refused to discuss details with anyone. Not that I pressed him to. I was as reticent as he was on the subject. Church folk are simply curious beings about such and when they quizzed Kirk, he merely pleaded ignorance.

Kirk conducted Roxie's funeral. His was a warm yet impersonal message in which he referred to the deceased's grief over her husband's death and her struggle to begin a new life. Then he quoted from the Bible Moose's favorite scripture, Matthew 7:11, "If ye then, being evil, know how to give good gifts unto your children, how much more shall your Father which is in heaven give good things to them that ask him?"

I read his features during the eulogy quite analytically, I confess. I watched for signs that never appeared. Kirk's wan features presented a warm, controlled mien of sad concern. No more. No less.

Callie sat to my right, Heather to my left, both supporting me in ways known only to us. Charlie Tessner sang "Because He Lives," Moose's favorite song. In some ways, it gave closure to his disappearance. A *goodbye.*

As Charlie sang, Callie, teary-eyed, leaned to whisper in my ear. "I hope she made it." Her face shimmered and swam before me. I snuffled, blinked to loosen tears, and nodded.

Because Roxie, despite her ill deeds toward my family and me, had asked my forgiveness – some of her last words. I prayed she'd asked God's pardon, as well, knowing she probably had, such was her desperation that day.

So I closed my eyes and tried to picture her in Heaven.

You don't have to handle this, came the familiar voice I'd learned to trust.

Just turn it loose. Give it to me. I did.

CHAPTER SEVENTEEN

I fought daily to be normal when I was anything but, trusting no one with the truth. Somewhere along the way, I'd adopted the notion that if one went through motions long enough, they became real. Maybe, I surmised, I could outlast it. So, I choked back apprehension and smiled when I felt like weeping, creating a desperate cheer to drive gray from my days and black from my long dreadful nights.

Heather entered the local junior college. She dated Ralph Stevens – now enrolled in his second year at Clemson – long-distance. Toby, precious Toby, with his innocence and affability, skimmed through time unaware that his mama teetered on a tightrope so flimsy, a gnat's sneeze could send it crashing.

Dawn was my balm, anchoring me to sanity. Our nightly ritual was to bathe together, she astride my birdlike soapy thighs, as we chatted about everything under the sun, giggled like Doofuses, then sang to the rafters her current favorite, bouncing between *You Are My Sunshine, Bingo was His Name* and Frankie Valli's *My Eyes Adored You.*

Afterward came cuddling time, piled in my bed, singing softly her choice spiritual verses. Music was, and would forever remain, intrinsic to our bond. Then prayer...that soft little voice asking God to *bless Mama and Daddy and my Heaver (Heather) and Toby* never failed to leave my throat knotted like a pretzel.

I didn't stop praying in those days of hazy suspension. Had I done so, I'm convinced the strength to nurture and sustain my family would simply have fled.

Truth was, the only time I felt *right* was when Kirk held me in his arms as he did so often now. His warm touch would – momentarily – seize that loosed, clanking thing inside me and press it back in place. His wonderful hands and lips, in private, calmed and validated.

Kirk's libido had, most definitely, recovered from its sag.

Seemed like honeymoon at times, what with the sexual awakening.

Yet, without fail, the morning-after found me desperately engaged in battling *it*, that elusive, unnamed thing inside me that, sometime between lovemaking and dawn, disconnected.

It clamored in my gut like rocks agitating in MawMaw's old wringer washing machine. It left me gaunt-eyed and vigilante. Of what? I had no idea. And despite life's uneventful, outwardly peaceful flow, it flailed about, groaning, *Something is wrong.*

"How's it going, Chuck?" Kirk thrust out his hand to my bedridden brother.

Chuck's face burst into a grin, transforming his gaunt features from torpid to alert. "Great! Just *great*, Kirk! C'mon, pull out a chair and sit a spell." We were up for Friday and Saturday, having gotten the news, via Anne, of Chuck's rapid slide into despondency.

I leaned to kiss his cheek and his frail arms engulfed me in a fierce hug. "Ahh, Sis," he said gently, "it's so good to see you." He released me and wobbled his head around, searching. "Where's that Toby?"

Like a rowdy hummingbird, Toby swooped in, alighted on the bed, and in a flurry of hugs and furious pats, uncle and nephew renewed affections. Heather was next. Her endearments, though more composed than before, were just as warm, leaving me misty-eyed at the mellowed change in my brother.

Anne and Dad arrived shortly thereafter to spend family time together with Chuck. We all wanted desperately to give him the sense of family he needed, a thing he'd so lacked. Now, we could rally for him, carry him on our shoulders and backs if need be to lift him above his placelessness. Of all the family, I could most sense Chuck's desperation to belong somewhere. It twisted my heart.

"Anne," Chuck said, reaching out to take her hand between the bed's guard rails, "I want to eat with ya'll tomorrow." He weakly rotated his head till he sighted Daddy. "Can you come get me, Dad?"

My father nodded, nostrils aflare. "Wild horses couldn't stop me."

Chuck's tired, pale face relaxed. Glowed waxy white.

That evening, after leaving the convalescent home, we prepared for bed at Anne's and Dad's.

I raised my brow at Anne. "Will they let Chuck come?" *They*, meaning the convalescent home staff. In view of Teresa's territorial, power stance, it was doubtful.

Anne bit at her bottom lip, eyes worried. "I don't know, Neecy."

"We've got to do some *tall* praying," I said.

"Yeah," Anne nodded slowly. "I don't want to fight Teresa."

"Me, either," I agreed. "We can't *make* Teresa do *diddly*. We can only take care of our own attitudes and leave the rest to the Almighty." Something in me leaped at my own words. Something fearful. Nausea squeezed my stomach and tapped at my throat reflex.

The kids escaped to Anne's small back den – a converted porch – to watch television and teen-gossip.

Dad, Kirk, Anne and I sat in the den for a long time, contemplating. I tucked my bare feet under me and snuggled against sleepy-eyed Kirk, who melded to the sofa's crook like a sprawled lab retriever. His fingers played over my arm in an abstract yet intimate caress. Callie had just this week told me she could see Kirk's renewed *reaching out* to me. Tonight, as usual, the warm reciprocal thing in me twanged like a happy banjo at Kirk's touch, even as the subterranean thing in me shrieked *why?* I had consciously – desperately – buried my doubts about Kirk's fidelity when Kirk buried Roxie. Literally. But in moments like these, just the words, "..*we can't make Teresa do diddly,*" spewed them up like angry seltzer bubbles.

Remembering Kirk's full speed ahead, blinders devotion to Roxie in my hours and months of need, left me shaken and sick anew.

I can only work on me, I reminded myself. Just the thought made me feel exhausted.

I abruptly sat up and glanced at the wall clock. Kirk stretched and yawned, rubbing his abdomen sluggishly. "I think I'll turn in, folks," I forced lightness into my voice. "A long day ahead."

"Good Lord willing," Anne stood and began picking up empty tea glasses. "we'll eat lunch with Chuck tomorrow." She stopped and, glasses dangling from limp hands, gazed desperately at me. "I pray he'll get to come this time."

Fear shot through me, but I managed a smile. "He will." *Please, God.*

Shortly, we retired for the night. Kirk fell asleep instantly, his arm tangled around my torso. My own sleep was sporadic and restless. I was on automatic pilot again, my norm for twilight time, and was relieved to hear Anne puttering around as the sun rose, rattling pots and pans early the next morning.

Daddy and Kirk left for the convalescent home at ten thirty-five. Anne sent our lunch menu for the nurses to check against violations. Chuck's diabetic diet had to be kosher.

"Why don't you call?" I suggested. "No use sitting on pins and needles wondering."

Anne rushed to snatch up the phone and call. I went to check on Toby, who romped with Lynette outside while Heather hung out with Dale. Cole had gone to get Leigh, his current and according to Anne, *serious* girlfriend, to join us for lunch.

I chatted a minute with the teens, folded into white front porch rockers.

On my lazy return, Anne nearly slammed into me, grabbed my arms and squeezed. "The nurse said Teresa left a note saying we could pick up Chuck any time we wanted to."

We gazed at each other through tears.

"Only prayer could have changed Teresa's heart on this," I whispered.

"For now." Anne's face sobered for a long moment, then brightened up. "But we've got *today*."

"Yes'm," I nodded, tilted my head and smiled, linking hands with hers. "That, we do."

"Teresa didn't want to come?" Anne asked Chuck as, complying with his wishes, she disconnected him from his portable oxygen-tank.

"Said she had plans."

"What about Poogie?" I asked, disappointed. I'd so wanted to see my niece.

Chuck languidly shrugged his shoulders. "She's with her other grandma. Busy." Pain, beyond physical, marred his handsome features as – with Dad's solicitous assistance – he moved slowly, laboriously, to the table and took a reserved place of honor at its head.

I fought down a niggling feeling of nausea as I seated myself. Nervous stomach, no doubt. It settled as I began to eat and soon, we all laughed and bantered as though back in carefree teen years.

Chuck ate two helpings of Anne's macaroni-cheese pie and two pieces of fried chicken. "Lordy, this is good." Eyelids half-mast, he grinned a dopey grin as his scrawny hand rubbed his swollen, distended stomach.

Afterward, Trish sang Chuck's favorite, *Amazing Grace*, and on the second verse, became so choked she fell silent for a full minute. Anne rose abruptly and fled the room, but not before I saw tears spiraling down her cheeks.

I swiped mine away and was relieved that Chuck, laid back in the La-Z-Boy, had his eyes closed, enjoying, soaking up the love and fun time with his family. Trish resumed her song and finished it, eyes glimmering with unshed tears.

All too soon, the day was used up. Chuck hugged us all 'bye' as Daddy prepared to take him back to Pinehurst Convalescent Home. We, too, piled into the VW for the long drive that would put us home near midnight, pulling out of the drive just before Daddy's white Toyota. I craned to see my brother's face, pressed to the car window watching me leave. I smiled and waved.

His wan face brightened and I saw the pale hand lift.

My brother. Myself.

Take care of him, please?

My nervous stomach continued to plague me. One morning, I vomited.

It *can't* be, I thought, wiping my face with wet washcloth, peering at my white face in the bathroom mirror. Terror seized me. I can't be.

I spun away from my reflection and fled the idea.

A week later, I could no longer escape. Terror clutched at my gut.

"Kirk, I'm pregnant," I blurted out as I washed dishes at the sink.

Kirk's reaction baffled me. "It's not – right," he muttered, taking my arm to turn me, gazing at me with tortured eyes. "It's not fair. Not now. Not when –"

"What?" I asked stupidly, hurting that Kirk rejected our creation. Procreation, our children, had always been sacred. My world shifted and tilted. My fingernails bled as I clutched at meaning.

The flailing thing inside me grew more pronounced.

"You had such a difficult time with Dawn, Neecy," Kirk reminded me softly, his hand running gently through my hair and cupping the back of my neck.

"I know," I whispered, fear spiraling through me like crazy bursting balloons shooting in all directions. Ice water filled my belly and my head spun. I closed my eyes and felt Kirk's lips brush mine, then his forehead sweetly mesh with mine as our breath mingled.

"Neecy," his face lifted only a fraction, so that his eyes locked with mine, "I can't – *can't* let you risk your life again."

I gazed at him, stunned. "Kirk – you don't want me to...to have an abortion, do you?'

His eyes clouded with such agony, my breath caught. "I can't let you go through that again." His head rolled back and he groaned, "I feel like such a *heel*, letting this happen."

"But Kirk –" My eyes filled with tears of confusion. And gut-wrenching fear. "I can't do that. I couldn't live with myself –"

His mouth went grim and his fingers closed around my arms like vises. "You might not live at all if you do."

His quiet words exploded through me like glacial anacondas, slithering, choking, squeezing...plowing a path of panic. Its blast toppled me from my flimsy highwire, plunging me into instant, numb capitulation.

His hands rubbed my arms desperately. "Don't you see, Neecy," his moist, tormented eyes pleaded with me to understand, "*I can't lose you.*"

❖ ❖ ❖ ❖ ❖ ❖

I was somewhere else. Not in me. I cannot explain how I became misplaced. How I became someone else reflected in Kirk's eyes. In the coming week, I moved in a petrified trance. Kirk gathered Heather for family counsel. She surprised me by agreeing that she, too, was concerned about my going through another childbirth.

"Too, Mama, I wouldn't be here to help you. I'll be away at school next year."

I wilted away a bit more.

Heather put her arms around me. "The main thing is – Mama...I don't want anything to happen to you. We need you more than ever."

Need. Don't want anything to happen to you....

I seemed to have ice water for blood. Panic attacks seized me between bouts of nausea.

Kirk arranged for me to see Dr. Temple, a Christian doctor. We went together for counsel. "Do you want to have this procedure?" my physician friend asked, having heard Kirk out.

I looked at him through a haze. "I – I can't go through this again," I spoke past dead lips.

Dr. Temple took my hand. "I understand Kirk's fears. But it's you I'm concerned about, Janeece. Because you're the one who will live with this decision in years to come."

I looked dully at him. I tried to make sense of the terror in me. Of my numbed heart. Of my non-functioning brain and code of ethics. Where *was I?*

"I can't face childbirth again, Dr. Temple." I slowly shook my head, felt panic rise until I could barely breathe. *I can't...I can't...I can't.*

"There, there," he soothed. "I'll make the arrangements for you."

"Please –" I looked away. Shut my eyes tightly. "Make it as quickly as possible." I couldn't bear to know the little heart already beat inside me. Dear *God!* Why am I in this position? No matter what decision I made, I faced agony. Possible death. Somehow, I *knew.*

I would die.

I turned to look at Kirk. He was so certain. He wouldn't lead me astray.

Kirk loved me.

"Make the arrangements, Dr. Temple," I whispered, tears in my eyes.

I rushed from the room.

We told no one, save those close. Only once did I allow Cal to hold and comfort me. Gene and Trish drove down that terrible week just to be with us. Lend support.

"I'm behind you, Sis." Trish, dear Trish, always *there*.

"I understand," Gene took my hand, then Kirk's. "God understands."

After that, I refused to discuss it. My body moved lethargically while my mind, a bizarre, mid-film video, repeatedly played that moment during Dawn's delivery when death's jaws locked about me, crushing the breath and life from me. Cocooned in sorrow's opium, I'd survived, content to remain with or vacate earth.

Things had changed. No opium coated my raw nerves. *'Things will only get worse with each pregancy, Janeece,"* came Dr. Jennings' warnings to haunt me, *"you need to have your fallopian tubes tied before you leave the hospital."*

Now, anxiety curled and frayed my entrails. My emotions either sliced out the top of terror or checked out completely. Nighttime found me perched like an old crow on a gnarled, rotten limb, rocking and teetering toward an endless, bottomless pit. I dared not move lest I topple off.

My children *need me*. *My children need me.* The desperate litany held me there, safe.

No. Not safe. *Will I,* I wondered, *ever again feel safe?*

Kirk daily, hourly checked on me, encouraged me that it was the right thing.

I loved him. Trusted him with my life. If Kirk said it was the right thing. It was.

"I can't go any farther than here," Kirk held me in his arms outside the clinic door. He stepped back, hands grasping my arms. "I wish I could do this for you, honey," he whispered, tears in his eyes. His features were ravaged, as though carved by Da Vinci.

I took a deep breath and let it out on a long, sad sigh. "That's life."

He kissed me, tenderly, with all the love in him. I realized then, that he, too, suffered.

I entered the waiting room like an apparition, white-faced, silent as death. Young women filled brightly colored sofas and love seats, chatting amiably.

Dear God. Let this be over. "Is –" I faced the girl across from me. "Are you nervous?"

Her young, sculpted jaw rotated on chewing gum. "No." She snorted softly. "Nothing to it. This is my second one."

"Are you married?" I asked and hugged myself, feeling my teeth begin to chatter from the chill of dread.

"Oh, yeah." She filed her nail, then closely examined it. "We aren't ready for kids yet. Still got two years of college left." Then she looked curiously at me. "How about you? Any kids?"

"I have four. That is – three. Living." I could not leave Krissie out. *Would* not.

"Oh? Did you lose a baby?" She snapped her gum and dropped her file back in her purse.

"No." My dull gaze fell to my pale, clenched hands. "An eleven-year-old."

"Mrs. Crenshaw?" A cheerful nurse motioned me through a white door, down a white hall, into a white room. So antiseptic.

I paused inside the door. Frozen into place. A masked medical team, *pac men*, stared at me with compassionate eyes. The nurse led me to a dressing room, helped me undress, then assisted and settled me onto the table.

"Please –" I stretched out a trembling hand to the nurse. "I feel so –" Pooled tears spilled down my cheeks, into my hair, onto the pillow, "*desolate.*"

She took my hand. "I know." Her voice was kind, caring.

Her face shimmered and floated. "I don't take this lightly," I whispered. "I want to die."

If not for my children, I would welcome death.

"Oh, no, dear. It will soon be over." Her fingers squeezed mine. "Just relax."

I closed my eyes and prayed. *God, you know I don't want to do this....*

The nightmare snatched and swallowed me up – to the *whirrr* of a vacuum's sucking sting to my midsection – then spit me out onto a cold recovery table, where I lay stuporized. A fetal-curled zombie with no brain and no feeling.

An hour later, Kirk came by for me, his face nearly as ashen as mine.

"You okay?" he asked in a husky whisper, blotting with his palm cold sweat clinging to my brow.

I blinked. "Let's go home."

He took my hand and led me away.

Away from the horror. Away from death's threat.

To my three children, who needed me.

I did not look back. Not then. Not for a long, long time.

I could not and live.

Survive. Because that's what I did in those coming months. Simply survive.

Healing came so slowly I wasn't aware of it at the time. Did not recognize it. I needed to go back to school and finish my last two semesters. But I didn't want to miss a moment with Dawn or Toby. Heather, well, she'd migrated again to peer-land, a place not always open to me. We had our close times, but they became fewer and farther between in those coming months.

Kirk and I never talked about that day at the abortion clinic. It was as if, by our silence, it had never happened.

One day, Anne called, upset. "Oh, Neecy. I wish you lived closer." She snuffled. "Chuck's signed a paper donating his body to medical science."

I gripped the receiver. "So –" I grasped to understand Anne's angst. "You're saying?"

Anne's furious intake of breath exploded in explanation. "Teresa hassled him into doing it, Neecy. He told me he didn't want to do it."

"Then, why did he?" I'd always admired those who nobly gave their remains to the study of medical science but felt it should definitely be the donor's choice.

"Said she got on her knees beside his bed and pleaded with him to spare her the expense of a burial when the time comes."

Anger cannon-blasted through me. "How *could* she?" I closed my eyes and clenched a fist. "She has no right, Anne. Chuck's a human being with rights."

My stepmother sighed, a long ragged sound from her toes up. "She's got all the cards, Neecy. Holds 'em over our heads like a whip."

"A power trip," I muttered, disgusted. "That's what it is to her. A danged power trip!"

"If we want to see Chuck, we'll have to bow to her wishes."

I swallowed my fury. "You're right. We do. But doggonit. I don't like it one bit."

There was nothing I could do. Later that night, I told Kirk about it.

Kirk's face clouded, but he said little. Seemed off somewhere. He never said it, but lately, I'd felt, *sensed* unspoken needs behind that strong mask that rarely slipped. When it did, I glimpsed a look I'd never before seen. One quite like worship, that hitched my breath and stirred my love to new heights.

Yet, my feet still sought solid ground. I was convinced Kirk's flirtation with Roxie was just that – a flirtation – but its undermining of my security had left ugly scars. Would they ever fade? I harbored deep, shameful emotions I could share with no one.

One was my concern that Kirk felt so comfortable with Callie. Another was her devotion to him that, until the traumas, had pleased me. BR (before Roxie), I'd never had a jealous bone in my body. It changed me in ways I did not like. It was as though, having brushed up against the fiery threat of Roxie, I was driven to protect, at all costs, my marriage.

Jealousy is a terrible, terrible thing, Neecy.... Kirk's words haunted me. Stopped me, many times, from making a fool of myself.

I took great care to hide my knee-jerk anxiety when, at home one night, after supper, Kirk asked Callie for a cup of coffee rather than me. I later discussed it with Kirk, who chuckled and said, "Neecy, Cal and I are together all the time at the office. She makes coffee for me every day so it's just a habit." Then, disappointment filled his green eyes. "Can you understand that?"

I did. But it still bothered me on some level. Kirk's allegiance to Callie wasn't unfaithfulness, per se. But *because* of it,

I'd become, again, the invisible person, the unnecessary one. It was not a case of simple jealousy. But then, is jealousy ever *simple*?

I prayed desperately to rid myself of it. Still, over time, my relationship with Callie suffered.

"I'm going to have to move away soon, Neecy," Callie told me one day in my kitchen. We'd just lunched on chicken salad sandwiches and potato salad left from the night before and faced each other across the oak table. "I hate to leave ya'll, but Mama's gonna be needing me."

She gave me a little smile of regret.

The battle-shocked part of me did not see the plea in her eyes nor hear her plaintive *'at least make a gesture of protest, Neecy!'* Not then. Not until years later. So, I picked up my frosted glass of iced tea and drew on it with my finger. "I understand, Cal." I looked at her then. "I really do. You know I love you, don't you Cal?"

Something sad flickered in her chocolate gaze. "Yeah, Neecy, I know."

CHAPTER EIGHTEEN
"A Time to Lose...."

I didn't see it coming. God only knows what I'd have done if I had.

As it was, when Kirk woke me up early that Saturday morning – I'd now begun to sleep through the night – kissing me, I was delighted. Somehow, the clamoring in me had begun to subside and peaceful interludes blossomed and burgeoned.

"You're already dressed," I croaked sleepily, stretching and rubbing my eyes.

"Yep." He watched me, with that adoring look in his eyes, for long moments. Then he smiled. "Throw on some jeans and a shirt. Let's go for a morning drive on the beach."

In minutes, we were out the door, leaving Toby in the den spooning Captain Crunch into his mouth and watching Scooby Doo – he still loved his ol' doggie-buddy – while the girls slept.

The sun climbed a silver horizon as our VW made tracks across the damp shoreline, then halted to a rest. Salt air filled my nostrils as sea gulls scattered and soared lazily overhead. I smiled and lay my head back on the rest. "What a beautiful day. I'm glad you thought of this, honey." I turned my head to look at my husband, who gazed across the water, his face suddenly solemn.

"I've got to talk to you, Neecy." His eyes lighted on me, so full of emotion I was stunned.

"Is something wrong?" I asked, antenna rising from every pore.

He melded into the crook of his seat. Relaxed, yet tense. The mask was gone. Kirk faced me, my Kirk – with vulnerable green eyes pleading with me in some way.

"What is it, honey?" I asked gently.

"Neecy...this is the hardest thing I've ever done." His features morphed into the most desperate composite I'd ever seen.

No! I stiffened, yet turned completely to face him, knowing instinctively I didn't want to hear what he was going to say.

But Kirk had already dived in. Now, he struggled to complete his mission.

His face suddenly dissolved into tears. *Oh, God.* This was major.

"Neecy...I've got to make it to Heaven. I promised Krissie –" He wept as he had when Krissie died. Loud, unrestrained sobs.

I knew. Suddenly, I *knew.* "Oh – no, *no, Kirk.*"

He lifted his head in shame. Nodded. "It's true."

My mouth went dry as cotton matting. "How much?"

"All of it. All you suspected is true."

I faced the ocean, blood draining, draining, *pouring, gushing* out my toes, my nose, my fingertips until I was nothing but cold numbness. "You had sex with Roxie?"

He nodded. "Yes."

"Why?" I whirled to face him. "Why, in *God's name?*"

Kirk tried to brace himself. "It wasn't what you think. It – she seduced me...while you were away. After Moose disappeared. That night when she claimed to be having a nervous breakdown. She knew what she was doing, Neecy."

I gave a bitter huff of a laugh, staring unseeing at the silvery rolling surf, thinking how my insides could be so numb yet hurt so. "Why am I not surprised?"

"Neecy –" His hand moved toward my arm. "I –"

I jerked my arm away from his touch. Something in me snapped in that instant, breaking me free of my restrained self. He flinched and withdrew, watching me with such humbleness I choked up. I closed my eyes and an image flashed – of Kirk and Roxie tangled in the act of sex. In that instant, the pain of losing the one thing left – our exclusivity – was so sharp I thought I'd die from it. The wail that rose from my bowels crescendoed such that it put my labor sounds to shame.

I heard Kirk's sobs mingle with mine. "Don't –" he moaned, squeezing his hands together to stop from reaching for me, "please don't, Neecy. It was nothing to me –"

"*Nothing?*" I shrieked, tears dripping off my cheeks, chin, nose. "Nothing?" I peered at him as I would at a lunatic. "It was *everything...*" I threw back my head and howled, "*Everything! And you gave it aw-a-ay. It was mine!*" I clutched my chest, then beat it. "*It was mi-i-ine.*" When my breath ran out, I glared at him through tears. My voice, hoarsened, now rasped. "You gave away all that was left." I slumped from the effort of saying it. "There's nothing left." I stared dully at the distant horizon, not seeing anything except my husband and this other woman. Copulating.

"She asked me to forgive her, Kirk." I looked at him. "Did you know that?" I threw up my hands. "And I did. I gave her peace. She gave me *this.*"

"Dear Jesus," Kirk said quietly, gazing upward. "What have I done? I shouldn't have told you. You can't take –"

"Ha!" I sliced him a look of contempt, ignoring the way he flinched. "Too late. You *did*. And as for my not being able to *take it*, don't worry about *poor lil' Neecy. Poor lil' Stupid Neecy*, to quote the late Roxie."

I wanted to fight. For the first time in my life, I wanted, could *taste*, hand-to-hand combat.

"I'd kill her if she wasn't already dead." I barely recognized my thick, even voice nor the rage behind it.

"Oh, God," Kirk moaned, rolling his head back, then dropping it forward to rest on his chest, his fingers pinching his bridge. I glared coldly at him, not feeling a shred of pity for him. He'd killed me. As surely as I sat there breathing, he'd destroyed me. All those months of *her* rubbing my nose in the fact that Kirk treated her preferentially.

"The two of you probably laughed at me behind my back?" It didn't matter. I closed my eyes. Nothing mattered anymore.

"No! I *never* dishonored you, Janeece, outside the –" Kirk shifted to face me, reached out and seized my resisting hand. "You've got to know...I've never loved anybody but you. You must believe that. And I didn't want what happened to happen. It was a trap I fell into – that many, many men fall into all the time."

I turned my wooden head and peered at him through leaden eyes. "You're not just any man, Kirk. You're a man of God." I watched it wound him, glad that it did. He needed to feel some of what I felt.

I felt like a squeezed out lemon. All substance gone, leaving only an empty, dried rind. Kirk slid over and pulled me into his arms. I stiffened and pushed against him, but he wouldn't let go.

"Janeece," his voice was rough velvet, "I made a terrible mistake, but I'm not crazy enough to let go of you. Please – please try to find it in your heart to forgive me."

His big hand took my chin and guided it around until our gazes locked. Oh, it hurt so dreadfully to look into the face I loved above all others. Even humble and repentant, he was splendid. Manly and all quiet dignity and I began to cry and he held me, soothing and crooning to me.

"I love you, Neecy," he murmured, pressing his lips to my hair, my cheeks, eyelids and finally, capturing my lips. My tears continued to flow. Crazy thing was, he was the only one who could fix my pain. He, who'd caused it. "Do you love me?" he asked in an uncertain, little boy voice.

I laughed, a harsh, hysterical sound. "Of course I love you. Love doesn't just *stop*. Why do you think this hurts so much? *Huh*? I wish I *didn't* love you," I hiccupped a sob, then finished on an exhausted whisper. "It wouldn't be as bad if I didn't love you."

"Honey," Kirk's arms tightened and he leaned to look down into my face, eyes dark with pain. "If there's anything you want to know, ask. I don't want any more secrets. It was hell..." He shook his head and gazed off. Then he looked at me again, determined. "Once Roxie seduced me, she resorted to emotional blackmail to keep me dangling. You need to know that. The times you saw us together, I was appeasing her – praying she wouldn't destroy us. I never wanted you hurt. Now, I want everything clear between us."

I turned my head to stare out the window, woozy with exhaustion and confusion. My terror was gone. Desolation replaced it. Facts swirled through my mind. The worst had happened. I faced yet another struggle: to survive. I thought of the recent abortion. Tears puddled up again, then spilled over.

"That's why you felt different about the baby –"

Kirk resisted me pulling away. "No – I told you why I didn't want you to go through –"

"But Kirk," I peered at him through tears, my mouth in rictus between words, "always before, everything about our making babies was so spiritual...so sacred." I bawled then like a three-year-old who'd lost her doll, with Kirk's arms holding and bolstering and his voice murmuring I knew not what, only that it lulled me into quietness once more. "I knew. In my gut, I knew something had changed."

"Janeece, listen to me." Kirk turned to see me better. "You've got to believe me when I say that the thing – between me and Roxie – had no bearing on that situation. I told you then, and I'll say it again," his eyes darkened and speared mine, "I couldn't bear to lose you." His emotion-rough voice, this time, pierced my haze. Suddenly, during that heartbeat, he was my Kirk again and when he hauled me against him, I closed my eyes and breathed strength from him.

"Honey?" he rumbled softly in my ear, "You're not going to leave me," he raised his head and gazed into my eyes, "are you?"

I looked at him, heavy-lidded and addle-brained, hardly knowing where I was. And I let out a sound between screech and howl, a crazy bray of a laugh that ended on a sob. "Kirk! I've *never*, for one moment, considered not being with you." I gulped and swallowed another siege of hysteria. "That makes me crazy, doesn't it? I shouldn't love you – don't even know if I *do* love you. I don't know *what* I feel anymore."

"Neecy," he cupped my wet face in his hands, then lowered his head, reverently, to kiss me. "I'll make you love me again. I promise you, you won't be sorry."

The next day, Sunday, my body moved about from sheer habit. Having slept very little, if at all, I charged on adrenaline one minute, crashed the next. My emotions gave no warning when they'd do a column-left, column-right or an abrupt to-the-rear march. I simply rode them, a Lamb Chop moppet jerked around betwixt Dr. Jekyll and Mr. Hyde.

Strangely, the anger protected me from myself. Defiance kept tears at bay during church, kept my back straight and my eyes unwavering. Made me present myself strong and all put together. Often, during his message, Kirk's gaze sought and held mine. I had nothing left from which to draw, so I returned his soft little smiles with stony stares or averted my gaze altogether.

When I'd *snapped* – *was it only yesterday?* – the lights inside me disconnected, leaving cold, dank emptiness. Anger had ambushed me so brusquely, was so alien to me, I had no defenses against it. No prior knowledge armed me, so fury propelled and steered me, spewed words from my mouth, turned me silent as death and made me cynical.

Cynical. For the first time ever, I saw Kirk through the eyes of a stranger. Because, to my way of thinking, he was. The Kirk I thought I knew, the one who'd vowed, *"I'll always love and protect you, Neecy,"* didn't exist.

"Why did you lie, Kirk? That day, at church, you said there wasn't anything between you and Roxie." I'd reminded him through the hellish night before, as we lay side by side in bed, talking softly so the children wouldn't hear.

Kirk's tortured face, all angles and dusky shadowed planes, creased deeper. "Because, Neecy, I didn't want to hurt you." He reached over and slid his fingers over my arm. I stiffened and moved away. "Can't you understand that?"

"Please, honey," his voice vibrated with emotion, "don't pull away."

I tried to relax, to be sensible. *Sensible? Ha!* "Well, it didn't work. I hurt."

"I'd give my life to go back and not have you know." He rolled to his back and gazed at the ceiling. "I suppose I'd wrestled with it for so long, analyzed it so thoroughly, seeing how Roxie set me up – I guess I thought you'd see that right away, as I did after the fact. Not that it excuses me. I take full blame for my actions. I prayed and asked God to forgive me. He has. I know that. Then –" He grew quiet for long moments. "Then, I felt He wanted me to confess to you, ask your forgiveness. Set things right. I've felt so wretched for so long...it got to the place I couldn't pray. Couldn't preach without feeling like a hypocrite."

I turned my head to gaze at him through the darkness. He was Kirk again. In that heartbeat, he was my Kirk.

"I've got something else to tell you, Neecy."

I tensed but remained silent.

"Callie knows."

Ice water filled my belly. "Why – how?" The frigid liquid slithered through my veins.

He sucked in a long ragged sigh and exhaled, then linked his hands beneath his head. "You see – more's been going on than you know. Cal and I have tried to protect you. Sarah Beauregard saw my car at Roxie's apartment while you were gone, during Chuck's crisis – more than once. Seems she began to ride by there and came up with the conclusion that –" He broke off. Then gave a disgusted snort. "Well, you know Sarah."

I stared at him. Regardless of what Kirk had done, I still cared about the ministry. On this, we remained together. "Did she say anything?"

"Tillie came to Cal, upset that Sarah had told her mother about her suspicions. That's all it took to get a wildfire going."

So Tillie's heard, too. I felt walls closing in, suffocating, exposing me. I sat up, plumped my pillow behind me and leaned into it. "So? Has it spread?"

Kirk joined me by adjusting his pillow, too, and propping upright. "Fortunately, I think Cal was able to douse the rumors by vouching for me...saying she knew about the sessions, had gone with me on some of them."

"Lying." I said flatly.

Another long sigh. "Well – yeah. I suppose that's exactly what it was."

The aftershock rocked me. "So Cal knows. For how long?" I didn't know the air had been squeezed from me until I began to gasp at oxygen.

His head swiveled and I felt his green gaze pierce the darkness. "Not long. Honest, honey. I needed somebody to confide in, to steer me. I felt I was losing my mind. I didn't trust anyone else."

"Not even another pastor?"

He gave a dry laugh. "*Especially* not another pastor." The old secretive, cynical Kirk only mildly surprised me. "Anyway, Callie told me I needed to tell you."

"How did she take it? Your –" I fought the ball of restiveness that wedged in my belly.

"She forgives me. Didn't bat an eye. Said we just need to put it behind us and go on with the ministry."

So easy for her to say.

"How do you feel, Neecy?" he asked, a quiet, concerned appeal in his voice.

"About what?"

"The ministry."

"You mean about staying on here? As though nothing has happened?"

He nodded slowly, then grew unearthly still, his eyes filled with hope. "Could you?"

I looked away, my heart pounding as though I'd sprinted cross country. "Kirk –"

"I know it would be difficult, honey, but my life is in this work. My heart. It would mean so much to me if you could –"

"I'll have to pray about it, Kirk." I lay down and turned away from him.

Oh, Kirk. How could you have done something so stupid? So irrevocable? I've always tried to 'fix' everything for you. This, I can't fix.

I'd not even dozed after that. With the adrenaline surge, I could go without sleep. For a time, anyway.

Today, as Kirk ended his message and the congregation stood, I found it no easier to reconcile to this turn of events than I had at the moment of Kirk's confession. I turned and would have left the church without speaking to anybody had Callie not caught up and grasped hold of my arm in the vestibule. "Neecy? What are lunch plans?"

I turned to face her. "I don't have any." The words thudded like ice cubes between us.

Cal's face emptied and she gave me a hesitant, sidelong look. "What's happened?"

"I know, Cal." An instant alarm dawned on her face. I slowly nodded. "I *know.*"

She touched my hand, gingerly – tentatively. "You okay?"

"Sure," I shrugged briskly and pulled my hand away. "S'true, you know."

She stepped back in wounded wariness, her gaze narrowed. "What's true?"

"The wife is the last to know." I spun and walked away.

Callie was with Kirk when he got home. "Toby and Heather took off with the Tessners for lunch at the Fish Camp." He looked around. "Dawn already down for a nap?"

From the sofa, where I sprawled barefoot and indifferent, I took in their together-stance. "Yep."

Kirk shot me an uneasy, measuring glance. I met it levelly, recognizing and hating the shadow of guilt I saw there. He gestured to Callie, "Take a load off, Cal."

She took the chair opposite me as Kirk slid onto the sofa next to me, throwing his arm over its back so that his fingers almost touched my neck. I could feel warmth coming from their tips and it stole the oxygen right out of my lungs, leaving them heaving and struggling to refill. When alone, I lulled myself into thinking it wasn't true, his power over me. In reality, my reaction to his nearness bewildered and distressed me. I shifted, curled my feet under me and laid my head back, saying nothing.

There was not the usual spontaneity today. I didn't have the strength to care.

Kirk, after long silent moments, began to speak. "Honey, Cal and I have been discussing the ministry and the – situation. I think –"

My head jerked upright. "Don't you think this is between *us* – you and me?"

Callie sprang to her feet, palms thrust forward. "I'm outta here, guys. She's right, Kirk." She was already in the foyer when Kirk caught up. I heard them murmuring, voices rising and falling. I sat unmoved, unmoving. Disassociated. Not caring if I ever saw Callie again. Or Kirk, for that matter. In that moment, I could have moved into a barn in Shanty Town, with Toby, Heather and Dawn, and faced the tomorrows. Knowing that, I felt an amazing strength begin to flow into me.

The voices continued, "...it's too soon, Kirk. She needs time to...."

"...worried about her. She's not eating and...acts out of it."

Anger stirred, then buzzed like hornets. "Hey!" I yelled. "I've got ears! I'm not going to melt like sugar in a rainstorm, *ya'll*. And I'm not crazy. *Not yet.*"

The front door slammed and Kirk returned to the den, his eyes clouded with concern and a touch of fear. "Honey, you've got it all wrong about Cal. She's worried about you, too. And –"

"I know. I know," I snapped. "I just want everybody to stop – acting like I'm a time bomb, set to blow into tiny bits."

He dropped down beside me, curving to face me and lean in, so close I could feel his warm breath on my cheek. My body responded. That he had the power to sway me after such a betrayal proved something terrible was wrong with me. Was I so unlovable I grasped at crumbs?

"Neecy?" Kirk spoke softly, his finger running over my shoulder, neck, ear. Goosebumps scattered all over me. I didn't look at him. Wasn't ready to. Humiliation stirred thickly in me. And need. I hated it. Anger began to rise again.

"Neecy, have you thought – *prayed* about staying here in Solomon? Could you find it in your heart to stay here, where we could work together here in the church and –"

It was the desperation in his voice that pushed me over the edge.

My head whipped around. "I can't, Kirk," I said firmly because suddenly, I knew it was true. "That's one thing I *am* certain of." I turned from the pain in his eyes. Had to. "I'm sorry. I truly am. But I can't stay here."

Where rumors run rampant about the preacher and that woman who was murdered. I couldn't face the pity in folks' eyes. Worse still, the contempt, because if he was running around, something *had* to be wrong with his wife, doncha know? I'd said it myself – not about Tillie, however – but the old adage of two sides to everything now haunted me.

I'd already seen it, this morning in church. In Zelda and Alton Diggers' not so subtle, measuring gazes. And others of their clan had cast knowing looks from me to Kirk and back.

"'Know what Sarah said to me this morning?" I asked in a weak whisper.

I felt Kirk stiffen. Then, a quiet, "what?"

"She said, '*why you losing so much weight, Janeece?*' I told her I'd been so busy lately, I'd forget to eat."

She knew. Deep down, Sarah – skeptic that she was – knew. She wouldn't have taken Callie's word on Kirk's innocence, with such juicy evidence as she'd collected. It was only a matter of time before it blew up in Kirk's denial-face. I didn't want my children subjected to such shame and disillusionment. They didn't need to lose respect for their father. He was a good father.

Above all, I wanted to protect the children.

And to do that, I had to keep my sanity.

Okay, so the Prince of darkness had found my Achilles heel. It had always been there, the hidden, unlovable part of me. But I'd always managed to juggle my self-worth while capitulating to Kirk's wishes, to his dreams. I'd been his appendage, his cheerleader. I'd helped him row his boat all these years.

Now, it was time for me to paddle my own canoe to a safe shore.

I can survive this. I will survive this. It wasn't Kirk telling me. It was *me* telling me.

What a marvelous discovery: I trusted me to make my own decisions. Something I'd not done before.

"Are you going to leave me, Neecy?"

I looked at him, my husband, his eyes bottomless pools of green pain, the most gorgeous specimen of manhood I'd ever known. And I knew I loved him with every fiber of my being and nothing would ever change that. Another thing I knew: I could no longer entrust my welfare to another mortal.

"I'm leaving Solomon, Kirk. If you want to come with me, that's fine. If you don't, I'm going, anyway. Because I can't live here. What we had here is gone. I don't want to leave Krissie behind, but someday in the future, her grave can be moved. Life here is spoiled for me. For us. It could never be the same. Too many bad memories." Fatigue caught up with me. Somewhere between words, I'd grown limp and it took great effort to talk. "I'm weary of fighting. Life shouldn't be all battles. There has to be peace somewhere."

Kirk had moved closer as I spoke, I felt his breath stir my hair. "Neecy, I can't lose you. That's all I know." He pulled me into his arms and held me so tight I could feel his rapid pulse. His was an embrace of desperation, of devotion and respect and, God help me, worship. "Whatever happens," he murmured, "we're together."

It was something I'd have given my kingdom for years back.

Today, it came at too great a cost.

"Let me help," Callie insisted, hovering hesitantly in Toby's bedroom doorway, watching me purge his closet of toys he'd not played with for at least three years. I'd just finished emptying the drawers in my room, knowing soon, we'd be moving and this had to be done. Another thing was, it kept me busy working off this new humming energy, one fed by anything re-motely wired to anger.

"I'll be moving out tomorrow," she said inanely, shifting uncomfortably from one foot to another.

When I didn't reply, Cal grabbed an empty plastic gar-bage bag and began to stuff discarded items into it. A week had passed since Kirk's stunning revelation. Callie had given me space to work through things, had not pressed me one way or another in my dealing with Kirk, though I felt her sympathy was more with him than me. It didn't matter.

"Women have more to give than men," was her pat blan-ket for most marital conflicts.

So, she'd simply gone about her business when I visited my husband's office for one reason or another. My old compliance had done an abrupt about-face. The Janeece of old would nev-er have appeared during working hours without a valid reason, simply out of respect for the Pastor's office. Now, my esteem for its sovereignty was jaded.

"Neecy," Callie paused to set down her bulging bag, tight-en its drawstring and plop down onto Toby's cluttered bed, "We need to talk."

Ice water trickled into my belly and I cast her a sidelong glance as I sorted through old ball gloves and worn-out balls. "So, shoot." *No more revelations, please.*

She leaned forward to rest elbows on denimed knees and cup her chin in her hands. "Why don't you talk to me about it, Neecy?" she asked softly. "We used to talk about everything. Remember?"

"Yeah," I turned the frayed basketball over and over in my hands before tossing it aside. "That was before I knew there wasn't a Santa Claus." I looked at her then. "You were the one who told me. Remember?"

She gave a tiny huff of a laugh. "Yeah. I remember." Her dark eyes grew misty, faraway. She shifted to lean back against the pillow-garrisoned headboard, deep in thought. I resumed my task, ignoring the silence, glad for it. Finally, she said, "When did we stop?"

I tumbled the ball bat into the 'SAVE' box. "Stop what?"

"Talking to each other."

My hands idled and I thought for a long moment. "When you started dating."

"Really?" She looked astonished. "That long ago?"

"Um hum." I pitched a Hopewell Methodist ball cap into the box with the bat.

"You know why?" she asked, stretching out her legs on the bed and crossing her bare feet at the ankles. "Because I didn't want you to know how bad a person I was."

I snorted, a little too sharply. "I got the idea you didn't worry about *what* I thought of you, Cal. Or what anybody else thought, for that matter." I tore into the pile of sweats.

I heard her long sigh. "I didn't think I gave a rip in those days. But later – after being hurt so dreadfully by a man I thought would always love me – I realized I was so angry, it ate me alive. I went along that way through two marriages...and then I met Jack Farentino."

I slid to prop my tired back against the far wall, facing her. "Bad, huh?" It helped – as she knew it would – to focus on someone else's problems, if only temporarily.

"He made the other two look like Mary's little lambs." She slowly shook her thick mane and lowered her gaze to mine. "It nearly destroyed me. If I hadn't come here and—oh, well," she shrugged, "the rest is history, as they say. Thing is – in God, I found the strength to forgive Jack for –"

"Whoa." I lifted a palm toward her as my chin fell onto my chest. "I'm not ready for all this just yet. I appreciate what you're trying to do, Callie. I just – I'm still numb in places. And the other places scream in pain and rage. I've got to –"

"Listen, Neecy," she scooted into upright, tailor position, elbows planted on thighs, eyes level with mine, "I've got just one more thing to say to you...Kirk is a good man."

I closed my eyes against the jagged lance. "I – know...."

"Honey," Cal struggled for words, and sighed with frustration. "All I'm saying is, I was there when Roxie put the make on him. Kirk didn't have a clue. Oh, he was sorta flattered. He couldn't help but be, it's human nature. But his main concern was to help her through Moose's vamoose. I know that. Problem was Roxie didn't. She used tears like a machine gun and –"

"Stop." I took a long, deep breath and blew it out. "Please, Cal – no more." I rolled my head back and flexed my neck from side to side, hoping to dispel the dizziness crashing over me as this discussion progressed. "As for forgiving Kirk – I think I can. It's just – so fresh. Everything."

And I resent having it paraded and inspected and catalogued by you or anybody.

Callie leaned forward, an earnest appeal stamped over her lovely features – a beauty that, for the first time ever, stirred me to uneasiness. *Jealousy is a terrible, terrible thing, Neecy....*

I looked at her then, forced myself to remember that she was my friend. *Callie, for heaven's sake!* I felt the thing curled inside me slither to a dark corner.

"Neecy, Kirk didn't know. He didn't know what Roxie was capable of...not until it was too late. He was so innocent...I work with him and know him. I tell you, *He was like a lamb led to the slaughter.*"

I groaned and buried my face in my hands. It was too, too graphic. Callie could sit here and talk about my husband with an objectivity that ripped me to shreds.

I threw my head back and leveled her an angry look. "I'm sorry, Cal, but this is not something I can be as detached about as you can. Kirk and I never – well, we were the first, the *only ones* with each other. That's like," I grimaced and spread my hands in search of apt words to describe our exclusivity, "a gift. The greatest treasure you can give one another. To lose that...." My voice trailed off, and I stared unseeing out the window as the leaded sickness settled inside me again.

"I do understand, Neecy, but you –"

"No." My gaze whipped to her. "You *don't* understand, Cal. I'm sorry, but you haven't a clue as to what I've lost. I know you feel I'm not giving Kirk the consideration –"

Callie was on her feet in a blink, in the doorway, squared off, "Seems you've already decided what I'm thinking. So, since you've got it all figured out, I won't explain myself any further. I'll be moving this weekend. If you need me, you know my phone number." With that, she vanished in a puff of the old Callie-grandeur.

I sat there for a long time, trying to make sense of my relief that she would soon be gone. That I wouldn't have to face anybody who *knew*, who analyzed and sifted and threw back at me what I needed to do or needed not to do. What I should or shouldn't be. Fact was I had no more control over *now* than I'd had over *then*. Few would understand that. Least of all Callie, who hadn't treasured monogamy a day in her life. Not to say she wasn't a changed person, but even so, she had no exclusive relationship experiences from which to draw and compare with mine.

I crawled onto Toby's bed, curled into a ball and shut my eyes against what had happened, still happened daily, to my world. It was a situation in which I found myself isolated, *wanted* to be isolated. I trusted no one, yet, to impart wisdom to me. Women, my former *sisterhood*, posed threats as base as breathing and gender. Men, were they truly so fragile? Oh, I didn't slide completely off into the deep, but I wrestled – oh, crazy pun – oceans of new notions

I never consciously moved away from God. I'd simply crash-landed so far removed from Him that I knew not in which direction to begin searching for Him.

Kirk resigned that Sunday evening, leaving a shocked congregation slack-jawed as we rushed from the church before being swamped with questions. I felt only relief while Kirk – well, he looked as if he'd taken a bullet between the eyes and had yet to fall.

Heather's reaction to moving was, to my surprise, mild. Her courtship with Steve had cooled, what with him away at school and Heather's increasingly busy college social life. She'd begun going to dances and socials that jerked Kirk's eyebrows up and down like a wired Howdy Doody. My, but he was a territorial Dad. Too, Heather's indifference to leaving evolved from a tiff with Dixie Tessner, her pal, who'd betrayed Heather's confidence, by divulging to Kirk Heather's tryst with a man she discovered later to be married.

I understood Heather's hurt but at the same time, was grateful for Dixie's courage in stepping forward with her information. "I know she hates me right now," Dixie's golden-amber eyes simmered sadness, "but I couldn't stand by and watch her destroy her life, Mrs. Crenshaw."

I hugged and thanked her. "She'll get over it someday, Dixie," I assured her.

And Heather did, they later reconnected by writing and phoning religiously. But at that precise moment in time, it was a difficult mountain for our daughter to span, especially when her Dad went along with her for the next 'date.' An angry Kirk Crenshaw is not a pretty sight. He scared the spit from the poor guy, who promptly vanished, but not before Kirk got his license number and called a local policeman-friend to get the man's address and phone number.

A quick telephone call to the man's wife – who'd delivered a baby only days earlier – filled in the blanks on her absentee husband's antics. "He's a *heel*," Kirk snarled after hanging up. "She deserved to know and make right decisions." This came after his confession to me and I knew that his righteous indignation was, in part, anger at himself, as well.

Somehow, that little statement drew respect from me.

Today, as I packed, I realized it was a first step in the right direction.

"Mama," Heather rushed into my room later that afternoon, after Callie left, "Come talk to me while I pack some more of my school things. I can't *believe* I'm going away to college in two days! No more sitting at the church piano week in and week out." She hugged me effusively and jabbered about things to take and not to take as I joined her, sitting on her bed as she moved about, all energy and youth and dreams for the future.

"Mama," she suddenly paused and peered at me, shifting from one bare foot to the other, "I'm sorry about...you know, about the baby. I know how hard it was for you." Her hands clasped and wrung, then slid down her hips to dry. "We'd talked about how horrible it is for a woman to have an abortion. And it *is*. But with your health problems and all –" She dropped down on the bed, facing me, took my hands in hers as tears shimmered along her lower lids, "Thank you, Mama," she said past quivering lips while I watched a tear slide down each satiny cheek, "for choosing *us*. I was so afraid you wouldn't and – and I don't know what I'd do without you." Her arms were around me for a long, long, fervent moment, and then she was up and moving again.

In the wake of her hummingbird's departure, something in me sang of reprieve. And forgiveness. And hope.

My heart mushed as I watched her morph from little girl to woman and back.

Thank you, Lord, that she doesn't know.

Was it only last year I'd dreaded her going away like I would a pestilence? That I couldn't bear the thought of being separated from her? Local college had merely whetted her appetite for the real thing and I'd agonized at her *I-can't-wait-to-be-outta-here* gusto.

Now, I was grateful to see her go. I couldn't hide from her indefinitely the thing between her father and me. I was casualty enough, thank you very much.

I'd faced many things over which I had no control

This was different.

My silence could, and *would,* buy my children two things: *peace and security.*

Many voices clamored in my head as Kirk and I said furtive goodbyes to church folk, only doing so when forced to. Once decided, Kirk seemed as driven as I to get out of Solomon sans fanfare. In his resignation, he'd stated '*effective immediately,*' hoping, I'm sure, to disengage himself with minimum emotionality. At any other time – given my near-maudlin nature – I would have balked, would have declared Kirk's maneuver unethical and crudely insensitive to the flock. This time, however, I was in total agreement.

The blind cannot lead the blind.

I had to get away. To begin to sort out the mess of my life.

Tillie Dawson dropped by to say goodbye. Kirk and I were loading the moving van. We had little to no assistance. Only Charlie Tessner put his shoulder to Kirk's and helped. I knew the churchmen were hurt by Kirk's sudden, non-negotiable resignation. And the fact that we left them high and dry, without preacher or pianist, since we'd hauled Heather, trunks and baggage, to Winthrop the day before, was a slap in their faces. Of course, shifting Dixie from organ to piano would work. An organist would eventually be found. Charlie Tessner could, in a pinch, lead the choir. There were ways, I'd learned early on, to accommodate ministry voids.

A new pastor – well, the conference would sort that out. To them, Kirk had pleaded *health problems*. Which was not untrue. We were, the two of us, basket cases.

Tillie's appearance at my door hit me below the belt. I'd never before known what *below the belt* meant nor that it applied to emotional, as well as physical, jolts. It was a drop kick to my gut, one that exploded pain in every direction, leaving my lungs deflated, struggling to suck in air, and my legs like rubber. Because Tillie *knew*. I read it in her big, red-rimmed Bambi eyes and her quivery lips, in every gesture of her Tinkerbell body as she reached for me and squalled on my shoulder. Her arms held me as a mother holds her babe, to protect and shield.

I felt it, her pity. Her compassion. The new me did not want to reciprocate the passion, floundered against it because doing so acknowledged my loss, a thing I could not expose to others and survive. It was one of those base *Id* reactions I did not – still do not – understand. At that moment in time, it propelled me in directions uncharted. But with Tillie's stick-figure arms squeezing me senseless, love overrode my self-revulsion and I returned her offering squeeze for squeeze, pat for pat. And when she released me, I smiled at her, a genuine smile of sisterhood. She was one of the few who remained in my order.

I knew Tillie would not mention my quandary, as I had not hers. She would allow it to remain my private hellhole because she'd been there. Hers had been tossed out there before the world while mine remained, at that precise moment, hidden away from all but a few eyes. The difference being that Kirk's indiscretion, if broadcast, carried far more potential to atomize than Rick's ever would. Of course, Tillie's simplified vantage revealed only two women in like-peril. On that level, we were. When we bade one another fare-thee-well, with the customary promises to keep in touch, we both sensed this was truly goodbye.

Despite closet and drawer purgings, the Crenshaws left behind on our lawn, for the garbage men, tons of attic treasures, including all of Toby's football gear and Dawnie's baby paraphernalia. I suspected – what with all the trunks and bags transported to Winthrop with Heather – she had carried most of hers. As Kirk and Toby pulled out in the moving van, I followed in the car. My eyes did a wistful sweep of crib, carriage, play pen, high chair, cleats, balls of every shape, shoulder pads and football helmets. At least, I thought, Kaye Tessner had helped me pack up all of Krissie's clothing, Barbie dolls and outfits, toiletries and school effects into a cedar chest she'd insisted on giving me.

"Take it, Neecy," she'd insisted. "You need something to keep her things in." Her rapid blinking kept tears back and I was grateful for her stoicism, more than I'd ever been before.

"Thanks, Kaye," I hugged her hugely. "I won't ever forget your kindness."

She gazed at me with amber donut, no-nonsense eyes. "You'd *better* not," she snapped comically. "I expect you to stay in touch. And that's an order. Y'hear?"

I grinned at her. "Yes'm."

Her face gentled. "And don't worry about Krissie's grave. I'll see to it when you're not able to get here."

Tears pooled, despite my resolve, then spilled over. I couldn't speak, spread my palms helplessly, then hauled her into my arms for a final hug.

Today, driving slowly from the parsonage, remembering the good and the bad, I allowed my gaze to meander through Crenshaw booty littered about the lawn, the sentimental me torn asunder at leaving so much of us behind. Yet, another part of me rejoiced to leave the hurtful behind. I swiped tears away and laughed suddenly.

The garbage men will think they've done died and gone to Heaven.

I stomped the gas pedal and looked ahead, beyond the van, to new horizons.

And a new homefire.

PART FOUR

"A time to Keep..."

1981-Present

CHAPTER NINETEEN

Life's timing sometimes sucks.

Why couldn't Kirk have adored me all those years sim- ply *because*? Why *now*, with me furious and raw and bleeding *because* of him? In that next year, I was militantly territorial of my newfound autonomy. I did not consciously evolve into a self- absorbed person. It simply happened as I fought my way back to self-respect.

Actually, I was not aggressively difficult. It was just that, the contrast from my former docile easily entreated self to one obsessed with self-preservation and emotional space made me, on occasion, *feel* like a shrew.

"I know I'm different." Kirk and I dined at the Truck Stop Restaurant, keeping one eye on our moving van parked outside and visible through the window. We sipped second cups of cof- fee while Toby and Dawn fed money to game room machines. "I'm simply being normal. Like I should have all along. I mean, I'm just acting like you've acted all along. You've *always* been viciously protective of your space." Which was absolutely true. Only thing was, in the past, I'd always capitulated to Kirk's whims. Now, I did not. "If you can't handle this, Kirk, I'm sor- ry. That's the way it's gonna be from here on out. If you want to bail out, now's the time."

"Darlin,' I'm not letting you out of my sight." Kirk was so happy I stayed with him, and was so eaten up with guilt, he took it all in stride. "I know I've been lousy and demanding. I was a real butt, honey. You should have spoken up years ago."

"I was *stupid*," I retorted, meaning it. "Nobody should think less of themselves than of those around them." That my words carried the sting of a swarm of wasps failed to daunt my pristine candor. For the first time in my life, I spoke with blunt honesty, letting the chips fall where they may. That fact gave me no great pleasure. For my survival, at that point in time, it simply had to be.

Kirk took my hands in his, gazing into my eyes. "We'll get through this together, honey. I want you to do whatever you have to do to get past all this."

Bottom line was, I needed to know me again in order to face the tomorrows. And to know me again, the *me*-pieces had to be joined together in a different order. The old no longer fit.

Was it true, after all, that *nothing* could put Humpty Dumpty together again?

All I knew was it was easier to fume than to hurt. *Easier* appealed to me simply because I'd shorted out in the cataclysmic explosion of adultery. It had depleted my emotional reserve. No quiet, lagoon refuge waited to embrace me and reflect in its still waters the real me, one I knew on some subliminal level. Now, indignation braced me for each leg of the arduous odyssey back to balance and purpose.

Quiet rage shaped my reasoning and simplified life for me. It told me I must never again be vulnerable. It was a knee-jerk certainty in my mind.

Thing was, I didn't know my way out of the murky maze.

Moving from Solomon had, in a way, shut the door on *then*. Made me take a step from it. Nighttime still brought horror flashes and bad dreams that drew me to my feet and away from Kirk, who tried so hard to be there for me.

"Come on back to bed, hon." His deep voice would rumble from the den doorway and he would come, take my hand and lead me back to our soft mattress-dent. "Let's work our way through this together." And beneath the covers, he would wrap his warmth around me and lull me from the nightmares, to *now*.

I had no agenda. Could not even fathom one. Nor, I think, did Kirk.

New beginnings did have their effect on our family. The first day in our new residence turned into a memorable event. We'd all four, after putting away clothing and fishing out towels, sheets and pillow cases, dashed out to Winn Dixie for groceries. Afterward, we put them away and explored the apartment, made *ours* by familiar pieces of furniture.

"*Man!*" Toby whooped, sitting and bouncing on the side of his single bed in the cramped quarters; a two bedroom unit. "This is like *camping out!*"

Four paces across the room, Dawn sprang rubbery and flat-footed, on her mattress, squealing, "*Campin' out! Campin' out!*"

The siblings would, until we found a house, share the room.

"We gon' have hot dogs for supper, Mama?" Toby, thirteen now and all legs and arms, fidgeted with the small television rabbit ears.

"Sure, why not?"

Kirk's arms seized me from behind, swooped me off the floor and swung me round and round until I screeched, *"Sto-o-op! You crazy man!"*

We tumbled into a heap atop Toby's mattress. *Plop, plop...* the kids ascended on us like squiggly worms, tangling us into silly, giggling knots

"Stop, Toby!" Dawn shrieked, her little face red as blazes.

I disengaged myself from the cluster and cut him a sharp, sidelong glance. "What you up to, Toby?"

Shifting upright, he was all round-eyed innocence, exposing and turning his hands as proof. "Nothing, Mom. She yells at *nothing.*"

"Aaaiiiii!" Another blood-curdling scream afflicted my ears. "You *lie, Toby!"* Dawn burst into earnest tears. Nobody, but *nobody* does *tears* like Dawnie. Today, with her mouth in square rage-rictus, eyes squeezed tight, tears looked big as clear glass marbles dropping off her chin.

I glanced in time to catch Toby's smug peek at his little sister. "Gotcha!" I growled.

He wiped his face clean, but it was too late. "I saw that look, son," I raised my eyebrows at him. "You know she's smaller than you and you've teased her mercilessly since she was born."

He flashed his boy caught-with-hand-in-the-cookie-jar grin. "I'm just playing with her, Mom. Dawnie, I just tickled your foot."

Dawn roared, "Don't *touch me! I've tol' you a hunerd times, Toby-y-y!"*

At four-and-a-half, Dawnie was becoming quite adept in self-defense, especially the verbal brand. "Toby, you know what happens when you over-tease little puppies while they're young, don't you?'

"Yeah," he conceded, still grinning. "They get *mean.*" His head swung to address Dawn on that last word, provoking another yowl.

"I'm not *mean!*" she shrieked, stiffening and clenching fists into tight little knots.

"Dawn, he didn't mean it that way," I lied and shot a meaningful look over her head at Toby.

"I'm sorry, Dawn," Toby said, not too convincingly. Dawn regarded him with a wariness far, far ahead of her years. It didn't help that his blue eyes still glimmered with mischief. I am convinced sibling rivalry never sleeps.

I sprang up, leaving Kirk sprawled on the floor, tickling Dawn's tummy.

"Last one in the kitchen's a rotten egg!" I yelled and sprinted. Kirk lost.

The day after our move to upstate's Harborville, a small foothills town, I went on a shopping frenzy. Our new location brought us within a reasonable driving distance to kin without having them popping in unexpectedly. Somehow, I knew family spontaneity would suffer for a season, but they would, in the process, be spared the heartache of knowing. Even so, the distancing hurt.

First thing I tackled was my hated reflection in the mirror. A Merle Norman makeover transformed sunken, fearful eyes into exotic confidence and gaunt features into highlighted – least it's what the saleslady told me – classic beauty. I knew the war paint helped, however, by the amazement on Kirk's face and the way heads now turned my way. I didn't seek attention. But it was there and like a warm springtime breeze lifts dead leaves into the air and gives them a life of their own, so did the unaccustomed favor lazily stir pleasure within me.

I would never again neglect that marvelous, feminine toilette ritual. Doesn't matter what Pharisaical church folk think anymore. The ceremony has little to do with vanity. *Au contraire,* I am truthful in saying I am not a stunning natural beauty. Few women remain so, past thirty, without cosmetics. I figured that when my husband turned to another woman, he gave me the green light to use every weapon available in makeup's arsenal.

Next, I bombarded department stores with money Kirk stuffed into my hands.

"Buy something pretty," he insisted, meaning it from the tips of his toes. In the past, when selecting clothing, I'd never thought past practicality and bargain. This freedom to be extravagant slightly overwhelmed me. But not for long. I was ready for something different.

Strobe images of Roxie hovering about my husband steered me to designer racks. I tried on clingy silk creations, romantic ruffles, and long-flowing skirts of wisp and soft colors.

Kirk's eyes, at first stunned, took on a gleam as he surveyed me moving decisively about in mere straps of shoes, transforming – with alluring creations – my skinniness into fashionable chic. After a detour to the perfume counter, a spritz of Chanel had him trailing me like a bloodhound.

I think, on some level, Kirk didn't want change. Was threatened by it. But his love and concern was such that he aided, abetted and encouraged my whims. And my desperate self-focus was such that I received it as my due.

"I love everything about you, Neecy," he murmured that night in our little Harborville apartment. Toby and Dawn, exhausted from "camping out," had crashed hours ago.

"I'd love you if you didn't wear a speck of makeup or a stitch of clothes," Kirk insisted huskily. When I burst into raunchy laughter, his eyes misted. "I mean that."

My lips still twitched. "I was laughing about the 'stitch of clothes.'" Another new freedom was spontaneity and it felt good to explore that side of me. I'd never, ever, been given that right. The new me grieved that I'd never taken it. Then, my laughter faded as our gazes ignited and we began to make slow, thorough love.

Kirk lifted his head from a tender kiss and gazed at me. "You look great in those new clothes." His eyes took on a deeper, sensuous glimmer. "You excite me."

Oh, I knew. We were both like little kids in a Disney park. Each new discovery brought out more unknowns about ourselves.

In spite of himself, Kirk, complex creature he is, grew to love the changes in me. His flexibility turned me on. The more urbane he became, the more my love grew. The old rigid, pugnacious Kirk became more and more obscure in those coming months. It was a magical time of laxity for both of us. It was like meeting again for the first time, seeing only the attractiveness and the good.

Yet, a part of me remained indelibly altered.

"You're beautiful – even without makeup," Kirk would say over and over. And he showed me in a thousand different ways that he meant it. Only thing was, I was no longer innocent and past actions drowned out his words. Roxie's exotic beauty had been – as any honest female would attest – artfully enhanced with makeup. Kirk could protest till Christ's return that it – the enhancement – did not affect him, and I would know better.

"I'm doing it for *me*, Kirk." My pat answer seemed to assuage his guilt. Oh, yes, Kirk was eaten alive with regret. I knew it would run its course. Everything does. My heart responded to his remorse. Couldn't help *but*. Yet, superceding that was the fact that I now *thought* for myself. The old me was dead. Killed. *Slaughtered*.

I was glad. Janeece disgusted me, her and her wimpy 'yes, dear, *whatever you say, dear*,' her *anything to avoid an argument* mentality. Her fearful, needy eyes and trembling hands made me wince and turn away in shame. Oh, I was indeed glad to see her gone.

It was not a calculated creation, the new me. It was survival in its most ignoble form.

Black and white emerged from gray, in 3-D clarity.

Between arguments – I was now a worthy opponent – we made passionate love. Kirk, who always had loved a good fight, got off on my new sauciness and became quite creative with ways to "court" and stir excitement. I reaped the very best of my husband in those months, knowing, *wishing* I could be more appreciative. Old habits die hard and an ember of the *I must make everybody happy* remained. I was like a bionic creation whose mechanical parts fit together but who needed an experienced technician to finely tune the intricate computer emotional system.

The two-sided drama mask was *me*. Especially during the following era, one that still, in my mind's eye, flashes past like a beautiful flaming comet, at a distance incredibly romantic but up close agonizingly hurtful.

I did not want to love Kirk to the degree that I had before. A measure that made me trust blindly and stupidly. That devotion had destroyed me.

Kirk was equally determined to win back that devotion.

Kirk, magnificent in battle, pulled out all the stops.

And me, even the new me, could not resist this hero, the man of my dreams. Heck, he was the man of every woman's dreams. Handsome, lean and strong, tender, considerate, an exquisite lover, outstanding father. Yet, I knew if he asked for the thing locked inside my heart, I would leave him.

I did not speak it aloud. And I knew if Kirk truly loved me, he would never require of me my *last ounce of dignity.*

Kirk, brilliant man that he is, knew. He'd discovered the key to my heart and handled it with utmost respect.

That, in the end, was what turned the tide.

It took two weeks to get our phone installed. I used a pay phone at Winn-Dixie to call Heather's dorm room at Winthrop College. I'd tried three times to catch her and failed. This time, a girl named Connie answered and I left a message for Heather. In the meantime, Kirk scouted out buildings for a hair styling salon. That would be our tent making. In the meantime, we lived off savings squirreled away by Kirk in years past.

"I don't want you out of my sight," Kirk teased, even as his eyes declared him dead serious. "I'll never tire of being with you."

"Someday," I said, "I'd like to finish up my teacher's accreditation requirements, but more immediately, I'd like to carry my weight for a change."

A shadow flickered over Kirk's features but was quickly gone. I'd explained to him that I'd felt inadequate through the years because of his ingrained tendency to measure worth by earning status. These days, I didn't hold things inside. Couldn't. Once opened, the door to hurts refused to close off again. They tumbled out and it felt good to examine and put them aside with constructive action.

Working with Kirk was a milestone to reclaiming myself.

I agreed to Kirk being my on-job instructor. That meant I could earn wages while learning the essentials of hair styling.

So began our day-to-day, hour-to-hour togetherness. A new frontier.

The phone rang as I drained spaghetti in the sink. I snatched the receiver from the wall.

"Hello?"

"Mama?" The query was tremulous and whispery.

"Heather?"

"Oh, Mama. I've been so worried. I didn't know where you were for the past two weeks. I had this terrible feeling that the Rapture had come and I was left and —"

"Whoa!" I laughed then, a loud resounding belly laugh. "Slow down, honey. Didn't Connie give you my message? I didn't have the phone then, but I told her to tell you I'd called."

"No." A long disgusted sigh. "She's a friend of my roommate and is sorta — flaky."

"Ah, honey — I'm sorry you didn't know how to contact us." I felt an instant jolt of guilt. "We've been packing and moving. And it's been such a mess. I figured you'd be so busy getting to know —"

I heard a distinct snuffling sound on the other end. "Heather? Honey, are you *crying?*"

A loud gulp, then, "Oh, Mama — I was so scared. It was weird, not being able to find you."

Her words smote me. "I'm so sorry, sweetheart. How *did* you find us?"

Another solid snuffle. "I called Callie. You know, at her Mom's? She gave me her address and phone number right before I left for school. I didn't think about —"

"But, she didn't have our number." I'd not been in contact with Callie since our last talk that day in Toby's room. Hadn't, in fact, been in touch with anybody, not even family. It was better that way. No questions. No explaining.

"No, she didn't. But she suggested I call Grandma again. I'd called her several times, but she hadn't heard from you, either. And when I phoned her again today, Grandma said you'd just called and given her your number. Mama, it was like — you just dropped off the earth. *Nobody* knew where you were."

"Oh baby – we've just been in over our heads. When can you come home for a visit?" I felt badly, but Heather had always been so self-sufficient I hadn't fathomed this turnabout.

"How about this weekend?" Heather began to sound more like herself again. "Can you and Dad come up and get me Friday afternoon?"

"Try and stop us!"

That Friday, Heather waited on the dorm curb when we arrived, bag in hand, and talked non-stop on the hour-and-a-half drive back to Harborville, gazing at us as if for the first time. Dawn, plastered against her sister's ribcage, gazed up into her animated features with bald adoration. Toby, too, was affected by the reunion, offering Heather not a stick, but his entire pack of Juicy Fruit gum, which she sensitively accepted, then shared with her siblings.

Later that evening, after Kirk turned in and the kids slept, Heather and I settled down on the cozy den's sofa bed for girl talk. My daughter watched me closely, as though weighing something.

"What?" I asked, pushing my newly cut, blonde-highlighted hair behind my ears.

Heather shrugged, then propped on pillows. "You look so different."

I wiggled my nose at her, bunny style, making her giggle like when she was small. "Different good or different bad?" I plumped my pillows and lay back, stretching and crossing my recently tanned legs at the ankles. I wore a new blue teddy and had just given myself a pedicure and polished my toenails Scarlet Rose to match my nails.

Heather's green eyes, so like Kirk's, remained vigilant while her mouth curved into a soft smile. "You're one of the most beautiful women I know. I'm glad you've finally started doing things for yourself."

I gazed warmly at her, struck that we'd transcended our old family ties to be friends. "Yeah." I grinned lazily, at ease with our new status. "S'about time. I got kind of tired being plain Jane. Y'know?" I fought back an urge to clench my teeth together.

"You deserve pretty things, Mama."

Heather's eyes did their little dance back and forth, sliding up and down over my features. Measuring – so like Kirk's it took my breath.

"What is it, honey? You seem to have something on your mind." I held out my hand to her, "Tell Mama about it." She sat up, scooted closer and took my hand. Only then did I see that she choked back tears.

"What?" I gently coaxed.

Her moist gaze locked with mine and I saw the stricken dilation of pupils. "Mama, I know – about Daddy and...Roxie."

My heart thudded to my toes. I tried to keep my countenance cool. "What do you mean, honey?" *Please, God. No.*

Heather's tears pooled along her lids, but she braced up and squeezed my hand. "When I called Callie, I said something that gave her the impression that I knew – though I didn't. She went on to comment that Daddy is a good man and I must forgive him."

I rolled my head away and squeezed my eyes shut. "Oh God, Heather. I didn't want you to know. Callie shouldn't have –"

"Mama, please don't blame Cal. She was so upset when she learned I hadn't known about it till then. You know, she's hurt, too."

I opened my eyes and looked at her. Everything feminine and caring and genetic poured from the green depths into my soul in that moment. "I'm so sorry, Mama, that you had to go through all that. I know you're hurting."

I smiled at her even as my eyes misted. Friend to friend. Mother to daughter. Heart to heart. Soul to soul.

"I love you, my darlin' daughter. You okay?" A tear spilled over my lid and down into my hair. I swiped it away.

"I'm okay," she said softly. Her chin lifted slightly and I saw she'd dealt with it, alone. And her eyes burned with resolve. "I saw how Roxie chased Dad." Her shoulder rose and fell limply. "I mostly hurt for you."

How strong she was. How brave.

So would I be. I pulled her to me and hugged her, long and hard.

"I'll be okay, honey." I pressed my damp cheek to hers and inhaled her clean *Charlie* fragrance. "Why, in time, I'll be as good as new."

Please, God, let it be true.

Kirk never knew of our talk. His greatest fear was that the children would hear and lose respect for him, like he'd lost respect for his alcoholic father. So, I shielded him. Heather was more comfortable with him not knowing so it made sense to keep silent. I was grateful that Heather's regard for her father didn't appear to have slipped.

I tried to imagine myself in her place. But I could not because my dad, handsome and winsome as he was with females, simply didn't have that venturous, on-the-edge personality that accommodates sexual duplicity. Dad also lacked a certain blinders-on *denial* required for marital deception. I was, by no means, an authority on the subject but one thing I knew: kids are casualties that ought not be.

Heather and I rarely mentioned Kirk's infidelity after that night. She came to terms with it on her own and seems not scarred by it. I don't think I'm being too Pollyanna. Heather has, increasingly, been open with me in all areas of her life and I think that, had it posed problems for her along the way, she would have told me. We have that kind of relationship.

I learned a valuable lesson: if the worst happens, we need not fold up and die. Life goes on.

CHAPTER TWENTY

"I enjoyed the message," I said as Kirk cranked our new blue VW hatchback. "Dr. Bergdorf has a smooth delivery." It was our first Sunday at the Harborville First Baptist Church; one of many we'd visited in recent months. Each time we entered a different vestibule – weekly – I always hoped it would click with Kirk. We needed a church home. Spiritual continuity.

"It was long," Dawn said, yawning. It had been.

"I liked it," Toby declared, and I knew why.

"She was cute," I said, tossing him a grin over my shoulder.

"Oh, Jane Smith," he said, blushing pleasantly. "Yeah, she is cute. She goes to my school."

"Ah." I settled back, tensing a little at Kirk's continuing silence.

"Did you really like it?" he asked suddenly.

I looked at him, fighting a niggling annoyance. "The service? Overall, it was nice."

Kirk looked thoughtful. "I felt he could have been a little more enthusiastic over the beatitudes. And he rambled at times."

I made myself smile and relax. "Everybody's not the pulpit dynamo you are, Kirk."

"*Were*," he said quietly. "Past tense." The muscles in his jaw knotted and his voice dropped to an octave lower whisper. "And I don't think I'm hot stuff."

There it was. Resentment. I frowned. "I didn't say you did. I wasn't comparing –"

"It didn't sound that way." The quiet words, raw and palpitating, gouged me into fury.

"I can't believe you said that," I hissed through my teeth. I wasn't nearly as successful as Kirk in arguing quietly, but I did try.

Later, alone in our room, we had it out. I didn't back down an inch. Which made it quite heated because it was not in Kirk's nature to capitulate. Now, however, he forced himself to do so. The victory was not a thing I relished. I didn't want to argue to begin with and resented being forced to do so.

"We need church, Kirk," I said. Dear *God, how we need church*.

"I agree." He raked fingers through collar-length hair, whose darkening waves made my fingers itch to tangle in them, even now. A full mustache cast his features more Tom Selleck than I liked. It thrilled and frightened me. Just as his strong sex drive did.

I spun away in frustration, away from his blaring masculine appeal. "You don't act like you agree. All I hear is this on-running put-down of each message."

"Can't you understand, Neecy?" His hoarse supplication cut to my heart. "I can't be a spectator. I'm far too emotionally involved to simply sit on a pew and – exist."

That jostled me. I whirled. "You can't be a follower, can you, Kirk? You never could. What's so terrible about taking time out to listen for a while? Is it so *beneath* you?" My anger far exceeded the subject. I couldn't even understand it myself, not completely.

Kirk stood at the window, hands shoved in pockets, his back to me. "You don't understand." His words were so quiet I wondered if I'd heard right.

"I *do* understand. You refuse to submit to another man's ministry." I knew the oversimplified statement was sharp, but I also knew it to be true. Kirk Crenshaw didn't trust another man to guide his thoughts and destiny now that he'd experienced pastoral authority. I didn't know that he ever would. Just as I tried new untested sod, so did Kirk.

He turned slowly, his expression so sad it took my breath. "It's much, much more than that, Neecy." He walked past me, on his way to help the kids decide on a restaurant for our Sunday lunch trek. At our bedroom door, he paused, looked over his shoulder and gave me a smile that didn't reach his eyes. "I know I deserve what I'm feeling." His green gaze darkened with pain. "It's just so hard." The door closed softly behind him.

Kirk and I pitched ourselves into building our four-chair hair styling business. Two of the chairs we leased to other stylists.

"I don't want a boss," I stated flatly when the subject arose. Kirk, sharp looking in his black shirt and slacks – that matched my own outfit – leaned indolently against the trellis entrance to my stylish stall and measured me with shuttered eyes. I knew I forced him to shuffle tactics to integrate me into his business scheme. His was a black and white approach.

"Every business needs a boss," he declared gently, raising my ire another notch.

"I might not be sharp with numbers," I sniped, fluffing my platinum blond bob and checking out my new red lipstick in the salon mirror, "but I'm smart enough to make appointments, turn out a great hair style, collect money and make change without major problems. So," I faced him squarely, "I don't want a boss."

When had I begun to welcome confrontations? It had to be a perverse charley horse reaction to anything I sensed in myself as remotely compliant. I detested my old submissive self and would run around the block and back to avoid her. Today, Kirk simply walked away, saying nothing. I marveled again at the man he'd become.

His silence could have baffled me, made me wonder if he conceded to my wishes because he truly respected my intellect or could have made me ponder why, after all these years, his self-confidence had geysered out the top. The latter explanation seemed feasible since he'd always, in the past, had some macho something to prove. Now, he seemed at peace with me as an equal. In my new matter-of-factness, I regarded the current relationship as one long overdue.

It was, to me, one of mutual respect. All I'd ever wanted from my marriage.

Now, when I wanted time to myself, I went shopping. Kirk played golf. I didn't care that sometimes this stretched into dusk. I loved my solitude. He was the one who complained I read too much or spent too much time writing in my endless journals. Of course, he did it teasingly, distracting me and playfully demanding a kiss or mussing my carefully coifed hair. We'd end up tussling and making love.

Despite occasional tensions, Kirk and I maintained a sense of togetherness for our children, saving serious discussions until Toby hung out with neighborhood teen buddies and Dawn was tucked away with kin. She spent most weekends with Trish, now her cherished 'Mema.'

"That's as close to being 'Mama' as I *dare* go." Trish tweaked the small turned-up nose. "Gene's satisfied with being 'Uncle Gene' and protecting her from monster-Toby." She leaned and kissed the puckered up lips. "I'm so glad your mama and daddy came to visit our church today."

Trish looked at me then, concern furrowing her face. "Everything okay?" Because Trish knew Dawn's time with her was a double blessing for them both: it gave Trish the child she never had and spared Dawn the unpleasantness of homefront skirmishes.

"Yep." I smiled lazily from the parsonage's overstuffed floral sofa. "I love sharing her with you. You should have had five of your own. I'll never, ever, *ever* understand God's reasoning in some things."

Trish shrugged, kicked off her heels and shuffled in hosed-feet to the adjoining kitchen to check on Sunday lunch heating in the oven. Her weight had slowly crept up through the years, but she was still, to me, beautiful. I could see her from where I lounged, swollen feet propped on her glass-topped coffee table. The long salon hours took their toll, leaving me near collapse by Sunday mornings.

"Need any help?" I asked, rolling my neck to dispel tiredness.

"You just stay where you are, Sis," Trish insisted, pulling a pan of steaming barbecue chicken from the stove and gingerly peeling back the foil. "You deserve a day of rest."

"But I feel guilty," I muttered.

"Don't." Her busy hands soon had chicken arranged on a silver platter. Effortlessly, she orchestrated a dining table array of mashed potatoes, coleslaw, whole green beans, yams, buttered rolls and a three-layer chocolate cake that made my sweet tooth gasp.

"You're so creative, Trish. Such a homemaker."

"Reg'lar ol' Julia Child." She blushed becomingly. "If I'd thought of it in time, I'd have gotten Gene to go fetch Chuck to eat with us." Trish padded to the refrigerator for her gallon tea jug and filled the iced glasses parked on white counter space.

"How is he, by the way?" I hadn't seen my brother in so long, I'd lost count of time. I was ashamed my life's problems had pushed him aside, same as they had MawMaw.

"Teresa finally signed over her power of attorney to Anne and Daddy."

"Praise be!" I breathed, closing my eyes in relief.

Trish turned to face me, grim. "She's asked him for a divorce."

"What?" I gazed at her in disbelief.

"Says she needs to get on with her life and Chuck's not part of it."

"Oh Lord – how can anybody be so cruel?" I blinked back tears. "I've got to go see him. Soon."

Trish wiped her own eyes and placed napkins beside her stacked china. "He's brave, Sis. I know it hurts him like crazy, but he's putting on that big grin of his so nobody will know. Fact is, if a kidney donor doesn't turn up soon, our brother will die."

"Let's don't even go there, Trish. Let's believe for a miracle, huh?"

Trish winked. "I'm game."

I sat there, thinking how courageous my brother was. In contrast, I was a wimp.

But I *had* come a long way.

"Let's eat!" Trish called out the back door, heralding our males to lunch.

And I knew in that moment I still had a ways to go.

The next eighteen months saw me plowing much new, hard terrain. Kirk and I met our nightly Cosmetology School requirements to place us in the upper-income bracket of the business. I found a profound sense of accomplishment in earning wages that, many weeks, exceeded Kirk's. We were, in every professional sense, a team.

One day, Anne called in tears. "Neecy, sit down."

"W-what is it, Anne? Is Chuck –" My voice choked off as my pulse raced away.

"Remember my friend at the nursery, Janice Towery?"

"Uh hm."

"Well, her brother was in a bad automobile accident three days ago. He was only thirty one years old. The doctors had him on life support. I was there with Janice when they had to make the decision to disconnect him.''

"That's terrible," I muttered.

"I heard them say he had an organ donor card and this thought came to me, Neecy. I just came out and said 'Can you donate his kidneys to anybody you want to?' And the doctors said they could. I asked them to donate a kidney to Chuck." She began to weep.

"Oh Anne." It was like a big fist squeezing my heart. "What did they—"

"They said *'yes.'*" My weeping joined hers for long moments.

"Anne," I finally managed to croak, "Chuck's gonna *live!*" And in that moment, I realized how truly terrified I'd been that he would not.

"He sure is, Neecy. My boy's gonna make it."

I called Trish right away and told her the good news.

"God gave us our miracle, Sis," Trish said. "Anne was used to instigate it, don't you know? If she hadn't thought to ask –"

"Got that right, Trish. A good sermon illustration for Gene. *'Ask and ye shall receive.'*"

Chuck was immediately prepared for surgery. His family was there to lend love and succor in those pain-filled hours. But he came through like a trooper.

His first slurred words after surgery were "See, ya'll? I tol' you I was strong as an ox."

Kirk's attentiveness never wavered. I didn't seek it, but it was there. Slowly, it began to affect me. I'd never been immune to Kirk. Never. But the adultery trauma had closed off a part of my gentle, sensitive side. Now, his unceasing gallantry tugged at the binding ropes until, little by little, their knots slipped loose to release feelings I was loathe to acknowledge. They would render me entirely too vulnerable.

Kirk told me so often and so fervently that he adored me and could not live without me that I began to trust it to be truth. Something in his need broke down some of my last defenses. I now felt free to crawl into his lap, as a child would, and ask him for a hug. Or a stroke. Or a word of encouragement. I'd never felt this liberty with another living being.

The dark times still came, but they were fewer and farther between. I thought I could even see a light at the end of the proverbial tunnel, especially with Kirk's support.

Heather came home on weekends and summers. Dawn spent after school hours at the salon with us, doing homework, watching television, coloring and doing crossword puzzles. After a year of private Christian education, we entered Toby and Dawn in public school so Toby could play football and other sports and ready himself for college.

"It's so-o-o nice being an ordinary person," Heather exulted one summer afternoon as we lounged around the salon, sipping canned sodas and munching chocolate chip cookies the two of us had baked the night before. "I got so tired of being a PK."

"Yeah," Toby echoed. His chocolaty grin belied his gripe. "Everybody watches you like a hawk."

As the day wore on, I grew more and more silent as clients came and went. Depression, which had hovered for days, dropped and wrapped me like Saran. I didn't recognize it until I choked and struggled against its invisible force. I felt Kirk's gaze but didn't return it. I could not reassure him that I was fine when I wasn't. My despondency wasn't flagrant. I'd simply stopped pretending. Kirk never had. Now, he at least put as much effort in diplomacy as I did. I'd always given him space to struggle through low points. That's all I wanted now. I didn't want Kirk to feel responsible for my moods. That wasn't fair to him.

Nevertheless, I felt the strain of his concern and struggled to ease myself free by staying busy.

"We're going home, Mom," Heather called from the door. "Pizza okay for supper?"

"Sure." I shot her a smile and finished polishing my mirrors. Kirk's big hand captured mine and he pulled me around to face him.

"What's wrong?" he asked softly, his green gaze probing mine.

I shook my head, averting my eyes. But he would have none of it.

"Look at me, Neecy." The command was gentle but firm. "Something's bothering you. We need to talk." He took my hand and led me to the waiting area, where he seated me on the plush navy sofa, closed the vertical blinds and locked the door. Then he lowered himself into the almond and navy striped chair facing me. He hooked a tan ankle over his knee and steepled his fingers to his lips, his gaze riveted to my face.

I gazed dully at him, feeling only melancholy. Loss. Anger at myself. At him. At the world. Yet – none of these feelings were as powerful as they'd once been. And they would run their course in a day or two, then dissipate.

His voice sliced through my stupor. "What do you want from me, Neecy?"

I frowned. "What do I want? Kirk, I don't know of a thing I don't have that you could give me."

He stared at me for long moments, as if not seeing me. "Except what you feel I stole from you."

I opened my mouth, then closed it. It was true, in a sense. I sighed. A long, ragged sound. "I wish I could say it doesn't matter, Kirk. Do you think – if the tables were turned – that you could say that to me?"

A dark shadow flickered across his face. "I can't say, Neecy. Because I'm not in your place."

Anger stirred inside me. "You can't just – imagine?" I asked, knowing full well he could.

"No. I cannot do the hypothetical thing. It's not me."

Old denial Kirk. Smooth as an eel. So much for genuine empathy.

"What do you think would help you not feel so – deprived?" he asked evenly.

The question took me off guard. "I've never thought of the situation as something to be 'fixed,' Kirk. I'm trying to get past it. We've come a long way, actually."

His gaze sliced to me, electrifying in its intensity. "I don't think so."

I threw up my hands. "Kirk, you know I've worked hard at putting this thing in the past. You've been wonderful," I reminded him that I *noticed*. "If you hadn't – I couldn't have made it this far."

The green laser pinned me. "Did you know that I'm suicidal?"

"Why?" *Dear God in Heaven.*

"I've lost everything. My ministry, my wife...."

My stomach knotted. I would not succumb to guilt. No way. "Kirk, that's ridiculous. We've got this business and you haven't lost me."

Some infinitely sad shadow passed over Kirk. "Where is my sweet little wife? Whose voice was like a soft bubbly brook. And who would have died before speaking sharply to me? Where is that woman?"

The question was a bullet to my heart. Because Kirk knew. Deep down, he knew.

Like a balloon with a tiny prick, I began to leak life.

"You'd better get used to the new me, Kirk," I said dispiritedly and stood, reaching for my purse. "Because the other woman is dead."

"Why?" Kirk was on his feet, eye to eye with me. "Why does she have to be dead, Neecy?" he asked in his velvet-husky way.

Forces inside tore me asunder. How could he push me into this corner, demand I return to a place no longer accessible, *be* the tormented person I'd fled?

How could he dump the whole mess in my lap and insist that it's all *mine?* How could he force me to say what I didn't want to say?

"She's dead," I gazed at him through a wet, shimmery haze, "because you killed her, Kirk."

"Mama!" Toby rushed through the small apartment den, lanky waist wrapped in a bath towel. "Help me," he moaned as he flopped across my bed in the next room.

I rushed to him. He'd just come in from a neighborhood stroll with a pal and taken a bath.

"What's wrong, honey?" I leaned over him and smoothed his wheat-colored hair from his cold forehead. "Sick?"

His head began to roll from side to side. "I won't *ever* do it again, Mama."

Alarm shot through me when I saw his pulse jostling him like he was hooked to a gigantic vibrator. "Toby, tell me what's happened." I sat down and took his icy fingers in mine. His eyes gazed unseeing at the ceiling.

"That man," he swallowed and tried again. "That man in a downstairs apartment, he got me and Wayne to puff on a cigarette. Mama, I feel like I'm dying." He jackknifed and arose in panic, pacing to the door and back, arms clutching midriff, trying to escape the demons tearing him apart.

"Drugs, right here in this building," I muttered, heart in throat. "Kirk!" I cried.

Kirk rushed from the kitchen where he'd been having coffee and reading the paper. I relayed Toby's quandary in angry tones as our son sprawled spread-eagled, prostrate on the floor, every hair on his head quivering from his young heart's exertion.

I quickly called Heather at school, knowing she'd seen drugs' effects at college parties.

"He's gotten a laced weed, Mama. He'll be all right in a few hours. Takes three to four hours to sleep it off."

"You sure, honey?"

"Yeah. Chill out, Mama. He'll be okay. I promise."

"Love you, honey." We rang off and I sat with Toby, holding his hand until, gradually, his heartbeat wound down from runaway to tranquil. Toby had, I knew, quietly prayed all during his ordeal. It tore at my heart that an adult had talked him, my innocent Toby, into inhaling something so terrible and potent.

"Where you going?" Kirk looked up from his television golf match as I marched through the den on my way out.

"To find that man who gave Toby drugs."

"Whoa!" Kirk, instantly pale, was on his feet blocking my way before I could say scat. "No, Neecy," he said gently. "You don't tangle with drug people."

"But Toby –"

"No." The command was soft but firm. "Toby's learned his lesson, honey. That's what's important."

The starch went out of me and I plopped onto the sofa. "I think it's time we started house hunting."

I inhaled the brisk, late September air as I grabbed my textbook from the car seat and dashed into Harborville Community Tech College. An early afternoon shower had left the world smelling of newly washed earth. Autumn is my favorite time of the year – well, it actually ties with early springtime. The freshness of both presses cerebral buttons that spin me back to courtship days when Kirk and I exulted in each other and in hopes of bright horizons.

I'd decided to wade through a self-paced evening math course required for my teacher's certification. My mind needed more engagement than hairstyling gave it. Kirk's subtle denouncement of our successful business nudged me to press on for my teaching credentials.

In one predawn moment, I'd faced the fact that my future was no more certain than it had been four years earlier. Kirk's quicksilver moments of unpredictability kept me ever vigilant.

The class was just beginning when I slipped in and tried to unobtrusively claim a seat, managing to step on the toes of a good-looking dark-haired male student. I apologized profusely and took the seat beside him.

And as the professor divided us into self-help groups, I found myself paired with Johnny Revel, the hunky Stallone lookalike. That his gaze kept alighting on me and he chose the seat next to me rustled a certain excitement in me. Afterward, when he asked me to join him at the Campus Quick Shop for coffee, I decided it was a perfectly innocent thing between friends.

Perfectly innocent.

Another downpour had me sprinting into the house when I arrived home. We'd lived on Oak Street for nearly a year now. The hedge-wrapped, tri-level was roomy – my idea of Heaven after the tiny apartment stint – spread over a big lot with lovely crepe myrtles, dogwoods, azaleas, hostas and every imaginable seasonal blossom.

"Closets," I'd badgered the realtor because our tiny cramped quarters left me ravenous for storage space. "Lots and *lots* of closets." This house had them tucked away in every nook and crevice. I could actually find my out-of-season clothing without crawling into an attic.

"How'd class go," Kirk called from his La-Z-Boy in the sunken den, his hands tucked behind his head. Was the soft, underlying tension in his voice my imagination?

"Great. Looks like it will be fairly easy, what with the self-paced thing." I commenced fixing myself a quick ham and cheese sandwich. "You eat yet?" I asked.

"No. I was waiting for you."

I pulled two more bread slices from the loaf. "Where are the kids?"

"Gone to see a Disney movie." He stood at my elbow, touching, gazing at me with an adoration that kept bouncing back even after our most vicious conflicts. "They won't be back for a couple of hours."

His quiet, simmering suggestion turned me into his embrace and we kissed as if our very survival depended on it. "Oh, Kirk, I love you so." I wanted to crawl inside him and plaster myself there.

"Me, too," he murmured. Soon, our sandwiches were things half-made, forgotten....

Christmas came and went and another year began, one that, in retrospect, blurs at times with its erratic emotional roller coaster. Kirk impulsively drove on campus one evening and discovered me having coffee with Johnny at the Quick Shop.

I introduced Kirk to Johnny. Kirk was his most cool self, embarrassing me. Johnny was unruffled, warmly shaking Kirk's hand. I excused myself and Kirk and I left together.

"How long has this been going on?" he asked as soon as we were outside.

"All semester," I answered truthfully. "We use that time to study for our weekly math tests. Johnny helps me understand the algebra and trig. You know how dense I am there."

Later, in bed, he asked, "Why didn't you tell me right away?"

"Because – what was the point? Why make an issue of something so – so *piddly?*"

"Piddly? I don't think so." His quiet voice took on an edge.

"Well, I do. Honestly? I didn't think you'd mind." The truth.

Kirk's possessiveness of me, inch by inch, declaration by declaration, had moved me to a pinnacle of confidence that drove back my numbing lapses. Tonight, when he saw me with Johnny and I glimpsed the flash of green fire, it didn't occur to me Kirk could feel fear. Through the years, Kirk had always been spontaneous with both positive and negative reactions. And if his love for me now encompassed, as he proclaimed, unconditional acceptance, could it not delight in the new honest me? After all, my self-talk insisted, I'd always tolerated his less than perfect philosophies.

Now, in bed, he wanted an explanation of my silence. "Because – I didn't want you to be concerned about it, that's all."

I felt the shuttered gaze pierce the darkness. "Have you seen him off campus?"

The succinct probe stirred old, ingrained annoyances. It was so demanding. So – Kirk. He'd always placated his qualms with blunt forthrightness while denying me the same right. The reminder immediately tied my insides into pretzels.

"Why do you ask?" I turned my head to meet his gaze head-on, letting him know he crowded me. I'd never given him reason to doubt me.

His eyes, jade pools in his shaded, angular face, measured me for long moments. Then he sighed, as though harnessing something runaway. He locked hands behind his head and stared at the ceiling. Still as death. I remembered how this silent treatment once had sent fear careening through me and how I'd begged Kirk to talk it out, not insist on "sleeping on it," holding it over my sleepless head until dawn drove back the night and I was so sick I could barely remember what had set him off. I recalled how he'd set all the rules with the cast of his features, the timber of his voice and the cutting off of his emotions.

Most of all, I remembered his sovereign refusal to explain himself, as though I didn't require clarification. The double standard had peaked with the unfaithfulness. Now, he resented that I might be attractive to another man.

"Do you want to find out how – *exciting* it is?" he asked flatly.

My head swiveled on my pillow and I stared at his handsome profile, hating that I'd never, before or since his betrayal, looked at him without a jolt of sexual awareness. I knew what he spoke of. In some of our recent heart-to-hearts, when he'd encouraged the "little girl" in me to reveal herself, to tell him exactly how I felt, I'd begun to truly trust him as my friend. So, I told him I'd resented that he'd tasted of different fruit than ours and had wondered if I'd missed something by our exclusivity. The admission had been purely honest, without rancor.

Without prayer.

Tonight, I turned my face to the ceiling. "I only want the pain to go away."

"Do you think having a fling with someone will help you?"

"I don't know. All I know is I've lost something precious and you haven't. And I know you can never understand my perspective."

"No? I've lost your trust. You don't think that hurts?"

I sighed and fidgeted with the bedspread. "It's not that I don't trust you. It's just −" I looked at him. "You know I've never slept with another. I know you *have*. You can compare. The feelings inside me are not any you can imagine. I can't even explain them except to say that if I could stop grieving for what isn't, I could get on with life."

"Well," he drawled, "I can tell you that having sex with someone outside your marriage is not exciting. It's hell. It leaves you feeling like pond slime. The whole experience made me realize what I have in you. Can't you understand that?" The appeal in his voice only stirred my resistance to his one-way view.

"In a sense, I can. It's just − I wish I didn't feel this desperation about the whole thing. I need a purging."

"At one time, you would have prayed and been rid of it."

"Yeah." I gave a sad little laugh. "Every other situation on earth, I could have prayed away. This − this has sapped the part of me that reached out to God." I shook my head. "I don't think God even wants to have anything to do with me now. I've pushed Him so far away...."

In reality, prayers stuck in my throat, undelivered. Something in my post-trauma psyche remained locked against the old Janeece and her ways, something turbulent and implacable.

Kirk turned to face me, his eyes glimmering in the silvery dusk. "If you need to have a fling, Neecy. Do it. I want you to get over this."

I gazed at him, shocked at his words. "Kirk, I've never wanted a man on this earth other than you. Johnny Revel included."

"Thanks, honey," he whispered. Then he took my cold hand in his. "I'm serious as I've ever been. If a fling is what it takes to get you past this – do it. But I can assure you of one thing: it won't be what you think."

"Why, Kirk Crenshaw," I gasped, horrified, "You'd never forgive me if I slept with another man."

"I would," he said softly, reverently, stroking my cheek. "Because I know you'll not find what you're looking for there."

I stared inanely at him. "Where is God in all this, Kirk?"

I saw the shadow of his lips curve into an incredibly sad smile. "I haven't known where God is for a long, long time."

I don't know for sure when I first whiffed the foreign smell on Kirk's breath. We'd begun going out to dance on Saturday nights when Toby and Dawn were at Trish's. I consoled myself that at least *they* were in church. Toby, after the drug incident, had not missed a service, had taken to going either with Trish and Gene or Daddy and Anne. He'd latched onto the Almighty with a tenacity I'd once had.

I felt badly that Kirk and I slept in entirely too many Sunday mornings. Yet, when we did attend, Kirk's attitude nettled me to the bone. Why couldn't he simply let me glean what I could from the messages without sullying them with his negative comments?

"What's that smell?" I sniffed when Kirk kissed me on the drive home from Thursdays, a local disco. His arm draped my midriff and his fingers ran titillatingly over my hipbone.

"I had a drink."

"When?" I gaped at his profile. Something went off inside me like tiny fireworks, shooting icy sparks out my fingers and toes.

He shrugged as though it were of no consequence. "On my way to the men's room. It was just one mixed drink."

"Oh, Kirk," I moaned.

"Hey." Kirk smiled down at me, his eyes glimmering reassurance. "Just one, honey. I'm not a drinker. I've already gotten a headache from it."

"But I thought we agreed not to drink." My stomach had fallen to my toes, having been replaced by my dully thudding heart. "We were just going to have a little fun. Date."

"We are," he murmured. "Don't worry, darling. I'd never do anything to hurt you."

I sighed and gazed ahead into the night, keenly aware that he already had.

The episode pummeled me into knots during that next week. Kirk was so solicitous I felt almost guilty about the funk I was in. Almost. He insisted the drinking lapse was but a tiny thing. All the same, it was, to me, a significant one. He'd already begun smoking when the kids weren't around. That had upset me, but he'd laughed and teased my fears away, insisting he could lay them down any time he chose. The two things, together, gave me pause to consider where, exactly, we were headed.

I tried to pray. *Please God, make Kirk stop fooling around with alcohol and tobacco. It was such a triumph, spiritual and physical, when he'd denounced them years ago.* Where would his latest capitulation lead us?

Months passed and still, Kirk dabbled in the forbidden pleasures. My silent fear was that by catering to these appetites, he could easily slide into a lust mode. Too, I knew all too well that no matter how strong Kirk's declaration of love, I still had no influence over his urges.

The realizations affected my appetite and sleep. My quandary drove me to insulate myself by reading and writing more. I tried to talk with Kirk about my fears, but he smoothly sidestepped them by promising not to do either again.

"We need to begin to take time apart – have some breathing space," he suggested one day as I wiped my salon station clean at the day's end.

"Oh?" I organized my brushes without looking at him, a sense of dread washing over me.

"We're together all the time. No husband and wife should spend every waking hour together like this." He spoke casually, shoulder resting against the trellis, hands shoved into neatly creased slack's pocket, ankles crossed. "I want you to go to the beach to rest next weekend. You need that."

I looked at him then, searching for a hidden motive. He looked levelly at me, concern marking his good looks. "I'm worried about you, Neecy. You barely eat and you're too quiet."

"Why don't we go to the beach together?" I asked, propped against my work backstand, my arms crossed.

"Because you need time to just rest. I want it to be your birthday present from me." He moved to take me into his arms. My stiffness soon dissolved when he began to kiss me and murmur his love against my neck, turning my joints to liquid. "Do it for me, huh?" he whispered.

"Hmm?" I'd already forgotten the question.

Kirk put the last of my suitcases in the car trunk and slammed it shut. We'd only a couple of hours earlier dropped Dawn off at Trish and Gene's. Heather and Toby were spending the weekend at Dad and Anne's. Grandma was elated and planned a virtual feast for Sunday lunch. I didn't even deal with the fact that my family, by now, knew I was going to Myrtle Beach, alone, and being the conservative souls they were, would wonder *why?*

"So," I said, turning to face my husband, "when can I reach you tonight? The hair show will be over by nine, won't it?"

He looked at me almost vacantly for a long moment, then – *as though programmed,* the thought flashed meanly through my mind – smiled and hugged me. "I'll be home late. I'll have a sandwich, then drive over to the Hilton for the hair show. I'm not sure when we'll break up. Now," he hiked up his watch, peered at it and pointedly assisted me into the car, "you'd better get started so you won't be too late getting in. I don't like the idea of you driving after dark."

Then why are you sending me off alone? I ground my teeth together, flashed a dry smile and waved as I drove off. For the next five hours, I had that off-kilter feeling that something was not quite right. Was it *me?* Was it Kirk's determination to rid himself of me? Was it a combination of everything, the smoking, drinking and his subtly taking control again now that he felt secure that I loved him as blindly as ever?

I thought dryly that the homefires I now tended were ones I could do without.

For some reason, MawMaw flashed through my mind. *I need you now, Neecy. You'uns will have to stand by me now Papa's gone....*

Dear Lord. I couldn't even hold MawMaw's hand when she needed it, after all the affection she'd shown me all my life. We'd driven to Asheville at Christmas time and brought her down to stay a week with us. She'd been weak but happy being with us. She and Dawn spent the days together at home while Kirk and I worked at the salon. Each evening, we took her to a different restaurant to eat and she felt like Queen for a Day. Afterward, she and Dawn would demonstrate new little dance steps Dawn had taught her during the day and we'd laugh 'til tears at her little rotund shape jiggling about.

Only thing was, behind the scenes, Kirk and I locked horns. I was so afraid MawMaw's sensitive nose would pick up on the foreign scents of alcohol and tobacco, but Kirk refused to back off. I also feared she would overhear our arguments, which were becoming increasingly more heated, as Kirk's golf times stretched longer and longer and his afternoon treks on un-named *errands,* during my scheduled appointments, increased.

Helpless fury almost paralyzed me as his personality became more and more erratic. The last day of MawMaw's visit was a scene from Hell. While she sat in our sunken den, I tried to reason with Kirk to stop drinking and disappearing all the time, which, I figured out by now, were connected.

"You stink like a stale ashtray," I hissed at him in our upstairs bedroom, where he sprawled on the bed, grinning like an idiot, "not to mention the beer. Kirk, you were a *preacher, for God's sake.* Don't you even care what your image is?"

His slumberous eyes blinked slowly. "Can't say as I do, Neecy."

"Neecy?" MawMaw called from downstairs. "Honey, why don't you come down and sit with me for a while before I have to go? I'm getting kinda lonesome."

Her quavery appeal pierced me to the core. I'd shot Kirk a disgusted look and left, quietly closing the door behind me.

Tonight, rain riveleted my windshield and I remembered driving MawMaw home that day, alone, because Kirk was in no condition to be around her. I knew, someday, he'd be ashamed. But not now. He'd won his mission to conquer me. He'd made me love him to distraction again and now, he'd become bored with the whole thing and had turned to drinking and God only knew what else.

I turned the windshield wipers on, barely able to see the highway ahead. Rain and tears blended in a melancholy symphony of grief and pain.

Grief for something vital and pure within the hallowed walls of marriage. Gone. Something inside me knew, *felt* the slimy spirit of betrayal.

Pain from my indomitable inner-self, who refused to accept its demise.

"Bloody rain." I leaned forward, wiping the foggy windshield with damp wadded tissue, focusing my teary-blurred gaze on the road ahead. I slowed the VW down to a more tranquil forty-five mph.

I checked into the Landmark and settled in, tired and hungry. It was nearly eleven o'clock by the time I finished a sandwich from room service, a splurge I felt I deserved after the long drive. I called my home number. No answer.

I watched television for the next couple of hours. Then tried to begin a Fern Michaels novel but couldn't concentrate. I tried again to reach Kirk. No answer. I looked at the ornate wall clock. One-ten am.

Only then did I give in to the tears that had threatened since I walked into the lavish setting surrounding me. I cried until I hiccupped and was out of breath. I pulled on my housecoat and went out onto the private balcony to fold myself into a lounge chair, where I watched the dark ocean until dawn turned it silver and the sun climbed up to paint its horizon golden and banish my nightmares. I went inside, closed the drapes and pulled the covers over my head and slept.

❖ ❖ ❖ ❖ ❖ ❖

I gathered my writing paraphernalia, shoved sunglasses on my face and walked to the elevator down the hall. Inside, alone, I stared at my reflection in mirrored walls. I didn't look as skinny in the turquoise swim suit. Just – *thin*. The two-piece was not bikini, but when I tied the string on each hip, the result was modest yet chic. I took off the shades and my eyes, though huge and sunken in my near-gaunt face didn't look as feverish as I'd imagined. Fact was shadow and liner camouflaged fear's glassy earmark, presenting instead a gaze shimmery and self-assured. Aloof.

Didn't matter what I felt inside. Nobody was the wiser.

Anything was better than revealing fear.

Detached, I tilted my head and studied the total me. I looked sort of like a petite version of your high fashion model. The emaciated, mannequin kind, hat-rack hipbones and shoulders, while bright slashes of color marked drooping lids and mouth.

My little dry laugh didn't reach my flat eyes. Fact was, I didn't care doodly about how I looked at that moment. I'd not reached Kirk on the phone until just before I came outside. He'd been at the salon.

"Oh, honey," he said, "It was a great hair show. There was a reception thing afterward so I stayed and chatted with folks and lost track of time. When I came in around midnight, I was so tired I fell asleep on the den sofa. I didn't hear the phone."

I let it go, too dispirited to do otherwise. Truth was I didn't think I could handle the details. "I'm going to get some sun," I told him.

"Miss you, honey," he said huskily.

"Me, too," I replied quite honestly, even though still miffed at him for pushing me into coming alone. And though I could manage sequestration, *forced alone*ness had never truly been my thing. Only during writing was I happy in it.

I exited the elevator and moved to the pool deck, searching for an empty lounge chair. I spotted the only remaining vacancy, next to a huddle of college age males, and made my way to it. I stretched out on the webbed seat, pulled out a pad and pen and began a poetry exercise, which usually got me going.

Within moments, I abandoned that and worked on a romance novel. But the sounds of fun coming from the young men made my despondency more pronounced. I replaced the pad in my beach bag and shifted myself to lie flat, hoping to doze off.

Soon, the slightly uncomfortable pinch of the lounge's wicker weave told me the beach towel had slipped beneath me. I rose to adjust the towel and only when I lay back down and shifted my sunglasses did I notice the three college guys staring openly at me.

Dully unimpressed, I flipped over on my stomach and closed my eyes. But each time I neared drowsing, a wave of memory hit me...Kirk drinking, his personality doing its chameleon thing, slithering from sweet to indifference, a mode that numbed him to everything around him, including me. Sleep danced around, eluding, seducing me and then taunting me to wakefulness.

Finally, I adjusted my seat into an upright position and noticed that only one young man remained in a nearby chair. He still stared at me but his was an openness – an innocence I likened to Toby's.

"Hi." I found myself smiling at him.

His face brightened. "Hi."

I had not, until that moment, realized just how lonely I was. The realization made me hang onto that moment of human contact for just a little longer. "Where are you guys from?"

"Canada."

"Wow. A long way from home."

"Yeah. We go to college together. What were you writing?"

I hesitated briefly, then, "would you believe, romantic fiction?"

"Really?" He looked impressed.

"Um hmm."

His name was Chris and he was twenty-two years old, a clean-cut, not unattractive young man. His questions, about my writing, were impressive, intelligent ones.

"What sort of hero do you usually come up with?" His blue eyes twinkled teasingly. "I mean...what does he look like?"

"Ohh," I laughed, a little self-consciously, "I'm partial to green eyes and coppery brown hair."

"Like mine?" he flirted charmingly.

"You could say that," I went along with his good-natured teasing. "But sometimes, I do a complete flip-flop and create a dark, Latin hero."

"Oh." His demeanor did a comical collapse.

I gurgled with genuine laughter at his transparency. "Romance writers can't be too predictable, you know."

Our chat continued a while longer, until I felt a burning sensation creep over my skin – the side exposed to the afternoon sun.

"I really must be going inside." I started to rise.

"Janeece," he said so imploringly I remained seated, "you were telling me about the good live band at the Coquina Room?"

I nodded. I'd gone there for a few minutes the night before, during my restlessness, and enjoyed the music. "The band is pretty good."

"Well...my friends will be going to another club. But I – well," I watched his Adam's apple bob as he swallowed, "would you come with me to the Coquina Room tonight?"

I stared at him. *Careful, girl, don't hurt him.* I paused long moments before replying.

"Chris – I really feel flattered. But you don't have to invite me out." *Did he see through to my dreadful loneliness?*

"But you don't understand, Janeece." He leaned intently and scooted to the edge of his seat. "I *want* to take you out."

My head moved from side to side. "That's probably – not a good idea." He looked so hurt, I hastily added, "I mean – not as a date."

His shoulders slumped. "If you don't like me, just say so."

"Oh, it's not that." I felt compelled to spare him from a brush-off. In light of my own rejection experience, my sympathy crescendoed. "I truly like you."

His countenance lifted. "You're such a beautiful woman, Janeece. I'd be proud to take you out."

Get out of this one, old girl.

"Look," I said gently, "If you want to come along to the Coquina Room as a sort of – escort, then do so. But only on the condition that you dance with other girls and have fun."

"But I want to be with you," he insisted, a sun-bleached curl falling over his forehead, "If I go, I want to sit with you, dance with you. I can't imagine another female being more attractive than you."

I sighed tiredly and stared at the ocean, hands dangling between tanned knees. I'd already traded one set of problems for another. The sting of my exposed skin prompted me to my feet. "I simply must get out of the sun, Chris." I reached for my carryall bag and briefcase.

"I'll carry that for you." He rose quickly, picked up my briefcase and scooped up his small ice chest and hurried to keep up with me. He was, I realized, at least a trim six feet tall. Toby's height.

"I'm really not very good company," I said flatly.

"I don't see why." He threw back broad shoulders in challenge.

I pressed the open button on the elevator. "I'm married." From beneath lowered lashes, I saw his expression shift, then settle again.

"So? If it doesn't bother you, it doesn't bother me." I felt his gaze rake me again as I closed the elevator doors. "You really are a beautiful woman." His voice was edged with awe – uneducated in flattery for flattery's sake and I felt a warmth envelope me, the striking of a chord somewhere deep within that drove back the iciness of rejection. He followed me off the elevator, so close I could hear him breathe.

Watch yourself, Janeece Crenshaw! He's only a boy. And you're a prime target for rebound stuff right now. I unlocked the door to my room and the cool air-conditioning hit me deliciously in the face. "Set that over there, please." I motioned to a corner. Chris unloaded both case and ice chest.

"Do you mind if I have a drink from my bottle?" he asked politely.

"Go ahead." I remembered all the alcohol Kirk had imbibed, always somewhere else – away from me. I quickly pushed the troubling thoughts aside, hoping Chris would soon leave. Another part of me was glad for the company. I wasn't alone. With him here, I wouldn't think on all the damaging things.

"Would you like a drink?" He held the bottle out.

"Uh – no, thanks. I'll have some diet soda."

He looked disappointed. "Are you sure?"

"Certain. I don't drink alcohol."

"Why?"

"It doesn't agree with me. But you go ahead."

Live and let live, I thought dryly. After all, what influence had my misgivings had on Kirk's drinking? None. He failed to consider, for one moment, what effect his indulgence had on me.

There I go again. Stop it! I scooped ice into my glass then poured Diet Coke over it.

I turned on the television and went to sit on the bed since the room's two chairs were not very comfortable. I drew my legs up, propped against the headboard and tried to get interested in the game show. Chris lowered himself very gentlemanly onto the foot of the bed, sipping his drink and casting half-shy glances my way.

"Wanna talk?" he asked, grinning.

"Sure," I said. "Why not?"

Our topics ranged from cars to college curriculum. Chris lived with his divorced mother and majored in business administration. The conversation was so warm and flowed so spontaneously I barely noticed he refilled his glass several times.

"Wow!" he laughed suddenly, flopped on his back, stretching out across the bed, then propped on his elbow facing me. "I can't *believe* this." He slowly shook his head, grinning like a little boy.

"Can't believe what?" I sipped my watery Coke, curious.

"That I'm doing this...*me*, Chris Jenkins in a woman's bedroom. I'm really a shy guy, Janeece. The guys tease me all the time."

"This is a *suite*, Chris, not –"

"I don't have much luck with girls." He laughed again, oblivious to my narrowed gaze as he sat up again, shaking his head.

I sighed. "I can't imagine why," I said tactfully.

"Too shy." He shrugged. "Sure you won't have a drink?" He gestured toward the bottle.

"Absolutely sure."

"Here." He inched closer, his courage growing. "Have a taste." He held the glass out to me.

I shook my head. "No. Remember? It doesn't agree with me."

"Oh. Yeah. I forgot." He grinned and stretched to set the glass on the floor. "I still can't *believe it!* " He flopped backward, laughing. "Me. *Here.*"

I tried drawing my leg up, but his shoulder pinned my ankle to the spread. Too late, the effects of his drinking became all too apparent to me as he lay on his back and swiveled his head to gaze at me. "With a beautiful woman."

"Old enough to be your mother," I said flatly.

His grin dissolved. "If my mom would've been in a situation like this with a young guy like me, she'd have already been teaching him the ropes."

"Chris —" I wiggled my foot from beneath his shoulder and shifted my position.

A mistake. His gaze dropped to openly study my anatomy. A bald, unblinking sweep.

"Chris. Listen to me." He seemed hypnotized, his features slack. "*Chris.* Do you know how old I am?"

"Probably somewhere in your early thirties. It doesn't matter."

"I'm forty-two years old."

He got very still.

"How does that grab you?" His gaze slid downward again to my tanned skin. Suddenly, I felt absolutely naked in the bathing suit. Why hadn't I pulled on my beach jacket?

"It doesn't matter." His eyes leveled with mine. "Just look at you —" His hand arced through the air. "Your body is gorgeous."

My heart thudded to my heels. "Chris, I have a son nearly as old as you."

"I don't care." His hand had tentatively inched until it now caressed my thigh in feathery little strokes.

"Don't, Chris." I shifted, but he was so close it didn't help. "I told you I'm having marital problems. You don't need to be here." I exhaled on a long shaky breath. "My life is a mess. *I'm* a mess." *Such a mess I allowed loneliness to sucker me into this stupid predicament.*

His glazed gaze moved up to my face and he smiled lazily. "You don't look a mess to me." His features sobered. "God, Janeece — you're beautiful."

Then in one swift movement, his arms slid fluidly around my hips and his face pressed against my exposed midriff. It took me so by surprise I gasped. I raised my hands away from him, horrified that I'd let this happen.

"Janeece," he moaned against my flesh as he began to lose control, his hands and face climbing upward.

Dear Lord, help me. I froze – I was getting aroused. "Stop, Chris –" My words had no more effect than a fly swat against a smart gnat.

I heard a moan as his hand moved down over my abdomen. The sound had come from me. I slithered from beneath him and was on my feet, frantically adjusting my top into place. "You've got to leave, Chris."

He was on his knees on the bed, his features bewildered. "Why?"

"*Because,*" irritation seized me, "You just *do.*" I turned away and began to pick up things scattered over my room – instinctively trying to restore some measure of order.

But I suddenly felt his arms slide around me from behind – his lips moved over my neck and shoulders.

My knees turned to water. "Chris –" I whispered, "stop." I felt myself turned by strong hands and pulled up against the long length of this young man, revealing my effect on him. "Please –" but his mouth moved over mine in hungry exploration. I fought against a wild urge to respond.

God, please help me! I pulled away from his kiss only to have his hand slide into my hair and press my face to his neck.

"Oh, Janeece," he cried out, "I want you."

"No." I pulled back and felt his soft cheek brush against mine.

His soft cheek. A boy's cheek. That was, for me, the bottom line.

And I realized that, perhaps even subconsciously, I'd fostered the idea of retaliating against Kirk's cruel betrayal. But this young man could be my *son.*

"No." My voice, this time, was more firm as I pushed him away. "No, Chris!" I stepped away.

His glazed eyes turned tormented. "You can't do this to me, Janeece!"

I felt only a niggle of guilt. For only a moment.

"Why, Janeece?" He reached out to me imploringly.

"Because," I snapped, annoyed with him, with myself, with the whole thing. "Just – because. I can't."

"Oh, Janeece." He fell backward across the bed. "I want you so bad...." He rolled into fetal position. I struggled against the sympathy rising in me.

"You've had too much to drink, Chris. Get your things and go. I'm going into the bathroom and taking a bath. When I come out, I want you gone."

"Let me take a bath with you, Janeece." His voice was husky.

I rolled my eyes in exasperation. "Oh *God.*" I slammed the door and quickly locked it.

"Janeece!" He hammered on the door as I filled the tub.

"Go away!" I slipped into the water and lay back.

"Janeece? Please let me in. Open the door." More hammering. "Let me take a bath with you."

"No!" My sympathy evaporated. I felt like shaking him as I would a petulant child.

"Janeece? Please..." he whined.

"Chris?"

"What?"

"You're being an imbecile."

Silence.

I finished my bath and dried off.

"I'm leaving, Janeece. I'm getting my things."

"Goodbye, Chris."

"I'll bet you won't even talk to me tomorrow. I know I've been an imbecile."

I wrapped the thick white towel around me.

"Janeece?"

"Yes?"

"I'm sorry."

"Okay."

"Will you talk to me tomorrow?"

I stifled a laugh. "Yes, Chris. I'll talk to you tomorrow." It was my fault – the situation.

"Bye, Janeece."

I heard the door open and close softly. I emerged from the bathroom and gazed about to make sure it was empty. I released my breath on a long sigh, then pulled on a short teddy and slipped between cool sheets.

"Oh Kirk," I moaned, his beloved angular features my last vision before sleep came.

CHAPTER TWENTY-ONE

As it turned out, I didn't talk to Chris the next day. When I arrived at poolside with my paraphernalia, the area was deserted. Relief surged through me as I settled into a lounge chair and pulled out my writing pad. The words came readily today. I'd found that the more circumstances cornered me, the more my creative juices flowed. I recognized my need to escape reality. By creating plot and characters, I was in control. All my endings would be happy. If only I could arrange my own life so easily.

Mid-afternoon, I phoned the salon.

"J and K's on Main, Kirk speaking," came my husband's vibrant voice.

"Hi."

"Hi, darling."

I closed my eyes and let his words caress me and snap my world in place. "Are you busy?"

"Just finishing...Bye, Mandy. See you next month." He laughed at something the regular, middle-aged client said in parting. "Okay, honey, I'm back. God, I've missed you."

Good.

Then, "Having fun?"

"Mmm. So so."

"That mean you're ready to come home?"

I thought about it for a moment. "It might."

"You've already paid for the next twenty-four hours. May as well enjoy it." I heard him greet his next client. "Gotta run. My appointment is here. Love you, honey," his voice vibrated with emotion.

"Me, too."

"Have you missed me?"

"Mm hm."

"Sure?" Did I imagine tension in the word?

"Yes, I'm sure."

"Bye, sweetheart."

The line went dead. For long moments, I stared at the receiver in my hand, wondering what in blazes I was going to do to fill up the rest of the day.

The Coquina Room was nearly filled. I sat alone, sipping my watery Seven-Up. Loneliness drove me there. By nightfall, I'd had it up to here with my quiet room and silent phone. When I'd called home, I got no answer. A quick call to Dad and Anne's confirmed Toby was still there. Dawn and Heather were at Trish's. Where was Kirk? It had been my understanding he was going to pick Toby up earlier today. Why had he changed his mind?

"You okay, Neecy?" Anne's voice had relayed her worry. "Kirk said you'd been depressed."

"I'm fine, Anne. I didn't really want to come, but Kirk insisted it would do me good to get away."

"It probably will. You've been working too hard, according to Kirk."

I heard, behind Anne's kind words, her disappointment that I'd closed them all out in recent years. But it wasn't in her nature to be intrusive or demanding and now, more than ever, I was grateful. I'd quickly ended the conversation.

Tonight, I gazed about me. The lowered lights cast an enchanting spell over the party atmosphere. Everybody seemed carefree yet glamorously postured. Except me. The scene would have been Norman Rockwell funny had I felt light-hearted enough to laugh. As it was, my chest felt weighted with an iron anvil – cold and heavy.

I'm different. I've always been different. Any other woman would have been having the time of her life but not old Janeece. My fingers curled against palms until I felt the long nails cutting blood. *Kirk has to run you off to get you out of his hair.*

Where *was* Kirk? Why had he been so desperate to get rid of me anyway?

Anger, a white-hot force, gathered inside me.

"May I?" A male voice pulled my attention to my left, where a neatly dressed man with a nice smile held out a hand to me.

Feeling more than a little reckless, I took his hand and let him steer me to the dance floor. The little black sleeveless knit dress with its dainty gold buckle had cost a fortune and tonight, I was glad for its classy look. I enjoyed the respect I saw in the man's eyes.

The slow song was not one I recognized, but my partner was a good dancer, easy to follow and I began to relax. As we chatted, I learned he was a tech math teacher from Orangeburg attending an educational convention. "So that's why the Coquina Room is so packed out," I said, "A convention."

"Undoubtedly." The song ended and he politely thanked me for the dance.

When I sat down, the anger I'd felt earlier returned full force. I got to my feet and sought out a pay phone. After twenty rings at the Crenshaw residence, I slammed down the receiver and whirled around to backtrack –

"Oops," male hands steadied me.

Startled, I gazed up into a familiar face. "Chris –"

"Janeece," a very big grin slid across his good-looking face "I thought that was you heading out the door. I followed to make sure."

"Wh—where are your buddies?"

"Split to see some girls they met."

"You mean you haven't run into an irresistible female down here?" I teased.

"Yeah. You."

I gazed at him with narrowed eyes.

He rolled back his head in laughter. "I know, I know. You think I followed you here, but I promise – scout's honor—I only came after getting bored at the Sandlapper Bar." He shrugged, looking so boyishly innocent, I burst into laughter.

"So," he gently took my elbow and steered me back to the main room, "don't let me spoil your fun. Just act like I'm not here. Okay?"

He settled me into my chair and asked, quite uncertainly, "Would you mind if I join you?"

"Oh, sit down, Chris," I said, fighting back laughter, suddenly thankful somebody wanted to be with me. Heck, even Kirk wanted me gone.

Mine was not self-pity. It was a cold acceptance of place-lessness. Whereas the old Janeece worked at making people happy and charming them into loving her, the new woman accepted that she was not solely responsible for others' contentment and was resigned that she was not always loved in return.

The band, accepting requests, struck up *Special Angel*, and I felt my eyes moisten. It was one of my and Kirk's favorite love songs. I pinched my forehead to squelch tears, knowing what a mess I'd be if they spilled over and trailed through my makeup. I'd look like a raccoon with scars streaking down my cheeks. Even Chris would be mortified.

"May I?"

My head jerked up. "Of course, Chris." Gratitude shot out the top of my head and my fingers eagerly linked with his as I followed him to the spotlighted area of the room. Much of my starch dissolved as he took me into his arms and, very gentlemanly, whirled me onto the dance floor. Then he began to make little harmless descriptive asides about some of the more eccentric dancers. By the end of the number, he had me laughing till my sides hurt.

"That's better," he gazed down at me like a fatherly figure. "You need to laugh more, Janeece." I was impressed with this more mature emergence of the young man.

Chris ordered himself a mixed drink. I sipped my flat Seven-Up as he stirred his fruity concoction. "That smells heavenly," I said, chin in hand.

"Want a taste?" he asked.

"No." I shook my head firmly.

The band launched into *Sixty-Minute Man* and Chris and I danced a lively shag, laughing and mugging all the way back to the table. Then in a sheer reckless gesture, I picked up his drink and took a long pull on it. "It's delicious," I said.

"Here," he said, "keep it. I'll order another one for me."

So, I sipped the drink, feeling sophisticated and free and all the things that, through the years, I'd disdained in others. Little nudges to my brain irritated me – I kept pushing them away. I didn't want to think and feel guilty.

We talked and danced a couple of more dances. Chris ordered me another drink. As the evening passed, I felt better and better. My tongue began to get lazy and I laughed about that.

"I mean," I said to Chris out of the blue, "didn't even Jesus drink wine?"

"I believe you're right," he said quite seriously. "Look – don't drink that if you don't feel right about it."

"I've about finished it anyway," I said.

Chris scratched his head, eyeing me soberly. "How long – I mean, you really don't drink at all?"

"Nope. I'm a to-teeler." I giggled. "Tha's not right, is it?"

He didn't laugh. "A tee-totaler." His brow furrowed. "Janeece, I'm sorry I gave you the drink. I feel terrible."

I laughed a full, froggy belly laugh. "Not me. I feel good."

Chris watched me warily. Like I was going to blow up or something. "How about some coffee?"

"Huh uh." I grinned at him. "Can I have another juice drink?"

"I don't think that would be wise, Janeece." He looked worried now. Really distressed.

"Don' look so sad, Chris," I said, trying to prop on my elbow. It kept slipping off the table, making me giggle. Which made Chris more anxious but I couldn't help that everything was hilarious. After such a long, long stretch of sadness, it felt good to turn loose and be free and have such a wonderful time with such a good friend. My best friend in the whole world, in fact.

"Hey," I leaned close and whispered, "I feel good for the firs' time in years." He stared at me and I nodded solemnly. "Tha's right. Kirk made me come here. I din't want to." I took another sip from the nearly empty glass, jerking it away from Chris's hand as he tried to take it away. "Nonono. Mus'n be a – an Indian giver," I scolded, then another giggle

"Why did Kirk make you come here?" Chris asked, watching me intently.

"Cause –" I thought for long moments, trying to remember. Then I cut my gaze at him and grinned. "Ask me again."

He frowned and then looked very sad. "I asked why you're here."

"Cause Kirk didn't want me – with him. He wants me here." My finger jabbed the tabletop. "So I'm *here.*"

"Why didn't he come with you, Janeece?" The question was soft. "If you were my wife, I'd never send you off alone."

I shrugged and nearly lost my balance. Why was the room moving? "He's doin' somethin', Chris. I don' know *what*. He's drinkin' – oops." I covered my mouth. "Not s'posed to say that."

Suddenly, I wasn't feeling so good. "I need to go, Chris," I mumbled and began to rise. He caught me before I hit the floor. "Jus' tangled my foot on my purse string is all," I muttered, trying to shake loose of the shoulder strap. Chris's strong arms hoisted me into upright position and he somehow managed to walk me the length of the room and into the corridor as though it were an ordinary thing for the two of us.

"Christ," I heard him mutter.

"Don' take the name of the Lord in vain, Chris," I scolded, then smiled at him.

I thought I saw tears in his eyes but just as quickly forgot about it. "Give me your key," he said, then checked my room number on it. On the elevator going up, I began to feel bad in earnest.

"I don't feel so good, Chris," I groaned and burrowed my head against his shoulder.

"Hang in there, Janeece. We'll have you in your room before you know it."

Another corridor – ten miles long and Chris propped me between his shoulder and the wall before I heard the key inserted into the lock. He caught me as I toppled.

I felt myself lifted then lowered onto a bed that moved. He turned on a lamp.

"Chris," I lolled my head over to look at him through a red haze. "I'm dying."

"No, Janeece. You're not dying. You just lie there and –"

"Get the waste basket. Hurry –"

He grabbed it from beside the dresser and had it under my head as I began throwing up. I have to hand it to him – Chris not only had guts, he had a strong stomach. Pregnancy nausea was Minnie Mouse compared to my purging that evening. When it subsided, Chris washed my face with a warm soapy wash cloth. He slipped my shoes off and tucked me in.

"Don't leave me," I moaned, clutching at his shirt. "I really *am* dying."

"I'm not going anywhere, Janeece." He gently pried my fingers loose. "Try to go to sleep." I heard him slip off his shoes and lie down on the sofa across the room from me, but I was already spinning back into the Netherland of nightmarish twilight.

"God is punishing me, Chris," I groaned.

"Shhh."

"He is."

"Go to sleep."

I lapsed into the awful twilight. Sometime later, I curled over on my side, fighting down another tidal wave of nausea. "Chris – the waste basket. I might...." I swallowed several times as I felt the weight of Chris's athletic frame lower onto the side of my bed.

"Here," he said gently, holding the basket near me.

"Just – set it there on the floor." I swallowed some more and moaned. Presently, I felt the wet cloth wipe my face again. It began to soothe and settle the quandary inside me. "Thank you."

"You're welcome." I felt his weight lift from the mattress and heard him resettle himself on the sofa. I realized he'd emptied and washed out the small trash can when I –

"Chris," I croaked, "I owe you. Big time. You cleaned up that mess and –"

"Janeece, you don't owe me a thing. I'm glad I was here to help you. It's the least I can do considering it's all my fault, you being sick." He shook his head woefully, "*Dang!* You told me it made you sick. It's all my fault."

"No. It's not. Nobody made me drink." My voice was whispery weak, my guilt and remorse overwhelming. I knew better than to ingest alcohol. I'd found that out when trying to sip a little wine for insomnia. It did not agree with me at all. Besides, I had no business drinking. I'd never seen its purpose, at least not in my life and not in those close to me. I'd only seen its bad results.

I heard a scraping noise and raised my head. "What was that?"

"I didn't hear anything." Chris came back to the bed and looked down at me. "I'm afraid you're wrong, Janeece." He looked utterly miserable. "I – I shouldn't have tempted you."

"Don't blame yourself. It was me."

"My, my," came a voice out of the night. A dry, sarcastic *familiar voice.* "Whose fault was it? Who tempted who?"

"Kirk!" I lifted my head and squinted at the shadowy figure standing just inside my door. "What are you doing here?" I moaned as nausea rose up in me again.

Chris spun around. "Kirk?" he said, moving toward my husband. "It's a good thing you came. Janeece is –"

Cr-rack!

Through the red mist, I saw Chris hit the floor. Kirk towered over him, fists clenching and unclenching. "That'll teach you to tempt *my wife.*"

"Kirk!" I groaned. It was the last thing I could say before grabbing the bucket for another upheaval.

He hovered above me, gaping. "You've been drinking," he said in amazement. "All that nagging at me and look at you." He didn't lift a finger to help me.

I tried to glower at him but failed when my head collapsed back on the pillow. "Don't you think you'd better check Chris's pulse?"

"Why?" He was in my face, his anger a whispery *hiss.* "Does it matter?"

"Yes," I tried to match his belligerence but my voice came out like a sick woodwind instrument. "It does. He's only tried to help me. He's only a boy –"

"That makes it even worse."

Get out of this one, Janeece Crenshaw. Even in my near-death state, I knew I was in deep dung. Any leverage I had with Kirk – gone. In the best of times, Kirk was a skeptic. I didn't have a prayer of him believing in the goodness of Chris. Nor in anything good in me, for that matter, considering the scene he walked into.

Chris, poor Chris, had most effectively served as my executioner.

When he didn't come to right away, Kirk began to grow concerned. Oh, not about Chris but about his own skin. "If he's dead," Kirk said quite unemotionally, "I'll either fry or rot in prison." So, Kirk commenced splashing water in Chris's gray face. Lordy was he pale. "I don't really relish the idea of being punished over *Lover Boy*," he said through gnashing teeth as he hoisted his foe onto the sofa, propped him up and began to briskly smack his cheeks and call his name.

"Do you have to slap him so *hard*?" I turned my face to the wall, wishing myself anywhere else on the planet. "How did you get in my room?"

"I showed my ID at the desk, told them I wanted to surprise my wife." He gave a tight bitter laugh. "And just look who got surprised."

When Chris groaned and began to respond, I let out a long breath of thanks. I'd been doing a lot of praying since Kirk's untimely arrival. More than in the months leading up to tonight. When Chris spoke, one of those prayers was answered.

"What did you hit me for?" he asked Kirk, rubbing his jaw and flexing his neck.

Kirk, having paced to the window, spun and peered at him as though he'd grown toes on his chin. "You have to ask? I find you in my wife's bedroom and you have the gall to ask that?" Kirk advanced on him again with those clenched fists that looked big as boxing gloves.

"Whoa, man!" Chris raised a trembling hand. "You've already done that. Okay? Chill."

"Kirk," I croaked. "Listen to reason. It's not –"

He advanced on me then, so swift I shrank back into the covers and though I didn't think he would strike me, his white-hot gaze and furious words were just as lethal. "Reason? Listen to *reason*?" His laugh was mirthless. "Send Lover Boy away and we'll reason."

"Chris," I said, knowing it was a control thing with Kirk, to insist I say the words, "You'd better leave."

"No joke," my friend rose to his six-foot height and moved unsteadily to the door. There, he turned to Kirk. "I just want you to know, Kirk – you really should count your bless –"

"Get out." Kirk's order was so quiet it roared. He didn't move a muscle, stood rooted to that floor like a mighty oak, his green gaze sparkling with fury. Chris slid me one parting, sympathetic glance – or was it pity I saw? – then quietly closed the door behind him.

It was the pity that made me lash out at Kirk. "Why are you standing there, so *all righteous*, spewing hatred at me?" I spat at him, surprised I'd regained the strength to raise up on a trembling elbow and glare at him.

He glared back. "I sent you here in good faith. I thought if you could just rest and —"

"*Aha!*" I pointed a trembling, accusing finger so fast his features emptied with surprise. My gaze narrowed on him as I swung my legs over the side of the bed and sat up, holding on as the room moved. "You *set me up*. I didn't even want to come. All that talk about how I should have an affair and you'd forgive me...manipulating me into doing something you could hold over my head and get me back under your almighty control."

His brow furrowed. "What are you talking about? *Control*. I've treated you like a queen for years now. Seems you're the one in control. And I'm tired of it." He pointed a finger and gazed slit-eyed down it like it was the barrel of a gun. "Things are going to change."

Those words, *things are going to change*, smote me, caused something in me to plunge and spiral down, down, down until everything drained from my head and heart, until I'd gone limp and all I felt was the room doing a slow, slushy spin.

I fell backward and when the room grew still, rolled over into a fetal knot.

"Come on, Neecy," Kirk's voice, right at my ear, taunted me. He was hot for battle. "Let's *reason.*"

Then I did what Kirk had done for years. I went to sleep.

CHAPTER TWENTY-TWO

The coming days merged into a psychedelic strobe-lit procession of happenings. The morning after Kirk flattened Chris on my hotel suite floor, I awoke to find my husband sitting in a chair he'd dragged up next to my bed, ankle hooked over knee, hands steepled to lips, watching me with grim detachment.

All sleep fled me. I sat up, disoriented and apprehensive, trying to unstick my tongue from the roof of my mouth. After a wobbly trip to the bathroom to relieve myself and wash my face, I returned to curl against the head of the bed, facing Kirk. He hadn't moved. Not an eyelash. His stillness threatened to finish off what of my nerves had survived the prior night.

I have to say that I've never known anyone else whose *still quietness* shrills and invades like Kirk's. To me, it's like screaming sirens, freight train whistles and a squad of jack-hammers bursting loose all over me at once. And the fact that I know this is exactly the effect he desires does not make it less so.

Okay. I squared my shoulders to face the ambush head on, to get past *it*.

It is nearly always something about which I haven't a clue. This morning, I did. But I hadn't a clue as to how to defuse my simmering spouse. The suspense, as usual, was my undoing. And the guilt – not of wrongdoing but a reaction to what Kirk *thought* he'd seen.

"Kirk – say something."

No blink. Nothing. Only those green lasers riveting me to the headboard. I rose abruptly, suddenly angry, and snatched my suitcase from a corner. I began stuffing my belongings inside until it bulged. All during this time, I felt Kirk's gaze probe, poke and assault me. I whirled and glared at him.

"Spit it out, Kirk. You might as well be beating me as the way you're watching me like I'm some germ under a microscope." I plopped down limply on the bed, drew my legs up and hugged my knees. I felt incredibly sad and tried to keep my gaze steady with Kirk's.

I couldn't. My eyes watered from the strain and I shrugged, looked away and thought, It's not worth the effort. He always could out-mean me. No contest. That didn't mean I had to be his punching bag.

That thought ricocheted my gaze back to his. "What are you thinking?" I asked sharply.

I nearly jumped when he spoke. "There's nothing left," he said, his voice a near whisper. His eyes never wavered. How in God's name did he not blink for so long?

"What do you mean?" I sniped, inordinately irritated. "Nothing left?" I gave a derisive sound in the back of my throat. "We've got everythi –"

"It's all gone," he continued as though I'd not spoken. I hated it when he crawled out onto his isolated berg, alone with his calculations of what *is*, regardless of what my perception might render. It's like talking to somebody on a television screen and they're off somewhere else entirely. At those times, I hated his drive, one that propelled both the good and bad in Kirk.

"Kirk," I said sharply, "If you're talking about the situation you walked into last night, it was *not* what you think. Chris and I didn't –"

"I've lost everything. My wife. My –"

"Will you listen to me – you've not lost me, Kirk!"

" – ministry. I'm a man without a country." His voice droned on, his gaze fixed hypnotically on me. "I guess you know I'll most likely go blow my brains out, Neecy."

"Kirk!" I scooted upright and swung my legs to the floor, recognizing the sheer possibility of his words. "That's foolishness, you –"

"No." His eyes suddenly turned dark. "That's not foolishness. Foolishness is what I've been doing for the past years, catering to your every whim and –"

"Oh," I threw my hands wide, "so *that's* it. You've –"

" – treating you like the Queen of Sheba, giving you everything –"

"I didn't ask you to." Anger boiled out my fingertips and toes. "You chose to do that. And as far as your ministry, I didn't require you to leave."

"You said you were leaving."

"I would have. But you didn't have to. I had a choice. You had a choice. You chose to stay with me. It's not my fault you left it behind."

"I wouldn't say that." His voice and scrutiny grated my already raw nerves.

"Look, Kirk," I rose to my feet, "I've got to shower and dress. I will not accept this guilt trip you're handing me." I spun away and headed for the bathroom. At the door, I whirled back to face him. "This is all about the fact that you found a man in my room last night and –"

"That's not all this is about. But it hurts like crazy knowing he –"

"Hah!" I planted my hands on hips and glared at him. "So now you finally know how I felt when I found out you'd been throwing yourself away on Roxie. And all the recent drinking, acting like it didn't affect *me* in the least." I couldn't help the bitterness in my railing. That he'd rendered me invisible again filled me with desolation.

He was on his feet in a flash and in my face. "*Don't*," he ground between his teeth, "ever talk to me about drinking. Never again." If looks could kill, I'd have been plastered to the carpet in five seconds flat and ground underfoot. "And I'm sick of your manipulation and –"

"I do not manipulate you," I thrust my chin out and glowered back at him. Only thing was, my voice rose and his didn't, making me sound more shrewish than ever. "Just because I finally speak up for myself and refuse to kowtow to –"

"I'll show you what independence is." His timber changed in a heartbeat, as did his emptied expression. "You're so all-fired liberated, I'll just back away and let you have it all. I think it's time to see a lawyer." With that statement to clinch his control, Kirk, my hero, my protector, turned his back and marched out the door, slamming it behind him.

Abandonment.

Everything elemental in me lurched...panicked. I dashed to the door and flung it open. He was disappearing down the corridor, his gait military, back straight.

"Kirk?" I cried, fighting the sickening fear rising like bile in me.

His step never faltered. He did not look back.

I didn't see Kirk for several days. I told his salon appointments he was sick. He was, I told myself. In the head. I dreaded seeing a police car pull up to our house or business and hearing them say, *"Mrs. Crenshaw, we're sorry to tell you your husband is dead."*

Underneath all that, I felt responsible for some of his distress. I'd had no choice in some matters, such as having to leave Solomon for a fresh start. But during long sleepless nights, I'd seen with stunning clarity that I had not truly forgiven Kirk of his infidelity. Oh, I thought I had. But looking back, I saw that I'd placed myself in tempting situations I once would have shunned, subconsciously hoping to punish him.

I prayed. Kirk's suicide threat haunted me. Some part of me knew it could happen. The brutal side to Kirk could turn inward.

By now, Toby and Dawn knew trouble brewed, but I soft-pedaled like crazy. "Daddy's taking a rest," I told them. "He's been overworked for a long time. He needed to go away for a few days, by himself and – rest."

I could see in Toby's eyes that he sensed more, but he didn't ask. And I knew. He didn't want to know. Dawn was more blunt.

"Why doesn't Daddy want to be around us anymore? We don't make lots of noise or anything." She worked her crossword puzzle, her wheat-colored sheet of hair falling forward to hug her adolescent cheeks. I'd recently given her a wedgy bob that had her constantly tucking it behind her ears.

"Oh," I sat beside her on the salon sofa, looking over her shoulder, hoping she didn't notice my trembling hands, "he'll be home any time now, all rested and dying to see his little girl."

"What's a six letter word that means 'residential district'? Begins with S."

Her savoir-faire attitude struck me anew. Dawn seemed far beyond her twelve years in ways. "Suburb," I replied and watched her pencil it in.

"Can I go to the Bijou tonight?" she asked blandly, knowing what my answer would be.

"'Fraid not, Dawnie."

I felt her stiffen without her face losing its bored mien. "All the other kids go."

"Can't help it. Daddy and I don't think it's too good an idea to turn you loose in a darkened movie theatre with a passel of teens dying to find a nook in which to neck."

"Daddy's not here," she drawled. "What's a four letter word that means 'labels'? Starts with a T."

"Tags." I wondered again what to do with this girl-woman of mine who kept me busy devising ways of saying 'no' without making her feel deprived. Yet – she did anyway.

"You could let me go if you wanted to." Her fingers gripped the pencil that meticulously filled in the blanks with artistic lettering.

"Mm hm. But I love you too much to do that. I remember when I was your age, and I know what went on in such circumstances."

She swung her head to look at me with narrowed sky-blues. "You mean you necked with guys?"

"No. I didn't. But I had a friend who did." *Callie.* My heart lurched at the thought of her. How I missed her. "So – I can't, in good conscience, let you get caught up in it."

The narrowed gaze grew cool, then flounced away. "You're too protective. All because of Krissie being killed. It's not fair." Her cheeks puffed out and the lips tightened in anger.

"True – we are vigilant as a result of Krissie's death. But had that not happened, Dawn, I'd be just as protective." I knew it was easier for Dawn to over-simplify our actions as being neurotic rather than being for her own good. I tried to spend as much quality time with her as possible. What with Kirk's and my problems, that wasn't easy to do. But I kept trying. She was, in fact, like an only child, what with Heather's college absences and Toby's teen activities.

"Where *is* Daddy?" she asked petulantly. Knowingly. Sometimes, I swore she had extra eyes and ears by the way she challenged me with questions – as though she already knew the answers.

Today, the phone's ringing rescued me from having to answer. After telling another of Kirk's clients he was ill, I hung up and for a moment pressed my face to the cool mirror behind his workstation.

Where are you, Kirk? When are you coming back?

Kirk, my dream man, never came back. Another version, the hidden man I'd dreaded all the way back to honeymoon days, appeared the next day. My good resolutions for change fizzled when he walked through the door, gilded in splendid fury.

He was the antithesis of the man who courted me so eloquently and gave me the greatest gift of all: unconditional love. This new man was convinced I'd squandered his affection and did not deserve his respect and devotion. My head swirled from the impact of it all.

In a heartbeat, I hated him. For one long moment, I felt pure hatred for him. "Why?" I asked, as furious as he. "Why did you want me to love you again? Why didn't you just leave me alone?" Tears spilled down my cheeks and I hated them, too. To this man, they spelled weakness. "Why did you give me the world and then – snatch it away?"

He stared at me with those blasted unreadable eyes until I wanted to scratch them out of their sockets. And I saw it delighted him that I humbled myself. Ice water shot through me and I instantly stopped weeping, wiped my eyes and took a seat on the den sofa. He remained standing, I suspected, to maintain the upper hand, determined that I not coerce him into *anything.*

Despair swamped me, but I would not let him see it. "So – where do we go from here?"

"Do whatever you want." He plopped defiantly into an easy chair. "Actually, I don't care."

The brutal response took my breath. The nightmare grew worse. Now, I had the dreaded stranger – one I'd only glimpsed in the past – living with me. And he was paranoid to boot.

Kirk, magnificent in battle, now wanted to destroy me.

"Kirk. Why do you hate me?"

He gazed at me with no emotion whatsoever. "Janeece, I don't hate you."

"What changed you, Kirk?"

He looked at me for a long time...I didn't think he was going to answer.

"I've been to Solomon while I was gone. Roxie's murderer was arrested. See, Janeece, the reason I got mixed up with Roxie to begin with was the letter Moose left her. Here," he pulled the tightly folded paper from his shirt pocket and tossed it at me.

I picked it up from where it landed at my feet, opened it and began to read Moose's big childish scrawl:

Dear Roxie:

This has got to be the hardest letter I ever wrote. I got my life in a mess. You been thinking I was on something. Well, I was. At times, anyway. I talked to Kirk about it, made him promise not to tell anybody, not even Janeece. I tried to get off the stuff, Roxie. I really have and feel that God's helped me a lot. But that's not what this letter's about. Here's the deal – when I was working in the Seven-Eleven Store, I left one day when the new hired guy came in to relieve me. When I was down the road, I missed my billfold. I figured it fell out of my back pocket when I used the men's room before quitting time. I turned the car around and went back. I found my billfold where it fell under the counter, then remembered I'd pulled it out to get some change, got busy and forgot about it.

The store was quiet and seemed empty when I got there. I got this spooky feeling, you know? Like somebody had held the place up or something and maybe tied up this worker – or killed him. So I snuck to the back of the store, as scared as I ever been in my life. I heard somebody talking in the men's room, quiet like. I tiptoed closer. That's when I heard them talking about drugs. Cocaine. Seems they was hiding some behind the sink in the men's room. They mentioned a couple of names I recognized and suddenly I knew I shouldn't be hearing about this deal. So I snuck out but hit my foot on the corner of a Cocola crate at the end of the counter and next thing was they come running out of the men's room. I was in my car pulling out but I know they saw me. I never did go back to my job. Thing is, I know they gonna kill me. Don't know when. But they will.

I wrote this so you'd find it if something happened to me. If I showed up dead, I know you'd go through my things and find it. Here's what you do. Don't tell anybody about this. Cause if you do, they might come after you. I didn't mention names on purpose cause that'll only get you in trouble.

Kirk will help you. Go to him. Only him. Don't ever forget I love you.

Forever yours, Moose.

"Kirk," I gazed at him through a teary mist, "Why didn't you tell me all this sooner? It would have made a difference."

"Maybe. Maybe not." He shrugged indifferently. "It wasn't safe for you to know anything. When Roxie was murdered, I figured the drug dealers might come after me, knowing Roxie had turned to me after Moose died. I haven't breathed a free breath until I found out last week that the killers were in custody and they'd confessed. Now," he stretched his mouth into a grim line and steepled his fingers to them for a long moment, his eyes hardening even more, "now, I've lost everything. There's no regaining. I've been stupid and foolish, but I went into it with the right heart. I wanted to fulfill Moose's last cry for help. It cost me everything."

Callie's words flashed before me: *Like a lamb to the slaughter.*

"Oh, Kirk," I wanted to take him in my arms and soothe him, but something in his countenance held me back. His eyes were green granite.

"You don't trust my motives at all, do you?" I asked quietly, shaking my head sadly.

I gazed into a stranger's eyes. They looked through me, didn't acknowledge I'd spoken.

Kirk knew. He knew he broke my heart anew. This time, he didn't care beans that he'd taken from me the one thing I'd vowed to never again relinquish.

For that – despite the love and pity I felt for him – I ceased to respect him.

CHAPTER TWENTY-THREE

Anne and Dad's house smelled of Christmas ambrosia, that unique blend of turkey, dressing, trimmings and traditional desserts seasoned with spices that tickle the nose and palate. The first whiff sent serotonin spiraling through me. While Kirk and Toby unloaded gaily wrapped gifts under a tall spruce tree that blinked endless multi-colored lights, I went to join Anne, Trish and Heather in the kitchen to add my dishes to the ones already sprouting atop groaning tables. Chuck, looking more alive than I'd seen him in years, entertained our clan with Saturday Night Live jokes and monologues. I still marveled at his wit and recall.

"He hasn't lost his touch," I whispered to Anne.

She paused in spreading a tablecloth to reply, "He's more a part of the family than I'd ever 'a dreamed possible."

"Yeah. Amazing what hard times can accomplish." I gave her a hug and we finished setting out bright red holiday cups, plates and napkins.

Long ago, Anne had invested in folding tables for family occasions and today, recruited all for service. Each had a long white cloth with red tapered candle centerpieces. Trish lit the candles while the other females – excluding Dawn, who disappeared like magic when the work began – arranged food according to genre on the big oak dining room table we'd eaten on since Ann had come into the family.

"Joe," Anne called, "go get the folding chairs out of the shop."

Daddy and the guys promptly complied, knowing it brought them closer to chowing down. Since Daddy's heart surgery, he'd been like a lab puppy. Today, he kissed Anne's flushed cheek as he plopped a chair next to where she stood supervising the order of heavenly carbohydrates.

"This woman's something else," he said to me and winked.

I nodded, grinning, ecstatic to see him so happy. His devotion to Anne did not leave her unaffected. She still spit out orders to him, but he now rushed to do her bidding. His hospital stint, during which Daddy declared himself an "outright coward," had unveiled to him Anne's selfless nature.

"I not only had my heart fixed, I had my eyes opened," he told me repeatedly. "Anne didn't leave me during that two-week stay. She stuck with me night and day, meeting my every fear and need with sweetness and patience."

We always laughed at that point. "I'm the worst patient in the world."

I didn't argue, remembering Daddy's battle of wills with a tough drill-sergeant ICU nurse who refused to move him to a room until he stood and walked on his own.

"Lord, I hated that woman," he said today, but then his eyes warmed. "Mostly because I had claustrophobia and was so desperate to escape that windowless unit I'd have killed. Every time I tried to stand, I blacked out." He shook his head with grudging respect. "That battle-ax wouldn't budge."

"Daddy," I laughed till tears puddled, "I can still see you sitting rigid as a pole with her pushing you through those doors in a wheelchair. You were so mad you wouldn't even look at us. You could have spit nails."

"Yeah. But I was wrong to feel that way." I still marveled at the tenderhearted man evolved from my Daddy. "She was just doing her job, though. If she hadn't made me mad, I'd prob-ably *still* be laying in that ICU bed."

Later, we sang Christmas songs to Heather's accompani-ment on the old den piano. I noted tears in Daddy's eyes several times. When we finally hushed, he took me aside.

"Neecy," he took my hand, "I want us – you, me and Anne – to go up and visit your MawMaw. I been thinking about her lately, about how she's in that nursing home and all. I'd like to go see her."

My heart nearly burst with pleasure. I'd been to visit MawMaw several times in the past three years, cherishing each moment with her. "That would be great, Daddy. Just name the time."

The following Wednesday, both mine and Dad's day off, we arrived at Oakmont Nursing Home, where the normal Lysol odors assaulted our nostrils and the sight of MawMaw, sitting in a wheelchair that awaited someone to push her to lunch, was like a punch in the gut.

We approached my little grandmother, whose weight loss nearly destroyed her roundness, I grieved at the vacancy in her gray-blue eyes. She looked so – defenseless. So vulnerable.

"MawMaw?" I said gently when we stood before her. The bowed dark head, now threaded with silver and sporting a short carefree haircut, slowly lifted. Empty eyes sighted me and for long moments were confused.

"It's Neecy," I coaxed her memory.

Then, like a sudden sunrise, her countenance lifted into surprised joy. "Neecy," her frail arms reached for a hug. I stooped and gathered her into my arms, feeling her lips seek and kiss my cheek as she returned my squeeze with remarkable strength. I inhaled her clean familiar fragrance and as I released her, felt the soft loose flesh underneath her arms, shocked that it was no longer full and firm.

She became aware of her other two visitors. Her faded gray gaze scanned their faces for a clue as to their identity. Slowly, recognition broke over her features and the smile reappeared.

"Joe…" Up came the arms again, opened wide. "You're still my boy."

Daddy dropped to his haunches and gathered her to him, weeping. "I'm so sorry, Maude," he murmured, "for everything."

Her small fingers cupped his head to her bosom. "Joe…my boy. I love you."

"I – I love you, too, Maude," Daddy sobbed pitifully. "We had some good times way back."

"We shore did," MawMaw croaked.

Anne and I cried, watching the reunion. We spent several hours in the parlor, where MawMaw managed, with Daddy's help, to seat herself at the piano and entertain the other residents with her inimitable playing. Her fervent Pentecostal style soon had toes tapping that hadn't felt music's beat in years.

Exhausted, she finally let us settle her into her bed that evening. Daddy insisted we pray for her before we took leave. He knelt at her bedside and laid his hand on her head.

"Please, Lord. Heal Maude of her infirmities. She's still got a lot of life left. Please…." His voice choked off for a long spell before he managed a strangled "Amen."

I kissed MawMaw after Anne held her for a tearful goodbye.

"I love you, MawMaw," I whispered.

"I know, honey." She smiled at me. "I know."

I left with the most glorious sense of fulfillment. In recent days, I'd been talking more with God and in the process, found myself coming out of the fog I'd been in for years. I still had a ways to go, but it was a beginning.

One thing was certain: though thirty odd years had passed since I'd uttered them, God had finally answered some of my prayers.

My decision to become financially autonomous was, at the time, a sensible one. Kirk had never acted on his threat to "see a lawyer," but what with his coldness to me and his emotional hands-off stance, I figured I best prepare myself for the worst. My marriage seemed doomed. I say *my* because from the night at the Landmark Hotel, Kirk did not acknowledge any responsibility to me or the marriage beyond paying the utility bills as he'd always done. I began to feel like a kept woman. I didn't like the feeling.

No, that's not strong enough. I *hated* the feeling of indebtedness.

Knowing his contempt for me was excruciating. Worst still was not knowing *why*.

Beyond all that, I didn't want a divorce. Never had. A priority was concern for the children and how it would hurt them, innocent bystanders. It wasn't fair. Besides, I had no better agenda in the wings so I continued to work at reconciliation. At least, if all failed, I would know I'd tried.

I'd explained in detail to Kirk the events leading up to his discovery of Chris in my room that night. His attention had been that of a disinterested party. Kirk had dissected me from his life as succinctly as Daddy had MawMaw years ago. It was as though I didn't exist except as a bother.

Kirk, I decided, wanted his freedom.

Against Kirk's objections, I finished my math course at Harborville Community College. After I refused to drop the course, Kirk never mentioned it again. That, in itself, spoke volumes about his disdain. My refusal had nothing to do with rebellion; I simply needed the credits for my certification. Johnny

Revel and I struck an unspoken agreement to back off anything other than distant friendship.

He was lucky. I couldn't just walk away from everything.

Not until I could stand on my own.

So, it was with desperation that I began to plow through alien looking utility bills to acquaint myself with the idea of living alone and handling them. My initial terror had begun to subside and as I shuffled through phone bills, I commended myself on how far I'd come.

That was when I saw it. The unknown phone number. Calls were made to it on numerous occasions. I didn't recognize the area code. Times they were made varied, some late at night – one over an hour long.

A shrill alarm went off. The call was made during my disastrous beach trip, the second night of my stay. My gaze darted to other dates – consecutive ones. Shock *bzzzzzzed* through me. I sat there, paralyzed with it. Then adrenaline kicked in. I searched out the area code and discovered it was for near Asheville.

Anger. With shaking fingers, I dialed the number.

"Hello," came the pleasant female voice, "Cheryl's Beauty Box. Cheryl speaking."

I hung up. Sickness crept over me. The Hair Styling Convention Kirk had attended when he sent me to the beach. He'd met someone. She had a name. Cheryl.

I pulled my purse over my shoulder and drove to our salon. It was empty except for Kirk, who sat in his styling chair, reading the daily paper. I threw my purse on the sofa and advanced on him. Now, I knew what seeing red meant.

"Can you explain this?" I asked, shoving the phone bill under his nose.

Unperturbed, he took it from my fingers, showing annoyance at my invasion. He looked at the number, circled repeatedly with my red pen. Then, he looked at me as calm as I'd ever seen him. "So?"

"I called her, Kirk. You met her at the convention the weekend you sent me away."

Something flickered in his eyes, then settled into coldness. "What's your problem? I met a nice hair stylist is all. We've called each other a few times, discussing some business ideas."

"Kirk," I heard my voice rising but couldn't harness it, "You don't call a female this many times, long distance, without something going on." *Please, explain it away, Kirk.*

I plopped into a nearby chair, trembling with infinite emotions, spearheaded by terror.

Kirk stared at me for long moments, fingers steepled to lips, his eyes flat. That was the most terrifying of all, his cold gaze. Everything in me spiraled, spiraled downward, as though gravity was sucking it all from me.

Suddenly, Kirk dropped his hands and grinned.

I stared at him, frowning. "What are you grinning about?" I whispered. "I'm dying and you're smiling."

He shrugged. "What can I say. I'm caught."

Next thing I knew, I was on my feet and slapping him across the face. I'd never struck Kirk before and hadn't known I was going to do it. He grabbed my hands as I felt them preparing to hit him again. I knew I was out of control but didn't care. All I felt was rage and hurt.

I jerked free of his grasp and whirled away. I moved to lay my head against the wall.

"Oh, Kirk," I moaned, sliding down the wall until I hit the floor in a heap, weeping. "Why?"

He blurred and swam in my vision. "If you'd been thorough," he said flatly, "You'd have seen that there have been no recent calls."

I couldn't believe my ears. "You promised you'd never be unfaithful to me again," I heard myself whimper.

That hateful empty stare. "I lied. So shoot me."

"I don't want to live." I climbed to my feet and headed blindly for my purse. "I just —"

Kirk blocked my way. "You're not going anywhere like this."

He swam before me. "What do you care?"

"You've got an appointment." His statement jolted me from my red haze.

"When?" I whispered, swiping a hand over my wet cheeks.

He hiked up his arm and looked at his watch. "In ten minutes."

I quickly repaired my makeup, my fingers trembling so violently I could hardly maneuver them. When Mrs. Stone arrived, I managed what I hoped was a pleasant greeting and as I shampooed her, I heard Kirk quietly exit.

Somehow, I cut and styled my client's hair, then bid her goodbye. An hour had lapsed since Kirk had left. I sat down in a chair, trying to sift through what had transpired, strangely encouraged that I'd handled it as well as I had. The cold knot in my stomach reminded me that it was not over yet.

Kirk doesn't want me.

The certainty of that rippled a chill up my spine.

The door opened and Kirk walked in. He plopped down onto the sofa, not even joining me in the work area. On trauma-automatic-pilot, I moved to a chair opposite him. "What now, Kirk?" I asked, hating the tremor in my voice.

"All these years, you've never bothered your little head with the phone bill," he said, staring past me as though I didn't exist. "Now, suddenly, you just *had* to poke around and find something."

"I didn't go looking for anything, Kirk," I said, "I was trying to figure out how to handle utility bills. It's evident you don't want to 'take care of me' anymore." Sarcasm dripped from my words.

His green gaze slashed my way, pinning me. "Yeah. I believe that like I believe nothing happened in your hotel room that night." He gave a dry, humorless laugh. "You're going to be pitiful trying to keep up with bills."

Anger propelled me to my feet. "I know you despise me, Kirk. Now, I know why. Someone named Cheryl."

He was suddenly in my face. "This is not about another woman."

The smell of alcohol hit me like a mallet. "You've been drinking. Oh, God, Kirk – of all times to stay sober, this was it." I turned away. "I can't believe you couldn't stay sober for –"

His strong fingers spun me around. "Hit me now, Janeece," he said with that quiet lethalness I'd always feared. He gave my shoulder a little shove, "C'mon," he taunted, "hit me now." Another shove, a bit stronger. "Hit me."

I struggled to maintain my footing, staring at the huge fist swimming before my terrified wet vision. "I don't want to hit you, Kirk," I heard myself say in a dead voice.

And I knew Kirk was drunk. "I'm not drunk," he said as though reading my mind. "I know exactly what I'm saying."

I didn't doubt that for one minute. "I've got to go home, Kirk," I headed for my purse again, only to be blocked as he snatched it up and emptied its contents on the sofa. He grabbed my purse, extracted all the money from it and threw it onto the heap.

"You're what I made you," he said, eyes burning. "You couldn't make it on your own if you tried," he sneered.

"Then you shouldn't care that I'm leaving," I said, looking past him, waiting for him to calm down and step aside. I knew I must be careful not to push him over the edge. I'd always known violence lurked in Kirk. Somehow, I'd known.

"Leaving?" His gaze narrowed meanly.

I looked dully at him. "Going home."

Slowly, he handed me my car keys. I was suddenly glad for Kirk's strong work ethic that prevented him from simply closing down the salon and following me home to resume the fight. We welcomed walk-in clientele so we had to keep the door open during our posted working hours.

At the house, I'd just stepped out of my shoes when Kirk came in.

I stared at him warily.

"Don't," he said, pain flickering in his eyes.

"What?"

"Don't look afraid of me."

Tears welled, then spilled over as I gazed at him. He slowly approached me, then tentatively reached out to touch my wet cheek. "Oh, Neecy," he moaned and hauled me against him, his arms squeezing me so tight I could hardly breathe. "I'm so sorry. I don't want to hurt you." He lifted his head, then pressed his forehead to mine, whispering, "I've never wanted to hurt you."

"Kirk," I said, "do you love her?"

He stiffened, then said quietly, "No. I haven't talked with her in a long time."

"Why did you – ?" I couldn't put it into words.

He pulled me over to the den sofa and settled me onto it. "Neecy, it all began when I thought you were wanting to have an affair – to purge yourself, you said. I knew that guy – Johnny

Revel – was sniffing around you at school. That's when I realized I couldn't keep on hurting, either. I convinced myself it was stupid to feel so territorial and jealous at the thought of someone else looking at you. So – I let myself get caught in another situation that I thought would de-sensitize me, so to speak." He settled back against the cushions. "I came down to the beach that night because I realized what a fool I'd been but when I saw that guy in your room – I went crazy."

"I told you, Kirk," I said desperately, "there was nothing between Chris and myself. Not that night, not ever."

He looked at me with such sadness, it took my breath. "I want to believe you, Neecy. I think I do. But –"

"Kirk, I was so sick, I couldn't have –"

"What if you hadn't gotten sick, though, Neecy?" Kirk asked gently.

I gazed at him for long moments. I didn't have an answer for him because, looking back, I realized how vulnerable I'd been at that point in time. I'd been aroused by a man young enough to be my son.

"Kirk –" I licked my lips and decided to be honest. "I finally understand that sex isn't always about love. It can be – but doesn't have to be."

He gazed back at me and I saw questions in his eyes, but he didn't ask them. I was grateful.

"Janeece," Kirk's brow furrowed, "do you think we're gonna make it?"

"I don't know, Kirk." I reached out to touch his hand. "I really don't know."

I wish I could say Kirk didn't backslide into occasional pugnaciousness after that talk. But with Kirk's complexity, sailing didn't resume smoothly. The next week, Callie's mom died. Anne called me with the bad news.

"Where's the family going to receive friends?" I asked.

"At Forest's Funeral Home."

"Thanks for letting me know, Anne. How's Chuck's tech college studies going?"

"Great, according to him," Anne informed me. "You know he's into computer studies, something he can handle with his limited endurance."

"My my. He's indomitable. Is Poogie still spending time with him?"

"Whenever her Mama takes her. She's getting a little more pushy about being with her daddy, though. Brags on his good grades."

"That really warms my heart, Anne." I paused. "Thanks for taking care of him all those years he was sick and alone."

"He's my young-un, Neecy, just like you and Trish," she said softly.

"I know. See you at Forest's tonight. Love you."

"Me, too. Bye."

That night, folks overflowed the funeral home when Kirk and I arrived. I felt Kirk stiffen beside me as I signed the guest register. From the corner of my eye, I saw his head lift like a beast sniffing out danger. Wary, I turned to the target of his gawk. His old high-school nemesis Hugh Nighthawk huddled with other old high school friends at the far end of the large receiving room, unaware of our presence.

I turned on my heel and headed in the opposite direction, praying Kirk would follow. Callie stood beside the bronze casket with its spray of red roses, Mollie's favorite. Her burst of dark hair hugged her pale cheeks in a bob that swayed as her head dipped and moved in grateful animation. Her beauty still took my breath. I slowly made my way to where she greeted an elderly couple from Mollie's church. I stood silently, waiting my turn to speak to her, choking back sudden, overwhelming tears. I could see Mollie's lovely profile framed by a gust of white wavy gloss, horizoned slightly above the casket break. It could have been superimposed over Callie's face without changing much with its patrician nose set over generous, patient lips I'd never heard utter an unkind word. Even after Callie's worst shenanigans, Mollie had given Cal the benefit of a doubt. To a fault at times, but now I realized Mollie, with her husband's drinking and philandering, had handled things the best she knew how.

Increasingly frustrating battle-of-wills with Dawn had loosed my compassion for others in like situations.

The older couple moved on. Callie sighted me and her dark eyes rounded and filled with tears.

"Neecy," she whispered on a sob. We fell into each other's arms and bawled like babies.

"She's so pretty, Cal," I sobbed. "Like an angel. She *was* an angel."

"Got that right, Neecy." When we finally wound down, Callie pulled back to look at me through red, swollen eyes. "I'm so glad you came, Neecy."

"I've missed you."

She snuffled and tried unsuccessfully to blink back tears. "Me, too."

"Cal – I'm sorry about all the junk – and that I've not been to see you while you've been nursing your mama through cancer –"

"That was then and this is now. You've had your own battles, Neecy. I know that." Her hands gently squeezed my arms. "Let's not look back."

I smiled at her through new tears. "Okay."

"Oka-a-ay." She held up her hand and we did a high-five, tears coursing down our cheeks.

"Kirk!" Callie turned to give Kirk a big hug. I no longer felt threatened by their warm relationship. Felt, in fact, that I'd been stupid to ever have been. "Don't get gone." Cal grabbed our arms as we prepared to move away. "I want you to come over to the house when I leave."

Kirk and I meandered to the lobby area to wait for Callie. Hugh was nowhere to be seen. The disappearing act no longer amused me. Because I never knew what to expect from Kirk these days. Since I'd found out about the phone calls, not much had changed. Ours was an unspoken, spider-web fragile truce, the one-day-at-a-time and let's-see-what-happens brand.

I still whiffed the telltale alcohol smell on occasion. But not as often.

Kirk insisted I ride with Cal to her house and he followed in our Buick sedan. "He wanted to give us time alone," Callie murmured tiredly, exhausted from grief and all those months of hanging in there with Mollie. "How are things, Neecy?" she asked.

I hesitated, wondering how much to reveal to her during her own time of distress. "Okay," I replied, deciding it wouldn't be fair to dump on her. "Not perfect. Just – okay."

"Mmm. Takes time." She gave a long ragged sigh, slumped over the wheel as though it were the only thing between her and acute collapse.

"How about you, Cal? What you going to do now that both parents are gone?"

She didn't answer for a moment. Then a matter of fact, "I'll stay on in the house." She shrugged. "Why not? It's paid for and it's home." She gave a little snort that transported me back to younger days. "At one time, I couldn't wait to get away from here. Remember?"

I laughed. "Do I. You wasted no time in fulfilling your dream, either."

Her gaze settled dully on the road again. Her aborted grunt of laughter didn't reach her face. "Turned out to be a nightmare." Another tremulous sigh, then a conscious lift of features and shoulders. "Until I met God."

The sudden reference stunned my senses, like a brash intrusion. How far I'd drifted.

"How about you, Neecy? You leaning on Him?"

Paralyzed with revelation, I couldn't speak.

"Things like that – what happened to you and Kirk – can bring on bitterness, Neecy. I'm not saying you're bitter," she added quickly, seeing me tense. "That's not what I'm saying at all. I'm just saying that when a good person like you gets slaughtered by hurts, it's difficult as blazes to keep a straight head. I don't know what's transpired in the past ten years, but I know – *feel* – you've fought a horrific battle to stay sane."

She relaxed for a moment as she navigated her old plunker Ford around condolence-bearers' vehicles and into her teensy drive. Kirk had already joined the men occupying the front porch with its endearing white swing and neatly whitewashed, weathered rocking chairs. Cigarettes blinked like fireflies in the silvery darkness.

Callie turned to me, her silky dress rustling against the leather car seat, in no hurry to join her guests. Suddenly, I felt her intense love, one I'd never have dreamed, all those years ago, would have evolved. I swallowed a huge lump.

"Callie," I spoke impulsively, hoarsely, "you can't imagine how much your love means to me just now." I blinked rapidly, hating the free-falling tears streaming my face, revealing to her my need, my depletion. She took my hand and squeezed and in an instant, it didn't really matter. "Oh Cal – I don't want to burden you right now wi –"

Her fingers gripped mine so tightly I felt them begin to numb. "Don't you *ever again* close me out of your life, Janeece Whitman Crenshaw," she sniped in the old Callie vernacular, tart and concise and final. "We can't let go of each other again."

We fell into each other's arms and bawled it out. When we cranked down, sniffling and blowing noses heartily into Kleenexes, Callie looked me blearily in the eye. "Now, here's what I want you to do – my prescription, for whatever it's worth to you."

It's worth the world.

"This next week, you get alone somewhere, meditate and pray. Then – we'll talk again."

I stared at her, perplexed yet knowing she was right. There had to be a starting place for my odyssey back. I'd just needed Cal to remind me *where.*

"Thanks, Cal," I whispered, the darned tears puddling again.

She flashed a fervent smile. "Payback time, Neecy." She shrugged elaborately as her own dark eyes moistened. "Just – payback time."

CHAPTER TWENTY-FOUR
"A Time to Keep Silence….A Time to Speak"

The Starlight Motel room was small and plain. But it was clean. Kirk had kicked up a fuss when I told him my plans to withdraw for a time to meditate.

"So," he drawled, his face just short of a sneer as he paced the floor like a caged pit bull, "You're gonna go back to being little religious, Neecy, huh?" The smell of alcohol reached me halfway across the bedroom, but tonight, it didn't upset me as much. His words, however, punched me with the impact of Joe Frazier's boxing glove.

I gazed at him, struggling for calm. "I'm going to be *me*, Kirk, is all."

He glared at me as though wanting to say more, but he didn't.

"I'll call you when –"

He was suddenly in my face. "Why can't you tell me where you're going?"

"Because," I met his gaze levelly and spoke through clenched teeth, "I need time *alone*."

I did. I also needed an ounce of control over my life, as boxed in as it was, as stifling and desolate and damning as it was. Kirk had done it again: stripped me of everything.

Now, I had to find *me* in yet another definition. It wasn't fair. But that was how it was. And I would be damned to Hell, literally, if I couldn't at least have this one concession.

"Hah!" His abrupt derision startled me, left me shaking. "Probably got ol' Johnny tucked away somewhere. Or Nighthawk. I saw 'im eyeing you at the funeral home. He's a snake in –"

"Johnny nor Nighthawk don't play into –"

" – the grass. He's no good. Never was –"

"Stop it, Kirk. I'm only –"

" – worth the salt in his bread. Not even in high school. He –"

I spun and walked away. "I'll see you in three days," I called back and slammed out the door.

I took only bottled water and sandwich fixings to store in the tiny refrigerator. I would eat only when necessary, I decided. In the back of my mind, I still dreaded Kirk's assessment of me after I left here. He already laughed at my 'weirdness.'

Sleeplessness had rendered me vulnerable to weeping fits and nerves so raw as to be terminable. One recent night, Kirk had gotten up to go to the bathroom and found me outside on the porch, huddled in its dark corner, balled into a fetal knot. I'd long ago learned that he'd not come looking for me during my nightmare hours. Would, in fact, not miss a wink of sleep nor a daytime meal due to my distress. So, my disintegration was my own.

I'd never, in my worst hours, felt so alone.

"What're you doing out here?" he'd asked coldly, squinting blearily at me as though I were a mole invading his flowerbed.

I'd looked helplessly at him, depression slicing me to ribbons, hardly knowing where I was. "I – I don't want to live, Kirk," I whispered hoarsely, not expecting, not even hoping he'd care. Just – answering his query.

"Aww, you'll be okay, Janeece." He snorted then, "You're too selfish to kill yourself." With that, he yawned mightily and padded back upstairs and slept the rest of the night.

I kicked off my shoes in the motel room, closed the blinds and picked up my Bible. Another episode flashed from nowhere. One rock-bottom day, for some reason, maybe a slip of Kirk's tongue had led me to believe he'd begun to feel a bit of something for me again, or maybe desperation or survival instinct jolted me into crying out, "Kirk, I need just a little reassurance that –"

His laugh, a harsh snort of disdain, halted my appeal. "Reassurance? *Reassurance?*"

It was the burning look in his eyes that froze me into a *thing*. "Reassure yourself, Janeece. You're a middle-aged woman, for God's sake."

My fingers stilled on the Bible's pages and I cringed anew at his scorn. I knew his perception of me was distorted. Knew for a certainty that I did not harbor self-pity. Nor was I more selfish than – well, I'd learned through all this that everybody is basically a selfish being. I was no more self-absorbed than the next person, regardless of Kirk's taunting insinuations. What I did know was that I was in this alone for the long haul.

I couldn't change Kirk. I couldn't change anybody else in this whole world.

But I could change me. Somewhere, there was a place for me where I would find peace, where I could love and be loved, but first, I must find me.

"God, help me find me."

Guilt ambushed me as I whispered my first words. I'd left my Maker behind for so long. In retrospect, there was no justification for my abandonment.

A conflux of emotions dropped on me. I couldn't dissect the mass of squiggly snakes that crawled over, around and inside me.

Immediately, I locked the door, climbed on the firm mattress with its Cloroxed sheets and began to read my Bible and meditate.

On the fourth morning, I took a long hot, soaking bath. Afterward, I picked up my suitcase, gazed around the little room with its nondescript floral drapes and equally dismal bedspread and was astonished to find I dreaded leaving it. For three days, it had wrapped about me like a warm blanket and kept the cold world outside, cocooning me with words of life and a warm presence of truth. Within its confines, I'd forgotten food as I'd petitioned first for forgiveness, then canoed from harsh desolation toward a shoreline I'd never before known existed. I knew instinctively it was a land of renovation.

There, in the still oasis, I shut up and did more listening than I'd ever done in my life. A video of the past years ran nonstop, one I viewed through new eyes and emotions. This time, the scenes portrayed the humanness of loved ones who'd brought me pain. This time, when I wept, it was for them. With each victory, I felt strength rise a notch.

Words and phrases leapt from the Bible's pages to smite and enlighten. I was desperate to absorb as much of this inviolable atmosphere as possible, knowing I had nothing else. Without it, I was nothing.

It was there, on that thought that it happened.

As I lay flat on the bed, admitting that, without Divine help, I was nothing, I felt myself lifted gently from the mattress into a bubble of golden mist – where the air seemed stirred by angel's wings. I knew to describe it would seem hokey, but I didn't care. There I glimpsed a glowing presence that lit the entire chamber so brightly my eyes snapped shut against it. I wasn't afraid. I knew who joined me and tears squeezed from beneath my tightly shut lids and coursed down my cheeks.

And suddenly, I *knew*. Truth invaded me like a zillion fireworks exploding at once. I experienced a presence so powerful it still affects my life to this day. With complete clarity I heard the rumbling many waters voice: "The best way to *hold on* is to *let go. Neecy, you're going to be all right. I'm with you.*"

I began to laugh, humongous belly busting guffaws, propelled by joy that comes from liberation.

The truth shall set you free.

I alternately laughed and wept from sheer happiness, suspended there in that marvelous aura of purity and goodness until I opened my mouth to say, "thank you," and the words were not English. This time, I let the utterances flow, whooping and weeping and then, finally, feeling that warm honey pour over me until I was satiated as a wee baby burping from Mama's milk. The peace of it released me into a babe's slumber.

The next morning, in its aftermath, I was so different from the Janeece who'd walked in there days ago that I wondered if somehow my looks would reveal what had transpired. A glance in the mirror dispelled that notion because, actually, I looked thinner and more wan. But my eyes said it all. The fear was gone.

I walked out the door and for the first time in years, felt up to the task at hand.

My euphoria lasted exactly twenty minutes. The time it took to drive home. It being Wednesday, Toby and Dawn were in school. Kirk sat at the kitchen table, a study of morose brooding.

"Hi," I said warmly, then headed for our room to unload the suitcase, willing myself not to react to his silence.

As I unpacked and put my things away, I felt Kirk's presence in the doorway, where he lounged against the doorjamb, his dark gaze riveted to my movements, as though measuring and finding them inept.

"So?" he finally broke the silence. "How was your *season* of prayer?" The sarcasm in his words pierced my heart, but I refused to give in to tears this time.

I turned to face him. "I had a wonderful three days. Thanks for asking." I resumed returning my toiletries to their bathroom counter niche. I knew Kirk buzzed with anger. Craved a fight.

Takes two to fight, I reminded myself.

"I suppose Johnny's doing well?"

I didn't even look at him this time, just kept shuffling things into place. "I wouldn't know. I haven't seen him since the last day of classes." I did turn and look him in the eye then.

Kirk's face turned surly. "So – you're actually going to turn back into *little goody-two-shoes Janeece.*"

I didn't flinch from his sneering gaze. "Call it whatever you want Kirk." I lowered myself onto the edge of our bed. Then, feeling a sweep of tiredness, stretched out and rested my head on the pillow.

Kirk moved to the window, hands shoved into pockets as he stared unseeing into the trees. "Where do we go from here, Neecy? I'm not happy. You're not happy."

No rush of panic. With remarkable calm, I said, "I don't know. But whatever happens, Kirk, I plan to go with God."

His instant agitation was palpable. He shuffled his feet, glowered at me, then left the room in a huff, slamming the door behind him. I closed my eyes in relief. At least we didn't fight.

I went downstairs to pour a cup of coffee and was surprised to find Kirk sitting at the table, cup in hand. I thought he'd driven off somewhere to drown his ire. Instead, he examined the bottom of his cup as though it contained a formula for youth.

"Want yours heated up?" I asked as I poured mine, expecting silence. *All I have to do is my part, that's all.*

"Sure," he mumbled, holding his cup up for me to refill. "Thanks."

"Kirk," I said as I took the chair opposite him. "I want to apologize for all I've done to hurt you in the past years. I'm sorry I didn't truly forgive you for being unfaithful. Sorry for the harsh way I responded to you at times when you were kind to me." I shrugged sadly. "I take my share of the blame for what happened to us next. I regret many things. I can't undo them, but I can say I'm sorry."

He still stared into his cup. For long moments he continued to do so. Then, he looked at me. His green gaze was clear. "Neecy, I just want you to know – I plan to go with God, too."

MawMaw died that week. She'd always said she hoped that when the end came, she would simply go to sleep and wake up on the other side. She got her wish. My entire family attended the funeral in Asheville. Daddy took it as hard as anybody. I suspected he felt that, just when they'd finally made peace, when he'd finally reconnected to her, she was snatched away.

It was downright spooky how much – as he mellowed – Daddy and I thought alike. Toby, now past the gangly stage of youth, resembled Dad more than his sons did. And my son's disposition was a mother's dream. Though lively and fun loving, he never seemed to get truly angry. Didn't seem to have any teen-age axes to grind. Dawn, on the other hand, made up for the two of them.

"I'd *swear* she sits up nights dreaming up ways to worry me," I told Trish more than once.

"Aww," Trish poo-poohed my concerns, "she's just different. She'll straighten up one of these days. You'll see." I tried to take heart from her positiveness.

From her funky, all black clothes and garish purple nail polish to her offbeat sense of family, Dawn's desperate disparities grated on me like fingernails against a chalkboard. She and I didn't speak the same language.

Sometimes, I wondered if there'd been a hospital nursery mix-up. Kirk hated to hear me go on about her escapades. Got to the point that he dismissed my commiserations with, "you two just clash, is all. Too much alike."

An easy dismissal. But by now, I knew Kirk could only handle so much chaos before he folded.

It had not been a miraculous, instantaneous turnaround in our marriage. But my prayer getaway had been a pivot point. Months later, Kirk still was not warm to me. But I fulfilled my position as his wife and partner. That's all I had to answer for.

It was still a bit heady, knowing I did not answer to Kirk. Nor he to me. I stood alone under my Maker. My worth was not, nor would it ever be, tied to Kirk's assessment of me. Nor to anyone else's. My new spiritual psyche told me when to speak and when not to speak. Mostly, with Kirk, it told me to keep silent.

One day, I forged ahead, not listening to it.

"I miss the old Kirk. The one who teased and flirted and adored me," I said in one unguarded moment of lightness, thinking I could meander back into those lost times. I watched Kirk's face grow somber, then dark.

His eyes left the road to light on me. The old dreaded churlish gleam was back. "Would you rather have half a loaf or none at all, Neecy?" he asked in that almost silent way.

Shocked at the still present reality, I averted my gaze to the road ahead, saying nothing else. The soft side of me felt crushed. The other, newer, stronger side said, *So what? You've had nothing for so long anyway, it doesn't matter. If he wants to hold back, he's cheating himself out of lots of fun and joy.*

Callie and I got together for lunch one day at the Magnolia Drive-in while Kirk golfed.

"I do a lot of self-talk these days, Cal." I poured two Sweet'N Lows into my iced tea. "Kirk still holds himself aloof, refusing to contribute anything emotional to our marriage."

"Oh, come on, Neecy," Callie cut her chili cheeseburger in two. "Nothing?"

"Zero, Cal. I'm not exaggerating." I stirred the straw to dissolve the white powder. "Wish I were. Oh, Kirk, as you know, is the best financial supporter in the world. Though I feel more and more like a kept woman th –"

"Neecy!" Callie cut me a wry look.

"What I mean is – I try not to feel that way, but I know Kirk doesn't love me and doesn't really want to do anything for me." I held up a hand as she inhaled to protest. "And that's okay. I'm learning to live with it." I took a bite out of my chili cheeseburger as proof of my resilience.

Callie washed down her bite with a swill of tea. "I know you think that, but Kirk…"

"Cal," I took her hand and calmly relayed Kirk's half a loaf comment.

She stared at me, disbelieving. "Half a loaf? Or *none?* Doesn't sound like Kirk." She shook her head and looked away, mumbling under her breath.

"I know. And I don't want to make Kirk look like a bogeyman. He's just – Kirk, with limitations just as you and I have." I half-heartedly munched a french fry.

"Well, I must say, you're handling all this better than I could."

"I don't want to turn you against Kirk. I take my share of blame in all our problems."

Her dark eyes clouded as she watched me closely. "Don't let too much of yourself go, Neecy."

I laughed, surprising her. "You know, Cal, at one time, Kirk played me like a banjo. Now, I don't react as I once did." I'd told Callie about my three-day spiritual awakening. "Since my retreat, I've learned something invaluable."

"Oh?" Dark eyebrows lifted over the rim of the Coke glass.

"Pride is an illusion. Nobody can make you less than who you are, no matter what they think or say. I'd always, as far back as I can remember, acted as a mirror for what others saw or felt about me. I didn't go off the deep end with it, though, until Kirk – well, I gave him entirely too much power over me."

"So, it's a power struggle?"

"Not for me. It never was, except in the pure survival sense. But with Kirk, it's different. Why? I don't know." I propped my elbows on the table and cupped my face in my hands. "I get so starved for affection sometimes, Cal, I think I'll die. Had I not experienced that glorious romantic period with Kirk, I wouldn't *know.*" I sighed deeply. "I still grieve for the man who loved me so desperately when we moved back here. But I've faced up that he'll never come back. I just pretend he's dead. Buried. Makes it easier. Helps me keep my sanity."

"I'm sorry, honey," Callie murmured, her dark eyes moist.

"Only thing keeps me going is I know there's an escape hatch."

Callie gave me a long measuring look. "Oh?"

"Yeah." I sat back and drew with my finger on the frosted glass. "I promised God I'd stay with Kirk until he rids himself of alcohol. I owe him that. I'll give my marriage all I've got. A hundred-and-ten per cent. Then, if things don't change, I'm outta here."

CHAPTER TWENTY-FIVE

"I don't care who he is, no daughter of mine shacks up with anybody who isn't her husband." Kirk stopped pacing to address Heather, whose gaze was averted and features appropriately downcast. But we both knew, from past experience, Heather would make up her own mind. She was that much like her Daddy. She'd graduated, by a thin hair, from college with a degree in business management and now worked at a mortgage company, whose divorced owner was her new boyfriend.

The salon was quiet at that moment, with no patrons present. We'd decided to stop renting chairs to other hair stylists and keep our salon business all in the family.

"I love him, Dad," she said in a whispery, choked, *pleading* voice.

He stared at her as though she was mad and I marveled anew that he wasn't touched by the things that tore me apart. "Hey! If that man cared anything about you, he'd marry you. If you do this, you're no daughter of mine."

I gasped. *Oh my God.* "Kirk —"

"Stay out of this, Janeece." His gaze never left Heather's lovely chestnut head that bowed as she quietly wept and I knew she loved her Daddy so much, this thing was agony for her. "I haven't approved of your lifestyle for quite some time, you were raised to know better." His fingers swiped through thick hair, then both hands dropped to rest on his hips as he stood before his daughter. "This – this I cannot accept."

Heather wiped her eyes, stood, slung her purse strap over her shoulder and turned to leave. She glanced furtively over her shoulder at Kirk, who'd picked up the television remote and began clicking channels until he found golf, then plopped down onto the sofa, seemingly absorbed in the match. I knew better. He was more shaken than he wanted anybody to know.

I followed Heather outside and pulled her into my arms. "He'll come around, honey," I whispered in her ear as I hugged her. "He loves you. Give him time."

Fresh tears choked off Heather's reply, so she simply squeezed me back and kissed my cheek before she jumped quickly into her little green VW, a family hand-me-down, and drove away. I stuck my head back in the salon door and called to Kirk, "I'm going on home to start dinner."

"Okay." His eyes never left the screen. We always drove separate cars because our schedules zigzagged one another and stopped at different times. Today, Kirk would finish up later.

Toby bustled about in the kitchen when I kicked off my shoes in the den. "What's that wonderful smell?" I called, forcing joviality far from what I felt.

"A surprise," he replied, barely banking down the excitement in his voice.

I tiptoed to the doorway and sniffed appreciatively. "Spaghetti!" I rushed to hug him. "Oh, you wonderful guy, you!" He grinned, pleased at my response. He already had thick meaty sauce bubbling and noodles boiling. "You are so *neat*." I sliced a loaf of Italian bread, spread garlic butter on it and arranged it on a pan. "And in more ways than one."

"Thanks, Mama," he replied modestly, wiping off the last of onion peels from the counter. "Look, why don't you go sit down and rest. I'll treat you tonight."

I shot him an adoring gaze. "I'll just take you up on that, son." Sighing and thinking again how blessed I was to have Toby, I plopped down on the den's navy-blue floral sofa, one plush as a baby's favorite teddy bear. My feet ached.

But not as much as my heart. I fought back tears, replaying Heather's impassioned appeal for her father's understanding. Yet – I understood Kirk's feelings because I shared some of them. I didn't agree with her cohabiting outside marriage, not only fornicating but also setting herself up for heartache. And Kirk was basically right. If the man loved Heather, he'd marry her. But I didn't agree with cutting Heather off from us.

I flipped on the television and tuned in a talk show, only half listening. Until the doctor being interviewed said, "these adult children of alcoholics all share a syndrome of anger and mistrust. Because they were not parented as children, their social development jelled there. Forced to parent themselves, they come up with their own special behavioral code."

Fascinated, I turned up the volume. *My Lord, that's Kirk Crenshaw up one side and down the other.*

By the end of the program, I felt a stirring of hope for Kirk. I scrounged in an end table drawer for my ever present pen and writing pad, flipped to the back and wrote down the doctor's name, Dr. Wayne Kritsberg, and the book's title: *The Adult Children of Alcoholics Syndrome.*

The next day, I bought it at Waldenbooks, took it home and read it from cover to cover. I wept, laughed and experienced goosebumps at intervals. By its end, I had the first inkling of what Kirk Crenshaw was about. If it affected me so profoundly, would it not be as revealing to my husband?

My first hurdle was getting him to read it. With his present paranoia, would I be able to lead him to help? I shrugged. I'd do my best, that's all I could do. Somewhere along the way, I'd learned to switch mindsets when needed. I rarely thought as a wife anymore. Rather, I looked on Kirk as a friend who needed help.

Later that evening, during a relaxed moment at the dinner table, I said, "Kirk, I heard the most interesting theory about adults from dysfunctional alcoholic homes – such as yours was. It was on a talk show. I went out and bought the book and read it." I sipped my coffee casually while my heart did crazy tap-dances. "Interesting." I said, studying the bottom of my cup while slowly swirling the dark amber liquid. "Very interesting."

When I looked up, he watched me with empty eyes. The weight of responsibility was heavy – this might be the only chance Kirk would have. I went for the kill.

"You ought to read it. I think you'd discover some things about yourself and your family you've never suspected."

He didn't blink. I yawned and settled back in my chair, a calculated picture of levity. "If you decide you want to read –"

"I don't want to read any self-analyzing book." He rose and his leave-taking was as indifferent as his words.

My heart thudded to a new low. Hope for any meeting of minds fizzled for me in that moment. I would continue to fulfill my promise to the Almighty by living each day as though it were my last while preparing for many tomorrows. I'd also treat Kirk with unconditional courtesy and love until he'd beaten alcohol completely and could stand alone. That was almost funny...Kirk, the Superman, depending on me, who, in his estimation, couldn't think my way out of a paper bag. Only thing was, during my spiritual meditation, Kirk's emotional frailty had revealed itself. At this point, he'd rather die than admit it, but Kirk needed me.

I stood and began clearing the table. *Perhaps,* a sudden thought struck me, *that's what he fears most.* I grew still as an at-rest heartbeat, mulling it over. I shook my head. *Nah.*

"Anything wrong, Mama?" Toby hovered at my elbow, all concern.

"Everything's fine," I trilled, reaching to kiss his cheek.

He didn't look convinced. "Y'sure?"

"Yep. But if you want to cheer me up, grab that casserole dish and scour it quickly for me so I won't mess up my acrylic nails."

"Okay." He happily complied and we worked compan-ionably cleaning up while Dawn did her disappearing act. I wouldn't scold her tonight. I'd rather busy myself and perhaps keep disappointment at arms' length.

I reminded myself to let go of Kirk. I reminded myself I was responsible only for what *I* could do. I reminded myself I was no less a person because Kirk rejected me.

I reminded myself that soon, if nothing changed, I would leave. I would free Kirk and somehow, with God's help, I would make a new life for my children and me.

❖ ❖ ❖ ❖ ❖ ❖

It came unexpectedly, with no drumrolls, on a rainy Sunday afternoon. I rested in my tiny reading room, an upstairs nook I'd claimed and decorated with pastels, a small navy-blue sectional and floor to ceiling library shelves. Beautiful smoky beveled wall mirrors and bursts of greenery opened and vital-ized the area. Toby was visiting a neighbor pal and Dawn was still at Trish and Gene's so the house was quiet as I began a Pat Conroy novel. The only sound was a golf commentator's voice drifting up from the downstairs television, where Kirk lounged. He rarely sought me out anymore. Hadn't for a long, long time.

So, when he sauntered into my lair, I was mildly surprised. He stopped, scratched his head and gazed at my stuffed book-shelves. "Uh, where's that book you were telling me about?" he asked.

My heart leaped, but I made myself rise almost indolently. "Up here." I moved to a shelf and extracted it. He took it from me and left the room as uneventfully as he'd entered. I resumed my reading, telling myself not to get too excited. Kirk was entirely too kaleidoscopic to second-guess.

Later that afternoon, I drove to pick up Dawn, leaving Kirk sprawled on the sofa, book in hand. Usually, he dozed but not today. I visited with Trish a few minutes then left. Back at the house, Kirk now lounged in the La-Z-Boy, eyes riveted to the book.

I began to prepare an early dinner. Dawn, glad to be home, helped. In moments of camaraderie, she could be incredibly sweet. We peeled and diced potatoes to boil. I taught her to dip chicken in a buttermilk and egg mixture, roll it in flour, salt and pepper and place it in a skillet of sizzling oil. Toby arrived and pitched in, doing the mashed potatoes in his inimitable way, lots of mayo, butter and milk, then battering it all into whipped cream consistency.

"Neecy," Kirk nudged my arm with his elbow and I turned from the stove, leaving Dawn turning a drumstick. "Listen to this –" He read me a long passage in an incredulous voice, then peered at me from eyes no longer vacant but astonished. They made me think of a person born blind, who, by some miracle, suddenly *sees* and is amazed at how different reality is from their imagined world.

"There's a reason for my – our family's dysfunctionalism. We had no parenting. From the time I was twelve, I had to buy my own clothes. I had to make my own way. Nobody took care of me. That's why I can't trust others for – anything. God –" He smacked a palm to his forehead, still gazing at the pages, "all that misery. All that anger comes from that helplessness and –" He trailed off, already into another passage.

"Makes sense," I said, encouraging his openness and checking on Dawn's progress with the marvelous smelling chicken. "Good job," I commented on the perfectly arranged, golden browned pieces. Her eyes did their little *oh, Mama* roll even as she blushed with pleasure.

"Listen to this." Kirk still shadowed me. I relaxed then, knowing he'd follow me as I moved about – icing glasses and pouring tea – to read highlighted text to me. The book remained next to his plate that evening as he ate.

I said a silent prayer of thanks. Regardless of how our marriage went, Kirk could now get help for the crippling syndrome that besets adult children from alcoholic homes. One where rage is a roaring tornado that destroys everything in its path. Maybe he would discover a new, better Kirk than ever before.

It was revealing to me that I loved Kirk in a new way. Now, as a friend. Unconditionally. *Sad*, I thought, that to survive Kirk's coldness, I'd had to smother romantic love. I couldn't have survived with it burning in me.

I caught Kirk watching me across the table, a strange look in his eyes. The distance he'd wedged between us made it impossible to read him anymore. So I smiled at him as I would at a good friend. He gazed so intently that I instinctively grabbed a napkin to blot my chin, thinking I had dribbled gravy. His brief, answering smile held a tiny glimmer of warmth.

Not much. But then, a half a loaf *wasn't*.

At one point in time, I'd thought I couldn't live without Kirk. Now I knew that I could. He'd not truly been with me for years now. For whatever reasons, Kirk had not loved me for a long, long time. That fact no longer pierced me as it once had. It just made me incredibly sad.

Strangely, Kirk still sought sex with me. Our marriage bed gave us a sanctuary where we escaped the stifling reality of where we'd come. For brief moments, we joined physically, silently pleasured one another, then Kirk went back inside himself, leaving me bereft and keenly aware that our former intimacy was gone. Yet, Kirk had supported me financially. He'd given me time to prepare myself to stand alone.

Tonight, across the table from him, my smile turned genuine and my eyes misted with gratitude as we gazed at one another. I realized I could now, finally, set him free.

"Neecy," Callie paced my living room floor, "our class of 1960 had one hundred twenty graduates. The response to our thirty-year Chapowee Class reunion questionnaire is a measly seventy." She threw up her hands. "Ridiculous!"

"Give it time, Cal," I soothed her. She'd worked hard on the invitation letter, one I should have helped with but was too engrossed in my present marital crisis. "There're still two weeks until the deadline."

"Neecy," Cal stopped pacing and grew stock-still, peering at me. "You serious about asking Kirk for a divorce?"

I released a long shuddering sigh, momentarily regretting my divulgence. "Yes, I am, Cal. Kirk's hung in there with me far too long – being as how he hasn't loved me for ages. I owe him his freedom. Maybe he has someone he would be happier with."

Cal's dark eyebrows winged toward the ceiling. "Whatever happened to 'thou shalt not commit adultery'?"

I shrugged. "It's no sin to divorce. The other – well, I don't intend to indulge. I've kept Kirk leashed to me long enough. He's a good man. We just – don't blend anymore, y'know?" It *still* hurt to say those words.

"Could'a fooled me." Callie's gaze narrowed, narrowed.... "You aren't – I mean, you don't have somebody else tucked away, do you, Neecy?" I heard a shrill note of fear in her question.

Laughter burst from me. "Lord, *no*. I've never *wanted* another man. Only Kirk. But I can't have him." I was astonished when a lump tried to centralize in my chest. I thought I'd exorcised all of those feelings long ago. "So –" I took a deep breath and flashed an over bright smile, "I've accepted reality. But I simply can't ask Kirk before the reunion. And Heather's wedding. Y'know? I don't want to spoil either."

"Yeah. He would probably be too upset to enjoy them."

"No. I mean *me*. It would spoil them for me. Not Kirk." I gazed sadly at Cal. "I doubt he'd bat an eye. Nope. I'll wait till after then."

Cal yawned hugely, stretched like a cat kept still too long, then slid her bare feet into slippers. "I'm outta here, Neecy. You done poured cold water on this party." She swooped down to kiss my cheek. "See ya later."

What I didn't tell Cal was that I suspected Kirk's relief to rid himself of me would be overwhelming.

Until after the two events, I didn't want to *know*.

CHAPTER TWENTY-SIX

"Do I pass?" I checked my reflection one more time in the freestanding bedroom mirror. Keeping in theme, I wore my old fifties' color-guard outfit. The short flared crimson skirt and jacket still fit. It was the one outfit I'd kept meticulously stored throughout the years, along with the white leather boots and crimson tassels. Enough summer tan lingered to lightly bronze my legs. I'd cut simple side bangs and arranged my hair into a slightly rumpled Monroe bob.

"Mmm, let me check you out." Kirk nuzzled my neck, inhaling my *Passion* fragranced skin. "Smell good." He straightened and swept an appreciative gaze over me, lingering overly where the snug jacket hugged my bosom. "*Look*s good, too. I'll keep her." That had become our little joke, the *'I'll keep him/her.'* As though anything else was absurd.

Role-playing. Because Kirk's gestures and cliches had no depth beyond sex.

My going-through-motions existence had equipped me to slide into dialogue I needed to keep things on an even keel in our marriage. There were moments when, mind reeling from memories, I'd assume the business partner approach of negotiation and professional courtesy. Other times, during Kirk's quiet times, I'd become his best friend and pal. I no longer regarded appeasement as a demeaning thing.

"Life's a trade-off anyway, Cal," I'd told her one day during one of my mind-purgings. "Think about it," I popped peanuts in my mouth and munched as we visited in her den, barefooted and drinking ice cold Diet Pepsi. "From the time we're born, we trade out. Mama tickled and fed us and we gave her big drooly smiles and goo-goos. In school, we studied, the teacher gave us good grades." We rolled our eyes at each other over *that* one, snickering for long moments before settling back into sobriety. "We behaved and our folks treated us well. If we didn't, we – at least *I* got grounded. Courtship –" I shrugged, "and marriage ordains *the* dilly of all trade-offs. What can I say?'

"Not with God," Callie began to protest. "His love is un-conditional and —"

"Oh absolutely, His love is pure and unchanging. But *yes,*" I wagged a finger at her. "The Bible is full of *If you will do this then I will do that.* Even the Almighty sets conditions for us to reach Heaven. There's never a time we're not responsible to something or someone, even if it's only to ourselves."

"Hey!" Callie stretched her back. "This is heavy stuff." She guzzled Pepsi. "And you're right. I'd just never thought of it that way." She cocked an irreverent eyebrow then, transporting me right back to teen days. "You ought to be a writer, y'know?"

"Hey! I *try.*" We sat in companionable silence for long moments, reflecting on the conversation.

"The trade-off concept — it's what's kept me putting one foot in front of the other. No joke. For so long, Kirk has been simply someone I'm —" I wrinkled my nose and squinted in concentration, "sorta responsible for. Y'know?"

"Yeah," Cal's countenance fell somber. She, too, had been hurt by the whole drama that started in Solomon years earlier. "I'm sorry, Neecy, that you had to go through all that."

"Hey," I poured more salted peanuts into my palm. "That was then and this is now. I do my best not to look back." I laughed then. "Y'know, Cal, I've heard folks say 'I just can't forget what he did to me' —" I shook my head. "Things can get so bad, you either drown in the sludge or you swim out the other side, shake it off, take a good bath, and leave it behind."

Cal now lounged in her easy chair, feet tucked under her, head lolled back against the backrest, watching me with an intentness that made my throat go all tight.

The words shot out of my mouth. "I'm glad you're back into my life, Cal."

"Me, too, Neecy. I sure missed you. What you've shared with me today — by the way, *thanks* — is pure gold. There's no friend like an old friend." Her eyes misted; she blinked and roused up to reach for the Planters Peanuts jar nesting on the glass coffee table between us.

"You're absolutely on target about acting out roles." Her chocolate eyes grew far away. "Maybe if I'd been more resil-ient — sensitive to my wifely role, I'd've stayed with Rog." She blinked then and took a deep breath and lifted her brow. "Who knows? I was too danged self-absorbed. Thought conceding one iota was belittling." Her head moved slowly from side to side. "Foolish, foolish, foolish."

"Strange," I said softly, "most folks *do* think playing games or play-acting is beneath them when it's really all life is about." I shrugged. "Just have to be careful not to *call* it game-playing or play-acting. Some folks are so *literal* they'd argue the question till Christ returns and others – of our Pharasetical *religious* order – would bust a blood vessel, thinking such a notion harbors deception." I rolled my eyes. "We won't even *deal* with our redneck friends' contempt for what, to them, is not totally, flat-footed *real.*"

Callie and I looked at each other and burst into laughter, remembering some of Moose and Roger's – and yes, at times, even Kirk's – crude interpretations of "to thine own self be true."

Callie caught her breath, wiped away tears of mirth and said, "Remember that day I was practicing for cheerleading try-outs and Rog sidled up to me and muttered out the side of his mouth, 'will you, for God's sake, quit showing out. You look stupid." She fanned her face and blew away the last of her exuberance. "A true redneck interpretation of honesty."

I nodded, understanding all too well. "What are totally honest actions? Try to define them in words, Cal. Are they feelings? No. We wouldn't get far if we acted only on feelings"

"Yeah. There were times – when Mama's cancer was so advanced – that I felt like running away and hiding in a cave. When she needed a bedpan, I couldn't go on feelings."

I went to the fridge and pulled out two fresh cans of Pepsi and brought them back. "Know what?" I handed Cal the drink.

"What?" She popped the top and took a long swill, thumped her chest and belched soundly. Some things about Cal never changed.

"You just defined love, Cal. Love isn't a feeling. It's a decision."

She looked at me a long time, crunching nuts, mulling it, then gave a solid nod. "You're right." She got it. Just like that. Some folks never do.

Tonight, as I anticipated the thirtieth high school class reunion, I gazed at my husband, in snug peg-legged jeans, open madras shirt collar peeking from navy blue sweater's V-neck and polished loafers. "You are one cool dude," I said, *feeling* every word.

"Still glad you married me?" Kirk murmured teasingly, yet his eyes were still flat.

My next words were as mechanical as Gilley's Broncing Bull from the eighties. "I'd marry you, anyway," I sang June Carter-like, "I'd have your ba-a-a-bies."

"I'd do it all over, too," he said, kissing me carefully, so as not to smear my Hot Red Berry lipstick or mess up my carefully disarrayed hair. "You're as pretty as you were thirty years ago. No. *Prettier.*"

"Thank you," I said, playing the part, as, I was sure, he was. Heck, to quote Shakespeare, the whole *world* is a stage. Then I whispered, running my fingers through his still thick hair, *feeling,* "I'm glad you're not one of those greasers."

He chuckled, sounding as sexy as Clint Eastwood. "Never could stand that stuff."

Kirk, the dream man, never came back. But, *hey!* For tonight, this version was no slouch. By the same token, Kirk's dream woman, his Janeece of old, was lost to him forever. But the present facsimile could adapt to meet his ever-changing needs in her own unique way.

In that light, for the present, the scales balanced.

Anyway – I switched into the party-girl role – change keeps things interesting.

The Dixie Doo-Wop Band burst into *Whole Lotta Shakin' Going On* as our small committee began welcoming class arrivals. Their middle-aged male vocalist, whose raven-dyed pompadour spilled unapologetically to center forehead, had the chameleon ability to be Jerry Lee, Elvis or Conway Twitty, depending on the song. On this one, he belted out a hoarse, desperate Jerry Lee rendition, sweaty gyration and all.

Excitement buoyed and propelled me to greet familiar, as well as unfamiliar, faces. Mine and Kirk's truce had lightened my heart. Kirk and I hadn't been able to attend the twentieth class reunion and so were shocked at how the years had changed all of us. Tonight, we both scurried about, making everyone feel welcome and comfortable. Every so often, Kirk would detour past me to sneak a kiss or "accidentally" rub against me. This was not unusual since, through everything, Kirk's sexual attraction to me remained steadfast. A thing that befuddled me, at times, left me wondering how it could be so without love.

Tootsie Gilmore, a petite ex-cheerleader, now married for the second time, could have stepped from her class photo into the gymnasium tonight wearing her Chapowee Cheerleading costume, a full, flared crimson skirt and V-neck sweater over white turtleneck, with black and white saddle oxfords.

"*Holy Moly*, Tootsie," I wailed, "you haven't changed a lick!"

Her eyebrows shot up over her small tilted nose. "You have, Neecy – and I mean that as a compliment. You were always pretty, but age sets well on you, honey."

I hugged Tootsie in everlasting gratitude as Callie, stunning in her white majorette costume and crimson-tasseled boots, grabbed her for a time of reminiscence. I gazed about me, at peers in their favorite high school attire, and felt a surge of incredible affection.

Callie rushed to clasp my hands in hers. "Last count is a hundred and *ten*, *Neecy.*" Her booted little leaps took me back to 1959 and made me laugh as I hadn't in years. "Some of these guys haven't been to either of the other reunions." She chortled then and whispered, "Look at ol' Nighthawk in his textile jacket. Not a bad fit after all this time. Lordy, Kirk hated him for rescuing him from the Grey High gang that night at our Junior-Senior Prom." Her gaze lingered on the object of her comments longer than was usual for Callie. As if sensing detection, the handsome head turned. His gaze narrowed speculatively on Callie. Then began to glimmer.

"Wheww" I muttered, turning away, "I felt that jolt all the way across the room." Cal merely looked thoughtful as Nighthawk sauntered in her direction.

You are My Special Angel stopped me in my tracks. Nostalgia paralyzed and had me spinning and yearning backward to our senior prom night all those years back. Tonight, I started as Kirk's hand, with just a touch, claimed me anew. And I was in his arms and we danced cheek to cheek and my soul yearned for it to be heart to heart, as when we were innocent teens.

Over Kirk's shoulder, I spied Callie locked in Nighthawk's embrace, her arms encircling his neck, chin resting on his shoulder, her eyes nearly closed in sentimental rapture. I grinned at her expressive features. Her misty gaze slowly roamed the crowd as she and Nighthawk moved together to the love song.

Suddenly, her eyes rounded in shock and she halted so abruptly Nighthawk nearly tripped over her. I glanced over my shoulder to see what had snared her attention.

"Oh, Kirk," I gasped. "It's *Roger Denton.*"

Callie rushed past us, leaving a bewildered partner in her wake as the song ended.

"Rog!" Callie shrieked and fell into his arms. Still lean, he wore his old football jersey with the big crimson C and pegged jeans. Kirk and I meandered closer to witness the reunion. Roger was, if possible, more handsome in middle age. His face, once pretty-boy, now bore character lines and shadows that defined it manly. His narrowed, gentle assessment of Callie's tearful face moved him further into mellowed humanity. After their divorce, he'd been stationed in exotic places all over the world. Callie, eventually, lost all touch with him. Last account, he'd not remarried.

Arm in arm, they moved to a quiet corner to catch up. I sighed, blinked back tears and gazed up at Kirk, whose unreadable gaze searched my features. "Tender-hearted Neecy," he murmured. After a moment, I decided it was not an unfavorable observance.

I snuffled hugely and delicately blotted beneath my eyes. "Is my mascara smeared?" I whispered, wishing I'd not revealed my insecurity to him. Kirk assured me it wasn't.

The band struck up *That Old Time Rock and Roll.* "You game?" Kirk asked.

"Why not?" I took his hand and we ventured into a not-so-swift shag that had us laughing like doofuses until out of breath. "Whew," I groaned, "age is telling on me."

"How many of you have still got *the stuff?*" roared the emcee's voice over the intercom. "Time for our shag contest. Winners get the two hundred-dollar jackpot! Contest begins in ten minutes. So guys, go grab your gals and *get ready to show us your stuff.*"

Kirk and I peered at each other. I wiggled my nose and we burst into laughter. One thing we agreed on: our dancing would win no prizes.

"Hey!" I gazed around the gym. "Where's Cal. She wanted to enter this. She and Nighthawk didn't do too badly." I ignored Kirk's dark reaction to the name and began searching. Five futile minutes later, we met at the entrance.

"You stay right here," Kirk insisted. "I'll scout around."

I glanced at the big wall clock. Only three minutes left until deadline. During that time, the Dixie Doo-Wop Band played *Rebel Rouser*.

The entrance door burst open. Kirk grabbed my arm and pulled me through it.

"Kirk!" I dug in, irritated at the heavy-handedness of it. "What –"

His fingers dug into my wrists and I noticed his stunned expression. "Neecy, you won't believe it." He tugged me outside, away from air-conditioning into the sultry May night where crickets sang, nearly tripping me over something on the lawn shortcut to the rear of the school gym.

Around the corner we careened and nearly collided with three dark silhouettes hovering in the shadows of the brick structure. Kirk brought me to an abrupt halt.

"Neecy." Callie, silver-gilded by a distant nightlight, gazed at me with a strange expression on her face. Roger, somber as a handsome movie-Mafia character, shifted closer to her and I noticed a supportive arm go around her waist.

Then my gaze slashed to the other dark, bigger, rounder shape. The shadow moved and the movement took my breath as my vision acclimatized to darkness and the features began to take form. "Neecy?" it said, the voice so familiar my head spun.

"Oh, my *God."* My hands slapped my cheeks. Goosebumps rose up on my chilled flesh. I felt Kirk's arms slip around me from behind, supporting me as my legs began to give way. "It *can't* be!"

"'Fraid so, Neecy," the specter said, moving to within breathing distance of me to reveal a goofy grin and half-mooned eyes –

"Oh Lord," I moaned. *"Moose."* I burst into tears and heard Callie join me as I squalled like a baby.

A big hand gently reached out to pat my arm. "Lordy, Neecy," Moose muttered, "didn't mean to scare you so bad." His large shoulders gave a frumpy shrug. "I s'pose 'shock' is a better word."

Callie and I finally wound down to snuffling and gaping at Moose as though he'd grown three heads. "W-why are we standing out here in the dark?" I asked in a shrill voice.

"Cause I felt kinda funny 'bout just showing up – y'know, a'ter all the worrying I put ya'll through an' all."

Moose shifted his bulk, now at least thirty pounds heavier than the last time we'd seen him. "Thang is – I'm back." The shoulders lifted, then fell limply. "I'm tired a'runnin'."

"Running?" Kirk tensed. "Those drug people were arrested and –"

"Yeah. I know." Moose's voice sounded dead. "Only I just found out from Roger."

Kirk frowned and stepped toward Moose. "How'd you and Roger connect?"

Rog spoke for the first time. "I ran into him in San Diego about six months ago, while I was on a business trip. We got each other's addresses and kept in touch. When I read about the class reunion in our local newspaper – I always bought one at the corner newsstand – I phoned Moose about it. When Moose explained his precarious situation, I convinced him to come out of hiding."

Suddenly, joy caught up to us and we began to laugh and hug Moose and bawl like three-year-olds, even Kirk had misty eyes.

Like the old Dead End Kids, we entered the gymnasium punching and poking and laughing together as though no world existed beyond us. Then some others spotted Moose and kidnapped him to catch up on the years.

My gaze sought out Callie and Roger, who, again, pulled aside to talk quietly, soberly. I resisted running to her, even as everything in me ached to commiserate with her over Moose's lost years, afraid of interrupting whatever she and Rog had going. Few had been Cal's references to Rog through the years but each carried regrets.

After that, the rest of the evening was anti-climactic. Kirk retreated into a world of glacial silence and brooding features.

Oh, he asked me to dance to the slow songs. But his mind definitely simmered to other directions.

"What's wrong, Kirk?" I whispered during one dance.

He raised his splendid head – more handsome tonight than ever – his eyes grazing my features as though hunting down a microscopic intruder to exterminate. Finding none, his gaze softened. "It's just – Moose's showing up...everything is so danged unbelievable." He sighed and pulled me back into his close embrace, shuffling his feet in time with Connie Francis singing about "Where the Boys are."

"Isn't it?" I pressed my nose to Kirk's neck and inhaled his Halston scent. "How in the world did Moose manage it – keeping his whereabouts from everybody all these years?"

"I don't know. But I'm going to find out." Kirk's quiet reply was edged in steel.

My head whipped up. "You aren't angry with Moose, are you?" Though, in all honesty, I was beginning to feel the first stirrings of anger myself. Moose could have let us know he was all right even if he'd wanted to keep his whereabouts unknown. I just didn't want Kirk to light into our friend on his first night back.

Kirk's gaze moved beyond me, grew far off. "I don't know how I feel. I've gotta think about things for a while."

We – our gang – managed to migrate back into the remainder of the evening's festivities, determined not to let fate cheat us out of one more moment in time. Kirk and I braved the medley of old dances, including the Stroll, the Twist, Hand Jive, Shag and regular old Jitterbug.

My husband and I muddled through the Stroll, but during the Twist, I did a fancy pivot away and slowly twitched my way around to find myself stranded on the dance floor. Hands on hips, I cast Callie, now grinding her feet into the polished floor with Rog, a disgusted *oh well!* look and dropped out.

"Why'd you just disappear?" I sniped at Kirk, irritated at his embarrassing vanishing act.

"Hmm? Oh – I didn't know how to do that dance," he said absently. "You know I've got two left feet." Did I ever? He'd not even taken umbrage at my nagging tone. Amazing. I watched him aimlessly wander off, his gaze faraway. Remote. Troubled. Alarm took hold of me.

Moose's old textile cronies kept him captive while Callie and Roger remained absorbed in each other, now touching even when not dancing together. Not sexual, just gentle gestures, a touch and light caress on the arm that ended in laced fingers or a finger brushing a stray hair into place.

At one a.m., the band shut down. Classmates' goodnights were reluctant and warm and nightcapped with "let's stay in touch." A few tears punctuated parting affections, as well as loud guffaws and raucous teasing. All served to bond us together and to this night of unforgettable memories.

By the time we got to Callie's house for one last cup of coffee together, dawn was blowing away the last of the stars from the sky. Moose had grown quiet. It was not, I suspected, that he was sleepy. Though he should have been after the long, celebratory, emotion-charged night. He seemed keyed up. Kirk, sitting next to me on the sofa, had gotten his second wind, and now watched our resurrected friend as we all lounged barefoot in Cal's den. Callie and Rog lolled cozily on the love seat. Longing – to have Kirk that blindly in love with me again – dropped heavily on me.

Suddenly, Moose pushed up to the edge of the easy chair he dwarfed, planted his elbows on thighs and clasped his hands between knees. "I learned about Roxie gettin' killed from my stepma. I kept in touch with Pearly 'cause I knew she wouldn't let nobody know where I was. Them drug people was a'ter me like crazy." He shook his head and his eyes moistned. "I didn't think they'd go a'ter Roxie." He swallowed a couple of times and twisted his hands together. "When I found out – I went crazy for a while. Blamed myself, y'know?"

"She made peace with God before it happened, Moose," I said, hoping to console him.

He blinked a couple of times, swiped his wet cheeks with the back of his hand and nodded. Then his eyes half-mooned, and I knew he'd put it behind him.

He began to speak like the old Moose. "I went to Solomon last week – before I come here for the reunion. I didn't know ya'll had moved back up this way, Kirk." His eyes glimmered like he knew some secret joke. "Anyways, guess who I run into at the church when I visited the pastor's office there?"

"Who?" Cal asked, curious as blazes, coming to the edge of her seat.

"Ol' Sarah Beauregard." Moose yuk-yukked. "Know what she said, right there in the vestibule? Said 'guess you know what that no-good preacher done after you left, don't you?' I says, 'Naw, can't say as I do.'" He yuk-yukked like crazy, slapping his knee, not noticing Cal's stricken look nor how Kirk had tensed up and now gripped my hand in a bone-crushing strangle-hold.

When Moose got his breath, he gasped, "That crazy woman says, 'he shore stabbed you in the back, man. Fooled around with Roxie is what he done. That's why he hightailed it outta Solomon, doncha know?' I told her, 'You're crazy, woman.'" He laughed until tears filled his eyes and ran down his cheeks.

"*Ouch*, Kirk," I muttered through my teeth, "that *hurts*." He abruptly released my white fingers and I flexed them to regain circulation.

Suddenly, Moose noted the silence. His face slackened and for the first time, I noticed his eyes were a hazel color. "Ya'll don't find that funny?" he asked, bewildered. "Couldn't wait to tell that on the crazy ol' –" He fell silent. His gaze narrowed on Kirk, whose features were shuttered. "It *is* just talk, ain't it Kirk?" he croaked, rising unsteadily to his feet.

When Kirk remained silent, Moose's gaze swung to Cal. "Ain't it, Cal? Just *talk* is all, ain't it?"

Cal flinched. She licked her lips and opened them to speak. Then shut them.

Kirk rose and went to him, put his hands on Moose's shoulders. "Moose, we've been friends for a long time. You know how I feel about you."

Moose stood there, looking as though he'd been shot with a stun gun. "Is it true?" Moose peered at Kirk and I heard in his voice the plea *tell me it isn't so.*

Kirk's level gaze held such pain I felt my breath hitch. "Yes." My husband's hands dropped limply from Moose's heavy upper arms.

"Oh, *God*," Moose wailed and his head fell back as he sloughed heavily in a circle, clutching his temples. I heard Cal's weeping as I snuffled back myriad emotions, the foremost being grief that the ugliness was resurrected. "I ain't got *nothin'* left," Moose moaned and stopped, his mighty limbs and head dangling as loose as Spanish moss in the wind. "Nothing."

"Oh, Moose," I rushed to throw my arms around him. "Please don't say that. You still have us." Moose stood like an uprooted dead oak, waiting to topple.

My heart pounded like Dezi Arnaz's bongos.

Moose pulled loose of me then took hold of Kirk's shirt and pulled him up till their noses nearly touched. "You encouraged me to disappear, Kirk. Said I could be killed by the drug people. We felt that with me gone, Roxie'd be safer. Remember?" He spoke through clenched teeth, shaking Kirk, who stood like a Raggedy Andy, loose and expressionless. But I saw the pain in his eyes.

Moose released Kirk so violently, Kirk nearly stumbled. Moose's great body heaved with sobs. "Did you just do it to get me outta the picture?"

Kirk sprang to life, touching Moose's quavering shoulder. "God, *no!* I knew those people would kill you, that's the reason I encouraged you to leave. I truly didn't think Roxie –"

"*Why?*" Moose wailed. "My best friend…." His body commenced trembling again and his teeth chattering.

"Take it easy, pal," Kirk put out a steadying hand.

"Naw. Not *pal.*" Moose's head swiveled so forcefully and he glared at Kirk so fiercely that a sob caught in my throat. "Not anymore, Kirk."

Moose turned and like a zombie, sloughed his way from the room. From our hearts.

Kirk had lost his best friend. Again.

CHAPTER TWENTY-SEVEN

"It's about time to begin." I straightened Kirk's black tie and picked a blonde hair, mine, from his black clerical robe. The church vestibule swarmed with wedding party members, costumed in lavender dresses and black tuxes, whispering frantic last minute reminders. Gene, its pastor, had only moments earlier made his mad, robe-flapping dash outside to the sanctuary's back entrance, where he joined the groom and his attendant.

I turned to kiss Heather's cheek before lowering her veil. She was a fairy-tale princess in her white gown and luminous smile. We embraced for a long, intense moment, our eyes misty when we locked gazes, knowing things would be forever changed but knowing, too, that the changes would be good and right.

My brother Cole, tall and handsome in formal attire, tucked my hand in the crook of his arm, escorted me to the front pew and seated me as gently as if I were made of eggshells. I sat alone, eyes ahead, preparing myself to lose my daughter to this man who had, after five years of cohabitation, finally proposed. Kirk, after his initial burst of outrage over their "living in sin," relented, and though not condoning their actions, had treated Heather and her companion with respect.

It turned out that Sam Chase was not technically a divorced man. When his ex-wife Sharon died of breast cancer three years after their divorce, he'd become a widower of a sort. Least that's how I viewed it. I tried not to think about his playboy reputation and the two live-ins before Heather. Kirk had stretched himself to accept Sam, a handsome, brash man who'd rarely darkened a church door in his entire thirty-two years.

I had a moment's unease that soon, Kirk and I would break our tradition of solidarity.

Heather needed us now more than ever. I consoled myself that Kirk and I would remain friends and that we could still "be there" for the children.

Today, against his better judgement, Kirk would fulfill Heather's wish that "Daddy marry us." Gene, Trish's husband, would assist – just until Kirk walked Heather down the aisle and gave her away. Kirk would then mount the pulpit and officiate the vows.

The wedding procession filed past me to the strains of Pachebel's *Canon in D*. Two-year-old Caroline, my brother Dale's daughter, tossed rose pedals along as she, blue eyes donutted in adject terror, spanned the crimson aisle in record time and stumbled onto the platform, spilling her baskets contents. Finding her X to stand on, she plopped thumb in mouth and sucked desperately as she watched the advent of ringbearer brother Billy, five. My Dawn, now fifteen, floated by, a chimera of pastel and flowing golden hair, to her place of honor at her sister's side. Following her was my little sis Lynette, the matron of honor, now married and sucking in her breath to conceal her fourth-month pregnancy. Soon as she lit in her spot, Caroline threw herself at Lynette, hugging and plastering herself to her thighs, pulling the long dress tightly over her aunt's rounding abdomen. I shall never forget my sis's stricken countenance for the duration of the rites.

A trumpet and piano rendition of the *Wedding March* brought me to my feet and I turned to watch Kirk walk our Heather down the aisle. A lump as big as Bald Mountain filled my chest. How beautiful. No longer my little girl. A woman.... A tear splashed over and I felt it trickle slowly down my cheek. I gently blotted with tissue and I felt Daddy's hand, from the row behind me, reach to pat my shoulder. I gazed at him through a mist and saw that his eyes, too, shimmered. And I knew in that moment what he'd felt when I married Kirk. I reached to squeeze his hand gently and watched Heather join the man she'd given her heart to.

Sam Chase was not an easy man to know. With us, he'd been polite yet distant, discouraging closeness. That he did not always treat Heather with respect did not set too well with me, but I'd held my peace and prayed for the best. Perhaps, I thought with a hopeful heart, today marked the beginning of a real foundation for them.

Toby, now a ministerial student at Asbury Seminary, sang *Only God Could Love You More*, in his smooth tenor that always moved me.

"Dearly Beloved," Kirk's rich voice soothed and buoyed me, "We are gathered here in the sight of these witnesses to join this man and this woman in Holy Matrimony."

Heather gazed at Sam. My breath hitched at the pure adoration shining there.

I decided in that heartbeat that if she loved him, I, too, would love him.

I recalled when Daddy had faced that decision. I had to smile, thinking how Dad was now positive that Kirk could hang the moon and the stars. I was thankful I had protected that frangible trust. I pushed away a surge of apprehension that things would soon change.

"I, Heather, take thee, Sam, to be my wedded husband –"

My breath caught at the emotion vibrating in her sweet voice. I closed my eyes. *Please, Sam – take her heart and shield it from hurt and harm. Nurture her and love her, as she deserves.* Oh, God, I prayed, *I give them into your care.*

"I now pronounce you man and wife."

"Now can I go pee?" Caroline shrieked at her Dad, one of the groomsmen on the platform. She did a little dance, hands fastened on crotch, knees locked. Grinning sheepishly, Cole rolled his eyes and passed her down to her mom Beth, a bridesmaid, who quickly exited the scene.

Cal's peals of laughter, from the vestibule door where she served with the registry, were as lusty as Mae West's.

Lips twitching, Kirk said, "You may kiss the bride." Sam's kiss was, characteristically, dramatic, as though for an audience rather than for Heather. I pushed the thought away, reminding myself of my new vow.

Trish catered the reception. "It's beautiful," I whispered, hugging her. "You outdid yourself."

"Well," Trish brushed back a stray tendril of hair above her flushed face, "Anne helped a lot. So did Joanie and Beth."

"Sure it wasn't too much?"

Trish dimpled. "You *did* buy most of the supplies, Sis. The labor, well – all that was my *gift* to the newlyweds."

"The most generous of them all," I whispered, kissing her cheek. "My, how I love you, sister dear."

Trish snuffled loudly, then mugged a ferocious frown. "Are we maudlin' or what?"

We mimed a "macho" slapping of shoulders and pants hiking before breaking into giggles and finally settling down to people watch.

"Hey!" Chuck moseyed up to us. "Did I do okay with the music tapes or *what?*" My brother gave me a high-five, grinning from ear to ear. His transplant had been tremendously successful and his tech computer degree made him the most sought after technician in the whole Whitman clan.

"You look great," I said and reached up to kiss his cheek before he dashed off to visit with relatives and to stuff his face at the refreshment tables.

"Joanie looks so pretty in her lavender bridesmaid dress. You'd never know she gave birth two months ago," I murmured, spotting her latched onto Dale's arm. *Dale, Krissie's soul mate.* My heart did a little dip and I took a deep breath, held it, then exhaled.

I gazed desperately about to dispel my sudden melancholy – Toby laughed with Heather, joking and ribbing affectionately as they always did. *Do they ever think of Krissie?* The thought sprang forth of its own volition. I sighed and accepted the inevitable mother reflections. *Mother's never forget.* Dawn talked passionately with a cousin about abolishing the death penalty and I thought sadly of how – though her curiosity simmered – she'd never actually *known* the sister she so closely resembled.

Kirk rarely spoke of Krissie. From our recent heart-to-hearts, I knew it was simply too painful for him. Though Kirk's attendance at ACOA support group meetings had dislodged many of his fixations, some remained static. As with an alcoholic parent, the adult child's recovery is a lifelong process.

One thing *had* changed. He was aware of his anger problem and worked desperately to dislodge it. At least I no longer felt myself its sole focus. He was more polite to me. But the passion of days past was, I was certain, gone for good.

"Hi." His voice, at my ear, jerked me to *now.*

"Hi." We gazed at each other, lost for a moment in some yesterday when youth's resilience sprouted unconditional hopes and dreams. There is, in that instance of pure illusion-idealism, a moment when dark reality intrudes and steals bliss. Today, I nudged aside the shadows as I would a blowfly trying to light on my feast.

Not yet.

Cole manned the tape deck and put on Anne Murray's *Could I Have this Dance for the Rest of my Life?* Bride and groom waltzed around the fellowship hall under the misty gazes of family and friends.

"I pray he'll be good to her," Kirk murmured huskily. I looked at him, knowing his heart to be as mine. Our differences, in that heartbeat, were of no importance. What mattered was this precious coalition, one formed over the years from a foundation of pure love.

"I pray he will, too." I smiled up at him and slowly, a flicker of light in the green depths grew and grew, until it burst into a warm glow.

The waltz ended with Sam, in grandstand fashion, dipping Heather nearly to the floor, setting her upright, then spinning her into a graceful curtsy. The applause was deafening.

Their departure for a Myrtle Beach honeymoon was as grandstand as Sam Chase.

"They fooled everybody," Toby muttered, throwing up his hands in good-natured resignation. "Took Sam's brother-in-law's car instead of the one we decorated so magnificently. All that art and talent *wasted.*"

Leave it to Toby to lighten everybody up.

I exhaled on a long sigh of relief, thinking *It is done.*

From our porch, Kirk and I waved off the newlyweds – Heather had convinced Sam to circle back to our place for a private goodbye – and watched them disappear over the twilight horizon.

"Whatever happens, Kirk," I impulsively laced my fingers with his and squeezed, "They're in good hands."

Kirk and I looked at each other, burst into laughter, then slowly, like a sudden sunset, he sobered and – as though catching himself – emptied his eyes of all feeling. My smile remained in place for long moments before his closing-off hit me.

Suddenly, it was too much. Years of deprivation, of no spontaneous "I love you," bear hugs or "I need you," crashed in on me.

We went into the den, where Kirk seated himself across the room from me.

"Why, Kirk?" I whispered.

His gaze darkened. "Why what?" The question reeked of disdain.

"I've given everything," I murmured, more to myself than to him, "still it's not enough." Tears began to gather in my eyes. I tried to force them away, but Kirk saw them, because his mouth thinned into an even grimmer slash and the eyes became granite.

That's it. Something in me snapped in place. I swiped the tears from my cheeks and clasped my hands in my lap. "Kirk, I want a divorce."

The eyes slowly shifted from glacier to amused. The mighty fingers steepled to the hard lips now. *He doesn't take me seriously.*

"I'm as serious as I've ever been in my life, Kirk," I said in an even voice that did me proud. I would not cry this time. I wouldn't give Kirk whatever satisfaction it seemed to give him. I supposed my tears were proof to him that I was as unstable as his poor mother had been in her lifetime.

I stood. "I plan to see a lawyer tomorrow morning. I suggest you choose one."

I turned to leave. "Why, Neecy?" he asked quietly, fingers still steepled.

I pivoted and gazed levelly at him. "Because you don't love me, Kirk." I shrugged. "I want to free you to see the person you've grieved over all these months and years."

His brow furrowed like trenches. "What in blazes are you talking about?"

I waved a hand at him. "Don't get upset. I'm not doing this in anger or haste. I'm simply setting you free to pursue your own life, Kirk."

He was on his feet, coming at me. Instinctively, my hand shot out as a shield. "Just – don't hit me, Kirk." The fear was there, stronger than ever. Now that I'd known the violent man, I couldn't deny Kirk's propensity to do harm.

He stopped like running up against concrete, his eyes blazing. "*Hit* you! My God, Neecy, how could you even think that? All this talk is crazy —"

I turned to flee, but he was quicker. I hated the terror that shook me like a rag doll, made me cower as he seized me with strong hands, hands that hadn't touched me in tenderness for so long I'd forgotten their magic. "Please, Kirk —" I whimpered as fingers dug into the soft flesh of my arm, "just let me go."

He stared at me as if I'd gone stark raving mad. "I *can't, Neecy.*" His wild green eyes desperately raked my features as I flinched and shrank from him. "Don't you understand?" he ground between clenched teeth, causing me to cringe with each word, "I *love you!*"

"No," I whispered, my head moving wildly from side to side as I tried to claw free. "No, Kirk, you don't love me."

He hauled me to him, crushed me with his arms. "I love you, for God's sake, Neecy. I love, love —"

"*Nononono!*" I pushed against him, but he only held on tighter, burying my face against his spicy smelling neck. I strained against him with all my might, resisting his words. They weren't true. I'd spent years with the truth. "You *do-not-love-me*, Kirk," I rasped, glaring at him, tears of frustration flowing freely, and I didn't care. "How can you say —"

"Oh *God!*" He threw back his head and wailed, "What have I done *to you? Oh Neecy,*" he began to sob then, great soul wrenching sobs, his arms still wrapping me like conduit. It was his desperate note of remorse that snapped me out of my hysteria, made me *hear* him.

I grew still in his embrace, stopped fighting. Bewildered. Confused. Numb. His hands began to gently move over my back, my shoulders....

"Stop, Kirk," I whispered, fear rising in me like steam on cold air. His arms were beginning to feel *right* again. "I know you think you love me right now, this minute — but what about tomorrow and the next day. Will you still love me? Or will your anger drive it away again? Oh, Kirk," I sobbed suddenly, "I can't live with the rage anymore. It's killing me. I've got to get away from it —" I tried to wrench free of the viselike hands only to feel arms circle my waist as Kirk slid to his knees before me, his face pressed to my torso.

"Please, Neecy," he whispered, his warm breath penetrating my blouse to seep into my skin, "don't leave me." He looked up at me, his eyes tortured green pools, his voice guttural, "I can't live without you."

As naturally as I drew my next breath, my arms slid around his neck and brought his face to my bosom. And I knew, in that moment, that my love had not died after all.

Kirk and I talked long into the night after Toby and Dawn got home from their Friday movie trek and turned in.

We made love at intervals, as if to convince ourselves we were truly together. "I've never, for one moment stopped loving you," Kirk murmured over and over. "There's never been an instant that I would have traded you for anybody or anything in this world."

When he saw my dubiousness, he took care to dispel it. I found I no longer believed his declarations as I once had. That fact didn't alarm me. I now accepted Kirk, clay feet and all, loving him still. I kept silent, hoping he'd simply accept, as I had through the years, that trust must sometimes take seed, root and grow. Perhaps I had the advantage, having lived for so long with no nurturing; I'd developed a strength to survive emotional abandonment. I listened to his perceptions, knowing *he* believed them.

"Neecy, my anger was at myself. Not you. Never you."

I smiled sadly at him. We lay side by side on our bed, legs entwined, faces together, touching. "It came out that way, nevertheless," I said gently. "I guess it's the coldness. The – empty way you look at me. Like I'm not there," I whispered. "That's the worst part, Kirk. You acting like I'm not there."

"Ahh, honey," he caressed my cheek, his face tortured, "I'm so sorry for all the pain I've caused you. I'm so screwed up it's not even funny." He rolled onto his back and cupped his head in his hands and glared at the ceiling. "One thing all adult children have in common is the numbing out, the turning off of emotions. We developed it for survival purposes way back when there was nobody to parent and protect us from all the violence and abuse. It wasn't *you* I turned off, it was the things in myself."

He shook his head. "I know it's hard to understand. I don't even understand it all myself. Not yet."

"Going to the ACOA meetings has helped me see myself in each person there. We're like danged *clones*, Neecy. Control freaks. Chips on our shoulders. *God*! You wouldn't believe the junk we carry from childhood. I'm only just getting an inkling of what happened to me back there when Dad raged and roared and ran us all into the woods with his car." He swiveled his head and angled me a tormented look. "Can you imagine running for your life from your own dad?" His gaze bounced again to the ceiling. "Does things to your mind. To your trust in mankind." He gave a soft huff of a laugh. "You were right all the time, Neecy. I *haven't* totally trusted anybody in my life, not even God. I have this drive in me to be in control – so nobody ever victimizes me again." He shook his head and grimaced. "It's terrible. I hate it."

"Well, at least you know where it's coming from now, Kirk," I licked my lips, determined to ask him. "I've had the impression that you were in love with – someone else. That was the only reason I knew that would make you turn on me so completely all this time. Were you?"

He rolled to face me, his eyes clear and intent. "*No*. Never, Neecy. That's one thing I'm not confused about. If you don't hear anything else, hear this: you're the only woman I've ever loved. I mean that with my whole heart."

I said nothing. Only nodded. I just – let it go. I could – in a sense – understand Kirk's claims that traumas could play with one's mind. I realized it would be a long, long time – if ever – before I would fully believe his words. Again, I took comfort in knowing that *he* believed them. I took comfort, too, that I still could feel compassion for him.

Another thing sustained me. I'd come through a dark, dark forest, where thorny kudzu-mazes entangled me over and over again through the years. Yet, I'd fought my way through and from them time and time again. I'd endured while my sanity prevailed and a new strength blessed me.

The old anxieties were gone. I knew that, if I had to, I could face just about anything.

"I love you, Neecy," my husband's arms slipped around me and our bodies meshed like warm silk.

"I love you, too, Kirk."

Not like I once had. Not yet. But I was glad he'd stopped me from leaving. Because there was nowhere else I'd rather be than right there, in his arms. There was no one else for me. Only Kirk.

His lips claimed mine again. Yes, I was glad he'd stopped me.

It came like a bolt of lightning. Kirk called me into the small kitchenette of our salon and closed the door. "The phone call –" he began and stopped, biting his lip. Kirk had taken the call in the salon's kitchenette ten minutes earlier, as I finished Mrs. Curtis' hair style.

"What?" I croaked, black premonition washing over me.

"I don't want to tell you this, Neecy," he whispered, his lips trembling.

"What's happened," I asked hoarsely, wanting with all that was in me to *not* know.

Kirk gripped my icy hands, his gaze holding mine. "There's been an accident – your dad's been killed."

The pain that lanced me was visceral, gripping my gut and twisting torturously around every organ in its orbit to burst into denial. *"No-o-o,"* I wailed. "Not Daddy. Please – not Daddy!" Kirk wept as I keened and howled my grief, his big warm fingers tethering me to him and to reality. His forehead pressed against mine and I knew his loss was as great as my own. Dad was the father Kirk had always yearned for. And now, just when I'd finally gotten to know the real Joe Whitman, the sweet, giving man who'd always hovered just on the perimeter of our experience, he was snatched away.

Orphan.

It hit me like a Mack Truck. My last biological brace – gone. Life's conveyer belt brutally plopped me into my father's vacated space. Until that very moment, I'd not known the weight of his position, not until I, myself, teetered, heels dug in, on the brink of the unknown, where mortality is a stark, grim fact that precedes forever. Now, incredibly, Daddy had already made that mysterious crossing to the other side. This fact separated us indelibly, pulled the rock-hard *father*-surface from beneath my feet and left me staggering, groping for footing.

I need Anne, my family.

Dawn became an unexpected fortress who took charge, gently washing my face and weeping with me, making calls to Trish, Chuck and other family members as I alternately fought hysteria then embraced it. Neither Heather, now living two hours away, nor Toby, both married and residing near Asbury Seminary in Kentucky, would arrive until the next day. Kirk would close down shop and join us later.

Later, as Dawn drove me to join relatives, another cold irrational fear blasted me. Daddy, my genetic link, was gone. I'd grown so secure with the Daddy and Anne alliance through the years that I'd simply taken family-solidarity for granted. Now, with Dad's abrupt departure, the chasm he left loomed murky and frightening.

Had *Daddy* been the glue? Did glue equate the *genetic*, after all?

Terrifying thoughts spiraled through my mind – *will I lose my family?* "*Blood's thicker'n water*" droned Grandma Whitman's ghost. Did Anne feel that way, too? Just a little? The small child inside me wailed and howled forlornly as I entered Anne's house.

Anne's house. Not Dad's and Anne's house anymore.

Will Daddy's void change her? She loved me, yes. But suddenly, I felt keenly DNA stripped, the stepchild of folklore. A sea of familiar faces filled the den. Yet, standing in the midst of them all, eyes streaming tears, I felt utterly alone.

"Neecy!" Anne's voice rang out and through a blur I watched her sail like a porpoise to me. "I'm so sorry about Daddy, honey," she murmured and gathered me into her arms.

Terror scattered like startled ravens.

What she did next took my breath. She looked me in the eye and said gently, "He's with your Mama now."

I snuffled and gazed into her dear face. "H-He always put flowers on Mama's grave –"

She looked puzzled, then smiled sadly. "No, honey, he didn't put the flowers on her grave."

"Then who –"

Anne looked a mite uncomfortable for long moments. Then she leveled her haggard periwinkle gaze with mine. "I did."

"You?" I asked, astonished. "All those years?"

"Yes." She wrapped me in her arms again and truth smacked me broadside. Blood is part water. Grandma just didn't get it. With love blending them, you can't tell one from the other.

Kirk arrived moments later, as if to punctuate my reassuring discovery. Like Kirk of old, he burst into the room with his head high, eyes searching until they lit on me. Swift as an arrow, he came to me and unashamedly gathered me close, murmuring in my ear that "everything will be all right, honey. We'll make it through this."

Through swollen, red eyes, I gazed at this man who was not blood kin, who was once a virtual stranger, whose love had elicited from me a vow to live with him – in unspeakable intimacy – until death. And in that instant, I was struck with the sheer implausibility of it all.

Then he smiled down at me as we stood there, surrounded by whispering on-lookers, yet *alone*. His big fingers lifted to gently touch my cheek as he lowered his face to brush noses with me. "I love you, Neecy," he whispered, his eyes, those magnificent green eyes, clouded. "I'm so sorry I ever caused you pain."

"But –"

"Shh." His cheek melded to mine as his breath ruffled the hair on my temple. "*Kirk's* back," he said hoarsely, "and I'll never leave you again." His arms tightened to still my quietly sobbing body. "Never."

And he won't. Because as implausible as two strangers bonding in matrimony seems, the fact of prevailing commitment stirs and sustains a mysterious chemistry that *works*.

"I'll take care of you, Neecy," he whispered brokenly.

"I know." I gazed at him through tears, saying the words because he needed to hear them. Saying them because they were true. "I know you will, Kirk."

EPILOGUE
THE PRESENT

"And I will restore to you the years that the locusts hath eaten, the canker-worm and the caterpillar and the palm worm, my great army that I sent among you. And ye shall eat in plenty and be satisfied and praise the name of the Lord your God that hath dealt wondrously with you."
Joel 2:25-26 KJV

The moment had come. I stood beside the open sepulchre, breathless at dashing from work to be here at the cemetery at this appointed time. I trembled with emotions long buried and now resurrecting. I'd opted to work today, as usual, and await the summons from the funeral home when the truck bearing such precious cargo arrived. I'd thought it would help to keep my mind occupied until this moment.

The past two weeks had been hell. The decision to move our daughter's remains began soon after Dad died and was buried, according to his wishes, in the little church cemetery where generations of Whitman ancestors lie. No Ph.D. inscriptions mark their headstones. My kin were poor, simple, *good* folk who were too busy surviving squalor to worry much about schooling. Not until my dad's generation was education upgraded to "important."

My gaze swung to his headstone, a low-cut marble one that not only meets Anne's fashionable criterion but also allows the custodian to mow flush and maintain a well-kept look. I stood between Dad's green mound and the gaping earth readied to receive my daughter's corpse.

My attention skittered to Dawn, whose long, denimed legs dangled lazily from her perch on a nearby, older tombstone, a pose so at odds with her grief-ravaged face that my breath hitched. Last week, she'd waged a fierce appeal to view her sister's remains.

"Mom, it's not unthinkable, you know," insisted my wonderful strong-willed girl-woman. "Medgar Evers was disinterred after thirty five years and was so well-preserved they held a wake. Krissie's been dead at least ten years less. There's a good chance she could be viewed."

The room had begun to spin as I gazed at her, not knowing how to react.

Dawn's voice rose slowly, steadily, like an elevator. "Wouldn't you like to see her once more, Mama? I mean – just *once more?*" Her stricken azure gaze beseeched me to agree.

Tears filled my eyes and I pinched my forehead. "Oh, Dawn – I don't think I could say goodbye again...I said goodbye all those years ago. I don't know that I can do it again."

"But Mom – *I've never seen her.*" Her declaration was a whimper, an unheard of thing for Dawn, one that pierced me. Of course, she wanted to see her sister. Everybody in the family remembered the live Krissie, could still hear and feel her energy, her laughter, her goodness and her love. We'd all *known* her.

All except Dawn. Now she stood before me, her need a throbbing passion.

I took a deep steadying breath and gazed at her. "I'll talk with the funeral director and see what he says, honey. I understand how you feel. I'll do everything I can to make this happen."

And I had. But in the end, it wasn't enough. "Discourage Dawn," had been the mortician's counsel. "Occasionally, a viewing is possible, but more often, it isn't. Once the vault's seal is broken," he shrugged, "It won't reseal. Not only would you have to go to the expense of a new vault, there is no guarantee you'd get a viewing."

Kirk had made the final difficult decision not to risk it. For once, I yearned with all my heart for the affluence to disregard monetary concerns during that emotional decision. But we'd already spent well over two thousand dollars to disinter and relocate the burial site. New vault prices began near a thousand, not a sum to sneeze at nor one that fit into our already strained budget. By now, I'd curtailed to part-time work in order to spend more time writing and had published some short stories. All with Kirk's blessing. Kirk was, again, the main breadwinner. Without his finance-juggling genius, we'd not have enjoyed as many comforts.

Had I been in charge, we'd have been destitute.

Still, it stung that we couldn't simply order the vault seal broken. I keenly felt Dawn's disappointment and lost dream. But an amazing thing happened. Dawn took the defeat with remarkable grace and pitched herself into planning the memorial service set for the upcoming Sunday afternoon.

Today, on its eve, our family congregated at the cemetery to watch the earth-stained vault poise majestically in honeysuckle-flavored stillness to bid us a brief, somber greeting. Warm golden

May sunlight kissed its metallic surface for the first time in twenty-odd years. Our moist-eyed regard was hushed and reverent, almost apologetic for disturbing the eternal rest.

Dawn hovered closely, her features grim and deferential. Her banker husband, Charles, an Al Pacino, drop dead gorgeous look-alike, watched her with concern, his arm draped protectively around her.

I missed Heather's calming presence. She, Sam and their daughter Angela would arrive late tonight, along with Toby and his family, for tomorrow's ceremony. Sam had begun attending church with Heather in their first year of marriage and experienced a conversion experience that still had my eyes rolling with astonishment. *Watch out, world!* Sam Chase would be a pulpit-dynamo.

He and Heather's move to Asbury, Kentucky, situated them two streets from Toby's family and settled the brothers-in-law, elbow-to-elbow, in the seminary's theological school. At times, I had to tack my feet to the floor to keep from leaping into infinity with joy. They would all drive in a caravan, arriving late tonight, Toby, wife Joellen, three daughters Michelle, Tiffany and Kennedy and Heather's family.

That supportive family unity helped me through today's sadness. It helped me watch the crane lower the casket into earth once more and stifle a piercing cry at life's injustice. It helped me face tomorrow.

Sunday dawned fair and sunny. Today was my bittersweet, poignant Mother's Day gift. A sweet gardenia-laced breeze caressed my face ever so gently, and I knew she was present. I felt her essence, that indefinable, *ageless*, unique aura that depicted Krissie the baby, toddler, child and adolescent at once. I experienced anew the splintering regret that she'd not experienced adulthood. Never been kissed and romanced. Never known motherhood. So many nevers.

I took a deep breath and watched cars arrive, lining themselves along the quiet country lane that wound through the cemetery. Only family and intimate friends were invited. I wanted no curious gawkers. Not now, after all these years when I was more aware. At the long ago funeral service, I'd been trauma-anesthetized, seeing only those caring, life-sustaining gestures at the end of my nose. All else had blurred into merciful insignificance. Today, clarity and hindsight jarred me. The idea, that time had wiped away much of the pain, shattered.

I blinked against a red haze and watched Dawn, tall and blonde and elegant in a hunter green silk pants ensemble, solemnly place an artist's easel at the head of the new flower decked mound. Charles handed her the eleven-by-fourteen portrait of the beautiful blonde, smiling Krissie in her favorite strawberry dress. The resemblance between the two sisters still took my breath at times. Dawn reverently placed it on the easel and draped blue ribbon streamers from a bow mounted atop the stand over the corners of the picture and stepped back to honor the moment's gravity.

Heather moved to put an arm around her sister as the gathering settled into hushed stillness. Toby and Joellen linked hands, with Michelle, five, Tiffany, three, and Kennedy, just turned eighteen months, pressed to their legs like cherubs to a baroque column in old Rome.

Kirk began the ceremony by leading in the Lord's Prayer. At its end, my siblings, Dale, Lynette and Cole harmonized, *a cappella*, the gospel song *Sheltered in the Arms of God*.

Oh my, how *clearly* those words spoke to me now. Strange how, after the *fact* of separation, those words comforted me so profoundly. Kirk's strong fingers laced with mine and squeezed just before he stepped forward to speak a few words.

"This service is purposefully informal. We – Janeece and I – want each of you who knew Krissie to feel free to share your most meaningful memory of her with us all. I'd like to begin with my recall of daily, early morning drives to school. I was chauffeur, of course, and we listened to the Carpenter's music tape every day as we rode together. When they got out of the car, Krissie always turned to wave goodbye to me and then escort Toby as far as she could before turning to go to her class. I can still see her –" Suddenly his voice broke and he began to weep. I took him in my arms and held him as his body quaked with grief and I realized that, all those years, this sorrow had been just below the surface.

I heard, behind me, Dawn's sobs as Heather and Charles comforted her. So my Dawnie had *connected* with her sister. Finally, she *shared* our loss.

Immediately, my brother Dale began to reminisce about his and Krissie's last time together, a month before her death, when, during our Christmas visit home, the two of them had wrapped Dale's gifts to friends, then traipsed over the village, delivering them. Then, Lynette recalled how, during her visits to Solomon, she'd loved wearing Krissie's pink jeans and sweater ensemble. "Knowing Neecy didn't have more laundry to do in the machine, Krissie would hand wash and hang the outfit in the bathroom to dry by morning so I could wear it. She was always doing things like that to make me happy," my sister, now the mother of a son, said.

One by one, relatives and friends spoke of Krissie, some provoking laughter, some tears, many sharing things before unrevealed, giving further glimpses into an extraordinary life ended too soon. I listened, too moved to say anything throughout the service. I noticed, too, Heather's silence and Toby's.

Has time distanced them from the emotions now sucking me down the drain? I wondered. Neither of them, who'd known Krissie's sweetness, wept. Dawn, who'd never known her, cried forlornly. I'd never used a yardstick to measure emotions – except for that brief lapse with Toby following Krissie's death. And then, unconsciously. I could not assume Heather's equanimity today indicated lack of love. Nor Toby's. Yet, it tugged my heart.

Kirk's hand gently squeezed mine. I looked up at him and saw me mirrored in his face.

No words were necessary. His was the affinity I sought. Not my children's, whose loss was unspeakable. Only Kirk's toll equaled mine. Only his grief had held out against time as had mine. Time had not, nor would it, dim our sorrow, which was not an incessant, indulgent angst. Time *had* erected diversions along our odyssey, some ecstatic, some agonizing, some simply a smooth running river of happenings. Life had bequeathed tomorrows with promising horizons. Yet – at times such as this, when smacked broadside with the fact of Krissie's absence, our anguish erupted violently, as though no time bridged us from *then* to *now*.

It wasn't, as one well-meaning friend recently hinted, a simple fact of Kirk and me "getting on with your lives now that you've relocated the grave." In other words, "Get over it." *Ahhh, such distanced assumptions serve well those who've never buried one's own child. A neat, pat rationale.* Problem was it rarely applied to reality. I clasped Kirk's warm, big, callused fingers, marinating in the bittersweet, uncoveted bond we shared.

The service ended with Heather, accompanying herself on guitar, singing in her clear contralto soprano *Seasons in the Sun*, Krissie's favorite serious song. It's poignant, almost prophetical lyrics struck me as never before. *"Goodbye to you, my trusted friend, we've known each other since we were nine or ten; Together we've climbed hills and trees, Learned of love and A-B-C's, skinned our hearts and skinned our knees. Goodbye my friend, it's hard to die...when all the birds are singing in the sky; Now that Spring is in the air, pretty girls are everywhere, Think of me and I'll be there. We had joy, we had fun, we had seasons in the sun: But the hills that we climb were just seasons out of time."*

As the music faded, the only sounds heard in the hushed country setting was that of quiet snuffling, men blowing their noses and birdsong from a nearby copse of elms. Something caught my misty peripheral vision – I watched a butterfly soar overhead, then light atop Krissie's portrait. My breath stopped. The yellow wings fluttered for long moments as everyone watched, mesmerized.

I know, Krissie, my darling. I know.

Then, as dramatically as it arrived, the beautiful creature lifted, arced gracefully and disappeared before our eyes. Nobody spoke for long moments, then slowly, reluctantly, folks began to stir and talk quietly amongst themselves. I continued to gaze at the portrait, blue ribbons swaying in the warm breeze.

"Janeece?" I felt a touch at my elbow.

"Cal!" I turned into her arms and we embraced for a long, long time. "I'm so glad you made it. Did Roger? I know he was supposed to work."

"He's here. Somebody else is here, too, Kirk," she hugged my husband and, holding onto his arm, turned to gaze into the gathering. "Moose?" she called.

Next thing I knew, Moose McElrath had his arms around Kirk, rocking back and forth and sobbing his heart out. "Ahh, Kirk," he said when he was able to speak, "how did things ever git the way they did between us? I knowed how Roxie was when I married her. No –" he shushed Kirk when he tried to speak, "I shouldn't'a flew off at you like that. Sure, I loved her, but if I was honest, I'd have to say she was driving me crazy with her spending and demanding and – well," he hung his head for a moment and murmured, "she'd stopped being a wife to me long before I took off. I suspected she was runnin' around. See –" He squared his shoulders and resolutely looked Kirk in the eye, "what I didn't tell you was that Roxie wasn't only a dancer but a high priced call girl when I met her."

His face flushed a bright crimson as he shot me an apologetic look. "I didn't know that part 'til a'ter we married. One of the last fights we had, she screamed it at me." He stopped for a moment, looking off, swallowing hard, fighting for control. "Called me a fat ol' clod hopper. Said she couldn't stand the sight of me." He mopped the sweat off his brow. "'Bout the same time, the drug thing happened." He gazed beseechingly at Kirk, who stood pale as death. "I really did try to kick the habit. My – the things I did in church was – well, *real*. Thing was, I got scattered when I run up on that drug deal thing in the bathroom. I panicked. It was just – too much happened too fast. I kindly – you know, tricked you into agreeing to my taking off." He gave a humorless huff of a laugh. "Truth was, I was glad to fly the coop." He blinked, wiped his mouth with the back of his hand and shook his head as if to clear it.

Kirk reached out. "Moose, I can't begin to tell –"

"No," Moose overrode Kirk's apology. "It was me who done wrong. *Me.* Kirk, you was my best friend and I run off into the sunset, disappeared, leaving you that letter begging you to take care of Roxie." His pain-filled eyes misted. "Kirk, I throwed you to the wolves."

His gaze swung to me. "You, too, Neecy." He bit his lip to stifle a sob. "God knows I'd'a killed myself before I'd'a hurt either one of you. I'm so sorry."

"Look," Kirk took Moose by the shoulders and gazed steadily at him, tears shimmering along his lids. "Let's make a fresh start, friend. We've all made mistakes. Failed each other. And that's bad. But the real tragedy would be that we don't learn from it, don't glean some wisdom. Please, Moose, accept my apology for all the hurts I've inflicted on you?"

Moose peered at Kirk as tears big as pearls slid off his round face. "You got it. An' I want you to forgive me for being such a butt – you and Neecy both?"

We three hugged and wept for long moments before giggles erupted from Toby's little girls. They'd gone to the car and now scampered back to the gravesite, each carrying a bunch of multi-colored balloons.

Michelle came to me first, reaching up her free arm to embrace me, to stem my tears. I squatted to hug her and got knocked flat on my fanny when Tiffany and toddler Kennedy ambushed me for equal opportunity. We dissolved into giggles and hugs and kisses until breathless.

"Mimi," Tiffany piped, "Aunt Krissie loved bubblegum and Snickers. And she loved babies."

"Aun' Kwissie," little Kennedy rejoined solemnly, "Her wi' Jesus."

"And – and she had blue eyes," Michelle gushed proudly, "just like *me!*"

I narrowed my red, swollen eyes on their exuberant little faces, so like seven-year-old Toby's all those years ago. "She had a small turned up nose like yours, too," I said, gently tweaking hers, drawing fresh giggles.

"Uh huh." Tiffany's head bobbed in agreement. "An – and Daddy said Aunt Krissie always –"

I listened, astonished, as they related, with amazing familiarity, anecdote after anecdote of Toby's antics with his sister "Aunt Krissie," whom, through their daddy's stories, they knew in an intimate way that moved me to fresh tears.

I swiped them away, not wanting to thwart my granddaughters' spontaneity. I felt Heather's arms slide around me from behind after she plopped down on the ground to join us.

"Y'know what, Mama?" she asked in a lilting, childhood carryover voice. "I've written at least fifty poems to Krissie. I do them when I miss her the worst. And I've bought her a little token gift every birthday...things I can always use later, but initially, I do it for her."

"Can you quote one?" I whispered, too choked to speak. "A poem." How many I'd written to her through the years.

"Mmm – let's see...Oh, here's one: "If I could ask you one question, Krissie, just what would it be? I'd ask you why you died that day – why did you have to leave *me*! Why, why, why? I'd cry, Do I miss you until I could scream? Why can't I wake up one day and find it was all a bad dream?"

Heather peered into my face and narrowed her gaze at my fresh tears. "Was it that bad, Mama?" she asked, a twinkle beginning in her eyes. She shrugged. "Heck, I told you I couldn't write worth beans."

I turned to hug her. "It's just so – moving."

Over her shoulder, I spotted Toby, tall and manly and blonde-ly handsome. He grinned at me and I saw that little boy of long ago, the night after proudly showing me his surprise pond-tribute. I'd sat with him on his bed as he tugged off his socks, readying for bed.

"I had to do something, Mama." He'd looked up at me and I saw the grief in the blue pools. I saw the grubby, callused little hands and thought of all the dirt they'd shoveled and the buckets of water they'd toted.

"Do you think she knows, Mama?" he asked that night.

"Yes, Toby. I'm sure she does."

Squeals of delight snapped me back to the present as little fingers released a bouquet of balloons. "Happy Birthday, Aunt Krissie!" the girls yelled in unison. Toby, Heather and Dawn joined in the clapping and whooping, a balloon-ritual, I've learned, that follows such party festivities.

Their grief – my offsprings' – is not tearful like mine and Kirk's. But it is profound.

They manifest theirs through celebrating Krissie.

And today, after more than twenty years, Krissie still *knows*.

I watched the colorful bouquet scatter and rise...rise...higher... *higher*....

Toby's and Heather's gift goes on.

In their hearts, she lives.

"It was a lovely service, wasn't it?" I turned to watch the wind ruffle Kirk's near-white hair, adoring every inch of his slightly sagging features. Time has not been too unkind to him. He's still as good-looking to me as he was nearly forty years ago.

"It was," he agreed, giving me that slow smile that still shoots a thrill out my fingers and toes. "It was hard – but I'm glad we did it."

He reached and took my hand. "Janeece," he paused and cleared his throat.

My breath hitched at the tone in his voice, the *get ready for an important announcement* one. I leaned toward him, keening for what was to come.

"Gene asked me to consider assuming an assistant-pastoral position in his church."

I stared at him, my mouth dropping open. *Déjà vu.*

Full circle.

"What do you think?" he asked uncertainly.

"It's been a long time," I muttered, emotions churning, flapping, *yeowling.*

He gave a long ragged sigh. "Too long." Then after long moments, he added, "but I won't do it if you'd rather I not."

In that heartbeat, I knew the depth of Kirk Crenshaw's love for me. I'd seen the lost, tormented look on his face through the years since he'd vacated the pulpit. I'd known – *felt* his desolation, his remorse in the wee dark hours. Now, a door opened up, casting sunshine over his world again.

And he'd give it up for me.

"I say go for it." *Heck! Why not?* What could happen that hadn't already happened?

I rolled my gaze upward. Oh, *Lord – pretend I didn't ask that.*

He crooked his neck and slanted me a dubious look. "Really?"

"Really." I gave him the most blazing, dazzling smile in me. And in that heartbeat of time, I let it go. All the hurts and disappointment, all the betrayals. I simply – turned loose. Like those released helium-filled balloons tied together, it disappeared into infinity. As far as the East from the West. And I felt the incomparable buoyancy and freedom that comes with forgiveness.

To forgive is – truly – divine.

Slowly, his lips began to curve up at the corners and his eyes shimmered with joy and peace and love – with gratitude.

"I love you, Neecy."

"I love you, too," I said, then burst into laughter. "Know what Toby said to me at the cemetery today – after everything was over?"

"What?"

"He said, 'thanks Mama, for you and Daddy holding our home together for us. And you, Mom – *you* kept the homefires burning. I've seen how JoEllen suffered through her parents' divorce and I – I really appreciate my parents staying together." I looked at Kirk. "That's what he said. And you know what?"

"What?"

"I'm glad, too."

He smiled at me, his eyes moist, his voice husky, "There was never a moment I could have let you go. Never, Neecy."

I sighed and laid my head on his shoulder. Was it true? God only knows. What I do know is that nothing or nobody was able to destroy our love.

And after all, that's the important thing.

Dear Reader,

I hope you've enjoyed the journey with Janeece and Kirk Crenshaw. Such enduring love as theirs is rare and to be treasured. I know you will miss the colorful characters you met along the way because I sure did hate to leave them when I finished writing the book.

In my next novella, *Space*, you will meet equally lovable, vulnerable characters in the Stowe family. This time, the parents have their twenty-nine-year-old daughter, Faith Kenyon, living with them. The once beautiful, "miracle child,"is a now a haggard, difficult, recovering drug addict, with all the problems and baggage that comes with that territory.

Deede and Dan Stowe, nearing retirement age, have worked and saved all throughout their marriage in order to enjoy unencumbered their well-deserved "golden years." But with Faith's constant presence, cloying neediness, and endless crisis, Deede and Dan find all their dreams of peace, a comfortable retirement, and togetherness stolen.

Faith not only is recovering from addictions but she has related criminal charges coming up, which require more financial assistance from the already fund-strapped family. Dan grows increasingly angry, resenting that he has become the sole supporter of this brilliant woman who has lost everything to her addiction habit, including husband and child. He also resents being forced into the role of "enabler." He hates that his home is no longer his haven. He wants his space back.

At the same time, the mother sees Faith differently. She knows all Faith's faults and failures but she feels there is still hope for a turnaround in their child's life. But her heart, too, cries out for her own space and sometimes she wonders if she can hang in there much longer.

Thus, the parents' opposing views reap dissension on the home front. It brews from day to day, tearing away at the foundation of their peace, security and marriage.

Faith feels the tension, too, and knows her father wants her gone but where can she go? There's nowhere to turn. Is there a place for her anywhere?

All three family members grope and yearn for that much needed breathing space that each can call their own. And the parents ponder, is there ever a time when one gives up on a wayward adult child? Is one ever justified in handing that once precious child over to be locked in prison?

The emotions here are too complex for a simple solution. Can love, faith, and forgiveness heal this family's dilemma?

Enjoy!
Emily Sue Harvey